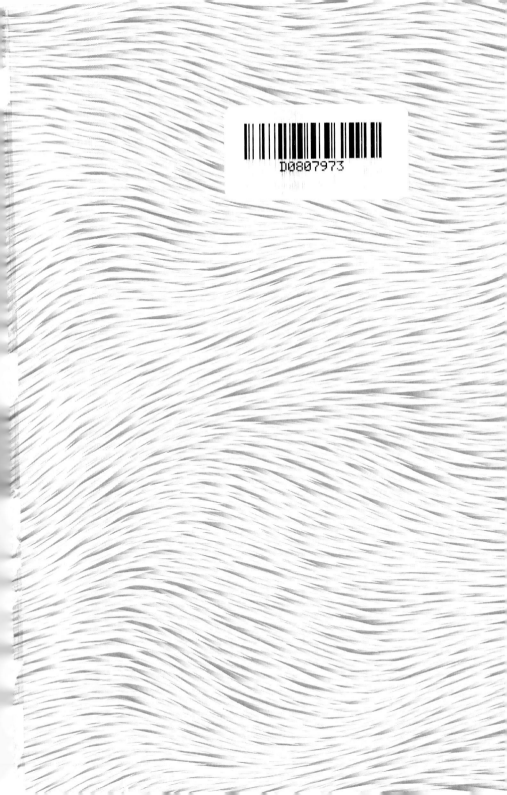

Also by Drew Hayden Taylor

NON-FICTION

Funny, You Don't Look Like One (1998)
Further Adventures of a Blue-Eyed Ojibway:
Funny, You Don't Look Like One #2 (1999)
Furious Observations of a Blue-Eyed Ojibway:
Funny, You Don't Look Like One #3 (2002)
Futile Observations of the Blue-Eyed Ojibway:
Funny, You Don't Look Like One #4 (2004)
NEWS: Postcards from the Four Directions (2010)

COLLECTIONS

The Best of Funny, You Don't Look Like One
(anthology from first three editions) (2015)
Voices: Being Native in Canada, with Linda Jaine (1992)
Me Funny (2006)
Me Sexy (2008)
Drew Hayden Taylor: Essays on His Works (2008)
Me Artsy (2015)
Me Tomorrow (2021)

FICTION

Fearless Warriors (1998)
The Night Wanderer: A Native Gothic Novel (2007)
Motorcycles and Sweetgrass (2010)
The Night Wanderer: A Graphic Novel, illustrated by Mike Wyatt (2013)
Take Us to Your Chief: and Other Stories (2016)
Chasing Painted Horses (2019)

PLAYS

Toronto at Dreamer's Rock (1989)

Education Is Our Right (1990)

Talking Pictures (1990)

The Bootlegger Blues (1990)

Someday (1991)

The All Complete Aboriginal Show Extravaganza (1994)

Girl Who Loved Her Horses (1995)

The Baby Blues (1995)

400 Kilometres (1996)

Only Drunks and Children Tell the Truth (1996)

alterNatives (1999)

Toronto@DreamersRock.com (1999)

The Boy in the Treehouse (2000)

The Buz'Gem Blues (2001)

Sucker Falls (2001)

Raven Stole the Sun (2004)

In a World Created by a Drunken God (2004)

The Berlin Blues (2007)

Three Tricksters (2009)

Dead White Writer on the Floor (2010)

God and the Indian (2013)

Cerulean Blue (2014)

Spirit Horse (2016)

Sir John A (2018)

Cottagers and Indians (2018)

Drew Hayden Taylor

COLD

a novel

M&S

McClelland & Stewart and colophon are registered trademarks
of Penguin Random House Canada Limited.

Library and Archives Canada Cataloguing in Publication data
is available upon request.
ISBN: 978-0-7710-0289-2
ebook ISBN: 978-0-7710-0290-8

Jacket design by Kelly Hill
Jacket art: (skyline) LukaszDesign / stock.adobe.com;
(clouds) SoulMyst / stock.adobe.com
Part opener art: polygraphus / Getty Images
Interior art: (snowflake) artemstepanov / stock.adobe.com;
(clawmarks) Odua Images / stock.adobe.com
Typeset in Adobe Caslon by M&S, Toronto
Printed in Canada

McClelland & Stewart,
a division of Penguin Random House Canada Limited,
a Penguin Random House Company
www.penguinrandomhouse.ca

1   2   3   4   5   28   27   26   25   24

To my n'dodem,
who always appreciated a good story and kept the cold away

THE STORM APPROACHES

Zoongaakwa'an G-nimadbiiw-g'jipzowin

(Fasten Your Seatbelt)

Below them, the sparse forest was deathly silent and still, a condition brought on by weeks of torturous cold that hugged the rough terrain. Only the occasional sudden crack of a stunted tree doing battle with the infrequent wind challenged the silence of the landscape. Up here, deep in the heartless muskeg of northern Ontario, silence and snow were the only things in abundance. It was late November, but the weather up in this territory seldom bothered to consult the calendar.

Most of the animals and birds were in hiding, conserving both energy and body heat. A seemingly white blanket with a pattern of green spruce spread to all horizons, challenging the perception of some that this land, this country, had been tamed. The vast expanse of mosquitos, tamarack, and moose begged to differ. The land had survived the grating of mile-high glaciers, and the more recent occasional presence of pesky two-legged creatures that frequently saw the need to rip materials out of its very belly and send to far-off territories or slaughter the four-footed or two-winged fellow inhabitants that shared their domain. But it was the quietness of this land that was its signature. And in temperatures this cold, the complaint of a single irate raven could be heard kilometres away.

Standing by itself, a testament to its fortitude against the bareness of the Canadian Shield, stood an unusually tall white spruce. A good five metres high, it towered above many of its siblings, claiming as much of the weak sunlight as it could grasp. Nestled snugly in the lower branches, rested an almost-invisible snow white ptarmigan. The cold had limited its ability to forage, and so it now waited patiently for its world to return to normal and the ambient temperature to increase. In its own bird-like way, it knew this was the calm before the storm. Something unforgiving and punishing was slowly making its way towards its section of creation, a force strong and life-threatening. Soon. But until then, the ptarmigan merely sat there, looking out at the world the ptarmigan gods had made. For the moment, it seemed all the universe was quiet and cold.

Well, cold anyway. Though barely perceptible at first, a roar disturbed the forest atmosphere. Gradually approaching, it interrupted the ptarmigan's meditation. It was an unfamiliar roar, an unpleasant and annoying disruption in the fabric of the land. Because of the cold's effect on sonic vibrations, the mysterious and loud growl sounded like it was coming from everywhere and nowhere. The only thing the ptarmigan was sure of was that it was getting closer and louder. The bird's curiosity had now shifted to concern. This was not normal in this part of the timberland, and anything that was not normal was usually bad.

Suddenly, the whole tree shook with thunderous vibrations, as if the ptarmigan gods had chosen that moment to vent their omnipotent anger on the hidden bird.

"Jesus fuck?!?!?! Was that a tree? Did I just see a fucking tree out my window?!?!"

Like an angry deity descending from a tumultuous heaven, a plane sheared off the top of the spruce, sending the ptarmigan flying off to pursue new, albeit quieter, adventures amidst a hail of needles and splinters.

"Yeah, I think our left wing clipped it. Hold on!"

"We're in a plane that's falling out of the sky into a frozen wilderness at two hundred kilometres an hour with a damaged wing, and seriously, you think holding on will help?!"

There was a dramatic pause before the pilot answered. "Well, it won't hurt."

Cessna 206s are generally designed to fly higher than this particular plane was at the moment. A good, reliable utility aircraft, barely twenty years old, it was currently finding the principles of aerodynamics versus the laws of gravity somewhat problematic. It was in an argument of lift versus acceleration versus gravity versus ice on the wing, and to be blunt, the plane was losing.

Luckily, only three of the eight available seats were occupied. Merle Thompson was the rather understandably stressed pilot currently attempting not to engage in a potentially dangerous game of tag with the landscape. Just behind her and to the right sat an equally stressed Fabiola Halan, a woman deeply regretting having gotten out of bed that morning. And in the back, huddled in a corner, sat a terrified young teenage boy returning home from an extended trip to a southern hospital.

"Do not tell me we are going to crash! Do not tell me we are going to crash!"

"Okay . . . I won't."

"You're just doing this to scare me. Locals like you love scaring the shit out of southerners like me. That's it! Right?!? That's how you get your kicks."

The older woman flicked a dashboard switch to the right of the steering panel. It seemed to do little good. "Do I look like I'm having a good time?" There was a sudden lurch to the left and then an immediate drop of five feet. The Cessna was not having a good day, and as a result, neither were its three passengers. Fabiola's nails dug into the armrest and she found herself praying to a god she was largely unfamiliar with. And nobody had informed her of the local ptarmigan gods.

As the plane fought its own mechanical difficulties, Fabiola kept closing her eyes for long periods of time, not wanting to see the growing catastrophe developing around her. Then, unwilling to be surprised by whatever dice random chance had thrown on her behalf, she would open them with a ferocious glare. The window, a scant foot to her right, reinforced her growing apprehension of her rapidly approaching fate.

Half to herself, and half to the woman sitting behind her, the pilot muttered, "I've been flying up here for fourteen years and I haven't yet lost a customer. Don't worry. She'll hold together."

A long time ago, in a faraway place, the dark-hued passenger had sworn she would never take another boat ride. If she walked away from this, Fabiola would have to expand her no-travel ban to include planes, which would essentially limit her to trains, Ubers, and carnival rides. From where she sat, the journalist could see the pilot wrestling with the craft's steering mechanism. For a brief moment, it seemed the woman in the cockpit was shaking a small child, before Fabiola realized what an absurd thought that was. The pilot, ineffectively, was fighting with the flippers and flaps and things that control the three-dimensional directions of planes. Looking out her window again, Fabiola saw another tree whiz by. And then another. And off in the distance, all she could see was more distance. She hadn't known there could be so much distance in the world. And all of it seemed to be centred around her.

Behind her, she could hear the boy muttering something. He had been silent when entering the plane, not even looking her in the eye, which was fine with Fabiola. The boy had remained quiet during the entire flight, up until now. To the journalist, it sounded like a prayer but in another language. Probably Cree. That was the predominant language up in this area, according to her research. And he definitely looked Cree—straight hair, almond-shaped eyes, high cheekbones. Once, briefly, she saw a huge smile. Still, her innate sense of objectivity found it odd that a teenage boy, other than one being from some religious cult, would be saying a prayer in whatever language. The few teens she'd come across in her life would have no doubt reacted substantially differently. But she was no expert on the motivations of youth.

There was another sideways lurch, followed by an unfeminine and colourful expletive from Merle, the pilot. *Shit*, she thought. What a place to die. This was not her land. Fabiola Halan came from a place where the only snow came in cones, and trees had fronds and coconuts. Water was warm and emerald, not cold and white. She had left that all behind decades ago for a better life. And seemingly, an arguably better death, too.

Amidst the cacophony she heard the woman up front, theoretically controlling the plane, yell "Brace yourself, this is gonna hurt." Whoever this pilot was—she'd only met her three hours ago—she was appearing increasingly impotent. And Fabiola hated useless women . . . well, useless anybody really. But anybody who couldn't keep a vehicle specifically designed to stay in the air . . . in the air . . . well, that kind of said it all, didn't it?

Fabiola noticed that the prayer coming from behind her was slowly morphing into more of a steady stream of anguished cries. Prayers and tears—two exceedingly ineffectual methods of dealing with a crisis, she thought. But admittedly, she didn't have any better alternatives. For the moment, she stifled the urge to tell the boy to "man up," as her personal trainer frequently taunted her.

Then the world inside the plane went silent. The coughing of the engine struggling to maintain its four-stroke internal combustion design stopped. For a brief second, she almost missed the obnoxious sound of the misfiring contraption. At least that had signalled it was trying to do something. Now, all she heard was the muttering of the pilot, the creaking of the plane, and wind buffeting the small craft. There was also the sound of a rolling bottle of water banging into things below her feet. It must've been the one she'd brought aboard not so long ago.

In one of her favourite poems, Dylan Thomas urged his readers to "not go gentle into that good night." It sounded good to her, and she had a few non-gentle things to get off her chest concerning her current situation. "Rage, rage against the dying of the light." Yeah, that sounded good too. Looking over her shoulder, she glanced at the boy, his hands clasped, eyes closed. His lips were moving but he no longer spoke loudly enough for her to hear. Suddenly, he opened his eyes, wide and scared, and in the chaos found Fabiola's eyes. For less than a second, they shared a moment—a moment of connection. And somehow, the journalist found herself smiling at the boy. It was unexpected; even she didn't know where it came from—perhaps a distant and dusty remnant of a maternal instinct she had hitherto been unaware of. She realized she didn't know the boy's name. Then she saw a tear run down his cheek as he found his own smile to share.

When Fabiola had been his age, she had cried too, frequently. A stranger in a strange land where she looked and talked differently, and everybody made sure she knew. For a moment, she almost felt like reaching out to him, taking his hand, lying to him that all would be okay. That wasn't normally Fabiola, but these were not normal times. Just as suddenly, he shut his eyes again, preferring the company of God instead of her.

Turning back around, Fabiola fixed her gaze on the back of Merle Thompson's head, managing to say through angry lips, "If we survive this . . ."

Everything went loud and then, just as quickly, quiet before she could finish.

Some time later, Fabiola struggled to open her eyes. Normally that shouldn't be difficult; they'd worked perfectly for the last three, almost four decades, but at the moment her eyelids didn't seem to want to obey. Even in her self-imposed darkness, she could tell it was noisy again. And cold. Maybe her eyelids had the right idea, but through years of training she had taught her body to do what it was told. Yoga, Wen-Do practice, meditation, and even a fleeting stab at Kegel exercises had given her full command of her body. She forced her eyes open.

Wind was battering and shaking what had once been the stalwart of the Cessna aviation empire. Lying at about a 30 per cent tilt to the right, most of the tail section had somehow been removed. Both wings had been severed and there was a large broken tree emanating from where the cockpit would normally be positioned. Evidently the storm they had flown through on their way to wherever they were had rudely decided to follow them. Most terrifying of all, Fabiola appeared to be alone.

In her life as a journalist, she had been in some harrowing situations. Potentially deadly ones that any sane person except reporters like herself would normally avoid—but frequently through an ability to read people, or the application of her intelligence, or on occasion just sheer willpower, she had survived, and even prospered. This was not looking like any of those situations.

Maybe she wasn't alone. The reality of the situation was all coming together now as Fabiola focused on the world around her. She noticed she was covered in blankets, and despite what little she knew about small-plane crashes, it was unlikely she would conveniently land comfortably propped up against the bulkhead covered in four blankets and relatively protected from the elements. Add to that, Fabiola could see half-covered footprints in the snow, exiting the rear of what used to be the plane. "If that bitch left me . . ." Before she could finish the sentence, something orange fluttered down over the back end of the plane. Puzzled, she watched it flap around in the wind then saw it gradually grow taut. It was a tarp of some sort, partially sealing off the rupture. Inside the craft, the gusts lessened to where they were now just annoying, not all-encompassing. Evidently, that poor excuse for a pilot was finally doing something productive.

Looking around, Fabiola surveyed what she could amidst the turmoil. There was still daylight streaming in the windows. Well, that was something. She hadn't been unconscious too long. Most of the windows were snow-covered, and from what she could ascertain through the split fuselage, the airplane had come to rest inside some sort of crater or beside a small ridge. All she could make out were rocks, trees, and snow. No horizon. Instinctively she knew this was not good. Even to a southerner like herself, she knew that made it more difficult to be spotted, especially if the depression filled in with snow.

And where was the religious teenager? That's when she noticed the tarp was being put up over where his seat had been, now a gaping hole in the fuselage. Scanning the interior quickly, she couldn't spot him. But he had to be somewhere? Maybe that was him putting up the tarp.

Pulling herself up for a better view, a sharp stabbing pain grabbed her attention. Her leg hurt. She hadn't noticed that before. Shifting her weight beneath the suffocating mass of the blankets, a sharp and intense explosion once again shot from her lower right leg. Right about where she thought her shin must be. Mentally, she debated extracting herself from under the blankets to survey the damage. But that would expose her to the cold, and if she was hurt, such an exposure, however brief, might rob her of vital body heat. No telling how long they might be in this new home. Opting to stay warm, she pulled the blankets closer.

Pushing the tarp aside, Merle Thompson entered, the left side of her face swollen and bloodied. As the pilot got closer, Fabiola noticed what little of her eye that was visible seemed not to move. *That couldn't be good*, she thought. And for a moment, she was worried about the woman.

"You look like shit. You okay?"

"That . . . that is a relative term. Of the three of us, I'm doing great."

On the ground near her feet, the pilot spotted the formerly rolling bottle of water. She picked it up and took a drink.

"I take it we crashed."

Fabiola watched the woman move her considerable bulk from the back, then settle in one of the seats facing her, wincing from the pain-incurring movement. Taking a deep breath, the pilot offered her the half-empty bottle. At the moment, thirst was the least of the journalist's problems.

"I appreciate a woman with a keen grasp of the world. Seems that storm we went through followed us here."

That was obvious. "So, what went wrong?" *Always the journalist*, Fabiola thought to herself as she asked the question.

"At the moment, don't know. Coulda been a frozen gas line. Maybe there was some ice build-up on the wings? Or might have been . . ."

Once again it amazed her. Sitting in front of Fabiola was the supposedly trained and experienced pilot formerly responsible for not only getting her to her destination, but also making sure she arrived there in some semblance of health—failing on all accounts. Instead, she sat there rattling off possible reasons for their sudden landing, as if it mattered now. Just one of the millions of people Fabiola had come across in her career that had a scant, if that, knowledge of whatever they had been hired to do.

"I get the point. You don't know. Let's try and find something you do know. So where are we then?"

The pilot closed her good eye for a second before answering. "That is a good question."

The journalist had known enough men in her life to understand the secret speak they shared, often avoiding a direct admission of ignorance. And in today's complex world of theoretical gender parity, women were not that far behind. "I take it you don't know that either." Ignoring the havoc around her, she looked directly into the pilot's good eye, awaiting an answer. She prayed once again to the god she seldom acknowledged, that the woman sitting in front of her who had really screwed up her day would provide a suitable and intelligent answer.

Merle the pilot managed a weary smile. "I'm pretty sure we're halfway to where we're supposed to be. Pretty sure."

Yet another person to disappoint her. "And what exactly is in the middle of where we are, and where we're supposed to be?"

For the first time, the pilot looked concerned. "Other than us, not a lot of anything. But we are alive and have decent shelter. That's a good beginning." Shifting in the small chair, the woman punctuated her mediocre attempt at positive thinking with as broad a smile as she could manage on her damaged face.

Oh god, Fabiola thought, she's one of those people with a missing front tooth who doesn't think it matters. That her personality will compensate for any deficiencies in her aesthetic charm. Well, reasoned the journalist, the pilot had dreams if nothing else.

Again, her eyes wandered over to the missing seat at the back of the plane. "The boy?"

Cracking the knuckles of her hand, Merle looked down, shaking her head. "That part of the plane hit a rock outcropping when we came down. He was . . ." She went silent. "It was quick. I found him, about twenty metres back, where we landed.

And also about ten feet off the right wing. It wasn't pretty. I . . . I . . . uh . . . I wrapped him in some material I found and put him under what's left of the wing. I'll make sure his family gets . . . him."

It seemed all that praying and crying hadn't helped after all. Almost immediately, Fabiola felt bad for thinking such cold thoughts. Though taking into consideration her immediate circumstances, the boy may have been the lucky one.

"What was his name?" she asked, surprised at her interest in such a currently unimportant fact.

"Don't know. I have it on the manifest somewhere but . . ." The pilot shrugged, indicating the mess around them. "Poor kid. Just had his appendix out. A nurse dropped him off at the airport and . . ."

"So we wait?"

Merle zipped her worn jacket up to her neck and pulled her fur-trimmed hat down below her ears. "Yeah, we wait."

"How long?" Though hidden by four layers of airplane-grade blankets, Fabiola's injured leg was going from mildly annoying to a raging pain. Having spent time in various conflict-oriented nations, and aware of the repercussions that could arise in such environments, she knew the shock from the crash was wearing off. Already she was feeling the unrelenting cold penetrating the tan/grey blankets, and a growing agony escaping from beneath it. "I think something's wrong with my leg."

"Yeah . . ." The pilot seemed unable to look at her, instead shifting her gaze back to the tarp as if it was directly responsible for what was troubling her leg. "Uh, I took a look at it just after the crash. I think it's broken."

"You *think*?" No matter the amount of pain, people whose tortured command of the English language would and usually did cause her more discomfort than a mishandled Brazilian wax and a children's first-year violin recital combined. It was, after all, her second language, and one that she had struggled to master and command. Being a journalist of her calibre tended to require that.

"Uh yeah, okay, it's broken. Definitely. Do you know what a compound fracture is?"

Was this woman underestimating her intelligence on purpose? Because she was from the city? A well-dressed woman with manicured nails? A Black woman at that? "A compound fracture occurs when a broken bone breaks through the skin." Well, there was no way she would be walking out of this situation. Fabiola couldn't even walk to the bathroom. As much as it was against her nature, she would have to rely on the talents and commitment of this offish woman, and any rescuers that would most definitely come looking for her. That, as much as the injury to her leg, she found galling. Her ability to get things done usually eclipsed the capabilities of those around her. But here, in this situation, she was essentially useless—a condition she had been largely and personally unfamiliar with for a very long time. She winced slightly as the fuselage rocked gently, unexpectedly shooting bolts of pain through her leg.

"I tried to set it while you were unconscious, but I'm no doctor."

Always the consummate professional, Fabiola knew this little accident would have a definite impact on the assignment she'd been sent to cover: the opening of a new diamond mine in the area. Canada was giving South Africa a run for its money with this first of three new mines expected to open in northern Ontario, which looked to corner a sizable share of the world diamond market. She'd deal with that when she was rescued and healed. Until then: survive. Fabiola had done it before, and she would do it again.

Ignoring the pain, she looked over at the pilot. "Well, shouldn't you be doing something?"

Nodding, Merle took a pack of cigarettes out of her jacket pocket and took a lone one out. Fitting it painfully between her swollen lips, she searched for a lighter.

"Want one?"

Fabiola most assuredly did not. Silently, she looked out the window, frustrated at her own inability to do anything. Merle watched her as she enjoyed her cigarette, till the silence became oppressive. "Ever been to the Caribbean?"

The journalist looked to the pilot, unsure of the question. "The Caribbean? What?"

Shrugging, Merle leaned back in her seat, wincing slightly. "Always wanted to go there. Sometimes, when I'm cold and miserable, I try to imagine what it would be like to live there. You know, a completely different kind of place. Sand instead of snow. Palm trees instead of spruce. Oceans instead of rock. Know a lot of people who've been to Barbados, the Bahamas, Mexico, Cuba, all those places. They say it's great. Always planned to go there. That's on my bucket list. Just wondering . . . that's all. Something to talk about."

It took a handful of seconds as Fabiola debated answering. Not one for small talk, but at the moment, that was the only kind of talk available. Still, it was a personal question.

"Come on," added Merle. "I can tell you gotta story to tell. Aren't you some sort of storyteller? Amongst my people, winter is the best time for storytelling. And let's face it, it don't get more wintery then this." With that she paused expectantly, her cigarette glowing in the encroaching darkness.

Fabiola's capacity for brooding silence had pretty much reached its limits. A door opened in her mind, and for a second, the walls she had built over the years gave in to the need for distraction.

Zhaabwii

(Survive)

Up until now, this had been the safest place in the world to the little girl. A place of comfort and security. All the evils of creation had no authority here. But today, on this raft, floating endlessly on an undulating ocean, there was no relief in her mother's lap. While her childhood had been one of limited resources, now a simple glass of fresh water would have seemed the most bountiful excess in the world. Three, or had it been four, days since the decrepit fishing trawler she and twelve of her family had been loaded onto had sunk beneath this same ocean. That was when she had last drunk anything.

Since then, fading in and out of awareness, she had sat delicately on what loosely amounted to a small wooden and metal patch that miraculously was holding the vast ocean at bay. A handful of tenuously attached debris, desperately amassed by the little girl's mother as they swam away from their no longer buoyant transport, had kept the small girl and her mother above the saltwater desert. Her mother's thin and worn dress still smelled of burning smoke. The location of her father and the rest of their extended family, the girl didn't know. She'd asked her mother, but the woman would only kiss her forehead and say that God was watching down on them—Papa and the rest were somewhere better, waiting for them.

Watching down on them. That phrase puzzled her. The little girl looked up into the sky that seemed as vast as the world of water surrounding them, hoping to see this somebody looking down, but she only saw the hot sun, and blue sky. If that was God, he hurt. Burned. Made them thirsty. She tried to hide her head under her mother's dress.

"Mama?" She'd been calling to her mother since the sun had risen that day, but her mother continued to sleep. The girl had tried to waken her several times but with no success. Why was her mother so tired? Just yesterday, as they got more and more thirsty, her mother had mumbled something in her sleep about wanting water. The little girl had been told very strongly not to drink the water that buffeted their little raft. But her mother had called out for water. Insistently and desperately. And, wanting to make her mother happy, the little girl did what she could. Soaking a rag in ocean water, she'd held it up to her sleeping mother's mouth and squeezed it gently, until a tiny but steady rivulet of water dripped down into the unconscious woman's mouth. Over and over she did this, until the woman drank no more.

That had been yesterday. Today, her mother did not seem to want any more water. The little girl did—she thought of it constantly, every minute of every hour—but she had promised her mother she would not drink the water. If that is what her mother had told her not to do, then she would not because she was a good girl. Maybe it was only for adults. Back home, they had lived several days inland, and the ways of the ocean were new to this little girl.

So there she sat, nestled in the lap of her silent mother, bobbing up and down as the currents decided their fate. There had been a slight rain the day before, but it seemed to the girl it was only there to tease her. Her mouth dry, her skin peeling from the punishing sun, wondering why her family had brought her to this horrible place. And where they had gone. Maybe if she slept, like her mother, she would wake up back home in the shack she shared with her whole family, and all this would have been just a nightmare to be laughed at. Snuggling as close to her mother as she could, young Fabiola closed her eyes, hoping she would wake up in a much happier place.

Naanaagdawendaan Waa-doodang

(Weighing Options)

Merle Thompson watched the journalist sleep, pondering her tale. Such a childhood this woman had. Everybody had a story, she told herself, even this rude woman. Such rudeness often came from either a place of privilege—which Fabiola definitely did not come from, despite how she dressed—or a sense of protection; it kept people away and provided a sanctuary. That was certainly possible. Sometimes it was the by-product of narcissism. The world was there for them, and woe befall anybody who didn't understand that. Also a possibility.

Their conversation had lasted seven minutes, maybe eight, before her medical condition made Fabiola pass out. Merle had a reputation for treating rude people in a much more aggressive and confrontational mood. Normally placid, she wasn't afraid to "get her hands dirty" when men made unwelcome advances or women gave her too much attitude. Her weight and physical dexterity made her a formidable opponent. And if she had met Fabiola in a bar or even on a bus, those beautiful cheekbones would definitely not have remained so perfect. Despite the fact that the current situation called for them to work together, Merle had been reaching the end of her tolerance for the journalist's brashness.

Though she'd not looked directly at the pilot while speaking, Fabiola's tale of origin had had an effect. Told in a distant, detached manner, it was like she was telling the story to herself, more than anything. And why she'd talked now, Merle couldn't say. The journalist didn't strike her as a "sharing" kind of individual. Merle was sure there was a bump of some sort underneath that perfectly coifed hair. Possibly a concussion. Fabiola would no doubt blame her personal confessions on that, should Merle ever bring it up. Who knows, maybe Fabiola wouldn't even remember. Still, Merle watched the woman sleep, wondering what their mutual short-term and long-term future would be.

Sleeping so much in these temperatures, in a weakened state, with such limited thermal protection, was dangerous. Hypothermia, it was called. The pilot could handle it. She had decades of experience making do in this environment. Some might even say generations of experience. Half Cree from a community unpronounceable to most non-Cree, Merle had grown up not only staying comfortably ahead of the dangers this part of the province provided, but revelling in it. Up until today that is. Using the vernacular—the plane, the journalist, and she were fucked. Every which way it was possible to be fucked. Just ask the Cree teenager. Except you couldn't. He was dead. Couldn't get more fucked than that. In fact, that was the final state of being fucked.

She wiped the unconscious woman's face, once again marvelling at her cheekbones. Both Merle's maternal grandparents had cheekbones that seemed chiselled out of the Canadian Shield, but this woman looked as if God himself had said, "Let there be cheekbones and let them be amazing."

The pilot could almost swear Fabiola was sweating, and sweat in a full-out northern Ontario snowstorm was not a good thing. It could freeze, precipitating frostbite, and further lower her core body temperature. Maybe that fancy coat of hers that Merle had thought was more suited to a windy day on Toronto's Bay Street than a wintery day a pissing distance from James Bay was warmer than it looked. Or it could be her broken leg . . . the pain making her sweat. Possibly the brief memory of that blistering Caribbean sun having a strong physical effect.

Merle did not know. Men, she knew. Hockey, she knew. Flying planes, she knew (contrary to what her current situation might imply). But the care and maintenance of a damaged journalist in a crashed plane who knows how far from anyplace useful was not a part of her resumé. Perhaps she should wake the woman up. In her debilitated state, sleep might, Merle thought, help recharge her batteries. After all, her own mother had told her a good sleep was never a bad thing. Sometimes it was the only thing. Then again, as she and her old Ford truck were well aware, the cold could also kill batteries.

Another day passed with little happening. Fabiola slept. Merle tried to make their shelter stronger. She gathered more wood and twigs. The wind blew. Hope dimmed.

It was night. Her watch told her it was twenty after midnight, but out here, in situations like this, exact times of the day were irrelevant. Two days they'd been here, hiding from a storm that seemed determined to bury them from existence. Four times the pilot had shovelled away some of the snow that had piled up against the bright orange tarp. She'd been counting on its vivid colour to be a beacon should a rescue plane fly overhead. But there'd been no rescue plane. Just continuous hours of wind, snow, and complaints from the woman. She'd not been an agreeable passenger and had been an even less pleasant patient for the most part. Fabiola Halan had reverted to her earlier incarnation. Once or twice, during her occasional moments of consciousness, Merle had again tried to engage her in conversation about the Caribbean but with only the occasional flicker of socialness.

"You get us out of here and I promise I will personally pay for your trip to the Caribbean. I'll make sure you start drinking in St. Kitts, sleep in Trinidad, and wake up in Aruba." That had gotten a smile out of the pilot.

Fabiola's leg was getting worse, and they had precious little left to eat. They'd been reduced to shovelling handfuls of snow into their mouths for moisture, which as experts would tell you aggravated the threat of hypothermia.

Merle was already feeling weak. Another two or three days of her body (and the journalist's) pumping out 37 degrees of life-giving heat with no continuous solid fuel to stoke their internal furnace, versus the inexhaustible and persistent encroachment of a Canadian winter . . . Merle knew this story did not have a pleasant ending. Again, ask the Cree teenager. So, she had to do something. Any of the options she was currently weighing seemed dangerous, but not quite as dangerous as just sitting here. Essentially, it was a lose/lose situation. It was just a matter of which choice had marginally the best chance of letting them live. Of one thing she was sure—she would rather die doing something than die doing nothing. All those who worked or travelled in the wilderness said you should never wander about aimlessly if you got lost. It was best to stay put and let yourself be found rather than get yourself more lost. As Merle rationalized, that precluded the fact you could be found. Where the plane had come to rest, the state of the snow build-up on the tarp, the insanity of the plane being painted a bright grey, essentially camouflaging it in the clouds of snow—all were contributing factors in her deliberations.

There were . . . other considerations to weigh. Somehow—and if somebody had asked Merle how she knew this, she would not have a logical answer—she knew this was not a normal snowstorm. There was something about it, something that made her more uncomfortable, if that was possible. She remembered some of the stories her kokum had told her when she was growing up on the reserve. Wondrous tales of beings and creatures in the forest that the Cree had lived with since time immemorial. Some fun, some sad, and a few terrifying. For unknown reasons, they had been on her mind the last couple of nights, keeping her up and aware.

If forced to explain, the pilot would say it felt like something was prowling around the outside of the wreckage, peeking in and exploring their improvised shelter, as if surveying possibilities. Of course, it made no sense and there was no such evidence. But Merle could not ignore what she was feeling. Occasionally, the roar of the wind—always when she was occupied and not listening to it—almost sounded like some great beast breathing. Fabiola never seemed to hear it, but most of her conscious time was spent venting against the world. There were never any tracks outside in the snow, but then again, the kind of beast she feared it might be did not leave tracks in the snow. Still, it was just one of several concrete reasons convincing her that some kind of action needed to be taken. Whatever she decided, somehow she knew her fellow survivor would not be happy.

The next morning, as she built up the small fire near the cockpit that she had managed to keep going, Merle told the now awake Fabiola her plan, and as she had correctly assumed, the journalist was not happy.

"You son of a bitch! What kind of person are you!?"

"The kind of person that's going to try to save your life. I don't know how much longer this storm is gonna last. A normal storm would have ended by now. And we have to do something."

"A normal storm? What the hell does that mean? And what the fuck am I supposed to do while you're gone?"

"Stay alive." With the few meagre possessions she planned to take with her, the pilot crouched awkwardly near Fabiola. In such a situation, a worried goodbye and good-luck hug would be normal. But Fabiola Halan did not strike her as the hugging type, under any conditions. "I'll be back as soon as I can. I promise. I will take you up on that Caribbean trip. So stay warm and stay conscious. If that fire goes out . . ."

For the first time since the crash—in fact, for the first time since she had met the once-haughty woman, a few minutes before their departure—there was a glimmer of something behind her normally defiant face. It almost looked like fear, mixed with a dash of concern.

"You're going to leave me here?" For a brief second, Merle thought it sounded like the voice of a young girl, not a mature woman. Fabiola was a woman who was very comfortable with being alone, but very uncomfortable with being left alone. That was a very big difference. Merle could see and hear all that in those six short words.

"I'll be back. I promise."

"You could die out there," the journalist said. It came out almost as a whisper.

"I could. But we will definitely die in here."

Shivering, Fabiola pulled one of the blankets up tighter around her. "Do you even have any idea where you might go out in this storm? I thought you didn't know where we were."

"I've been thinking about it. The storm came out of the north and took us with it. I've been doing some rough calculations, but if I'm correct—and that is a huge bastard of a 'correct'—there might be an ice road about thirty kilometres west of here. Or twenty kilometres . . . or forty kilometres. Whatever, I'm gonna try for that."

There was a silence, broken only by the gale force winds doing battle on the other side of the tarp. "Sounds like a long shot. Thirty kilometres. On foot. In that. I don't even think a marathon runner could do that, and you're not exactly a . . ." Fabiola finished her sentence with a small apologetic smile, the first one Merle had seen on her face. She returned it and slapped her still-sizable sides.

"Hey, this is better than any blanket, and is generally considered stored energy. I got enough baggage on me for a hundred." Things were really beginning to look up, she thought. The journalist was even smiling for a second time. "The sooner I go, the sooner I'll be back."

Fabiola only nodded.

"Bye," Merle added. Fabiola nodded again. There was a one-second shared glance before the pilot returned the nod as enthusiastically as she could under the circumstances and pulled the tarp aside. Instantly, the fury of the storm tried to enter their make-do hut, but Merle Thompson pushed it back outside with her body, redoing and tightening the knots holding the tarp. Any noise she made scrambling up the ridge and away into the wilderness was swallowed and digested almost instantly by the frigid tempest.

Nizhikewiziwin

(Alone)

The pilot had left. Fabiola was now alone. More alone than she had ever been in her life. Just the elements waging war on the other side of the remains of a once-overworked aircraft to remind her she was still alive, still a presence in the world. But for how much longer? Merle had not said what the odds were of her achieving her distant goal, but Fabiola was a realist. She was a realist to the point where all sense of fantasy and play had long been buried. The only imagination she allowed herself was in her work. Writing her stories. The normal imagination of a journalist. That was why she practically never watched entertainment television, rarely went to the movies, thought theatre was a total waste of time, and seldom imagined what could be, only what was.

Sleep, the pilot had told her, was her enemy. Especially alone. She had a fire, however small. It managed to keep her little section of freezing hell a dozen or so degrees warmer, which was not saying much. The pilot had brought her enough wood to last maybe another twenty-four hours if she used it sparingly. Of course, all of this was hypothetical. Fabiola was already exhausted, even though she had slept substantially while the Native-looking woman had watched over her. If she dozed off and the fire went out, Fabiola would become a popsicle until the spring. Then possibly a buffet for whatever creatures wandered these lands. The ultimate form of recycling. She'd had a chocolate bar . . . when was that . . . yesterday? Two days ago? She couldn't remember. Her whole life had now officially gone to shit.

Her mouth opened and one word came out. "Mother . . ." Fabiola had not spoken to her mother in decades, not since being adopted. That was the past, she had thought, and she had the future to deal with. That required more effort. Her mouth opened but she didn't know what to say. Should she pour out her heart, all the emotions she'd kept to herself for all these years, all the things she wished she could say? Deathbed confessions were always overly dramatic, she'd felt. Why should she change now? She closed her mouth, and unspoken declarations and admissions remained hidden in her heart.

She threw another broken branch on the small fire. If the storm outside had any benefit, it was that there was a constant draft—actually several drafts—that carried the smoke from the fire away from the interior of the plane. The dried spruce wood sparked with a crackle, giving the false impression it was generating more heat than it was. A coffin . . . she was trying to keep her coffin warm. A nice toasty coffin in which to die. Briefly, a memory from her childhood popped into her mind, making her think of the phrase "from one extreme to another." The thought, for a moment, amused her. Then the amusement was gone.

Something banged against the side of the fuselage, startling her. Must have been a branch from a weakened tree, or maybe a chunk of ice falling down the ridge. Or a part of the wrecked Cessna being blown across the crash site. Or maybe the poor dead teenager, angry that he had sacrificed a small useless organ from his body, and that his entire life and all his praying hadn't amounted to much. That would certainly piss her off. What she wouldn't give for the grating sound of a streetcar making a turn, or a car horn angrily insulting some oblivious messenger on a bike, or even noisy kids yelling from a nearby playground. Fabiola arrogantly thought this *Walden*-like, living-in-the-bush, being-one-with-nature shit was highly overrated. Any place you couldn't get decent Greek yogurt should not be allowed to exist. Right now, though, those thoughts were of a bygone era it seemed. She could not remember being warm. Being full. Being content.

Fabiola caught her eyes closing and her head dropping down. So cold and so tired. *No!* Retaliating against her own weakness, she banged the back of her head against the wall, hoping the action and pain would get some adrenaline going. But she was weak, and the balaclava she was wearing provided a surprising amount of cushion, all resulting in too little momentum and not enough physical surprise.

Fabiola doubted that she would see the pilot again. She doubted she would see anybody again. What an odd place and an odd way to die. Options . . . she wished she had options. She usually did, but they seemed to have run out. For the first time in a very long time, she felt tears falling down her cheeks.

They froze instantly.

Maajtaamgad Dnakmigziwin

(The Game Begins)

It started with an annoying rustle floating at the back of his brain, then a sliver of consciousness fought its way to the surface, like a mouse pushing its nose through a lush stand of grass. There was noise. And pain. Noise and pain. Not good things to wake up to. It was yet another morning where Paul North's consciousness waged a battle over whether it was worth all the effort of waking up to face a frequently unsympathetic day or clamouring for those few additional minutes of blissful unawareness. Today— this morning, to be specific—he lost to the reality of his previous night's exploits. Though he knew it would hurt, Paul forced his eyes open and was immediately hit with a storm front of light and self-induced cranial hurt. The rude brightness was from a lamp on the bedside table that had somehow been overturned in the night, and as a result it shone on his face like a searchlight piercing the darkness for enemy planes.

The source of the pain was obvious from the evidence surrounding what had once been a nice and neat motel room, but now could apply for disaster relief. Bottles of beer and rye littered the room. Half-filled cups of both stood ready in key locations should the drinking commence again. And the noise that had originally dragged him through those famed doors of perception was sleeping on his arm and snoring louder than you would think possible from someone with such a delicate and cute nose. It was a woman. A rather lovely woman, naked and curled up next to Paul, no doubt a thermal vampire desperately seeking his body warmth thanks to the thin sheets of an inexpensive motel. Mary . . . Marie . . . Melissa . . . Mindy . . . Right now he could not remember her name. He put remembering her name on his list of things to do once the rest of reality found its way back to him.

Toronto . . . he was in Toronto, or more correctly, on the outskirts of Toronto. The city itself had few affordable motels downtown, so the ever financially conscious manager of the team thought a quarter tank of gas getting the team to and from the games was smarter than letting the players sleep in decent beds and be closer to the action. He was fairly sure he was in the dark regions of a far-off primitive territory called Scarborough, where he'd heard dinosaurs had once been known to prowl the deserted ravines.

Paul North was a right winger in the IHL, the Indigenous Hockey League. A loose conglomeration of regional hockey teams representing various First Nations or groups of First Nations, it was at best a semi-professional league of Indigenous and Métis players of varying levels of competence. At worst, it was dozens of Native men of various ages raised not on the American dream, but the Canadian dream that salvation and prosperity could be found chasing a hard rubber puck through a net.

Paul's team, the Otter Lake Muskrats, represented the territory between Sudbury and North Bay,and south to Peterborough. Once amazing, now merely good, Paul played because that was what he had been doing since he left school. The drive he once had to succeed replaced by rote. Skate, stickhandle, shoot, fight, and if possible, score. He had been at it how long? At least since his haircut had been in style. How much longer could he keep his place on the team? That was up to his legs, lungs, and the coach.

Many on the team and in the league were hungry to taste the life the NHL dangled in front of them when they watched the games, as they had since childhood. It was still a dream in Paul's life, but the decades of unfulfilled hope had taught him the difference between a dream and reality.

Instinctively, Paul looked for his hockey bag. His entire life literally fit inside the confines of a heavy canvas bag. It was there, on the still properly made bed. There was a bra draped over the bag. A dull grey one. It took a moment before he remembered the woman beside him and quickly sighed in relief. Jamie Dawson, his roommate on the road, was not there. No doubt he was somewhere in the motel complex in a similar situation. It was amazing, the amount of adventure you could have in a mere ten hours. They had arrived yesterday mid-afternoon, in town for a tournament being held at a nearby university. Twenty minutes to check in and unpack, and ten minutes to find the nearest happening bar. Both he and Jamie had it down to a science by now. All those years on the road, the last four together as teammates, had made them a truly formidable pair—both on the ice and on the prowl.

Scanning the room, Paul noticed that the television hanging high on the wall had panties over it . . . actually, he was wrong. On closer inspection it was his underwear. For a moment, it unnerved him how similar they appeared to a woman's underwear. He remembered how they had ended up there. Some late-night television, some martial arts film they had been watching while they drank. Was it Donnie Yen or Jet Li they had watched? He couldn't remember. The hockey player had tried explaining to the girl his own fascination with the stylized fighting—that he had even taken Taekwondo for exactly five classes in his late teens before hockey pulled his attention and finances in a different direction. He still admired the fluidity of the practitioners. She, on the other hand, had been less than enthusiastic about watching two men whale away at each other. So they moved on to other physical sports.

Then Paul saw the time shining up from the clock radio located upside down on the floor. The coach would be pounding at his door in twenty minutes, dragging what he laughingly called his team out for morning practice. Everything in this room was exactly what the coach had said not to do. If his lord and master saw the state of the room, the woman, and Paul's life, there was a very real chance he could be suspended or even cut from the team. Again. That always seemed to be the threat. At his age, it was very unlikely he could find another team to take him in. Thirty-five, on the plane of hockey potential, sitting in economy. From there it was a short hop to luggage status.

As he had done so many times before, Paul began the math in his mind. Should he wake the girl and deal with that half-drunk conversation now? Or let her sleep and try to fit in a quick and quiet shower, and then ease out the door? If he got himself together quick enough, he could even be waiting out front of his room for when the coach pulled up, like a smart and professional hockey player. That would impress him. Or—and it was always the "or" that got him in trouble—he could wake her and see if she was interested in another quick round of "shooting the puck." After all, there were twenty minutes in a period . . .

Paul shook his head. There were too many questions bouncing around in his partly damaged brain. So, taking the road of least effort, he turned off the table lamp and delicately crawled out of bed, being careful not to disturb . . . Marianne . . . Marsha . . . Mona?

The shower was one of the quickest he had ever taken in his life. Not long enough to wash his short hair—it would get sweaty in a few hours anyway—but effective enough to wash the residue of the previous night off his still fairly muscular body. How many strange showers had he been in over the sixteen years he had been playing semi-professional hockey? How many puck bunnies had there been? How many nights of wild abandon?

Dressing quickly, he moved quietly across the room, grabbing clean things out of and shoving dirty things into his bag. He froze as the woman rolled over slowly, still asleep, and he saw her tattoo, a killer whale in a West Coast style curling around her belly button. Nicely inked. He took a moment to admire it once more, and the rest of her. Paul didn't think she was Native . . . it would have no more significance for the woman other than that she thought it was cool. Still thankful for the fun they had shared after the sun went down, in the darkness of the room, he saluted Marlene . . . Margaret . . . Marnie? Whoever she was, she was a noisy but sound sleeper. Thank god for small mercies.

As one final act of atonement, Paul took twenty dollars out of his wallet for the maid who would have to deal with the mess they had created. Quietly he put it in an envelope and wrote "maid" on the front, hoping Vicky—that was her name!—Vicky wouldn't think it was payment for her services and get insulted, or simply take it regardless. Wedging it between a rye bottle and a beer bottle, he opened the motel door and removed his bag from the room, still trying to move as silently as an Ojibway hockey ninja. The girl slept on. As the door gently closed, Paul let out his breath, completely unaware he had been holding it in.

"Hey." It was his buddy Jamie Dawson, smoking a cigarette, bags already packed and waiting. A decade of practice had taught Jamie to only unpack essentials when staying for a handful of nights. Basically, just clean socks, underwear, and several t-shirts.

Paul was about to ask an obvious question, but being close buds for the last few years eliminated a lot of useless chatter. "I got my stuff about an hour ago, while you and the killer whale were still sleeping. Didn't want to disturb you."

"Did you sleep at all?" asked Paul.

"I slept once. A few years ago. The novelty wore off." They both smiled in the cold morning. Outside the motel, there were piles of dirty snow, and Paul saw two vans pulling up.

Leaning out the window, the coach surveyed both of them. "You look like shit."

"I bow to a man whose knowledge of shit is far more extensive than mine will ever be." Giving the scowling man his best smile, Paul went around back to throw his bag in the trunk. Slowly the other players began to filter out of the motel, some looking better, others looking worse than Paul. Almost all were younger and definitely looked more spry than the thirty-five-year-old from the Otter Lake First Nation.

Another day in the life of Paul North, semi-professional Anishnawbe hockey player, had begun.

N'shaa Go Dzhiike Nooj'aad

(Playing the Game)

Katie Fiddler was the only one smiling in the class of thirty. But it was a secret smile, born of clandestine and ironic origins. Twenty-four years old and with a rare understanding of where she stood in the world, the young lady watched the man standing at the podium in front of her. Elmore Trent, well respected and handsome, gazed across the class like a seaman studying the ocean. Years of practice, he had once told her, had taught him the eddies and currents in the average sea of young students.

And she was his teaching assistant. That in itself wasn't worth the smile; it was their relationship outside the classroom that she found . . . amusing, for lack of a better term. But for the moment, she pondered the man's words. After all, it was part of her job.

"The Bible. The Koran. The Bhagavad Gita. What are they?" he asked.

Typical Trent, she thought. He always loved to start his first-year classes with a question. He felt it got the intellectual fluids he hoped were gestating in the minds of the students flowing. She saw him smiling patiently, waiting for a response.

There was none. The aforementioned intellectual fluids seemed to be constipated. Some students glanced surreptitiously at their cell phones, others were examining the peeling paint in one corner, the rest were trying to decipher what a "bag of gitas" were. Well, thought Katie, time to start earning that luxurious salary the university was paying her. If these students wouldn't think for themselves, she'd help jumpstart the process.

"Yes, Ms. Fiddler? Regale us with your wisdom."

"Books of worship, Mr. Trent?" She smiled again, playing a part in the pantomime they performed in front of the class.

Professor Trent smiled back.

"Yes and no. Yes, they are indeed books of worship, but they are also so much more. Above and beyond the sheer theological significance, they also play a much larger part in defining society than you might suspect. For one thing, these books explore the history of each individual culture. They tell us stories of the way things used to be and how they changed. They also set out philosophies and social parameters that make a culture unique. Some even set down very specific laws to follow. A few die-hard atheists would even add that they contribute fantasy and science fiction to our society. Superstition. Even elements of a good horror movie!"

Katie turned to see the students laugh, as they did every year when he trotted out that line. Though he'd never admit it, she knew he loved performing. Perhaps that was why Professor Trent was considered one of the best lecturers in the university.

"So, Ms. Fiddler, they are more than just books of worship. They are a blueprint for the social order."

"Hmmm, I see your point."

She saw him smile again before launching into the next phase of his act. "I thought you might. First Nation legends are no different. While not quite as totemic—no pun intended—they do provide us with windows into how the Salish, the Dene, the Cree developed into who they are. Within the context of those stories—whether they are about Sky Woman falling from the sky, or Nanabush creating this or that, or how the rabbit got its ears—they are more than just mere children's tales. Those stories have been honed through generations of experience, thousands of years of existence, no different than the Bible or the Koran or any set of beliefs that struggle to explain the world and our place in it.

"For the rest of the semester, we will be deconstructing many origin stories popular amongst the First Nations peoples in Canada. Hopefully, if you are all paying attention, peeling back the layers of these legends will show us who, what, when, where, why and how these cultures came to be. Remember, legends and stories are the DNA of any nation."

Katie turned again to see all the students looking sufficiently impressed, except of course for the two seemingly out-of-place jocks sitting in the back row. It was obvious they would rather be bouncing balls or running laps or doing whatever sports people tended to do. But in this world called a university, all had roles they had to play.

"First things first . . ."

Katie saw him pausing mid-sentence and glance down. His cell phone perched on the lectern, she theorized. Somehow, she knew his wife had just called him. Something must be up. Sarah knew he was in class and normally would not attempt to contact him, especially these days. No doubt it would not be good. Maybe Sarah was cancelling dinner. Trent would have to return her call when he had the chance. Katie found reading people was often easier than the books Trent frequently assigned.

"Okay, everybody take out their textbook please . . ."

Katie couldn't help herself. "You mean your textbook?" Once again the students giggled. She was referring to the book that Trent had written that was now part of the class curriculum, *A Legend for Legends*. A clever title, she had to admit.

"Very funny, Katie. I like to think of it as everybody's book. I just get the royalties." Once more there was laughter, and this time it was not just at the professor's expense. The natural order of the classroom had been restored.

Aadzookewnini

(The Storyteller)

Professor Elmore Trent had lived a relatively uneventful but somewhat productive forty-nine years. A respected academic at one of Toronto's finest universities, the man had tenure, an office with a window, two well-received books exploring the nature of First Nations traditional stories, a wife (for the moment), and a stylish house in a stylish part of town. On top of it all, he looked a good seven or eight years younger. All in all, it was a good life, and other than dealing with the minutiae of university politics, he knew it. And then there was Katie.

"Okay, I want to discuss the importance of anthropomorphism in early Anishnawbe stories. How the animals seem more human than the humans. I assume everybody's read the material?" A sea of heads nodded, except for the back row where it seemed two student-athletes were having difficulty realizing the third chapter could usually be found right after the second. The professor sighed.

Several hours later, in his office, he was dealing with another annoying consequence of his comfortable life. Sitting at his desk, ear to the phone, Trent was arguing politely with his wife.

"No."

As regular as the winter snows, they had this argument every time tax season came by, and while Sarah Trent, née Ireland, was by and large an intelligent woman, the simple fact he did not want to sell his "cottage" no matter what the financial logic might indicate simply failed to register in her consciousness.

"Look, Sarah, that building is all I have left from my family. You know that." There was a knock at the door, and he leaned over his desk with a groan, reaching across a university-issued chair to open it. There stood Katie, winter jacket on, backpack over her left shoulder, looking every bit as vivacious as her twenty-four years demanded. Trent waved her in as he continued relaying the information both he and his spouse were quite familiar with. "Yeah, I know we haven't been there in six years, but that's not the point. I'm willing to pay for the renovations. It's not that much."

"Twenty thousand dollars isn't that much?!"

Embarrassed, Trent glanced out the window. Despite the serious nature of his conversation, he could see Katie smiling at the problems of middle-aged people. "What you need to . . ." He paused, taking a moment to analyze the information his wife had just delivered.

Katie sat in the chair and dropped her backpack. For a brief second her feet rested on Trent's desk before he swatted them away, while keeping the momentum with his wife. "Doesn't matter. Doesn't change anything. My parents lived and died in that house. You know it's important to me." Trent gave Katie a weary roll of the eyes, and she suppressed a giggle. "Sarah . . . Sarah . . . when I get home, I mean to the restaurant, we'll talk about it. Okay?"

Elmore loved that house. He also loved his wife and the woman sitting in his office. Even with all his education, he constantly wondered why love was such a pain. As he talked to his wife, Trent saw the bored student get up and first look out the window onto the wintery campus. Then, for the hundredth time, Katie casually looked around Trent's office. Row upon row of books. Some well-known, others arcane in their origins. Trent knew she had read a good chunk of them already. Many were the mainstay of any Indigenous person with an interest in literature about, for, and by the original inhabitants of this land. The young woman pulled a fat one from a lower shelf.

Almanac of the Dead by Leslie Marmon Silko. He shook his head, amazed by her love of that book. Many discussions had been born exploring the tale it told. Katie felt it was breathtaking in its scope and amazing in its originality. It was exactly the kind of book she hoped to write someday. However, Trent felt the author was, as he put it, "wanking off"—trying to sound deeper than she actually was. But Katie did not agree or care. He knew she treasured it regardless, telling him it was not written for people like him. It was a tome to be felt, not deconstructed.

As he listened to Sarah prattle on, his gaze moved from the young woman in front of him to the various Native knick-knacks on the windowsill and walls. Most of the so-called trinkets were gifts from students, including the dreamcatcher Katie had given him three months ago that was hanging in the window.

"Great. See you in an hour." And with that, he hung up the phone, sighing in exaggerated weariness.

"Trouble in paradise?" Katie asked, putting the book down.

"It depends on how you define paradise."

The woman sitting across from Trent wore the usual and expected dabbling of Native paraphernalia on her person. A small and tasteful turquoise necklace adorning Katie's neck with a matching set of earrings. Thank god, he thought, they were not porcupine-quill earrings. Native students today overdid those. In his mind's eye, he saw the forests adorned with thousands of naked porcupines trying to keep warm, victims of contemporary Aboriginal fashion. Simple white cotton shirt, tight black jeans, boots, and a heavy bomber-style winter jacket to keep everything underneath those fashionable clothes nice and warm. Not bad for a Rez girl, he told himself. Katie Fiddler, from an obscure Manitoba reserve, cleaned up pretty good. Instinctively, he knew that was not a correct thing to say in today's politically correct world, but considering he was enjoying certain extracurricular activities with her, that was the least of his concerns.

"Evidently the house I was born in needs some repairs."

"New windows, shingles, that kind of thing?"

"A little more. It's been a while since we've been up there, and last spring my cousin who looks after the place . . . well, he found a family of bears had moved in over the winter."

Katie tried not to smile. "That's not good."

"No, it's not. Evidently bears can be quite messy and destructive. The floors are saturated with shit and blood. One of the sinks was torn out. Somehow the bears knew there was running water under all that porcelain, and run it did, all winter and a part of the spring. I could go on, but you get the picture. And some mining company wants to rent the land it's on. Anyway, never mind." Trent took a deep breath, trying to get the image of Goldilocks's antagonists out of his head. "What's up?"

"Just being social. Can't I just drop in and say hello?" Casually, she picked up a book on his desk, glanced at it, then put it back down. "Hello."

"Uh, Katie, you know that's not exactly advisable."

Smiling as only somebody with their whole future ahead of them could, the young woman took a copy of Trent's book out of her bag. "I think you're being a little paranoid. By the way, I really enjoyed your class today. I love this stuff. Puts a lot of what my grandparents used to tell me in a new focus."

"Paranoid? *Prudent* would be more the word. Don't forget, I could lose my job over this."

"Over what?"

Feigning annoyance, he said, "You know."

Rising from her chair, she moved quickly to Trent's side of the desk and kissed him—a very un-student/professor kiss. A kiss that would definitely be grounds for the revoking of tenure, and his dismissal. All in all though, it was a very good kiss. Almost worth it.

A few seconds passed before the passion managed to subside and their lips parted. Trent was the first to speak. "I hate it when you do that."

"That's why I do it."

Almost regretfully, he pushed her away. "I told you. Not on campus."

Taking her seat again, Katie leaned forward, elbows resting on the desk. "Okay then. Later tonight."

"I can't."

"Sure you can. I happen to know you have no classes tonight. And are currently dealing with some issues regarding your wife. So, let's do something interesting."

On occasion, Trent marvelled at the way young people at university approached life. Do something now and worry about it tomorrow. Living for the moment amidst planning for the future. The dichotomy amused him. Try as he might, though, he couldn't remember going through that phase when he was that age. All those years in residential school had given him focus. Others it had given nightmares, destitution, and other assorted horrors, but to him it had gifted a sense of never wanting to be at anybody's mercy again, and the best way to achieve that was getting as close to the top of the pyramid as was comfortable.

The view was definitely better up there. "Didn't you hear me tell my wife we'd talk about it at dinner?"

"Come on, the three of us know you only say that to end a conversation. You've done it with me."

"There are certain luxuries that come with being twenty-four that don't exist when you're forty-nine. One of them is a fluidity of time and obligations. Whatever it is you have planned . . . enjoy yourself."

Disappointed, she put on her best pouty face, and though he fought the urge, Trent smiled. If nothing else, she was adorable, in a dozen different ways. "I was going to suggest going to a reading tonight. But I assume you and your beloved wife are dealing with your problems?"

"Does it matter to you?"

"El . . ." That's what she called him. El. Not Elmore. Not Professor Trent. Just El. At first it had amused and flattered him. After all, who wouldn't want to be known as the twelfth letter of the alphabet? Now, it was not so amusing. It denoted a certain level of familiarity that made him uncomfortable. Even his wife didn't call him El. But he was stuck. "I have a lot of shit on my plate and I know I have a few faults here and there, but regardless, I do not under any circumstances want to be the cause of anybody's failed marriage. We're just goofing around. I like you and you like me. Not worth wrecking a marriage over."

"We're not getting a divorce." Was he trying to convince her or himself? "This is just a hiccup. Sarah and I will work it out. Nothing to get upset about."

"As weird as it may sound, I hope so. There are a lot more things in this world to be pissed off about, and I don't want me to be one of them—for either you or her. I'm just a little Cree girl from Manitoba trying to get by in this world. My time to change the world will come later. Right now, I've got my hands full dealing with you."

That was why the professor had let this charming young lady force her way into his life. There was something about her self-confidence, her outlook, that he found refreshing. And dare he say it, invigorating. Sometime down the road, he felt sure the world would indeed have to deal with a formidable presence known as Katie Fiddler. Given enough time, she could make a redneck marry a Jew . . . which was one of the less quotable sayings his father-in-law would trot out at inopportune moments.

"So, what's with this reading tonight?"

Katie had his attention. Katie always had his attention. "A journalist wrote a book about surviving in the wilderness. A plane crash or something up north. Supposed to be really gripping, and she's appearing in the student lounge tonight as part of a book tour. Thought I'd make an appearance. Check it out."

"Doesn't sound like your usual fare." Noticing the lateness of the afternoon, he brought out his backpack and opened it. This time last year he had carried a briefcase, but Katie had said that it aged him a good five or seven years. Through some subtle manipulations, she had convinced him to buy a backpack. A really cool leather one she'd seen another older man wear. At first, he'd been uncomfortable with it, feeling like a bald man wearing a toupee in an attempt to look young. Eventually though, he grew into the backpack, to the point he now took it everywhere. He packed his bag full of the necessary books, papers, his electronic notebook, and several files, all precisely and neatly aligned. "Doesn't sound like my usual fare either."

"I like supporting all kick-ass women in anything, and this one sounds like she did some serious survival ass-kicking. And the reason I am inviting you is what's in her book—the crash and everything—took place about a hundred kilometres north of your reserve. Thought that might pique your interest." She leaned back in her chair, raising an eyebrow, waiting to gauge his reaction. His packing pace slowed down as he assimilated the information. He hated to admit it, but it did intrigue him. As he closed his backpack, he glanced up at her.

"What time?"

"Eight-thirty."

Trent knew he should not. Things had been shaky with his wife since their paths had diverged less than a year ago—only momentarily, he had hoped. Mysterious evening outings might stretch the levels of her credulity a bit further then would be sensible. Sarah was not the type to hire a private detective, but still, she was not a stupid woman. As well as Katie knew him, his wife knew him better, and this event—he was sure—did not sound like something he would be interested in. A survival narrative ripped from the headlines—most assuredly not his cup of tea.

Normally, Elmore Trent's idea of roughing it was ordering the house wine. And there was a pile of books on both his desk at home and here—this year's avalanche of Native literature, all waiting to be read and digested by this professor of Indigenous literature. From what Katie had told him, this particular book sounded a bit too manipulative and reeked of opportunism. Still, there was also the lovely Katie at the other end of that equation. "Okay. Maybe I'll see you there once I finish with Sarah. No promises though. Usual protocols?"

"Usual protocols." Beaming in victory, she grabbed her backpack and gave Trent another kiss, half the duration but double the passion. Before he could respond, she was out the door and slaloming down the hall.

As he watched his door slowly swing close, the only evidence that Katie Fiddler had been in his office was the still-noticeable taste of her lip balm on his mouth. Every fibre in his body told Trent he shouldn't do this. This was not a good idea. But it was not the first time he had ignored those fibres.

Seventy-eight minutes later, Elmore Trent and his wife, Sarah, were sitting in a lovely Indian restaurant in a fashionable part of Toronto known as the Annex, tucked in the back area, secluded as requested. During their happier times, this had been *their* restaurant. A joke shared between them was that there was no problem excellent lamb rogan josh could not overcome. Of course, that was before. Now they were dealing with the after—an after that lamb just could not ameliorate. A feeling of suppressed tension emanated from their table like a bad aroma. Even the couple at the table next to them, on their third date and very much anticipating what the evening might bring, felt oddly awkward.

Trent cleared his throat. "It's good that you found a place so quickly. You keep hearing about the vacancy rate in Toronto and—"

"I'm a real estate agent, Elmore. If I can't find a place to live in this town, then I wouldn't be very good at my job, now, would I?" Even under stress Sarah still talked the way that had first got his interest. Every word clipped and perfectly executed. Succinct in pronunciation. Over the years he had realized it wasn't just an affectation. It was just the way her tongue, lips, and mind worked. Slur a word or leave off the *t* in *often*? Not likely.

"I guess not." Sarah was the only person Trent had come across in his life who made him uncomfortable to open his mouth and use words when she was in a mood. But if he did not, it would make for an even more prickly evening.

"Now, about the cottage . . ."

Forcing down a fork full of the lamb, he shook his head. "I don't want to talk about that."

Her eyes on him, she took a slow and calculated sip of wine. "You said we would. Another promise conveniently forgotten, Elmore? We must do something. That thing is just sitting there, eating up maintenance fees and taxes."

"I told you. It's on the reserve, it doesn't have taxes."

"Elmore." She breathed out his name, making it sound like it had more syllables than it actually did. "I am trying to get our affairs in order. That place serves no purpose. Yes, it's your family home, but you have only been there, what, four times in the last twenty years? Mostly for funerals. Sentimentality is all fine and dandy, but not in this case. It's a dangling thread that needs to be pulled, cut, or sewn back in."

Trent almost laughed at that. One of the trademarks of her family was weird proverbs that seemed to come from nowhere. He decided to try a different tact. "Sarah, how long is this trial separation going to last? I mean, I miss you. I want you back."

"As long as it has to." Sarah took another sip of wine, this time looking off into the distance. "Maybe permanently."

"I refuse to believe that."

"Of course you do. You live in your little world of academia and pretty young students. The idea of a divorce doesn't quite figure into your view of the universe, does it? It might make things a tad messy and difficult."

"My universe has you in it."

"Your universe also has that young lady, whoever she may be. I did not want the details then, and I don't want them now. But Elmore, your universe is getting a little crowded."

People at nearby tables were beginning to look their way. More than the lamb was heated and spicy. "I told you I was sorry. I told you a million times. It was terrible. It was insulting. It was a betrayal of trust. It was a mistake. I know. Can't we deal with it and just move on?" Aware of the hypocrisy of his words, Trent wondered if it was his imagination that made him briefly taste Katie's lip balm once again. He did genuinely love the woman across the table from him, of that there was no question, but he was also aware of his own weaknesses, and he could only do battle with one major problem at a time. He had not yet told Katie about the weakening of his relationship with his wife, for fear that her fluid sense of morality might make her bolt, leaving him completely alone. It seemed that being alone scared him.

Often, he wondered if it was a repercussion of those years at the residential school, where amongst a hundred and seventy other students and a dozen staff, he had felt incredibly alone.

"Elmore, we have been together twenty-four years. And in those twenty-four years, I have learned many truths about you, one of which is you are a man of habit. You tend to repeat yourself. Your routine in the bathroom, your choice of restaurants, your method of sex . . ." This got a few more heads turning towards their table. ". . . and so, I have no doubt that this . . . incident has more than likely happened before, and quite probably will happen again. I know perfectly well that women are also capable of having affairs, but let's face it, it seems it's primarily endemic to men. So, my husband, I need to process all this before we can, as you say, *move on*. In what direction, I do not know."

Throwing her napkin down, Sarah pushed her chair back. "And, I just realized, I'm not hungry. If you will excuse me?" In one smooth motion, his wife rose from her chair, threw her purse over her shoulder, and took her coat from the nearby stand.

"Sarah—"

She shook her head, cutting the words off in his throat. "No. You don't want to talk about the cottage? Fine. As with so many other things, let us leave it unexamined. I'll be in touch, Elmore." Then, just as quickly, she was out the door, and he was alone as feared. Sort of alone. Half a dozen people were looking at him with curious but seemingly accusing gazes.

Not surprisingly, Trent had lost his appetite too. Putting his napkin over the lamb, he leaned back and looked out the window at the busy street. He knew he was to blame. He was at fault. He was responsible. And he had a date with Katie later that evening. A memory from a Shakespeare class he took a thousand years ago came back to him. About the difference between something being a tragedy and something being tragic, in the theatrical sense. Tragic was just when something bad happened to people. In a tragedy, bad things also happened, but the difference was the central character was fully capable of preventing such events from occurring, but because of their own weaknesses, was incapable of avoiding them. *Great*, it occurred to him, *I am verging on becoming a Shakespearean character.* Sighing at his own fallibility, he gestured to the waiter.

"Yes sir, can I get you anything else?"

Nodding, Trent said, "Yes please, a double Scotch. No ice."

Gegoon Baabiitood

(She Waits for Something)

Fabiola Halan sat in what was frequently referred to as a green room. Green rooms were seldom, if ever, green. This one was more eggshell white, with noticeable stains scattered about the walls and on the two couches. In her right hand was a cup of coffee, half-full and cold. In her left hand, a cigarette. She had briefly dabbled with the habit in her early twenties, but for some reason, now she craved the experience. Or so she thought. The cigarette had remained unlit. Outside, on the other side of the big window facing her, it had started to snow, and Fabiola watched the delicate flakes fall gently downwards.

What was this, the sixth or seventh town she had been in hawking her book? Add to that all the radio and television interviews she had done; she was very aware of green rooms and their limited delights. At least this one had potato chips and peanuts, neither of which she had consumed. Instead, she just sat there, looking out onto the dark, cold city. Fabiola wondered if what she yearned for was out there. Officials had said the pilot had died out there. There was no way she could have walked all that distance, in a tortuous storm like that. The large, gap-toothed woman could not have gone even half the distance. Although by all dictates of logic, Fabiola should not have survived either. Her whole situation was just a fluke and should never have happened. So once again, people were wrong. And if they were wrong about her, they might be wrong about the pilot. Two flukes were rare, but in theory they could happen. Taking a deep breath, once again she wondered if that woman's heart was still beating.

Fifteen months. Almost sixteen. So much had happened since the crash. She looked down at the leg that had been broken . . .

"Ms. Halan? We're ready for you."

The voice with the slight East Coast accent was Janine Sonny, the woman running the university event tonight. Perky and enthusiastic to the point of annoyance, she stood at the door, smile beaming. Fabiola returned a practised but not quite so bright one. Putting down the cigarette and coffee, she smoothed out her black and silver dress—stylish, but not enough to make the audience judge her. Standing, she presented herself to the author-wrangler, knowing being asked for her opinion would make Janine's day. "How do I look?"

Her fist pumping with irritating enthusiasm, Janine said, "Perfect. They'll love you."

"Good. I like being loved. Shall we begin?" One after the other, the two women left for the auditorium. It was show time.

Anwaatin Jibwaa Gtaamgwak

(Calm Weather before the Storm)

Paul had been to the city of Toronto a dozen times, but never for this. Standing on the cold and windy street of Carlton with his teammates, Paul looked at the building with a rare sense of reverence. There, in front of him, was what was left of the famous Maple Leaf Gardens, once the portal to heaven itself if you were a hockey fan of yesterday. He'd grown up watching the games coming from this very building on TV and listened to his uncles talking non-stop about the players and history of the Maple Leafs, frequently coming near to violence over disagreements.

Now he was here to play on the sacred ice itself . . . kinda. The Leafs no longer played here. They played at that modern facility that had no character or history, and Native people were all about history. Standing here, Paul was sure he could almost smell the sweat coming off the glory that was Darryl Sittler or Doug Gilmour. And who knows, maybe even the great George Armstrong had stood on that very block of cement. A Leaf for twenty-one years, captain for thirteen seasons, Anishnawbe all of his life—and most amazing of all for Paul, Armstrong had also been a right winger. As a result, the man was a personal hero of Paul's.

There was a local popular story of Armstrong paying a visit to Paul's reserve on a goodwill hockey tour. Needing to relieve himself, he found the first available tree during a walking tour. Since then, the tree had become hallowed ground.

The Gardens, now a combination Loblaws and university fitness centre, beckoned to the small boy who still lived in Paul. Eager to play in the shadows of the greats, he opened the door, entering the building feeling that in this environment, with the spirit of George Armstrong watching over him, he would be no less than great.

Sometime later, Paul was having difficulty catching his breath. Leaning against the heavily scuffed boards, he sucked in air, gulped it, practically devoured it, but there did not seem to be enough oxygen left in the arena to replace what he was burning off on the ice. The end of a long day of practice always made him tired and winded, but this year, it was getting worse. He was only thirty-five for Christ's sake, and yes, most of the other players were a good ten years younger, but thirty-five was not old. It was not air-sucking, cramp-in-calf, seeing-dots-float-across-his-eyes old. Not more than seven minutes ago, Herbie Tort star forward and star asshole, had somehow come up from behind him and taken the puck. From out of nowhere, Tort had just swept the puck from his stick and left him stickhandling ice dust. Paul had tried to catch up, but the laws of unified gravity were warping underneath him and slowing him down. That had to be the reason.

Two more drills later, and both Herbie Tort and Miles Patterson had cross-checked him into the boards and skated off with the prized piece of hard rubber many sport empires were built on. A few years ago, Paul would have been instantly back on his feet and chasing after them, ready to give as good as he got. Today, as with many more recent days, getting up off the ice required his brain sending a specific and conscious order to his arms and legs, and especially to his back, to help him get up. It seemed his muscle memory had forgotten. As for giving as good as he got . . . could it possibly be he had a little less good to give? And what had happened to his lungs? Usually he never tired. That was one of the things that had got him on this and a few other teams: a sense of inexhaustibility. He could skate all day, drink all evening, screw all night, with a few minutes left in the morning for some bathroom time. Maybe he was sick or had some disease. That would almost be better.

"You're looking a little slow out there, North."

"It's a Tuesday, Coach. Tuesdays are always tough. It's a Native thing."

The coach, the only non-Native on the team, almost smiled. "You sure you're feeling okay, North? You looked kind of wiped."

Paul straightened up, wilfully slowing down his breathing to appear normal. "After that fabulous night of sleep in those lovely accommodations management set up for us, how could I not be rested and willing to give it my all."

"Funny, North, but you did take a nasty hit there. Just wondering if you pulled everything together, or maybe there's a few things still loose."

Spitting his mouthguard out, Paul responded: "Coach, the doctor hit me harder the day I came out of my mother."

That did get a reluctant smile from a man who generally did not smile. "Well, maybe you'll like the university residences better. We were lucky to get them. And stay away from the coeds! I mean it, North."

"I'm sure you do, Coach. And you know me, I don't really get along with women who are smarter than me."

Smiling, the coach laid an almost fatherly hand on his player's shoulder. "Then you're going to lead a very lonely life, Mr. North." Using his outside voice, the coach addressed his side of the rink. "Okay, I think we're done for the day. Might as well hit the showers." Turning to the other players scattered across the rink, the coach yelled above the din of skates and sticks on ice. "That's it, boys, good practice. Tomorrow morning we play the Haudenosaunee Warriors at ten. And they're good. So I want all of you to behave—have a quiet and restful night so we can kick their asses tomorrow."

Jamie and Paul shared a glance. There was a chance that might happen. But as life had taught the man from Otter Lake, many other things were just as possible.

Paul turned towards the door to the bench but was roughly pushed aside by Herbie—intentionally or not, the right winger couldn't say. Under normal circumstances, he would be on Herbie like black mould on an Indian and Northern Affairs house, but today that would take too much effort. He had just about enough gas left in his tank to withstand the kinetic power of a good shower.

Jamie skated up to the door and waited for Paul to go through first. "Thanks," said Paul.

"Age before beauty," responded Jamie. Paul groaned, but he wasn't sure if it was because of the pain he felt, Jamie's comment, or the potential truth of the joke.

Breathing hard again, Paul leaned against the boards, cursing global warming or whatever it was that persisted in taking the oxygen out of the air. This was only the third lap of the rink Paul had done so far that evening. This was so unlike him. He had already put in a full day of practice, but that whole breathing incident a few hours ago had really scared him. Yes, he should have been winded, and yes, he had worked hard out there, but never before had he almost collapsed, out of breath. It had been a slow start to the season, and as with most of his career, he had cruised along on natural ability. Being a damn good hockey player came naturally to him. It always had. Strength, endurance, speed, and knowing where the puck was and where it should be had made him a valuable asset for any team for a number of years. It had never occurred to him that could possibly change. But nothing was written in stone, let alone a man's talent on the ice.

Paul knew he'd be sore tomorrow, but he had to get his lungs back. Or the rest of his talents—which he knew were still there—might not get him through the season. A little extra training might be required, for the first time. That was why he'd left Jamie and the other boys, including that idiot Herbie, at the bar after only two beers and sought the necessary environment of the arena. Another hour or two of basic power skating to force his lungs to do what he wanted. Scattered across the rink were a potpourri of other ice enthusiasts. Several couples skating slowly, holding hands, obviously on dates. What appeared to be two figure skaters trying to nail a triple axel but with limited results. A handful of other hockey players from the tournament doing their thing, trying not to kill any of the other skaters as they weaved back and forth imagining life as an evil Montreal Canadien, judging by the toque one was wearing. This left half a dozen other amateurs just trying to perfect the art of standing up on frozen water.

He had never played in the Gardens before, which in itself was unusual as he'd slapped rubber in practically every arena from Halifax to Winnipeg. Though roughly comparable in shape and atmosphere, there were distinctive differences to each building, brought on by the tastes and practices of its patrons.

Hockey rinks smelled somewhat different from curling rinks. Add to that the different decor and architecture, each one could be identifiably different to the practised eye. Fingerprints practically. Paul North had one of those practised eyes.

As much as he loved the game, he could feel a dark cloud hanging over him. He wasn't sure what the future held; it had never been an issue before. Maybe this was his future. A little less partying, a little more hardcore practice. If he could keep to that regimen, it might get him through the next three or four years. After that . . . who knew? He'd worry about that tomorrow.

Just before stepping into the showers, he noticed a torn university t-shirt on the floor of the dressing room. Paul smiled to himself, thinking that his mother, were she still alive and watching her precious soap operas, would be so happy that he'd finally made it to university.

"Mr. North, perhaps you'd like to answer the question?"

Twelve-year-old Paul suddenly realized he'd been caught daydreaming by the teacher. Mr. Henderson was not a pleasant man under the best of circumstances, but when he came to the conclusion that one of his students, this time Paul, was not paying attention—well, entire walls in the boys' bathroom were dedicated to comments about their teacher.

Paul had been trying to imagine where he'd be in ten years. It had been part of a discussion on the playground, and he'd discovered he didn't have an answer. He'd talked to his mother about the concept of having a long-term game plan, but like many of her generation, planning had little to do with it. Rent and the appearance of children frequently grabbed you by the scruff of the neck and forced you to go where they did.

Some of his friends had mentioned being cops, firemen, singers, and some had talked ambiguously about saving the world, either by going into politics or getting bit by radioactive spiders. But Paul was having difficulty coming up with a future. In a vague sense, the young boy felt this should worry him. But right now, there was another crisis to deal with.

"Ah yes, sir. I'd like to." It occurred to the young boy that it would help if he knew the question. Meanwhile, everybody in the room waited patiently, and then not so patiently, for him to answer. There were a few snickers, and Tommy, behind him, kicked his chair.

"Would you like to hear the question again, Paul?"

"That might help, sir."

Mr. Henderson sighed. "The question was, who was Socrates and what was he famous for? It was part of this week's readings."

Indeed it was. And Paul had fully intended to read everything last night, but the game on TV went into overtime and it had looked, however briefly, like the Toronto Maple Leafs might actually clinch a playoff position. At the end of the game, a disappointed Paul had forgotten about everything and gone directly to bed.

"Well, Mr. North? Do you have an answer?"

Desperate, Paul swung for the outfield. "Socrates . . . he was a straw man, kinda. And he wanted a brain of some sort." And missed.

Some kids giggled. Others rolled their eyes. Mitch, near the back corner, nodded in agreement. Mr. Henderson—the only reaction he could muster up was a deep and weary sigh.

"Well, I hear you're good at sports."

The first seed of Paul's mistrust of education had been sown.

Maaji Dibaajmowin

(The Story Begins)

"I was used to almost dying."

The room was silent, all listening to the one voice as it read from a book. "It had happened frequently in my life. Escaping by boat from a destitute Caribbean island with my family—that was my first trial by fire. I alone survived that. Later on, in my teens, I did battle with meningitis, leaving me bedridden for many months, hovering on the edge of existence. Somewhat later, after university, I left Montreal and sought my fortune as a journalist. There was an entire world out there I wanted to see, and stories that needed to be told. I ended up in places like Afghanistan, where a mortar shell took the leg off my photographer. In Egypt, a mob took a disliking to my Western apparel and swarmed me. I was later told I was minutes away from it turning into a gang rape. A dozen different countries and a dozen different ways to put my life in jeopardy. But I did not stop. I had drive. I had ambition. I wanted to know the world and I wanted the world to know me. And there were the stories I wrote. Always the stories.

"Unexpectedly, that's how I ended up flying across the harsh skies of northern Ontario. It certainly wasn't for the money, as any experienced journalist would tell you. I was looking for THE STORY. I was always looking for THE STORY." Fabiola looked up from her book, a slight smile on her face. "That's in capitals by the way." A modest chuckle from the fifty or so people arranged in a semicircle around the podium. The woman stood in a standard lecture hall, with ten rows of seating climbing up to the low rafters.

Katie sat halfway up the centre of the auditorium, in semi-darkness. Most of the other patrons were seated closer to Fabiola Halan, but Katie was more comfortable at the rear of the crowd. That way she could watch the people as well as the authors. That was part of the fun. She enjoyed reading people as well as books. In addition, it provided a more secluded opportunity for Trent to join her—part of the so-called protocols. He was late as usual. Fabiola had been ushered on stage fifteen minutes ago and was well into her reading. The journalist was amazing, an orphaned refugee who now travelled the world and had managed to survive what was essentially a death sentence . . . several times over, it seemed. How exciting was that? Part of Katie envied such an exciting, different life, while the other part of her was more than happy both parents were alive and delighted their only daughter was a success in university. Katie had only been to the United States and Mexico, but when the time was right, she planned to blanket the world with her size-seven shoe prints.

"Sorry I'm late. It's started to snow outside. Did I miss anything?" Trent slid down into the seat just behind her and to the left. Katie could smell Scotch on his breath.

"Not too much. How's the missus?"

"Same as always."

Katie wondered about that. Normally, El was more than content to unload his marital discord onto her as a disinterested sort-of third party. But lately, the professor had been quite closed-mouth about details on the home front. Katie had been sincere about not wanting to be the source of a divorce. Her relationship with Elmore was casual and amusing. Men her own age left something to be desired . . . actually, left a lot to be desired. Katie felt men were like the moose carcasses her uncles would hang in the backyard. They needed to age appropriately before they could be properly enjoyed. White people had their wine metaphor; the Cree had their moose metaphor.

Katie whispered over her shoulder, "She's fascinating."

Leaning back in her seat, she took in Fabiola Halan. About five foot eight, maybe a hundred and thirty lean pounds. Her hair pulled back almost too severely into a fashionable bun. Tailored skirt suit. Stylishly pretty. Her skin dark, the colour of Trent's walnut desk maybe. And those cheekbones. They sat high and proud, looking like they could cut diamonds. And confident. Her voice commanded the lecture hall, and as her story sunk into Katie, she found herself somehow enamoured by the tale the author was telling. She got the feeling the woman was afraid of nothing, and given the experiences detailed in her book, who could blame her.

"THE STORY, as I call it, is like a drug. When you taste it, when you are writing it, when you know it could change the world, you feel the rush. Simply put, I knew nothing of northern Ontario, the land or its people. Though I had travelled the four corners of the world in my job, this mysterious land just a thousand miles to the north and northwest was an alien domain for me. Like most Canadians, I had spent most of my life in this country no farther than maybe three hundred kilometres from the American border. I knew the cities, the farmland, the forested cottages, but not this snow-swept bush that surrounded me. I had spent my life looking outwards from this Canada, and now I was looking in—or more accurately, looking to this raw and untamed habitat. Yes, that is a cliché, but a true one. I was in this hostile land because of THE STORY I was looking for. You see, beneath its virtual permafrost and muskeg, little morsels of carbon, very similar in molecular composition to coal, had been discovered. Add a few million years of heat and pressure, you get this substance called diamonds. To the layperson, diamonds are often thought of as a girl's best friend. I never had that opinion, not then and not now. But it was a story. A journalist's best friend. Perhaps THE STORY that would turn me from a journalist to a JOURNALIST." Fabiola looked up from her book, scanned the room, and smiled. Her tone became more casual. "Again, in capitals."

The audience was appropriately amused.

"To all the budding journalists in the room, and all those who write essays and reports, never underestimate the power of capitalization. Many frown on it, call it trite, but when diplomatically used, they can be quite effective. Don't be afraid to assert your 'capital' rights." This got a modest round of applause, and cheers from many of the students scattered throughout the audience.

"Oh great," muttered Trent. "You do realize now everybody's dissertations and compositions will have multiple capitalizations seeded throughout the text?"

"Shhh" came Katie's reply.

"Diamonds are interesting. Of themselves, they serve no useful purpose. You can't eat them. You can wear them, but they won't keep you very warm." More laughter. "They are a substance that by definition should be worthless. As I said, they serve no useful function, unless you operate an industrial drill or are in need of a very accurate watch. Yet we dream of them. We lust for them. We dig for them. Diamonds . . . more valuable than gold. Entire empires have spread greed across the planet looking for diamonds and their close relatives. For something so pretty, so representative of love and devotion, they have been responsible for an unimaginable amount of misery and disappointment. I was just the latest victim."

"A bit overwritten, don't you think?" whispered Trent.

"Try rereading your own books," Katie countered.

"Jeremy Acapetum, a Cree teenager, had already lost his life in the crash, ironically returning from a life-saving medical operation in Timmins. It's assumed the pilot Merle Thompson's existence was also extinguished by the events perpetrated by the crash. Both people, whose ancestry had for thousands of years been shaped by the northern Ontario land, had become part of THE STORY. THE STORY was no longer the diamond mines that were sinking deep talons into the Canadian Shield. These mines were now being referred to laughingly as 'the New Buffalo,' and that metaphor indicated it was a new path or a way for the Indigenous people located around the infant mines to, if you'll pardon the pun, mine new economic potentials. To become self-sufficient. Of course, with irony being what it was, buffalo were not indigenous to the area.

"The new STORY—as it was turning out to be—had taken an unexpected turn. It now focused on how a lost daughter of a far-off tropical sea would survive a land so hostile, so different, and was succumbing to the bitter wind and biting cold. Was it the end of that STORY, of her STORY?" Closing the book on the lectern, Fabiola looked up to her audience, again with a slight smile. "And with that, I think you know the answer to that question. And if you don't—well, as luck would have it, we have some books here for sale that will fill in those blanks."

The room erupted with applause from a hundred different hands. For a minute, Fabiola soaked up the appreciation before bowing slightly. Near the door, even the woman selling books for the university bookstore was applauding. Katie clapped her hands enthusiastically, while Trent's ovation was a little more subdued.

D'zhindmowaad Iw Enokaadmowaad

(Talking Shop)

Of the four dozen or more people that had attended the reading, Trent judged by the length of the line that more than half had been intrigued enough to purchase a copy of the book. *A Frozen Heart*, the book was called. On the cover was Fabiola Halan, dressed in a contemporary parka, and behind her a bog of tamarack and spruce had more than likely been superimposed. Feeling obligated, Trent bought the book, rationalizing it by admitting he had probably read worse things. And he could write it off. Personally, his tastes leaned towards more academic pursuits, and Sarah had a fondness for more classical influences. She rarely read anything published after World War Two. But this was entirely Katie. Pop culture and feminist authors. Trent shuddered at the thought of what her bookshelves must look like.

Her sharing her apartment with a roommate meant he had never been to her place—it would have been too obvious. But it was a proven fact people's abodes frequently reflected their personalities. Still, to many people, a good professor, while being an expert in their field, should be willing to explore beyond their realm of expertise. And as Katie had pointed out, this story had happened a hundred or so kilometres north of where he was born.

Looking around at the people in line, there were some Trent knew and had given the prerequisite head nod too, but most were unfamiliar. Situations like this always made him uncomfortable and conscious of who was seeing him and Katie frequently in the same room. The fact she was his TA made things a little more plausible, but people could still be suspicious—especially when there was a reason to be suspicious.

After twelve minutes in line, Trent could see Fabiola at her table, smiling mechanically as she signed books. Katie was busy reading the back of the book, mumbling to herself, "Geez, for twenty-nine bucks, there better be a lot of sex in it." As they moved up in the queue, Katie took a diplomatic step backwards behind Trent. "You go first," she said, uncharacteristically shy.

Stepping up to the seated author, Trent handed over his book and Fabiola took it, appraising the new man standing in front of her. "Hmmm, you practically breathe academia. This your university?"

"Not mine personally. Just renting." This got a small laugh from the woman to his right stacking the table with new books. "Make it out to Elmore Trent please."

Fabiola started writing his name on the first page of the book. Trent noticed a very delicate hand, with perfect nails painted in a subdued pinkish hue, signing in a very measured script. "And just what are you a professor of, Mr. Trent?"

"Human sexuality." He didn't know why he'd said that. Especially with Katie standing right behind him. It wasn't as if he was a natural flirt . . . it had just sort of come out of him. The point of saying it, he did not know. Maybe Sarah was right. Maybe he was incorrigible. The momentary thought of Sarah briefly brought a pang to his heart.

At least this warranted a brief and amused glance from the woman. "Really?"

"My work is my life."

"Like every other man I've met. You are amusing, Mr. . . . Professor Trent. I bet you say things like this to all the women authors who sign your books."

Trent cleared his throat. His flirting—or whatever it was— was going too far. He was a tenured professor at one of the country's finest universities. Surrounded by people. Including one behind him that he was sleeping with. And this wasn't exactly a bar. "Not quite. I was looking at your program. You've been on quite the tour. Winnipeg, Calgary, Vancouver, Edmonton, Regina, Thunder Bay . . ."

"Yes, marketing is easily sixty per cent of publishing a book. And I do want this to be a successful enterprise. Literally, this book almost killed me. But if I'm being honest, I thought eking out my existence in that dreadful plane was hard, but a book tour is crushing. And I've still got two weeks more to go, though luckily my magnanimous publisher has given me a few days off here in Toronto. Just media stuff, and I can sleep late. Thank heavens for small mercies, I suppose. Thank you, Professor Trent, and uh, enjoy your human sexuality research."

"Actually, that was a joke. I teach two classes in Indigenous studies, focusing on First Nations traditional stories."

Fabiola leaned back in her chair, appraising him once more. "Oh, I see. That was perhaps the trickster in you?" This time Trent smiled. "Forgive me, but there are people behind you." For all his attempts to be charming and provocative, he was summarily dismissed with a simple nod. "Hello, and you are?"

"Make it out to Katie Fiddler."

Trent couldn't help noticing the quizzical look his young lover was giving him. Was it the blatant flirting? Taking a deep breath, the professor wondered if he was in trouble. Again.

The office was dark but not deserted. Steamed an opaque colour, the windows hid the down-coming snow that was blanketing the city. On the couch, lit only by a diffused streetlight halfway down the block, Trent and Katie were enjoying a post-coital moment. The sofa, worn and lived in, was not the most comfortable of places to linger on after love, but other than the desk, an office chair, and a bookcase, their choices were limited.

Katie was the first to break the silence. "Were you flirting with that woman?"

"No, just some academic bantering. I knew you'd ask me about that." With his right foot, he managed to hook and pull the office chair over to in front of them, and he promptly put his feet up.

Snorting, Katie lifted her head up from his shoulder. "You forget. I know your flirting style. I know it very well."

"Oh, trust me, I don't think I have anything in common with that woman. Seemed kind of cold to me. I don't even know why I said those things. Very weird. Maybe I've been reading too much *Tales from the Smokehouse*."

"My god, you're still reading that book?!"

"Not in a while, but it was my first introduction to Indigenous sexuality." He kissed her quickly on the lips but, just as quickly, she backed up.

"Written by a white guy. Boy, I see I came along just in time."

"Herbert Schwarz didn't write it. He was an academic collecting traditional legend and put—"

"If I remember correctly, one of those legends took place at Expo '67. His research protocol was not exactly above reproach."

Katie was very bright, but frequently her enthusiasm for topics overcompensated for logical thought. Totally amused, Paul leaned back and smiled.

"Hmm, interesting. So, are you saying legends, in whatever their form, are restricted to time immemorial? There are no potential legends in the making today? The days of free-ranging legends or traditional stories regarding Indigenous people, places, and things are unfortunately a thing of the past? That's a very dim view of contemporary life, Ms. Fiddler."

The two naked people, in the middle of an academic argument, stared at each other across the worn couch. Katie was the first to break the stalemate.

"Oh god, I hope not. Sometimes legend and stories are all that make life interesting."

"Joseph Campbell could not have said it better."

Laughing, she rose to her feet. "Hey, where's the dreamcatcher I bought you? It was in your window this afternoon. You didn't throw it out, did you?"

He raised both his eyebrows at the question. "Of course not. I never throw out dreams, caught or not. It must be there somewhere."

Kneeling, Katie looked behind the couch. There she quickly found it on the worn carpet, leaning against the wall. "Must have been the condensation on the windows from things getting so hot and steamy." Subtly lit by the outside light, she certainly was a vision to behold. Definitely one of the Manitoba Cree Nation's best exports. It was a body that very few forty-nine-year-old men got to see in the flesh. Sarah had looked somewhat like that, when they'd first met, back before the millennium. Except she was a redhead and Katie was very much a brunette. "Can't be a good sign, a dreamcatcher falling to the floor. Bad mojo."

"Mojo. Is that Cree?"

"No, but *kiss my ass* is." Blowing an errant dust bunny from the dreamcatcher, Katie cradled it in her hands.

"You know I have my suspicions about the origins of those things." Elmore watched the light play off the contours of her body. It was moments like this that made him understand why he would put his marriage in jeopardy. And then, on the drive home, regret every single action that came from it. Infidelity had a yin/yang nature to it.

Grabbing a tissue from Trent's desk, Katie wiped some of the moisture off the window and rehung the suction cup attached to the dreamcatcher. "You would. Some of us like to believe in some things. Not everything can be researched away. I think it's a charming legend, like Santa Claus or the Tooth Fairy. It may not be a hundred per cent real but . . ." The rest of her sentence was a shrug.

Katie paused for a moment, looking out the clear part of the window. From where he was sitting, Trent could tell it was still snowing, though not as hard as it had been earlier. Her eyes seemed to drift to somewhere far away. "In Manitoba, the snow is kind of different. Does it snow like this where you come from?"

It had been snowing on the day he left for St. Andrews. Now it was his turn for his mind to drift far away. *Left* was such a polite word. *Taken* would be more accurate. It had been the tail end of the residential school era but still mandatory, and little Elmore Trent had been taken from his parents and shipped far away, in both geography and culture. The first snowfall of the season, big white flakes falling. Any other day the six-year-old would have been trying to catch them on his tongue. That day, as he'd left, he'd watched his parents disappear through the rear window of a large dark car. Living that far out on the trapline, Elmore had been overlooked in the mad scramble to harvest the children of the community. But it was only a reprieve, and a month later he'd joined the ranks of the assimilated.

Four years after the system had absorbed him, both parents died when their cabin caught fire, leaving him with no close relatives. An orphan living in a system of bad food, harsh correction, and alternate beliefs, that is where he stayed, even during the summer months. Sometime later, when he emerged back out into the real world, he continued in the general direction the people at St. Andrews had pointed him. Physically, spiritually, metaphorically, he'd never really returned home.

Many of his schoolmates had fallen by the wayside in the intervening years—victims of what he sardonically referred to as "post-contact stress disorder." A funny, complicated academic term Trent used to describe everything unfortunate that happened to many of his brethren. Luckily though—as if luck could ever find its way between those rust-coloured brick walls—the unholy needs of those holy people had bypassed the young boy. Sure, there had been much corporal punishment, but for reasons he was always afraid to ask about, it seemed he was not of sexual interest to those who served a higher god. A small part of him had felt he probably wasn't worth the attention.

At the age of seventeen, he proceeded on with the next leg of his life, post St. Andrews. In the intervening thirty-two years, he'd been back to his reserve four times, practically once a decade. Mostly for research, or a sense of obligation inspired by a funeral. He had even taken Sarah twice. On one of his trips, he had contracted somebody from the community to rebuild his parents' house, believing it would be a nice country getaway for him and his wife. And as coincidence would have it, the man renovating the ruins was a distant cousin. But there were too many memories—or, perhaps more accurately, not enough memories of the place. Trent would look around and wonder what he would have been like had he continued to grow and develop in this tiny place by the river. The more he thought about it, the more morose he'd become, and the anticipation of these visits gradually began to dissipate. It snowed on a day they visited. He hadn't been back since. And now Sarah wanted to sell the cabin. It made all the sense in the world to sell it, he supposed.

"Hello?!" Katie, in all her physical and naked glory, was now standing in front of him. She'd asked a question, about snow and his childhood . . .

"Yeah, pretty much." Reaching out, he grabbed her and pulled her onto his lap. "But that was then."

"You looked pretty sad there for a moment."

He could smell her hair—something coconut with a dash of sage. She must have been at the University Aboriginal Students Centre today. They always started and ended their day with a smudge. "You know, I never had lasagna till I was nineteen. Isn't that sad?'

Inches away from his face, she gave him a puzzled glance. "What an odd non sequitur."

For a few seconds, he leaned forward and rested his head on her chest. The trouble with carrying so much baggage—emotional or otherwise—was how tired it could make you.

Mnik Ko Bmaadizwaad Nimshag

(The Life Expectancy of Dogs)

Across campus, on a small residential side street, a little dog was taking its master for a walk. Standing barely eight inches above ground, Polly had difficulty navigating some of the snowbanks along the sidewalk. Add to that the accumulating snow, and these nightly toilet forays were becoming increasingly difficult for the miniature schnauzer. Justin Majors once again cursed the municipal workers for not doing a better job at keeping the sidewalks cleared. Obviously, none of them had small dogs to worry about. Probably all cat owners, he reasoned. So far, Polly was about twenty minutes into her sniff-and-reject excursion, not having yet selected the best place to "do her business."

The evenings had not been cold enough to make these outings uncomfortable in recent weeks—luckily February had yet to bare its vicious teeth—but still, the noise of the traffic bothered Mr. Majors. Vehicles on wet or snow-covered streets always seemed to generate substantially louder noise. And while it didn't seem to trouble Polly, Mr. Majors preferred the calm serenity of his little cul-du-sac. The city, thanks to all those goddamn condominiums that kept popping up everywhere, had gotten so much noisier since the eighties. That was a good three Pollys ago.

To protect his sanity against the sonic pollution, Mr. Majors had given himself for Christmas a set of expensive noise-cancelling headphones, hooked up to his cell. During these long walks, he'd listen to music, podcasts, or various CBC Radio shows, depending on what was of particular interest. At the moment, he was catching up on the day's news. A cold, professional-sounding woman's voice filled him in on what the prime minister was up to.

Up ahead and to the right was the entranceway to a small park. It was Polly's failsafe. If nothing else worked, she would never pass up the opportunity to drop her load amidst the maples and pines that populated the three acres of parkland. As usual, one of the four overhead streetlights was still out. It had been a good five months since Mr. Majors had first noticed it, and still it was not repaired. *Damn municipal workers*, thought Mr. Majors once again. Probably spending all their time fixing the potholes on their own streets.

At least this route was quieter. Already he was leaving behind the rush and storm of a busy Toronto street. The stridency of downtown urban life could still be heard, but the intensity was fading. As well, his anger towards the civil employees of this metropolitan sprawl began to lessen. Trees and park benches had that effect on him. And Polly was expressing a certain amount of interest in a patch of unsoiled snow.

The lady announcing the news reported that somewhere out west, Mr. Majors didn't catch the city—possibly Edmonton— there'd been a gruesome murder. Police were investigating. Well they'd better, thought Mr. Majors. That's how they earn those big salaries and pay for that union of theirs. And it followed another potential murder in Regina, too. Something about decapitation. Again, police were investigating. Mr. Majors detested this kind of news. He already knew the world was full of cat-loving psychopaths. He didn't have to be continually reminded of it, so he turned the volume down.

"Finally," commented Mr. Majors to himself as Polly began her circular dance. Centring a good chunk of his post-dinner activities around the bowel movements of a twelve-pound dog would have embarrassed his father. But Connor Majors was long dead, and Justin Majors no longer had to bow and scrape to the old man's wishes. As far as he was concerned, if he had the time and gas money, he would love the opportunity to take Polly to his father's resting place in Pembroke and let her go nuts on the old man's grave. The thought kept him warm and amused despite the growing cold.

The dog kept sniffing the ground, walking around in a circle, as if trying to find the proper aesthetic angle from whence to shit. "Hurry up, Polly. You eat your meals in half a minute, you should be able to do this in half a minute," Mr. Majors muttered. Nearby, he heard some snow falling from a shoulder-high cedar hedge. Must have been a squirrel running through or something. Stupid squirrels, he thought. They were supposed to be sleeping this time of year, in those houses made of leaves he could not help but see in trees all throughout the city. Mr. Majors knew he would sleep away these dark months if he could. But the problem at hand was that Polly loved squirrels—or more accurately, hated them. Already the small animal's ears were standing upright and she was facing the hedge in a crouched position, a low growl in her throat. Any interest in defecating was now replaced by something far more interesting located deep within the hedge. "Oh shit," Mr. Majors said aloud, unaware of the irony of his statement.

The man gave the leash a quick jerk, hoping he could coax his Polly away from savagely attacking some rodent that was barely smaller than her. He jerked a second time, but Polly would not be denied. Somewhere deep in her genetic history was a strain of savage hunting dogs, still strong and eager to do battle despite the size of the current generation. Lurching forward, the small dog managed to pull Mr. Majors's arm forward, and Polly disappeared into the wall-like green foliage.

"Goddamn it, Polly," yelled Mr. Majors, momentarily giving the dog slack before wrapping the leash around his wrist and giving it a much more solid yank, one designed to bring the dog tumbling back into the clear of the park. Tired and annoyed, Mr. Majors was willing to be a little rougher with his pet than he would normally permit himself. Except the leash did not give. It seemed fixed, unmoving. Perhaps Polly had somehow wrapped it around the base of the hedge or something. The man tried a second time, planting his feet and hoping his renewed effort would not hurt the dog. Only this time, something in the hedge pulled back. "Polly?" The dog did not answer, but the leash itself began to rise vertically through the wall of intertwined cedar branches, breaking some as it travelled upwards, bending others. Then, just as suddenly, the leash was pulled out of his hand and disappeared into the plant life like somebody sucking up spaghetti noodles, knocking his posh headphones off at the same time. This was no squirrel . . . At least he hoped not. With all the pollution in the water these days, Mr. Majors had always had an unspoken concern about animals mutating. He tried calling one last time—"Polly . . . ?"—half hoping there would be no response.

Again, no answer except for a leash flying through the air and landing at his feet, complete with a broken collar, but no Polly. Some other dog owners might have been angry. Some other dog owners might have gone foraging in the bushes for the demonic squirrel or coyote or fox or whatever, confident that their size and loud mouth would protect them. But Justin Majors was not that kind of dog owner. Standing there for a few seconds in the dark, looking down at the remains of Polly's birthday present on the ground, discretion strongly suggested that he walk quickly into where the streetlights were beckoning. Stepping on his headphones, he left quickly, almost evacuating his own bowels.

Now, it seemed, there was the possibility of a Polly 5.0.

Behind the bushes that hugged one of the ravines threading through Toronto, a large and impossible apex carnivore watched the man walk away.

Ogichidaa Maadaadiz

(A Warrior Starts His Journey)

Two blocks from the arena, three blocks from the residences used by the university for visiting dignitaries—which in this case meant hockey players—existed what could colourfully be called a "seedy" bar. Even though smoking in bars had been outlawed several decades ago, the Maple Leaf—as it was called because of its proximity to the arena—still reeked of ancient cigarette smoke, its chemical components layering the bar like a lacquer. Frequented by local university personnel, many a discussion had taken place over cheap draft concerning how deep the layer of primeval cigarette smoke residue must be on the walls, tables, floors, and people to still generate such a noticeable odour. Many even wondered if it could feasibly be a health hazard, but the beer was cheap and the location convenient. That was worth a carcinogen or two.

Two tables in the back were filled with young, healthy-looking men. The table was awash in beer, both in glasses and spilled along the scarred wood. The topic of conversation: the possibility of Herbie Tort being signed next season. Most of the players could spot a scout a mile away, and they had noticed this one guy at the last three games, paying close attention to the young man. Of course, if asked, Herbie would want to play in the NHL, for either the Leafs or the Canadiens—but, as of yet, he did not have such command over his career choices. As the cliché goes, he was just glad to be asked to dance.

Paul's buddy Jamie, the team's goalie, raised a half-filled glass of beer in salute. "To Herbie! To be voted Hart Trophy winner of . . . I don't know . . . 2025!" A round of cheers erupted, and the beer was drunk. Herbie drained his and jokingly took Jamie's beer and drained that too, to Jamie's mock indignation.

There was much mirth sitting at the table, except near the corner, at the opposite end from Herbie. Paul North, for several reasons, was not inclined to celebrate. Still drained from his extracurricular workout, this was the scene that had greeted him upon rejoining his teammates. At the tail end of his career, it hurt to find out an asshole like Herbie could be moving up in the hockey world, and in a few years might be on a trading card. He wasn't even sure if they still had trading cards. Awards seemed to gravitate to this particular teammate—he was last year's winner of the Player of the Year award in their unique league—and it was well known Herbie had been largely responsible for the team winning the Frederick Sasakamoose Memorial Cup as the best in their division.

Whereas he, Paul North, had a limited number of options in the upcoming years. He could return home to Otter Lake, move in with his sister (if she had grown forgiving in the past decade), and probably get some sort of training/recreation gig with the band office. Not quite the NHL. Could maybe go back to school. Spending the day walking around and training at this university had sort of opened his eyes to the potential of collegiate life, specifically all the pretty girls that were swarming the hallways and buildings. Paul was, after all, just thirty-five—thirty-six in five months. It wasn't too late to have a second life. He had always considered himself a smart, rise-to-the-challenge kind of guy. It was almost demanded by his clan.

It was the Eagle clan that Paul belonged to—at least that's what his father had told him. Supposedly a leadership-oriented clan, but Paul felt he related more to the animal's nomadic sensibility. When the eagle was flying high in the sky, you never knew when or even if it would land somewhere on the earth.

His father had left, disappeared when Paul was young, leaving behind a multitude of stories and a boat, which leaked. Paul's mother, when alive, had travelled around the powwow circuit, summer after summer. By his early teens, the young boy had been to nearly three dozen other Indigenous communities scattered across Ontario.

And his sister, Janine, she was a conference vet. Her job at the band office meant she was at some economic, political, or social symposium somewhere in the country at least once a month. Maybe this was why he felt more at home in a bus or a hotel room—someplace different from the night before. Family lineage.

He'd been on the road with a Junior A hockey team when it was time for his mother to meet her ancestors. Janine had begged him to come home but he'd refused. As much as he cared for the woman who bore him, he knew everything that was great and wonderful about her would not be waiting for him should he return. And his mother had always loved watching him play his game. Staying in the game was the best way to pay tribute. He could say his goodbye to a cold tombstone in a few weeks.

The end result: a very angry and resentful sister. The few times he'd made it home over the years, it was like he didn't have a sister. Or more accurately, it was like Janine didn't have a brother.

Every time he'd returned, he'd been pleasantly surprised to see he had another little nephew or niece. Once, absolutely delighted, he'd bumped into two at a local snack bar.

"Hey! I'm your uncle!"

"We have an uncle?"

Thus the road seemed warmer and more inviting.

Now, here he was, surrounded by buildings of higher education. And he couldn't help wondering, had he taken a different road, what he could have studied. Or, more aptly, what did an over-the-hill obscure-hockey-league player go to university for? At the far end of the bar, there were two young guys, noses planted deep in their laptops. When Paul had walked in, he'd seen on their screens columns of numbers with complex notations attached. Whatever they were studying was not for him. He had always liked movies—maybe something to do with that? But the simple fact he couldn't come up with the name of a university program that would include movies was a bit of a deterrent. 'Introduction to Movies'? Besides, what little he knew about making movies looked hard and complicated. Maybe Indigenous studies. He was Indigenous. How difficult could that be to study?

Paul had bumped into a cousin once, when he was in Winnipeg for a tryout. Jimmy Wabung. All the family talked about him as the guy from the Rez who was going to change the world. He was a university professor. Somehow the man had found out Paul was in town and tracked him down, wanting to say hello. Paul had dimly remembered the boy—now man—from his childhood. They'd gone squirrel hunting once or twice.

"Son of a bitch, look at you!" Jimmy was a lot bigger than Paul, horizontally. Dressed better too. He seemed to have a fondness for vests, like he was trying to hide his belly. There for a few days, Paul had decided to spend some time with family. They went to some games, closed a few bars, and found themselves at a fundraiser for the local Friendship Centre. It was nice to have family you could talk to, thought Paul.

"How's your sister?"

"Last I heard, pretty good. Four kids and a man who stays around. What more can you ask for?"

"I went on a date with her once. Did she ever tell you?"

For a second, Paul tried to imagine the well-fed man he was sitting with on a date with his pencil-thin sister. But then, Jimmy hadn't always been that big. "No, I didn't. Where was I?"

"On the road, I think. You were always on the road."

Still am, thought Paul, before taking another sip of his beer.

"Oh well, nothing really came of it. Just as well. I ended up here, and well . . . I guess she's got four kids now." They were both silent for a moment, remembering Janine North Ruston. Jimmy was the first to return to the present. "Hey, I'm teaching a class tomorrow afternoon. Why don't you come and sit in? It'll be fun. You can see what I do for a living."

Intrigued and with time on his hands, Paul had agreed. At 2:30 the next day, the hockey player showed up at the building and room his cousin had texted him. There looked to be almost a hundred students sitting in the lecture hall, all with notepads and computers, ready to learn interesting things about Indigenous people. That's what Jimmy's area of expertise was—Indigenous political structure. Sitting there, waiting for his cousin to show up, Paul found it amazing that all these people, most of them white, could be so interested in Rez elections and politics.

Regardless, Paul had spent all of his life as a Native man, and had been to more Indigenous communities and knew more Indigenous people than could be imagined. There was little he didn't know about Indigenous life, probably including its political structure. A course like this? Piece of cake.

Jimmy then entered from a back room, looking every inch a professor. With a nod to his cousin in the back row, Jimmy started his lecture.

"Last week we began to look at Indigenous governance and how it pertained to nation building and rebuilding. Today, I want to explore intergovernmental fiscal relationships, and if we're lucky, we might foray into defining contemporary Indigenous leadership, Crown government representatives, and civil society participants. I know, I know, all exciting stuff."

Immediately Paul's brow furrowed. Though he did not speak, everything about him said "Huh?" Twenty-five minutes into the lecture, Paul left, unsure of most of what was being said. Though he and Jimmy were from the same community, and essentially the same family, it was like they were speaking different languages.

Later, when Jimmy phoned him to ask why he hadn't hung around, Paul confessed his confusion over what was being said. "Sorry, Jimmy, but most of that stuff was way over my head."

There was a pause, then Jimmy Wabung said as enthusiastically as possible, "Well, at least you're good at sports."

"Paul!" Startling him out of his reverie, his buddy Jamie was refilling his beer glass from the pitcher. "Where were you this evening, man?" Four years off the reserve and Jamie still had a noticeable and palpable northern Indian accent. Paul doubted it would ever wash out.

"Out taking care of errands. Looks like I didn't miss much." Jamie handed his buddy a draft. Another rousing cheer erupted from the other end of the table. "Shit," Paul said confidentially to his beer. "Herbie sure looks happy."

Jamie nodded. "Wouldn't you be?"

Paul thought about that for a second. Yes, he quite probably would be. It had been a lifelong dream, but now his life was getting a little too long to sustain that dream. Once again it was becoming obvious to him that it was time to find another dream. And sitting here, listening to Herbie tell everyone what he was going to buy with his first million, was not the way to do it. "Jamie, I'm going back to the residences. I'll see you there."

"You okay?"

"Absolutely fucking fine!" he managed to say with an exaggerated bow and smile. Paul doubted Jamie believed him, but it was the best he could do. Friends let friends get away with lies like that.

Negotiating his way around the packed table, he caught Herbie's eye.

With a snarky nod of the head, Herbie asked, "Hey, North, leaving so early?"

"Nothing gets by you, does it? Oh, except a fast-skating German left winger!" Paul was of course referring to an incident last year during a game against a successful European team, the Hamburg Winnetous. The win had been within their grasp, and Herbie, high on hubris, had failed to notice Lars Glaap, star forward from Kiel, gliding gracefully behind him, then beside him, and then in front of him, having relocated the puck from Herbie's stick to his own and then between the goal posts. They lost the game and a possible trip to Europe. As with all good team players, Herbie had blamed himself for the incident and had put himself into a week-long funk for it. It was the only way Paul had to rattle the rising star's cage.

The table went silent as Herbie glowered across the rows of half-filled draft glasses. Smiling innocently, Paul added, "Just kidding. Have a great evening. You deserve it, you piece of shit!" The table broke out in uproarious laughter, except for Herbie. Hockey players could be loyal but inconsiderate buddies.

Freeing himself from the archipelago of chairs and bodies, Paul quickly cleared the entrance of the Maple Leaf, finally emerging into the winter night. Now depressed, he took a deep breath of Toronto air. The falling snow looked pretty when backlit by the streetlights. Watching nature do its thing—that was a good way for his nerves to de-agitate themselves.

Turning his face skyward, Paul allowed some of the flakes to land briefly on his face and then melt. The feeling reminded him of home and of his childhood. Also, it was refreshing—so refreshing he barely noticed a short portly man scurrying by, worriedly muttering to himself, "Poor Polly. Poor, poor Polly."

Paul loved snow. Most people hated it, but Paul was a definite winter guy—perhaps the reason he became infatuated with hockey. With that much ice whizzing by under your feet, it was hard not to feel cool, in every sense of the word. Summer had its moments, but usually it was hot and muggy with lots of mosquitos. And the only frozen water around was located in drinks. In another life, his mother had once teased him, Paul might have been Inuit.

Walking back to the residences, he noticed he was limping. That was very odd. Paul didn't remember hurting himself that evening. Yeah, Herbie and his buddy had checked him into the boards that afternoon, but he wouldn't be feeling that in his leg. That, he felt in his left shoulder. Besides, his leg felt more like a strain. Oh great, more evidence of his advancing years. If he put some ice on it when he got back, it might—if the hockey gods were with him—not be so apparent during tomorrow morning's game. Again, another practical use for ice. The list was growing endless.

Turning another corner, he didn't remember the trip taking this long. One of the things he didn't like about staying at these university places was that the windows in the tiny rooms didn't open—or at the very best, had only small glass slits that would slide open maybe a foot. There was barely any point. Many of these residences had been specifically designed to limit outside accessibility to those inclined to test the laws of gravity, either with beer bottles or their bodies. As a rule, Paul liked to sleep with the windows open during the winter, thus making the room cool and comfortable. For some reason he seemed to radiate heat as he slept, and found this the most comfortable way, outside of puck bunnies, to make it through the night.

Trying to ignore the pain in his leg, he found the footpath to the residences. All around him he could see the skyline of

Canada's biggest city. Quite impressive. Cities in general impressed him. Movies at one in the afternoon if he wanted. Food from fifty different countries if he wanted, delivered at all hours of the day or night if he also wanted. He could understand the appeal. In fact, he was getting a little hungry right now. Tonight's impromptu dinner had consisted of a hotdog, with lots of onion and peppers to make sure he got his vegetables, a Coke, and two beers. Perhaps he should have something a little more substantial, to assist with the healing of his tired and stressed body. But what? Downtown provided a myriad of possibilities—almost too many.

Thinking on the fly, Paul decided to walk around the block before turning in. Hunting and foraging, but not quite as his ancestors had done. What with this being student territory, there had to be numerous tasty and economical establishments within staggering distance. His tummy now grumbling, the man hunted.

Crossing the lawn to a larger street, a much brighter street, he saw a plethora of prospects lining both sides. The culinary world was an amazing place for a Native hockey player like Paul. Basically, raised on baloney, Kraft Dinner, assorted ready-made or canned spaghetti dishes, and Chinese-Canadian selections rich in a radioactive orange sauce, his taste buds had been pretty much dormant most of his life. Almost as if he was from England. But during his first years with a team in southwestern Ontario, he'd been introduced to cuisines originating from exotic countries like Vietnam, Thailand, Greece, Japan, and Brazil, and even creations from countries that no longer existed, like Persia, his current favourite. Unfortunately, there was no Persian restaurant in sight—but there, practically beckoning to him, he saw an unexpected delight.

On the corner, still open at this late hour, was a restaurant called Slice of Korea. Some kimchi and bulgogi would be just perfect now. Protein, starch, and a vegetable—practically a superfood. Ignoring the pain in his leg, Paul quickened his pace, and two minutes later was being ushered to a seat near the window. For this time of night, the restaurant was moderately busy—a dozen or so people scattered amidst the tables.

Before the waitress could even ask, he ordered his meal, complete with a beer. Suddenly, Paul realized how hungry he was. Looking around the room, he took in the cross-section of Torontonian society. To his right were some people of Asian descent. Making a logical assumption, he assumed they were more than likely Korean. Near the back, a foursome of white people, making an attempt to eat rice with chopsticks. Paul was amused. The rest of the patrons, judging by skin colour and facial structure, looked to be a mishmash of people and cultures from around the world, all here to eat Korean food. *Ah, Toronto.* And then, right behind him, was a woman that he was tempted to think might be Native.

She actually looked like his cousin Shelley in a way—longish dark hair, some bluish jewelry that he thought was turquoise, and a certain look that said, "Yes I'm eating Korean but that doesn't make me any less Native." Curious to ask her, he resisted the impulse. In the past he had been embarrassed several times by people who were Egyptian, Filipino, Spanish, and assorted other nationalities. His Indigena-radar was not as finely tuned as it should be. Instead, he looked for the waitress, who was a little late in bringing his beer.

Then, from behind him, he heard a voice, a very feminine voice, say in a low whisper: "Tansi. Or maybe it is *ahneen.* But I don't think it would be *sago.*" Paul was right. The woman was saying hello to him in Cree, Anishnawbe, and Haudenosaunee, otherwise known as Iroquois, covering most of the predominate Indigenous nations in Toronto. Armed with his best smile, Paul turned around to the same pretty young woman and said, "Ahneen." It was turning out to be a better night then he had expected. A mere turn of his chair and Paul was no longer dining alone.

"Ah, a 'shnab,'" the woman said with a smile, using an abbreviated and teasing term for an Anishnawbe. She was just finishing up her bibimbap, and gestured with her chopstick for Paul to take the empty chair opposite her. "My name's Katie, by the way." At the moment, the young lady didn't look as embarrassing in her chopstick manoeuvres as the table of white people. Smiling, the hockey player relocated.

His food came but he barely noticed. His friend Jamie was bright, even read books, but wasn't the greatest conversationalist. The two young people ate and talked with ease.

"I brought my parents to this restaurant when they visited me here last year. Let me tell you, Korean food was not to their liking. Said the ribs were too sweet, and don't get them started on the kimchi. Not great foodies, Rez people."

"I know. The last great gastronomic discovery my mother had was dipping bread into that mixture of olive oil and balsamic vinegar. She loved it. So, for her birthday, I went out and bought her two bottles of the stuff, the real good expensive stuff. You know, from one of those fancy kitchen stores. I mean, it was my mother. Well, she gobbled it up in two weeks and then went to a grocery store and picked up some oil and vinegar by herself. Of course, the cheap stuff. After telling me she did this, there was a pause, then she added, somewhat mystified, 'It tasted . . . different.'"

Both let out howls of laughter. Katie seemed pretty interesting, for a Cree girl, Paul thought. On the table, he finally noticed a book off to the side. Something called *A Frozen Heart*. "Oh, you're a reader," he said, picking it up. Something about a woman surviving a plane crash somewhere.

"It helps when you're a student. I just came from her reading, about three buildings down from where you're staying. You should get a copy."

"I'll wait for the movie." Again Katie laughed. *Such a lovely laugh*, Paul thought. "I saw on a poster somewhere about some sort of hockey tournament happening here at the university. Are you here for that?"

Paul nodded.

"Cool. Not much of a hockey person, much to my father's disappointment, but I didn't know there'd be Native players."

"You should have read more of the poster. There are seven other First Nation teams, and a handful of others, playing at this tournament. We have our own league now, but we like to mix it up with white people occasionally. Let them know who's boss." Paul finished the last of his beer.

"How kind of you," she said with a teasing smile. Paul smiled back. Katie finished the last of her meal, seeming to relish the flavour. "Well, Paul, I just may come and check out your team. A guy like you probably has a huge cheering section. Mostly girls no doubt."

Raising his eyebrow, he gave Katie his most charmingly boyish grin. "Me?"

Dabbing her mouth with her napkin, Katie rolled her eyes. "Nice try, but you forget I grew up on the Rez. Half my male cousins played hockey. I know the score—no pun intended. Anyway, what time is your game?"

"Tomorrow morning at ten."

Paul could see Katie mentally going through her agenda, eyes looking up at the ceiling. He hoped, even prayed, she could make it. With somebody like her in his so-called cheering section, however limited it was, it would be another added factor forcing him to play harder and better. It was unlikely that at this stage in his career, one really good game would catch a scout's eye, but it never hurt to dazzle the coach and manager occasionally. "Yeah, I can do it. I can make it."

How about it, thought Paul, *there is a God after all. And He likes hockey and pretty Cree girls.*

"Now, before you start giving me any sad and lame pick-up lines, I have to go. Some of us can't rely on our broad shoulders to make a living. I've got some reading to do before tomorrow. However, I wouldn't mind somebody walking me to my car. It's kind of late and—"

"Done."

Grabbing her coat, Katie took a small wallet out of the pocket. "Great. And don't even think of trying to pick up my share of the bill. I'm not against that, but I'm very picky about the men I want to feel obligated to. I'll pay for my own dinner, thank you very much. Especially since our meeting here was accidental." Knowing instinctively it would be futile to argue with the woman, Paul did an exaggerated bow and threw down money for his food.

Once outside the door, Katie tapped him on the shoulder and pointed north. "My car is up that way, about two blocks." She led the way with Paul racing to catch up with her, trying to hide his sore leg.

Wanting to appear as more than just a jock—and a potentially stupid one at that—Paul racked his brain for something interesting to say. All he could come up with were his thoughts from earlier in the evening. "It's kinda funny. Earlier I was thinking of maybe . . . I don't know . . . I was toying with the idea of going to one of these places. My mother always wanted me to get more of an education, and I had some opportunities for scholarships when I was younger, but I never really felt the urge. Thought I'd be playing hockey, and playing it, well . . . forever."

"And forever turned out to be a lot shorter than you expected?"

Without looking at her, Paul nodded. This woman seemed to get him. Maybe he had been spending too much time with puck bunnies. This conversation, this evening, it felt good. It felt right. "Yeah."

They ran across the street to a parking lot. "Well, you're still relatively young. What did you say? Thirty-four or something. Geez, I have a cousin that didn't get his B.A. till he was forty-one I think. Let me guess—a guy with your background, something in athletics. Kinesiology, a personal trainer, or sports medicine maybe?"

Paul almost stopped in his tracks. He had thought of exactly none of those as a post-hockey career. In truth, he'd always been a little gun-shy of academic life; it did not seem to like him, and reciprocally, he returned the sentiment. Could he have been wrong all these years? Was there more to life than just being good at sports? Had all those people been wrong?

True, in his sixteen years as a semi-professional athlete, he had personally encountered variations of all three of Katie's suggestions. He knew what they did. He could very easily, with the proper education of course, do what they did. Was this a possible new direction for his life? This would take some serious pondering indeed. "Yeah, yeah, something like that. I could do that."

The woman's car turned out to be a relatively new-model Hyundai, and she fumbled for her keys in the darkness of her purse. "They always say the best alcohol and drug counsellors are those who've gone through it and come out the other side. I would think the same could be said about trainers and therapists."

Leaning against her car, Paul's mind was racing. His hand resting on the hood barely felt the inch of snow that had accumulated on the vehicle. In just the past hour, she had commented on his broad shoulders, the fact he was not that old, and that potentially he had a whole new career ahead of him. More importantly, he would see her tomorrow. Where had this woman been all his life?

"Need some help?" he asked.

"Do you have a flashlight on your cell? That might help."

"Sorry. I have an old one." He held up an old-school cell phone—one lacking the ability to download apps of any kind. "I've been meaning to upgrade, but what with being on the road and . . ."

Taking out her own cell phone, Katie handed it to Paul after turning on the flashlight app. The tiny but powerful light lit up the side of the car. He put away his outdated model and shone hers into the her purse, adding, "Darn clever, those white people."

"Yes, they are. They've been maligned far too long." They both laughed. "Oh great, there it is. I was having a little heart attack. Thanks. Don't know why they keep these damn parking lots so dark. And all this falling snow doesn't help." She unlocked her door, but before she could open it, Paul quickly grabbled the handle, opening it for her like a gentleman of long ago. He was rewarded by an amazing smile. "Thanks. And I guess I will see you tomorrow. And my phone please."

Turning off the light, he handed Katie her cell phone. "Ten a.m. The university arena. See you there." Paul pushed the door shut, resulting in more snow falling from the side of the car. Seeing an opportunity for one last act of gallantry, he ran around to all the side windows, cleaning the snow off. He even made an attempt at the hood and trunk, but with only his hands and sleeves to work with, his effectiveness was limited. Still, the Hyundai looked a lot more road-safe than it had just a few minutes ago. Stepping back, Paul waved to the student. She waved back, and with a honk of her horn, drove off.

In later years, Paul would still remember the sound of snow crunching under her tires as she drove away, and the squeak of the windshield wipers as they battled the remaining snow on her front windows. It wasn't just a young, pretty, and smart woman driving away that night; she was a bookmark in the novel that was his life, showing him where he was currently, and holding the place from where the story could or should be started again.

Mdwejiigmizo

(The Tummy Growls)

In reality, Katie only had a few blocks to drive, but in order to avoid any embarrassing or unforeseen pressure from the man she had just left, she thought it better if Paul North thought she lived a substantial distance farther. It was only a stroke of luck that had made her park so close to the restaurant and student lounge that day. Some grocery shopping and a haircut, as well as some other non-essential errands, had made using her car of more benefit today than spending a fortune on subway tokens. Add to that the fact she'd almost been late for Fabiola Halan's reading, which had necessitated parking relatively close to the event location. All in all, it had worked out.

Soon—after just a couple of minutes in fact—Katie was home, parking in a secluded space behind the rented house she shared with Amy Madawan, a fellow student who was studying to be a nurse. Amy was from northwestern Ontario, not that far from the Manitoba border, and was of Oji-Cree background.

All the lights in the house were off. Amy was probably pulling some late hours at her job placement. Amused at her evening with this man who had suddenly popped into her life at a Korean restaurant, Katie smiled. This Paul guy was definitely not her type. Jocks rarely had much to offer in a conversation, let alone ones at the tail end of their career. And more importantly, they were well known to be hounds. All that testosterone they built up in training and in life bubbled up in so many unfortunate ways. Screwing around or having a nasty violent streak. Yes, she was aware she was generalizing, but if it was a stereotype, it was based on actual evidence.

Still, she could tell her relationship with El—if that's what it was called—was winding down. There was a natural rhythm to most relationships, usually fast and furious at the beginning with a natural entropy towards the end. And maybe that was for the best. It was going nowhere. Not that she wanted it to go anywhere, but there was a continued sense of stagnation or a spinning of wheels with no traction every time she left her professor. And that couldn't be good. Not that she saw any remote possibility of this Paul North guy worming his way into her life, but it was still nice to flex those flirting muscles, just as El had done tonight. What a guy ... actually, what guys!

Looking at the gauge in the car, she noticed that the temperature had dropped substantially in the last few minutes. Maybe one of those polar vortex things she had heard about so frequently in the news. For a world in the midst of global warming, somebody had forgotten to tell the weather patterns currently circling Toronto.

The overhead light that was supposed to illuminate the parking area wasn't functioning. Maybe it was broken, though from twenty feet below, it looked fine to Katie. Except, of course, that there was no light emanating. That seemed to be endemic in the city of Toronto. Must be something in the wiring, she speculated. Katie always meant to mention it to her landlord, but like a thousand other things in her life, she'd never got around to it. Maybe tomorrow.

She parked her car as close to the back door as was feasible, got her purse, and stretched her cramped muscles as she exited her vehicle. Then, after locking her car door, she fumbled for the right key to the back door of the house. Tonight, it seemed like it was playing hide-and-seek. It was late. It had been a long day. Time to close her eyes.

Eyes focused on her purse, she barely heard the snow nearby crunching under something heavy. Turning around, she had a few seconds to register what was approaching her. Her first impression was of a large man in a fur coat. Her second fleeting thought was of . . . a white Chewbacca of all things . . . but there wasn't time for a third thought.

Snow on the ground melts very quickly under a shower of thick red liquid measuring 37 degrees Celsius. In that dark back alley, there was nobody to comment on how something so horrible could happen so quietly.

There was barely a growl.

THE BLIZZARD RAGES

Bakadewin Bi-Naagozi

(Hunger Appears)

Detective Sergeant Ruby Birch arrived at the murder scene. Word had reached her that this was a real gruesome one. One constable, five weeks on the job, had already vomited up a sizable chunk of his dignity upon surveying the scene. As was the case with most murder sites, there were ribbons of yellow police tape circling the area, photographs being taken, and the odd passerby being urged to keep their distance by Toronto's finest. The only thing that seemed different to the seasoned murder investigator was that, instead of a single sheet over a single body, there seemed to be five separate sheets in five different areas of the dark parking lot. And the size of the body—or bodies—seemed to be oddly diminished.

"Why?" Birch mumbled to herself. All reports said there was indeed a single body here, but like a chicken from the butcher, it had been divided into several different sections. Immediately her mind began to function the way it had been trained. Such damage to a human frame required several different things: instrumentation of some sort; severe anger, or a form of dark psychopathy made physical; and time to do the damage. Answers to any and all of those, plus a victim background check, should give her and her underlings an idea on who might have done this.

Third Class Constable Jesse Wilson still looked a little woozy, standing by one of the spread-out blankets, leaning on some kind of spruce tree from a foreign land. He was looking in every possible direction but down. Birch watched him for a moment, wondering if the young man would make it through his inaugural year in uniform. The detective sergeant usually gave the new blood she worked with one puking incident before considering getting them reassigned. She was not unsympathetic, but having an iron constitution was part of the job. The constable had just used up—as it was ironically called—his get-out-of-jail-free card.

"You okay, son?" Birch asked without even looking at the young man, as she kneeled down to the blanket.

"Yes, Ma'am. We've already surveyed the area. No cameras. Doesn't seem to be any witnesses. No clear tracks."

Gazing at what appeared to be a lower calf—female by the sneaker attached—Birch looked up at the constable. "No tracks? With all this fresh snow?"

Looking down at his superior, Wilson could see part of the light green shoe poking out from underneath the blanket. He took a deep breath before answering, using all his willpower to keep those abs he spent a half-hour a day crunching to not heave in the general direction of his boss. She was a good seven inches shorter than him, and about sixty pounds lighter, but there was still a presence she emitted that many on the force implied was something akin to "I may look like your mother but I can hit like your father."

"Ah yes, Ma'am, but the athletic centre is over there, several fast food restaurants along this street, and a row of student housing behind us. Seems lots of students take short cuts back here."

It was true. Birch saw all the snow flattened and pushed. Some was frozen hard and could not take a footprint, other sections had been shovelled bare, and closer inspection by the woman's remains showed snow pounded flat. There was however some kind of impression, just behind a car, that looked like a snowshoe had been in that small parking area, but it was so distorted and out of place that she was tempted to ignore it.

"Wilson, can you make sure the photographer gets a shot of that print there? The big one."

"There's a print, Ma'am?" Wilson, who had already scanned the area, pivoted his head as he desperately tried to find what he had overlooked before, no doubt aware his boss was watching him and quite probably judging him. For a second, the young man reminded the older woman of when she'd had a dog and used to hide the poor animal's food dish, resulting in an eager and worried search by the animal. That practice had lasted only till her own mother did the same thing with her schoolbooks.

"Check behind the . . ." Birch paused as she craned her head, trying to check the make of the car.

"Hyundai." Without thinking, Wilson uttered it quickly, then seemed to realize he had potentially embarrassed his superior.

Despite years as a detective and twice as many being a constable, Ruby Birch still had trouble telling the years, the models, the endless makes of cars apart. "Yes, the Hyundai." With a subservient smile, the constable did what he was told, and the detective sergeant went back to surveying the scene.

It was indeed gruesome. Again, based on the shoe, it was a woman, she theorized. Young. Normally older women, Birch knew from unfortunate personal experience, would not wear fashionable sneakers that colour or style, let alone through snow. Looking under another blanket, her theory was confirmed by the scalp and hair, but unfortunately, not by her face. Judging by what she saw, Birch couldn't even tell if this young girl had two eyes. Equally grim—a quick survey of the other blankets told her about two-thirds of the body was missing. That wasn't good. Birch hated these weird murders. People taking out a gun or a knife, flooring the gas pedal of a minivan, or even just using a baseball bat—that was easy to figure out and deal with. But this . . . It wasn't enough to make her toss up her dinner, but it was enough to briefly sympathize with Wilson. And mourn for the human race.

Near the back of the door, just on the other side of what had been the head, she saw something in the snow. Crouching down over the shiny object, Birch saw it was keys. Car keys to be exact. Maybe for the Hyundai right next to her.

"Wilson!"

The young man quickly approached. "Ma'am, there's a young woman over here that says she lives here. She says this car belongs to her roommate, a Katie Fiddler. I'm just going to interview her."

"First, have Forensics retrieve those keys and make sure they go over the car. If a bird shit on it, I want to know what countries it flew through to get here." This evoked a smile from the young constable.

"I'm on it."

Pulling out his pad, Wilson went to carry out her instructions. Birch took position in front of the back door of the building, possibly where the girl was heading when attacked. Attacked by who? Birch was fairly sure the woman was Native: the key chain had a leather thong with two worn beads on it. Near the steps, she had been told, was a hand, with a small, delicate turquoise ring. And on the rear-view mirror of the car hung a dreamcatcher. She had a murdered (thirty-two years of experience had taught her it was more than likely not an accident) Indigenous woman on her hands. It was tragic when any woman—or man for that matter—was murdered, Indigenous or not. But this one had potential ramifications in today's political climate. Like most cops, she hated politics. Muddied up her work.

Detective Sergeant Ruby Birch just hoped this investigation would be a quick and easy job.

Mewzha

(A Long Time Ago)

"Jesus Christ killed all the little people."

"No he didn't. He didn't know anything about them."

Carl Benojee, a rough-and-tumble twelve-year-old, pushed the smaller and younger Elmore Trent harshly against the brick wall of the big school. In general terms, Carl ran the schoolyard, only giving up power when all the students were called in from recess. Once inside, power returned to the priests, nuns, and the god that lived in there.

"I saw them once. I really did!"

Carl shook his head. "Don't you pay attention? Jesus died so they would all go to hell." In technical terms, Carl was what some would call a collaborator. The Catholics were in power, so for the moment, he was Catholic. It just made sense to his junior mind.

And if the people in black said there were no little people, then there were none.

Like with so much of his culture, Trent was being forced to forget the mysterious diminutive people that lived along the shores of lakes. Rarely seen, they were talked about in hushed tones as spirit creatures that shared the land with the Anishnawbe. The boy had seen his parents put tobacco down every time a boat was put into the water.

Carl didn't seem to care. He just wanted to do his time and then get out. People like Trent tended to rock the boat and make kids like him look bad. Carl didn't like looking bad.

In his fourth year there, Elmore Trent was still trying to find his place. When they were still alive, his parents had taught him about the wonders of the world, and the many creatures that lived in them, real and mystical. And Elmore had believed them. Why would his parents lie to him? "They were down by the lake. I saw them. They even waved to me."

"Don't be weird." Carl spoke with a thick Cree accent, which hung on even though he hadn't spoken the language in half a decade. "They don't exist anymore. God excommunicated them or something." Elmore tried to push his way free, but Carl was unwilling to let the smaller boy go. "Don't make me beat you up. Just do what the Fathers and Sisters tell you." One final shove against the reddish brick made Elmore's head crack against it. Sliding down, he tried not to cry as Carl walked away.

That was essentially Elmore Trent's life at the school. Rules, rules, and more rules. Nobody would tell him why it was so bad to be him. Except, simply, all Indians were bad. The more like white people they were, the better they would become. That was the simple math. But what was the point? It was like telling a robin to become a blue jay. Both were birds. Both had a place in the forest. Wasn't there room in the world for them both?

Hobbling away, Elmore circled around the big building, then down to the creek that ran adjacent to the school. A short distance downstream, he came to the spot at which he liked to sit and think. Elmore knew he'd get in trouble when he got back. A quiet and studious boy, this was essentially his only sin in the eyes of the Church elite who watched over him. He thought too much. He liked to spend too much time by himself. He was moody, and quiet. He had the potential to become a serviceable and practical young man, once he was broken of his fondness for solace.

Once there, he sat down on the large rock. For a few moments, this topsy-turvy world would go away, and for a second, Elmore would dream he was back home, on the hill behind his house. It was a lie—and lies, he was told, were bad. Still, this lie to himself felt good.

And on occasion, if he was quiet enough and the world around him was just right, something would happen. When you expected things, they seldom happened. It was in those between times, when the world was going one way, and for some reason you found yourself in another direction.

The Memengweshii were what his parents called them—the little people of the woods. They were part of the larger world so many of these Christian people refused to see or accept. As he had told the bigger boy, he had seen them once, when he was fishing down by the water behind his house. A few inches high, hairy, they'd gone about their business, barely acknowledging the world around them, or the boy.

Amazed, Elmore had watched them, unable to move. Suddenly they stopped, and in unison, looked up at him. Frozen, he and the Memengweshii stared at each other. Unsure what to do, Elmore slowly raised his hand. And waved. Twice. If he'd had tobacco, he would have put some down.

There was a pregnant moment of silence, then all the Memengweshii—perhaps a dozen or more—raised their hands and waved back. As a rule, the little people were very fond of children. Then, as they were very busy people, they went back to work, loading their stone canoes. For the next ten minutes, the small boy watched them do their Memengweshii things before disappearing into the reeds.

"Mom, Dad, I saw them! I saw the Memengweshii!" he told his family, out of breath from the run. Both parents were silent, no doubt wondering if this was a new game their boy was trying to play. But the excitement on his face, the look of certainty in his eyes, told them their son was not this good a liar.

"Lucky you. Not everybody can see them."

"They're so hairy!" was Elmore's only comment.

"Just like Frenchmen!" answered his father with a small chuckle. That was immediately followed by a slap on the shoulder by his wife.

"Elmore, you know what seeing them means, right?" His mother always spoke with a tiny but noticeable lisp. Little Elmore shook his head, still trembling with exhilaration.

"It means, Elmore, they want you to see them. They like you. You have something important in you because only special people are allowed to see them. But be careful, sometimes they are there to help. Other times they can be little tricksters. You can never tell."

Still excited, Elmore's breath was ragged as he talked. "Will . . . will I see them again? I wanna see them again!"

This time, his father answered, and the weight of untold Anishnawbe generations could be heard in his voice. "Who knows what's in the minds of creatures like that, or what their plans are. They are our cousins . . . but very different cousins."

As with every morning, Trent woke slowly. His clock radio was playing some interview with a local politician about transit issues. It seemed to him that every morning there was an interview with some local politician about transit issues. What an odd, boring topic for people to wake up to and feel energized for the upcoming day. So, in response, he yawned.

Now a relatively newly single man, Trent had to augment his usual morning rituals. Sarah and he had usually shared the breakfast responsibilities. One doing the coffee, the other putting together a fruit and bagel platter for the both of them. Alas, the professor dealt with both responsibilities now. Once, their sparkling conversation had prepped them for the day. Now he listened to local politicians talk about transit issues on the radio. Otherwise, he'd have to deal with the silence of the house.

Slowly, he sipped his coffee, breathing in its aroma. Fresh coffee and baking bread, two of the few things that said "home" to those whose own home was dissolving. To his knowledge, however, there had never been bread baked in this house.

Distracted by his thoughts, he stared out his back window at the koi pond. There were no koi in it, but he and Sarah still called it the koi pond. Large and covered with a tarp, it had been a pet project for the both of them a decade earlier. Dug into their backyard, it was really too large for their Annex property, but their dreams of having huge multicoloured fish swimming around just off their deck had been a delight. Within a year, however, the fish had all died off, despite everything they did to preserve them. It had been both a financial miscalculation and a mystery. Then, they had turned it into a water garden of sorts, with water plants instead of fish. What would become of it now that Sarah was not here to look after it when the summer returned, Elmore didn't know.

There was a large lake a stone's throw from his parents' cabin. Now, this had to substitute. That thought made him smile, somewhat ruefully. Occasionally he would wonder what his parents would have thought of his Toronto home, of his job, his wife, his lifestyle. They had been simple people, and his life was so complex.

Last night he had toyed with the idea of bringing Katie back here. After all, he had the house to himself. There was absolutely no reason for him not to. Except he'd found he couldn't. Twice it had been on the tip of his tongue, but the words would not come out of his mouth. Also, there was some severe doubt about whether

Katie would ever be inclined to step through the front doors of this house. Having an affair with a married man was disrespectful in itself, but doing it in a house bought, owned, and up until recently shared by husband and wife was going a little too far. Then it became tacky, she'd told him.

On this particular day, Trent didn't have a class till noon, but as with all lives that centre around the operations of one of Canada's leading institutions of learning, there was always work to be done, much of it outside the classroom. Paperwork, grading, committee obligations, etc. Much of it could be done in his office right above the kitchen where he sat now, but he didn't tend to work there much anymore. It was too quiet, too big, and too lonely. Instead, he took every opportunity to be in his office or somewhere at the university. That was his world. Where he'd made a name for himself. This house—this home—was a shared world with Sarah. As a single man now, he felt he didn't really belong. He missed his wife. He liked Katie but he loved his wife. For such an intelligent and educated man, it was amazing the kind of stupid and clichéd situations he found himself in.

On the wall overlooking him was a print by the renowned Anishnawbe artist Norval Morrisseau, of a man changing into a thunderbird. *Copper Thunderbird*—that was the name of the play he and Sarah had seen in Ottawa, at the National Arts Centre. A rather surreal stage interpretation of the talented man's life and death, written by a Métis playwright—Marie Clements, he believed. Trent remembered he and his wife enjoying the production and discussing the imagery late into the evening. Sarah, not usually enthralled by Indigenous literature, had found the production and Trent's deconstruction quite fascinating, particularly her husband's revelation that Morrisseau was known as the Picasso of the North. An avid collector of Picasso prints, this sealed it for her. Upon arrival back in Toronto, she had urged Trent to get season tickets to the local Indigenous theatre company.

He had spent so much of his life studying and discussing other people and their work, and so little of his own life had ended up being noteworthy. Wasn't that always the way? More coffee, Trent thought—that's what he needed. While up, he turned on the radio and left his steaming cup of Brazilian-blend coffee sitting on the counter as he took care of personal issues. In the washroom, muffled by the closed door (closing it when he now lived alone was silly, but he was still getting used to the single life), he heard but could barely make out something unfortunate happening last night near the university. He was sure he'd hear about it when he got there. Gossip and news were the real engines of where he worked.

Shirt, pants, and tie were next on his list. It was to be an easy day, so nothing flashy. It's always been said you dress not for the job you have but for the job you want. He didn't know if he wanted any other type of job. Definitely not department head—so much bureaucracy and infighting. Maybe he'd just write another book. With only two under his belt, the academic vultures were beginning to circle. Publish or perish was the old adage. Or, if the marital gods willed it, he and Sarah could take that trip around the world, or at least a good chunk of it. At one point he had suggested a research trip to a dozen reserves spread across the country, and he'd put together a book about how traditional legends ebbed and flowed from one community to another. And, taking a chapter from Joseph Campbell, deconstruct creation stories from a handful of Indigenous nations and compare them. But poor Sarah had been less than enthusiastic about a cross-Canada reserve tour. She would be classified as a silver spoon liberal.

So much of his life with Sarah had been tabled for the near future. But she would come around. She had to. And when she did, Trent was absolutely one hundred percent positive he would get his life in order, and never again threaten his marriage with any shenanigans. It would all work out. Things in his life usually did.

Grabbing his coat and backpack, Trent made sure Waubgeshig Rice's dystopian novel *Moon of the Crusted Snow* was in it. Reading it for the third time, the professor still found the narrative creative—an isolated reserve thrown into turmoil by a sudden absolute silence from the civilized south—and he could picture several of his relatives enacting the scenario put forth by the author. Science fiction and futurism were a growing interest amongst First Nation authors and therefore their audience, and he was currently mining the latest generation of published literature for potential article and lecture topics. Trent found this new burgeoning field interesting. Usually Indigenous literature looked backwards—at what they had lost, were trying to get back or maintain. This generation of writers seem to be looking forward at what tomorrow might hold for the Indigenous in the late twenty-first century. If nothing, it was curious.

On his way in to the university, he mentally went over all his appointments and tasks for the day, only occasionally listening in on the news reports. Something about a missing student, a horrendous crime site, and her being Native. Hmmm . . . he would have to search the net for more about that. At the moment though—besides his current curiosity about sci-fi— he was putting together an outline for a new course he was interested in developing. Comparative traditional stories. Something like "The Trickster with a Passport: The Chinese Monkey King vs. Nanabush." Yeah, that sounded good. Indigenous academia was good business these days, with more and more colleges, universities, and even high schools making Indigenous courses, often in literature, mandatory. Stories, in whatever form, could cross more bridges than an . . . an Iroquois steelworker? Okay, bad metaphor. He would have to come up with something better later.

Then Trent heard a familiar voice coming from the radio. Fabiola Halan was being interviewed about her book. He recognized the measured tone, the hint of a French accent, and the slight laugh she occasionally released. Automatically, he looked in his bag and saw his copy of her book, exactly where he'd left it. There was a stack of books on his office desk that were demanding his attention, but he thought a little conceptual diversion wouldn't hurt. In fact, it was often refreshing. He would start it today. Waub Rice and his post-apocalyptic world would just have to wait. Besides, he knew how it ended.

Trent asked the Uber driver to turn up the volume on the radio. "Such an exciting book. I know it's cliché, but I literally could not put it down. This is your first winter since the crash. You wrote it really quickly. Does all this snow outside bring back any bad memories?"

Again, that slight laugh. "No. The snow I saw and experienced up there is a world of difference to what I see falling out your window. Let's just say I am very good at keeping perspective. I lost my family floating on a tropical ocean, with soft breezes and a tropical sun. Now, how many Canadians spend thousands of dollars of their hard-earned money looking for exactly that kind of environment, for pleasure? Not losing their family in the process, mind you. I am very good at compartmentalizing my life. All these tragic and potentially debilitating events could be traumatic, but I just put them in their individual rooms that exist in my mind. Think of it as a mind palace. I don't suppress them or ignore them. I know where they are. I just don't give them the key to the door. I control it. I am the master of what goes in and out."

The Uber was slowly approaching their destination, but Trent was reluctant to leave. This was interesting, and he wanted to see where the interview was going.

"Some mental health experts might not agree with your unique way of handling traumatic experiences."

He could almost hear her shrugging at the interviewer's suggestion. "Well, that's good for them. How else would they earn their luxurious salaries?"

Clearing her throat, the interviewer asked her next question. "In your bio, your childhood . . . it's very vague."

"I assure you, my childhood is not very vague. I remember it vividly."

"No, no, I worded that incorrectly. My apologies. What I meant to say was, your country of origin, where your mother was escaping from, with you, all it says is it was in the Caribbean. Is the mystery intentional?"

Trent could practically hear the author smiling a cold smile. "I am a Canadian. I've always thought it was bad manners to ask Canadians who don't look white where they came from."

"Of course, but—"

"Where do you think I come from?"

There was a pause as the interviewer struggled to respond. "Well, you have what appears to be a, for lack of a better term, a washed-out French accent."

"And what does that tell you?"

"Well . . . I . . . in the Caribbean, that means possibly Haiti. Martinique. Uh . . ."

"You're forgetting Guadalupe, St. Martin, Dominica, and even French Guiana.'

The host began to splutter. "Well . . . well . . . no but—"

"My mother thought our fortunes lay elsewhere. She was half right. Besides, we all need a little mystery in our lives, don't we?" Still leafing through the book, Trent smiled as Fabiola took control of the interview. "Who I am now says a lot more than who I was. I remember when I first came to Canada hearing somebody use the phrase 'there is more than one way to skin a cat.' What an odd saying, I couldn't help thinking. I have travelled the world, and to tell you the truth, I honestly do believe in my experience that there is only one way to skin a cat. You cut the skin and remove it. Not exactly brain surgery . . . and let's not get into how many ways they can skin your head for that, shall we?" The host laughed nervously as the author carried on. "However, in dealing with devastating events in your life and their psychological repercussions, there is no one solution. We are a complex species capable of finding healing in a number of equally complex ways. I have found one that works for me. I wouldn't be so quick to paint everybody with the same brush."

Chastised, the woman interviewing Fabiola cleared her voice once again. "Uh, very well put. I understand you aren't finished in our fair city yet."

"Yes, I have another speaking engagement at the university." Trent's ears perked up.

"I though your event was last night."

"It was. That was for the general public. But I have been asked to lecture to a specific class. The School of Journalism is where I got my original degree, and the new Chair asked me to come in to chat with some of the students. I guess I am to show them there is light at the end of the tunnel. You too can grow up to survive a deadly plane crash in the northern Ontario wilderness, defy death, live to write about it, and be on a radio show. I am sure that's every student's dream."

Again, you could tell the interviewer didn't know how to respond. Wow, thought Trent, the woman sure has a dark sense of humour. But she would be there at the university. He would have to go and check her . . . er, her lecture . . . out.

On the back of the book, her photograph looked a lot more approachable than she sounded now. Probably the result of a professional and experienced photographer. Still, the book was looking more and more interesting. Shoving it in his backpack before getting out of the car, he emerged into the cold winter air. 'Just two more months till spring,' he muttered to himself. Elmore Trent hated the cold.

Ozhiitaa'idwag Jibwaa-Nagmigak Gchi-Damnowin

(Rehearsal for the Big Game)

Fifteen minutes till the game started and Paul was as hyped up as he could get. He had actually gotten a good night's sleep—with a full stomach, practically no alcohol, and the memory of that lovely woman, Katie, dancing about in his memory. If all was good in the world, she was out there somewhere in the stands, a one-woman cheering force for Paul North. Definitely quality over quantity.

When he laced his skates up and adjusted his gear, Paul sometimes felt like a gladiator going into battle, complete with his deadly hockey stick of death. Other times he felt more like an overdressed clown being paid to chase a piece of rubber across an artificially frozen surface in a bizarrely designed outfit for the amusement of the masses. Still, it wasn't as bad or phoney as being a football player. At least hockey had some connection to reality, its history evolving from the need to move and operate on the frozen lakes of Canada. Football . . . he had no idea what that had to do with anything practical. Throwing a chunk of meat to each other to keep it away from all the sabre-toothed tigers!?

Oh well, time to get out there and shake his money maker— in this instance a mass-produced composite stick slightly curved at the blade. Standing at the door, the coach adjusted his baseball cap while looking up from his clipboard, and addressed his team.

"Okay, ladies, it's show time. Let's go out there and play some hockey. I want these bastards nailed to the wall. This is a do-or-die situation, so I want everybody's best. Let's go! Go!" He clapped his hands twice for emphasis, making all the players jump to their feet, unaware of the litany of clichés they had all been subjected to. Hockey changing rooms were not prone to linguistic originality.

Energized, Paul got to the door leading to the ice, but before he could go through, he found himself roughly pushed aside. Looking up, Herbie Tort stood in his way. With his usual arrogant smile, Herbie looked directly at Paul. "Make room for the stars."

"Stars? You mean those big balls of hot air and gas. Gladly." With an exaggerated flourish, Paul backed away, bowing ever so slightly to Tort. Herbie's smile evaporated as he took an ominous step closer to Paul.

"You are one smart-assed son of a bitch. Wait till we get out there, North. You and your mouth."

Stepping quickly between the two, Jamie turned Tort towards the door. "Come on, Herbie, he's on your team, remember? The opponents are through that door. They're wearing the green uniforms. Come on. Let's keep it on the ice. Fighting with your teammates does not impress scouts." Gently but firmly, the goalie pushed his reluctant teammate through the door.

"Later, North." With a final glower, Herbie disappeared out the door, followed by the rest of their amused teammates.

Shaking his head, Jamie looked at Paul, who was letting out a big breath of air. "What is it with you two?"

"I think he's racist."

Jamie shook his head. "No . . . what? Cause he's Métis?"

"I'm Status. Makes sense."

Jamie quickly tapped Paul's helmet with his goalie stick. "You do know I'm Métis, right?"

Feigning surprise, Paul stepped back. "And we drink from the same water bottle!?" Jamie tried to hit him again, but Paul was too quick, already out the door.

Wearing all his equipment, Paul couldn't help wondering if these long walks between the changing room and the ice were somehow getting longer. Even though he was wearing substantially more equipment, Jamie passed his buddy, lumbering quickly along the wall.

Jamie stopped short of the doorway. "Hey, you know what they say, mixed-breed dogs are a lot healthier, tougher, live longer, and are not nearly as neurotic as pure-bloods. I'm just sayin' . . ."

Stopping dead centre in the now deserted hallway, Paul turned to his friend. "Oh, great. Whose side are you on?"

Smiling, Jamie continued walking. "It's not a matter of sides. I think he doesn't like you for who you are, not what you are."

Watching his friend disappear behind the door, Paul yelled after him: "What if who you are is what you are?"

Jamie's head appeared briefly, peeking back in. "I don't know. I'm just a hockey player. That's who and what I am. And I noticed that you didn't ask what it was about you he didn't like." Paul opened his mouth to respond but Jamie had disappeared, only his voice lingering behind. "Let's go Paul, those goals aren't gonna score themselves."

While it had started out with such promise and potential, the day had rapidly gotten tarnished. Desperate for a glimmer of any silver lining, Paul reasoned that, with any luck, Katie would be out there to shine it up again.

Despite that hope, Paul still pondered Jamie's final words as he walked into the huge interior of the rink, ignoring a slight wobble coming from his skate blades. His friend in sin and hockey had to be wrong, he theorized. "I'm very likeable. Adorable in fact. My mother told me so." And she had. Once. When he was eight.

A quick scan of the seating told Paul another unfortunate truth. There was no Katie. The game was sparsely attended, as the Indigenous Hockey League had not exactly taken off in the zeitgeist of the settler community, so there was no way she could be hidden in the non-existent throngs of supporters. Skating around the perimeter of the rink as he limbered up, and then taking his position on the bench, Paul could see no sign anywhere in the stands of that wonderful woman he'd shared kimchi with. If it was possible for a thirty-five-year-old man to be heartbroken over one accidentally shared Korean meal with a woman, that man's name would be Paul North.

For the next couple of hours, the Otter Lake right winger fought for the puck and banged shoulders aggressively with the other team—and on occasion, a few members of his own. In the melee of this morning's game, he even managed a reasonably adept assist in the second period. But by far, the personal highlight of the game was seeing Herbie get hit just below the knees, making him cartwheel, landing in a lump just this side of the blue line. Even got the team a powerplay, so it was a win-win situation. Except for no Katie.

At the beginning of the third period, Paul began to feel a lapse of energy, both emotional and physical. This was fast becoming an all-too-common event. His additional training, all one night of it, didn't seem to be helping. He wondered if maybe it was the drinking. It had been part of most of Paul's life, and he had even joked that the more "proof" in his liquid, the more proof he was a good player. But alas, it was turning out he just might be alone in that belief.

Most health and sports professionals would argue alcohol was one of the worst possible solutions to an athlete's drop in energy. Alcohol just dehydrated you. In a precision game like hockey, it could even be detrimental to your safety, by inhibiting your reflexes and coordination. That was only if you drank too much, of course. A thousand years ago, before he disappeared, Paul remembered his father used to play hockey himself, frequently using a beer chaser, citing it as fuel for his "Injun." And besides, these so-called experts didn't play hockey in the Indigenous Hockey League, so what did they know?

"North!" Twenty years of playing and another twenty years of coaching had taught the man how to yell effectively in an acoustically horrendous environment like a hockey arena in full game mode. It brought Paul out of his reverie, as the coach bellowed, "You and Ferguson are up. Go!" As Paul stepped out onto the ice, a fight broke out down by the Haudenosaunee net, with a scrum of about five players. Paul skated directly into the melee, using his elbows and shoulders as his team did battle with the Haudenosaunee, their traditional enemies from centuries gone by.

A few minutes later the scuffle was over—mostly just clutching and grabbing—eight minutes of penalties were assigned, and the game continued. Paul took his place at right wing, and he did the best that sixteen years of semi-pro experience had taught him. Once again, he was good, but not great. And what before had been the product of natural talent was now, with every game it seemed, being replaced by sheer effort, desperation, and experience. Herbie kept skating faster, reacting quicker, and finding the puck the same way Paul had managed ten years before. At one point, Paul managed to expertly deke out a Haudenosaunee left winger and passed the puck to Mason, who managed to get it in the net, giving them a one-goal advantage. What Paul knew that the coach, his teammates, and the fabled talent scout somewhere up in the stands didn't was that the Haudenosaunee winger had, in a millisecond, mishandled the puck, thus letting the decade of experience layered in Paul's muscles take the frozen rubber and put it to better use. The result being Paul had looked better than was actually warranted. Paul hadn't taken the puck from the man; inadvertently it had been given to him, resulting in his second assist of the game. A goal would have been lovely, but today was turning out to be a day of few lovely things for Paul North.

If he had to leave this team and this sport, it would be fabulous if he could do it the way he came in, playing brilliantly and dazzling the fans. Just one good, amazing, memorable battle against an equally great opponent. But unfortunately, it looked like that was not going to happen today.

"That's the Paul North I know," said Jamie as he gave Paul a jovial head butt. Upon returning to his team's bench, both he and Mason were greeted with a hearty shower of hugs and solid pats on the back. Paul knew his assist wasn't as glorious as everybody thought it was, but at the moment, it was better than nothing. Even the coach gave him a reluctant nod.

Amidst the celebratory pandemonium, Paul took another look around the sparsely attended arena. Still no sign of the mysterious Katie from the night before. *Oh well*, he thought as he tried to celebrate his assist, *maybe she'd found something better to do.*

Makadewaanakwad Ishpiming
Gchi-Kinoomaagegamigong

(There Is a Dark Cloud Over the University)

There was a palpable gloom in the hallways of the university. One of their own had died. What was worse, it had been somebody young, full of potential, and well liked. Women walked down the hallways, unconsciously grouped together, hoping there was strength in numbers and that whoever had taken her life, uncomfortably similar to theirs, wouldn't jump out of a bathroom door and wreak horror upon their person. The men, frequently unsure how to express sorrow, merely looked glum. A multitude of grief counsellors, both Native and non-Native, were on their way to the campus. Should they need it, students and faculty were being encouraged to seek help.

Upon arrival, Elmore had travelled scarcely more than a dozen metres past the door when Maggie O'Neil, the departmental administrator, came running over to him, a look of severe concern and worry etched on her face. Maggie had many flaws, but gossiping was not one of them, a rarity in the university, so Paul knew whatever she had to say had relevance.

"One of your students! My god, Elmore, you must feel horrible. I'm so sorry." Walking from the parking lot, he had noticed a lot of rushing around. People—some students and cops or other professionals—milling about, going in and out of doors, talking on cell phones. At first, he'd wondered if maybe somebody had pulled the fire alarm. That was an occasional annoyance in an educational institution, but he didn't see any fire trucks. Just a few cop cars. Something was definitely up.

"Who?" he asked Maggie.

"You don't . . . It was Katie Fiddler! Lovely young woman."

Katie . . . For three seconds his breathing stopped. "What . . . what happened? What happened to Katie?"

"Elmore, they don't know. She's dead. At least, they think she's dead. There's so many stories . . ."

A flash of anger erupted from the usually stolid man. "What do you mean 'they think she's dead'? Either she is or she isn't. What are you saying?"

The older woman, who chaired the library fundraising committee, shook her head, realizing how vague and perhaps cruel her comment had been. "Stupid me! I'm sorry, Elmore. They found her—some of her . . . At least, that's what some are saying." That was not a great deal more helpful, and Elmore was about to get substantially more angry, but Maggie finished her sentence before he could amass the words. "Somebody attacked her. Sliced . . ." She noticeably gagged as she said those words. ". . . her up. Chunks. Pieces. They say it was horrible. Just . . ." Suddenly, she lost the energy to continue her explanation, which was just as good, as Trent was no longer listening. He walked past the woman, who started to cry softly, in the hallway. Maggie had met Katie a few times at various university events but didn't really know her. Still, Maggie was the kind of woman who was always willing to shed tears for other people's misfortune.

Alone, sitting in his office, still wearing his coat, snow melting on his boots, backpack on the other chair, he looked up at the dreamcatcher in the window. Twelve hours ago. Trent had seen Katie just twelve hours ago. And now she was dead. And in pieces—what the hell did that mean? He was almost positive he could still smell her in his office. He buried his head in his hands, bumping an almost-hidden copy of Daniel Heath Justice's *Why Indigenous Literature Matters* on the corner of his desk. It knocked a tube of lip balm onto the floor, and the tube rolled into the wall. Instantly, Trent knew it was Katie's. She must have left it here last night. He picked it up and smelled it. Yep, that was indeed hers, the familiar aroma reminding him of her. It was a fragrance he would never smell again. Less than the width of his hand, he stared at the tube. It was all he had of her. Closing his fist around it, the professor also closed his eyes, and for a moment could almost see her in the blackness of his mind. Young people weren't supposed to die. Especially those with such a future.

Leaning forward, elbows on his knees, Elmore shed tears for what the world had lost and what he had personally lost. He hadn't wept since that October day decades earlier when he'd been told about the fire and his parents.

There was a sudden blip noise on his computer. Perhaps the university was being closed for the day. That was a possibility. God knows the circumstances certainly warranted it. Teaching today—looking over at the seat where the young Cree woman usually sat—it was not possible. Instead, it was an email from the Dean telling English department faculty that, due to the current crisis, professors and instructors were being given the opportunity to cancel their classes for the day. *Smart move*, he thought, *emotionally for both the staff and the students. Definitely for him*, he thought as he wiped away the tears. There was also a recommendation to inform students, should classes be held, about the grief counsellors that were being made available. No doubt some of the staff, like Maggie, might just make use of the counsellors themselves.

But counsellors weren't for him. His feelings for Katie were complicated. As a result, his sense of mourning was just as complicated. This was a journey he'd have to complete himself, for he'd dealt with similar tragedies in his past. You could almost say he'd trained for it.

"We've been informed there was a fire of some sort. It seems your parents were unable to get out. They're with God now. You may have the rest of the afternoon off. We suggest you spend it in the church, praying for their souls. You may go now, Elmore."

Numb, he'd been escorted to the chapel by Sister Beatrice—perhaps one of the few nuns with a decent soul. She'd held his hand—one of the few manifestations of physical contact he could remember from his time there. In the chapel, he'd cried. Father James had given him six hours to grieve.

Other than those six hours, life at the school went on pretty much as it always had. There were lessons to learn. Dates to memorize. Problems to solve. It took his mind off his parents. Off the Memengweshii. Every time he got sad, he'd read about the Roman Empire. Every time he heard the chirping, laughing voices of those little people, he'd work on fractions. And when some of the other students would hesitantly try to talk to him in Anishnawbemowin, Elmore would shake his head, preferring to think about all the countries in South America. He was leaving the past behind.

Months later, he went home for the summer, but it was his last trip for a long time. Staying with his aunt, uncle, and six cousins, the house was already tight. Though he was treated nicely and welcomed warmly, Elmore felt out of place. Two of the other children were in residential schools, but they didn't talk about their time there either. In fact, a dark cloud seemed to hang over them whenever the topic came up. As hard as he tried, Elmore didn't feel at home with this part of his family.

Just before he was scheduled to return to the brick building, he made a reluctant pilgrimage to the creek where he'd seen the little people. Normally he would have been delighted to see them again, but for some reason, it would not be the same without his parents to tell.

It didn't matter. Though he sat by the water for several hours, they did not appear. He never saw them again.

It seemed he had lost everybody. What other horrors did the future hold, the boy wondered.

"Professor Trent?"

It was one of his students—Doug Morse, he believed—standing uncomfortably at the door. Third-year Criminal Justice. Claimed to be one-fifteenth Cree—which was an odd percentage—and at one point had tried to make "friends" with Katie. He'd never stood a chance, but she had always been polite to him.

"Sir, you've heard?"

Trent nodded, choosing to remain silent. Doug looked down, seeing but not really seeing Trent's dull grey carpet. "Just wanted to make sure you . . ." Again, he stopped. And started again. "There's all sorts of rumours going around. Weird stuff."

"Weird stuff?"

"Yeah, parts of her . . . are missing, they say."

He struggled with that statement. "Yes, I heard. But probably just hyperbole?"

Doug shook his head. "No. A student, Pamela Arkady—don't know if you know her—she was on her way home last night, taking a short cut, when she . . . found . . . her. Said she was spread out. Pieces . . ." Doug stopped speaking, unwilling to finish his sentence. "Anyway . . ."

"Thanks, Doug," said the professor. "Classes have been cancelled for today. You might as well go home. Take care of yourself."

As listlessly as was humanly possible, Doug nodded and lurched out of the office doorway, leaving Trent alone to marinate on the awful news. Pieces missing. Unpleasantness upon unpleasantness. Not knowing why, Trent stood up and left his office, travelling at a solid pace, heading up two flights of stairs to a balcony overlooking the rear of the building. Stepping out into the cold elements, Trent went to the edge, hands clenched on the metal railing, and looked off to the adjoining property. There, about fifteen metres away, he saw the yellow tape and several police cars circling the back area of a house. That was where it had happened. Where some monster had taken the life of an innocent young girl. And left her in . . . fragments.

An educated man, Trent knew there was no such thing as true evil, just levels of psychosis and sociopathy. *Who would do such a thing*, he wondered. *And why?* All the basic questions usually asked by society. And somewhere out in the city that frequently gobbled up people, the answer was wandering around.

Deep in thought, he only just noticed all the police activity happening behind the yellow tape. Cops and forensic teams carrying out their appointed responsibilities. And amid all the activity stood a woman next to an suv, drinking her coffee. She was relatively short and was bundled up in plainclothes. But she had bright eyes, and those eyes, it seemed to the professor, seemed to be following him.

That can't be good, he thought.

Waabndaan Mizhisha Teg
Kina Gegoon Eteg Maa Kiing

(The World Lay Before Her)

Fabiola Halan paced the carpet in her hotel room, occasionally glancing at the window to her right. On the other side of the glass, the city of Toronto lay spread out. This room high up in an upscale hotel showed the physical extent of Canada's largest city. Disappearing into the distance, for a brief moment this metropolis reminded her of her infrequent trips to New York. When she'd first visited this city so long ago, she'd been awed by the skyscrapers, as she was again several years later when stepping out of a cab in downtown New York. Since then, it had always seemed to her that Toronto was playing little brother and desperately trying to catch up. From her window alone she could see innumerable condos and buildings in various stages of construction, constantly changing the skyline of the city. Once, not that long ago, she had made a joke to a friend that Toronto was rapidly turning into Spider-Man territory. In a few more years, the downtown core could comfortably support a superhero swinging from high-rise to high-rise, battling crime.

But that was then, and right now Fabiola was worried, hence the pacing. She glanced at her watch. Places like this made her uncomfortable. She was close to finishing the tour and was wondering if writing this book had been a good idea. It had opened a door in her soul, allowing some of the pent-up emotions the crash had generated to be released. A good chunk of therapy was acknowledging the problem. A book currently number four on the Canadian bestseller list was a pretty solid way of acknowledging her problem. Some of the reviews had been brutal, but that was the nature of being an author.

There had been some criticism of her dispassionate approach to the two Indigenous people involved in the crash. Especially the pilot. Her editor had commented that she had seemed rather condemning of the woman. Fabiola had stated categorically that the pilot had been responsible for crashing the plane and then abandoning her. After some prodding, the editor managed to soften the accusations within Fabiola's book, but still the subtext was there. Her editor had said in a recent email: "If it wasn't for the fact you are darker than her, these critics would probably be a lot more vicious, claiming some sort of racism. Luckily, an inherent sense of middle-class white Canadian guilt prevents them from being so obvious about it."

But like any open door, regardless of its location, other things could enter, seizing the opportunity to subject her to other terrors. That was why she had agreed to this book tour. It kept her moving, far and fast. The country lay ahead of her, and behind her. But the experience of almost dying in that cold land to the north was never far behind her. She was always cold. And conversely, always seemed hot no matter what the temperature was. Too young for menopause, she reasoned. She stopped in front of the window, leaning her head against the cold glass. It felt good.

Places like Toronto, while momentarily exciting and exotic, frayed the edge of her conscience. Yes, she loved the treats the big city offered. Restaurants you would seldom find in small towns. Ethiopian, Tibetan, and a host of other unique and foreign cuisines she found delightful. And when she was feeling nostalgic and wanting to remember her mother, Caribbean food practically everywhere. High-end fashion stores that would die in smaller markets. Her tastes in couture practically demanded a city with a population in the millions. Yet she was a creature of the open spaces. That had been her childhood, and even a good chunk of her adulthood. Especially recently.

In Montreal she had an apartment in the suburb of Westmount. A two-thousand-square-foot apartment that gave her the semblance of space. It was monstrously expensive, but her driving work ethic managed to keep the landlord at bay.

Fabiola was hungry. She had missed breakfast, having slept in late. A bite of some kind was due before her next reading. Her head still resting on the pane of glass, she closed her eyes once more and she was there again, in that northern Ontario wilderness. She was cold . . . painfully cold. She was hungry . . . excruciatingly hungry. Her broken leg, half numb and the other half screaming for medical care. All she could hear was the wind, and the trees creaking as they moved rhythmically back and forth, as if praying to the spirits of the land. She barely slept anymore; the darkness when she closed her eyes always exploded with this imagery. She had changed out there. Being fixed and stationary for long periods of time, especially this time of year, reminded her too much of last winter. Eventually she would run out of places to run to. What would happen then?

Her existence in Montreal was still largely a question mark. Emile Nichols, lover and friend, had gracefully bowed out of her life.

"And how are we feeling today?" He'd asked that question every day after the crash, with a smile, when he'd visited her in the hospital. Always up, always positive, which was what had originally drawn her to him. He'd been there when she woke up in the hospital after being rescued. The eighteen months they'd known each other had been an unexpected change for the woman. Rescued from a tragic beginning, spending her life documenting stories of devastation and ruin, solitary by nature, she didn't normally have companions flock to her. Or care about her.

But a fundraiser for a local women's shelter had thrown them together. A year and a half of trips into the countryside. A year and a half of dinners and social events. Fabiola had grown quite fond of the head waiter who had entered her life. It was rumoured that many of the restaurant's clientele came more to chat and laugh with Emile than for the cuisine. He too was a storyteller, but in a different way. The man had a story for every occasion and frequently had Fabiola laughing when nobody else could. He was indeed a healthy and happy diversion.

Alas, he was no longer in the picture. Her new distant, moody nature had not been of interest to him. He'd tried, but Fabiola had grown cold to him. Add to that the persistent nightmares of being trapped in the plane, of the ghost of the Cree teenager looking accusingly at her, and that horrible woman who'd abandoned and left her. He had no stories to tame those images.

After a few weeks, Emile was gone, after a valiant but vain effort to save the relationship, and the journalist was flying solo again. She knew she'd changed, but didn't most people who survived major accidents?

It had been her agent who had made the suggestion. Actually, two suggestions. Maybe more than her body that had been tested in the northern landscape, he'd said. Maybe it was time to turn some attention to her emotional and mental state.

All those bad emotions and experiences were bouncing around in her head, looking for somewhere to go, driving her crazy. He'd told her to give them a place to go. To write a book about what had happened. Relocate the trauma to the page. Control it.

Fabiola had liked that idea. She was all about control, and she was at her best when she wrote. Fresh out of the hospital, spring in the air, it was something to do.

Secondly, her agent had suggested she start seeing a therapist. The normally private journalist was less enthusiastic about that idea, but he'd convinced her that time with a therapist might help her focus herself and improve the structure of the book.

Patricia Monk was her name. She'd come highly recommended from several people. At first reluctant, then grateful, Fabiola had found herself confiding in the woman. Accounts of the accident, her thoughts and agonies as she lay half buried in snow, then her miraculous rescue and recovery. She would spend three days of the week reliving the incident with Dr. Monk, and the rest of the time reliving the incident in the writing of her book. The events just poured out of her.

"Post-traumatic stress disorder. I'm pretty sure that's what you're suffering from. All the classic symptoms are there," Dr. Monk had told her.

Fabiola was silent for a moment. "I thought only soldiers and rape victims had PTSD."

The therapist leaned back in her leather chair, a slight smile on her face. "Yes, a lot of people think that, but it's quite prevalent. Anybody who's had a severe shock or trauma can develop it. And I believe you, my dear, have had a massive one."

Fabiola was digesting what Dr. Monk had just told her. PTSD. In covering wars and conflicts, she'd seen large and powerful men crying like babies, diving under tables when thunder rumbled, or getting violent when there was no reason to get violent. None of those symptoms were hers. "You're sure?"

"One can never be a hundred per cent sure about diagnoses like this but—" The therapist started counting off symptoms on her fingers. "You're easily startled. You have trouble feeling emotions and are generally numb. Feel depressed and anxious. Have a fear or obsession with indicators that precipitated your trauma—in this case, snow, the cold. Any of this sound familiar?"

It did indeed. Very familiar. "Alright then, what do I do about it?"

For a half second, the therapist chewed on the tip of her pen. "Do exactly what you're doing already. Face it. Do battle with it. Conquer it."

"Sounds a bit masculine, don't you think?" This brought a smile to Dr. Monk's face.

"I suppose it does. What I should have said was deal with it. Most emotional trauma gets worse when it's buried. It takes root and can grow under the surface."

"So now you're a horticulturalist?"

Another smile lit up the therapist's face. "You're deflecting."

"Okay, how do I . . . do battle . . . with this?"

"There are several ways. Perhaps join a support group. Also, you may want to—"

"I've been writing a book."

Fabiola blurted it out, like it was a terrible confession, not knowing how her therapist would react. Dr. Monk leaned back in her chair, as if waiting for more. "It was my agent's suggestion, but you know, I think it's helping. I was afraid to tell you . . . I mean . . . all the psychology articles I've read might indicate I'm wallowing in the experience, afraid to move on. What do you think?"

"You say you think it's helping. Tell me about your process."

"The writing is happening quickly. Very quickly. Almost too quickly. I did three thousand words last night. Four thousand the day before. I can't seem to stop. The story is just pouring out of me."

"Do you feel good about what you're writing?"

Again the journalist paused. "The nightmares have lessened. I still feel cold, but I think it's helping. Sometimes, it's like I'm there again, and I write it like I'm there."

"You didn't answer my question. Do you feel good about what you're writing?"

Smiling a rare smile, Fabiola answered. "When I'm working on it, it feels like I'm taking all of that negative pain out of my head, taking my experiences, and storing them away someplace else. I'm creating distance. I'm finding it freeing."

It was now the psychiatrist's turn to smile. "Now why would I be upset with that?"

Two weeks later, she finished the first draft.

Finally, Fabiola opened her eyes. She was still in the hotel, head against the window, looking down far below her. There she saw multitudes of people walking through their lives, oblivious to what was going on inside her. Once again, she looked at her watch. Three hours had suddenly disappeared, in what seemed like a blink of an eye. But she still had an hour to kill. What to do?

Fabiola Halan grabbed her coat. She was a practical woman, and pacing was not practical . . . unless you were racking up steps on a Fitbit.

Dbaajmotaadwag Megwaa Mnikwewaad

(They Tell Each Other Stories While Drinking)

Trent had spent the better part of the day sitting in his office, doing nothing, thinking yet not thinking about a world without Katie. He would have to find Katie's family's address, possibly send some flowers, or perhaps a delicately worded condolence of some sort. That would be the right thing to do.

Looking around him just a few streets over, Trent noticed the shock of what had happened had not migrated to the rest of the city. People milled about, either going to or coming from something that was important to them. Some were smiling, others frowning, but most were too busy to develop any serious facial expressions. Just a vast sea of blank people wandering around the city, blissfully unaware that some in their very midst might just be feeling something a bit more intense. And real.

Leaving his car, Trent kept walking. Street after street passed him, and the memories of his years in this city began to emerge. Soon, he walked by the restaurant where he'd first had dinner with his then-new girlfriend, an enterprising young real estate agent named Sarah, so many years ago. Next, he passed a movie theatre where he'd watched a movie with Katie less than a year ago. Then, across the street, he saw the office of where his wife's new lawyer worked and did his evil. Coincidently, right next to it was a favourite coffee shop where Katie would spend hours on her computer searching the world's vaults of knowledge for nuggets of information that would propel her up the academic ladder of achievement.

Unable to fight the urge, Trent entered that coffee shop, quickly finding a seat by a window. He'd neglected to order a coffee, but the barista was too busy with a half-caff macchiato with whipped cream for the moment to notice he'd taken up valuable parking space. The air was so full of the aroma of coffee that he wasn't sure he needed an actual coffee in his hand. Add to the fact he was not thirsty or hungry, any reason he had for being in that shop was purely nostalgic. So, he sat and looked out the window as the world walked by, unaware of the absence of the lovely Cree girl who used to ponder and research the unfair treatment of Canada's Indigenous people here, while eating a butter tart. He smiled a weary but loving smile at the memory.

Reaching into his backpack, Elmore took out Katie's last essay. It was for another class but she usually let him vet her work before submitting. He had read it again in the office and had brought it with him, unwilling to leave it behind. He put it on the counter in front of him. "Lee Maracle's I AM WOMAN and BOBBI LEE: INDIAN REBEL: An Exploration of Early Indigenous Feminism." Katie had always loved Maracle's work and had been thrilled when Elmore got the author to visit his class.

That's when he noticed the copy of Fabiola's book, which was also in his bag. That too reminded him of Katie. Leaving both on the table, the depressed man looked out at the world and, as was its wont, it ignored him.

Sometime later, still pondering his thoughts at that anonymous coffee shop, located on a random street in a huge city, Trent was at a loss for where to go. His office was empty and alone, and the whole university was currently bathed in an atmosphere of sadness and fear. The house he lived in did not offer him a brighter environment. There was no place else to go, so he sat there. Like a barge wedged high on a sand spit, he waited for the tide to show him a direction to go.

As if willed by the spirits, he spotted Fabiola Halan, ten metres across the street. Sometime during his daydreaming, she must have arrived. Comfortably ensconced on a bench, she seemed to be studying people as they walked by, phone to her ear, deep in conversation. Trent could see her eyes darting from moving figure to moving figure. There was an odd intensity to her surveying of the populace. Once again, he was struck by the unique bone structure of her face. She was indeed a handsome woman. As she tucked her phone into a jacket pocket, she looked up and saw Trent watching her. Her head tilted a bit, and Trent managed a feeble wave and quickly held up her book. One second later there was a momentary smile on her face, then she rose, doing up her coat.

"I haven't actually had the chance to read it yet," he'd said once they'd ordered and taken a seat.

"You didn't strike me as the kind who would buy this kind of book. Let me guess, a little too sensationalistic for your academic tastes? My editor pushed for as much of that as possible. The journalist in me fought it but there seems to be a substantial difference between a two-thousand-word article and an eighty-thousand-word book. Evidently you need to get their attention and hold it for sixteen chapters."

What appeared to Trent to be a student earning enough money to buy ramen noodles for the week delivered their drinks to the table. The latte looked inviting, but he was puzzled by her choice of a cold brew with cold foam. Noticing his curiosity, she took a luxurious sip. "Something my adopted mother drilled into me. Cold drinks for cold weather. Hot drinks for hot weather. Helps keep your metabolism unified and even. It's the mixing that makes you sick." Raising an eyebrow, she waited for a response from Trent, who merely sipped his steaming drink, weighing his response.

"I'll keep that in mind."

"This your hang-out? Demographically, the place seems a little young for you." It was true. Both the academic and the journalist seemed markedly older than the rest of the clientele.

Managing a wan smile, Trent looked down into his cup. "I got some bad news today. So, I was feeling nostalgic. I came here. I have some good memories of this place." And Katie, but he didn't say that aloud.

Nodding, Fabiola looked out the window, now seemingly lost in her own distant thoughts. Trent noticed it primarily because she didn't seem like a "distant thought" kind of woman.

"Think of something interesting?"

Briefly, it seemed to Trent, Fabiola was somewhere else in time and space. It appeared she hovered there in this faraway place, but then after a few moments she was back—for the most part. She answered, but her attention was still partially focused outside this world of the coffee shop. "Just some general paranoia."

"I'm sorry?"

"Ever get the feeling something is chasing you? After you? Wanting you?"

"How cryptic. Constantly."

"Really?" He now had her complete attention. Behind them were three students talking about a new music band they'd found online. Two tables over, somebody was playing a video game, the sound of explosions escaping the earphones the young man was wearing. Mechanical hissing and gurgling came from behind the counter as orders were being filled. A soundscape unfit for intimate conversation, but it did force Trent to lean closer, oddly delighted that he had piqued her curiosity.

Sipping his latte, now tepid, Trent nodded. "Oh yeah. I'm getting older. That's a factor for sure. I am very much aware that Father Time is creeping closer with every passing day. And on a less gloomy note, the university is after me to publish more. As is my . . . wife." For some reason—an obvious one—he tripped over mentioning Sarah. But just as quickly, he trudged on. "There are always bills. The more money you make, the bigger the bills get. But I'm positive everybody has those hovering over their head and thinks existence has a personal vendetta against them."

A dark-haired girl, obviously a student from the university, entered the café, desperately in search of hot, caffeinated warmth. For a brief moment, Trent saw her as Katie approaching the counter, and half expected her to order her normal macchiato. "Large black, please."

"If that's all that's chasing you, I'm envious." Fabiola scanned the people in the coffee shop. Again. The woman had wandering eyes. Always peering into the crowd. Following people. Like she was nervous, or memorizing people, or maybe just, as a writer, making mental notes of the world around her. "Those I can—and do—live with."

"Well, there are other things that—"

Fabiola leaned closer, smiling eagerly. "Finally, a nugget. Banal conversation bores me. What are these other things?"

Trent finished off his latte. Unsure how much further he should let this woman into his world, he smiled again, self-consciously. The woman was giving off an appealing fragrance, but he couldn't tell if it was a hair product, a skin lotion, perfume, or perhaps her natural aroma. Whatever it was, it was very pleasant.

He opened his mouth, planning to ask some question about the nature of the book she had written, but out of nowhere, he blurted out, "Well, I'm diasporic in my own country."

This got a raised eyebrow. "Interesting. Explain."

"I'm Ojibway . . . actually, the more accurate term is Anishnawbe, but being an old geezer like myself, I find myself using the old terms. I've even been known to use the word *Indian* once or twice. Honestly, I sometimes use it in class just to watch all those young, politically correct eyes widen. I was raised in a residential school, and don't really have any attachment to my home community. My parents are dead. My wife is white. I'm playing politics in a largely white educational system. I prefer filet mignon to moose. It seems I have excelled at living the Canadian dream. I have been called an apple so many times . . ."

"Apple?"

"Red on the outside, white on the inside."

Nodding in understanding, Fabiola smiled. "Ah, in the Black community, *Oreo* or *coconut* is the term frequently bandied about. Black on the outside—"

"And white on the inside. People can be so creative, can't they. You too?"

"On occasion. Okay, my turn. Let's see. I don't do 'Black' things. Black cultural things. There's a movement to support Black designers." She opened her coat, showing Trent a cashmere sweater. "This is Italian. By a white Italian designer. I wear what I want. Hip-hop. Not my cup of tea. I don't do the James Baldwin thing and write about the Black experience. I prefer to write about all experiences." Draining her cup, she smiled at Trent. "But I do support Black Lives Matter though."

"Good for you. Me too. Let's see . . . I don't speak my language."

"I was raised by a French Canadian couple that, I'm convinced, raised me more out of a sense of social justice than anything else. Because of me, they were the darlings of their social circle."

"I sometimes think the social and political demands of Native people are frequently unrealistic. There is a section of the community that believes reconciliation cannot begin until the land is given back. All of it. Good luck with that."

"There is no one Black experience. There's Africa. Then there's Caribbean, even Canadian. American. Many others. All substantially different. I'm finding it difficult to find shelter under so many umbrellas."

"Same with the Indigenous community. At time of contact, it's estimated that, in Canada alone, there were over seventy separate languages spoken, all reflecting completely different cultures. That's like discovering Europe."

Both sat back, smiling at the context of their discussion.

Trent raised his mug. "To living the Canadian experience."

Fabiola answered his toast with her now-empty cup. "And to all those that don't." Resting her arm on the wooden counter, she seemed to be taking stock of the man in front of her. "You mentioned your wife, but the first time you stumbled over it. Not an organic stumble. I would say a psychological one. I assume the two of you are having some difficulty?"

"I wouldn't call it . . . difficult."

"Then what would you call it?"

Fabiola raised an eyebrow, waiting for a response. Trent peered into his empty cup, choosing his words carefully. "I believe she wants a divorce."

Smiling in victory, the journalist looked out the window again. "I would call that difficult. So, who's the villain in this story, you or her?"

Trent took a deep breath before answering. "Not everything is so . . . black and white . . . if I may use that term."

"It must be so nice to believe that." Fabiola Halan smiled again, but this time it wasn't as warm. Trent didn't reply. "I'm so sorry. My view of humanity has soured some in the last year. I'm sure your situation is very complicated. My apologies. I wish I could help."

"I wish you could too. I'm meeting her at her office tonight. She's got a rather successful real estate business two streets over."

"I will cross my fingers and my toes for you. You seem like a good man. Not everybody deserves to be abandoned."

In this busy café in the centre of a very noisy metropolis, the two were suddenly enveloped in silence. Once again, Fabiola's eyes followed those who blindly walked by this little-known haven for coffee addicts, while Trent absentmindedly traced his fingers over Katie's final assignment.

"Your name, Fabiola. That's so unusual."

"Not where I was born. And I like to think I'm a very unusual woman, so it suits me." There was a loud hissing behind the counter, and it made her jump.

"You seem a bit unnerved," said Trent.

"That's one word for it. I'm told I have PTSD. It's very annoying." For a few seconds it seemed like the journalist had stopped breathing—her lips pursed, her eyes no longer darting around the street but again fixed on some far-off location. "Each morning I still wake up fucking cold. Every morning. Practically frigid. No matter how many blankets. My leg throbbing. I swear I can still hear the wind blowing through those stunted trees." She peered into Trent's eyes . . . but to Trent it looked like she was looking past his eyes, past him. "I'm seeing a therapist. She helped me work through a lot of what's in the book. I'll have to send her something really special next Christmas." Rubbing her hands together in yet another attempt to keep them warm, Fabiola added a cryptic comment. "Do you know one of the odd side effects of therapy? She's the only one I talk to. And because of that, sometimes I feel so lonely. So . . . abandoned."

After a pause, Trent recalls something Fabiola mentioned earlier. "The woman pilot . . . who left you? Is that what you feel is chasing you?"

She nodded.

"I thought she was dead?"

The journalist shrugged. "She was never found. After an extensive search, in such a forbidding and unforgiving land, it's just assumed. But I still feel, somehow, for some reason, she's out there, after me."

"But why?"

A fire engine went by their window. Fabiola watched it disappear down the street. "If I knew that, I would have put it in the book. Again, my therapist thinks it's the PTSD."

"I guess that gives you good reason to view people a little bleakly." That elicited a small smile.

"That's not what my therapist says." Quickly, Fabiola whipped her arms through her jacket sleeves, moving with clear purpose. "I've taken up too much of your time. I should be going." She was halfway to the door before Trent stood up to say goodbye.

"I . . . I was rather enjoying the conversation."

"Me too. You know what they say in show business: always leave them wanting more. It was indeed a pleasure. Mr . . ."

"Trent. Elmore Trent."

"Ah yes, you've told me that. A pleasure to meet you, Elmore Trent. From the university, right?" Trent nodded. "I will remember you. Definitely a delightful afternoon diversion."

"You're not the first person to call me that."

Once again, she smiled her distant smile. "Go take care of your difficulty. I wish you luck. It's never good to have somebody abandon you."

"Fingers crossed. And I hope you manage to shake that sense of being chased. See you tonight."

That provoked a puzzled look from the woman. "Tonight?"

Trent held up her book. "Yeah, I heard you on the news this morning. Your lecture at the journalism class. I just might find myself with nothing to do, and pop in to listen."

She gave the professor a sad smile, shaking her head. "I think not. The publicist just phoned me. It's been cancelled—or as she says, postponed. Evidently there's been some sort of incident at the university."

For a few minutes Trent had managed to forget the horror the morning had brought. He tried hard not to let it show in front of this woman. "Yes, a student was found . . . dead."

"How?"

"They're not sure."

"Young?"

"Aren't they all?" he answered, as Fabiola did up her coat.

"How tragic. Strange, isn't it, how it always seems it's never the ones who should die, but always the innocent."

"Yes."

At that moment, three people in big winter coats walked in the door, momentarily blocking Trent's view of the woman. And then there was no woman to view. Immediately looking out the large window, he tried to locate her as several dozens of Toronto's citizens made their way past. But she was gone. Sitting down, Trent looked at her empty cup, which happened to be sitting beside the book she had written.

Picking the book up, the university professor opened it and began to read the last book Katie Fiddler bought but would never read.

Miigaaziiwnini N'kweshkwaan
Miigaaziiwninwan Ebkaan'zinid

(Warrior Meets Another Warrior)

Paul North's team won their morning game. And the game after that. It seemed they were on a streak. "Passable" was his coach's description of his performance in those two games. For the normal hockey warrior, it was not exactly high praise, but from a coach who made a regular habit of raising the level of criticism of Paul North to a high art, the man from Otter Lake glowed in the mediocre review.

Meanwhile, Herbie Tort was having, of course, a brilliant time. Five goals in two games, and not just average goals. His manipulations of the puck, had it been nationally televised, would have been featured on all the sports networks' must-see plays of the week. His departure from the Indigenous Hockey League was no longer anticipated. It was now expected. Rumour had it that he had already been contacted and discussions with agents had commenced, but the prodigy said nothing, just smiled enigmatically.

As a result, Paul tried to keep out of his way. The right winger did not respond well to gloating. Especially considering he had an inch and a half, and twelve pounds, on Tort; and if push came to shove, Paul could do a lot more pushing, shoving, and everything else that was involved in a good hockey brawl. Beating up on the next great Indigenous hockey star, especially one on his own team, might not be considered a clever career move. Being a grinder usually involved a lot more fighting than being a star forward. Supposedly you could count the number of fights Gretzky had been in on one hand. Paul would need both of his, and the hands of practically all his teammates, to properly tally his score. Paul was who he was. Well, that's what he told himself.

For the moment, Paul sat in his shared room. Jamie was off doing Jamie things, probably in a bookstore somewhere. He knew Jamie liked to read, but Paul didn't hold that against him. The team's backup goalie, Hank Weensk, supposedly had a fondness for Scottish porn, but Paul always felt that what people did in their own time was their business.

So, it was a welcome evening off, and the team was busy chasing their individual interests. Except Paul. Jamie's exit from the room had woken him, and other than a trip to the toilet and putting some clothes on, he had remained relatively immobile.

Earlier that day, Paul had heard on the news about Katie. He barely remembered her last name, but it had to be her. The description, location, name—everything screamed out it had to be the kimchi-loving Cree girl. Death was always difficult for Paul. It was more the protocols of bereavement that made him uncomfortable. He remembered that for funerals, people sent flowers. Did you have to be close to the family to send flowers, or could anybody do it? When paying your respects, should you hug? Otter Lake had its share of people who had passed away, and ever since Paul could remember, he'd noticed his uncles never knowing when exactly it was proper to hug and who to hug. Did you shake with one hand and then pull them close with your free hand? Most of his childhood memories of funerals involved awkward hugging.

Herbie's rise and Katie's fall seemed to be reminding Paul that the world was changing all around him. New things, good and bad, were constantly happening, yet he remained the same. He was a plateau in range of mountains and valleys. Three or four years ago none of this would have mattered. Now it seemed to be growing increasingly obvious to him. In three or four more years, these revelations would quite probably be screaming in his ears. And then what?

His major introspection would have to wait. There was a loud knocking at his door. At first Paul considered not answering, but a second round of loud, insistent knuckles on wood forced his action. Stifling a modest groan as he pushed himself off the bed, he looked through the peephole located dead centre of the cheap university-housing door. It took a moment for Paul to comprehend what he was seeing—a floating head of hair. Brown hair. Then he realized the peephole was not designed to reveal short people.

Opening the door, his assumption proved correct. It was a woman, no more than five feet tall, maybe five-one. She regarded him with a look that would normally come from somebody not so short—definitely somebody who should have been a few inches over six feet for sure. Small glasses, a little fogged-up from condensation. Wearing a jacket over what appeared to be a blazer. And about twenty years older than him. Not somebody who would usually come knocking on Paul North's door.

"Hello. If you're looking for Jamie, he's—"

"Paul North?"

"Yeah . . ."

"I'm Detective Sergeant Ruby Birch. I'm wondering if perhaps we could have a chat with you."

Years of conversations with older members of his family back on the Otter Lake Reserve had taught Paul to be wary of police looking for you, especially by name. It was never about anything good, whether it was to take you to residential school or because you'd been joyriding in your high school principal's Toyota Camry. This was primarily because while in the white world, you were assumed to be innocent until guilty; in the First Nations world the authorities frequently believed the opposite.

"Mr. North?"

Paul was suddenly aware he was barefoot. For some reason that made him feel oddly vulnerable in front of this woman. "Uh, am I allowed to ask why?"

"We have some questions."

"Am I allowed to ask what questions?"

"Questions regarding the murder of Katie Fiddler."

To the woman's left, a male police officer—in uniform—leaned into Paul's field of vision, almost as if he'd been hiding. He had the opposite look of the woman, as he was indeed six feet and some change, but he had the attitudinal composure of a much shorter man.

Jamie had had the right idea. Today would have been a good day to go to a bookstore.

Thirty-five minutes later, all three were sitting in an interrogation room at the division headquarters. Almost as if directly accusing him, a set of keys sat in front of Paul. Encased in a small evidence bag half a metre in front of him, on a standard government-issued table, the keys sat attached to a key chain of the kind several of his cousins preferred. And on the other side of those keys sat Detective Sergeant Birch. Though Paul was substantially bigger than the woman, that did not seem to be an issue in the reality of this room.

"Did you hear me, Mr. North?" Mr. North had indeed heard the woman, but was struggling to come up with answers to her simple questions that he knew were far more complex than they seemed.

"Yeah. Yeah I did."

"Well?" She sat back, the chair squeaking under the shift in her weight. In all his years, Paul North had never been interrogated by the police. Oh yes, he'd had the odd run-in, the usual ne'er-do-well kind of stuff—again, the principal's Toyota Camry incident came to mind—but nothing worth bragging about. This was different, being interviewed in a murder investigation. It was like finding himself at centre ice, in the seventh and deciding game of an NHL playoff series, without knowing how he got there. And wearing snowshoes instead of skates. With a badminton racquet. This was not good.

"My fingerprints?"

"Yes, your fingerprints. How did they get on Ms. Fiddler's keys and on her car? Did you know her?" The room was a green, tan-ish quality. Very odd, thought Paul—who picked colours like that? His mind was finding as many tangents as possible to avoid . . .

"Mr. North, do I have your attention?"

Once again, against its will, his attention returned to the detective sitting in front of him.

"Yes. No. Kinda."

"Pick one, Mr. North."

If there was a god in heaven, the coach would not hear of this. Paul knew he was already on thin ice . . . Despite the situation Paul smiled—*thin ice*, and he skated on ice for a living. That was kind of funny . . . Then the woman's hand suddenly thudded on the table, bringing him back to his current situation. And the annoyed face of a woman whose patience was fading.

"Yes. I met her once."

"When?"

"Last night."

"The night she was killed?"

Paul was no detective, but he could tell that did not sound good. He could see a problem rapidly developing.

"It was just dinner. That's all. At a Korean restaurant. I mean, I didn't even know Crees liked Korean . . . did you? I bumped into her there. It was all accidental. I mean, she was just sitting there one table over, and I was sitting there by the window and she started talking to me. Really, she did. She knew I was Native and she was Native so we started making small talk. We do that, you know. That's all, and yes, I did walk her to her car afterwards 'cause, well, you know, this is the big city and things can get dangerous in this city and I didn't want anything to happen to her, so like I said, I walked her to her car. It was covered in snow and so I helped with that. That's probably how my fingerprints got on it and the keys. You know, just being a nice guy. There's nothing wrong with being a nice guy, is there? I mean, that's all I did. Oh, and I did invite her to my game . . . I'm a hockey player by the way. Don't know if I mentioned that but I'm in town for a tournament and I thought she might enjoy it 'cause Native people . . . we like hockey and she's, well, like I said, Native. Cree." Out of breath, Paul paused for a moment, before adding: "And I'm Ojibway. Anishnawbe. Me."

"So, prior to yesterday, you'd had absolutely no interaction with Katie Fiddler?"

Shaking his head vigorously, Paul gave himself a headache. "No! None! We only got into town three days ago. Like I said, we're here for the hockey tournament. 'He shoots. He scores!' That kind of thing. Before that, we were in Sudbury. Taking on the Giants." A smile split his face as he remembered the game. "Got a goal."

Bkadewin Zhaabwiimgad

(Hunger Finds a Way)

How quickly night fell frequently surprised Trent. During the summer he would be barbecuing till practically nine at night. But this time of year, by the time he left the university, darkness would have crept across the city. Katie's death still dominated the news. In a city like Toronto, grisly acts like the dismemberment of a woman tended to have lasting interest. Especially if it was an Indigenous woman. Several First Nation organizations were already in the ecstatic throes of claiming her death was a larger representation of the atrocities of Canadian society, frequently forced on Indigenous women by colonialism. The politics were quickly taking over the actuality of her death. On the news, Trent had seen interviews with a variety of political spokespeople, activists, and a plethora of others who had never known the woman but thought they had the right to comment about her death.

The Fiddlers, Katie's parents, had even showed up on one of the news shows. Not exactly the simple Rez folk most Canadians might have been expecting, Nathan Fiddler, her father, had recently found work in a branch of the provincial government in Regina. Suit-and-tied like the rest of them, he looked as if his heart had been broken. His wife, Alice, seemed to be holding him up, physically and emotionally. She worked for a local hospice and did most of the talking during the interview. Of course, there were the usual photographs of Katie as a child, and then a teenager, and finally the adult Trent knew. Only now was he becoming aware that there was a whole life behind the woman he had grown fond of. And somewhere out there, her murderer was still at large.

In the darkness of his living room, Trent drank all this in. That and the three fingers of expensive Scotch warming in his right hand. As always, the police never talked about an ongoing investigation, especially one this recent. Still, his mind wrestled with the kind of person that would, literally, tear another person apart. And keep some parts. Memories about a book he had read a long time ago, about the famous Jack the Ripper. About how the maniac had taunted the police and sent letters bragging of his exploits, even confessing gleefully to having consumed the kidneys of one victim. From there his mind bounced over to the iconic scene from *Silence of the Lambs* where Hannibal Lecter confessed to eating the liver of a census-taker with some fava beans and a nice Chianti. Both thoughts forced him to look over at the table where a lone serving of a filet mignon complete with Brussel sprouts sat, as if waiting for him. Tonight, the Scotch would be enough.

Except he had to leave the comfort of his house. Sarah wanted to see him at her office regarding some papers. Luckily, not divorce papers—at least not at this early stage of their quiet disbanding—but other documents regarding their various investments and holdings that needed attention. Two successful adults in the middle years tended to attract bits and pieces of complicated life that frequently needed attending to. Their brief meeting the previous day had dissolved before anything could be achieved.

Right now, Sarah Trent was waiting at her downtown office for him, no doubt unwilling to let him either know the address of or enter her new dwelling. "This will be quick, Elmore. I am not in a mood to discuss anything just yet. Do I make myself clear?" she said to him earlier today. Clarity was not a problem Sarah usually had. In fact, Trent sometimes wondered whether a little obtuseness might have improved her disposition.

But for the moment, their accountant needed some signatures. Tax season was coming up, and the Canada Revenue Agency was seldom concerned with the marital difficulties of two middle-aged people. He assumed Sarah would try again to convince him—her husband for the moment—to sell the property up north. Above all, he knew Sarah hated things that served no purpose. They had bought a treadmill a few years back. After a five-month flirtation with it, it had rapidly gathered dust and assumed a new career as a laundry rack. By the seventh month, it had been resold.

"Oh, and I heard about that student from your school. Very tragic. She was Native I believe. Was she one of yours?" Such a complicated question from a complicated woman. Trent was not sure how to answer that inquiry. His wife had known he'd been having an affair, but he was never quite sure if she knew with whom. Now it appeared that she did not. And now, quite probably, wasn't the time to confess. His difficulties with his wife did not need Katie's name being drawn into it.

"Yes, she was in my Indigenous Storytelling course. Smart woman. She was going places."

There was a slight pause on the line. "You have my sympathies, Elmore. Now, see you at my office at 7:30. And don't—"

"—be late. I know." There was a click as Sarah ended the conversation. Seven-thirty was in less than an hour. He'd better get moving. Uber was available, but unusually Trent decided a good walk was in order. With the gloom of Katie's death hovering over his head, and the prospect of seeing his potentially soon-to-be ex-wife, a good walk might just cheer him up. Unlikely, but possible.

Draining his glass, and then putting on his outdoor shoes and jacket, Elmore Trent left the comfort of his house. He missed her familiarity. And to him, it seemed the house missed her too. There were a lot of things recently that he'd been missing, but as he'd read in a book written by some Native author: "Life—the Creator's way of saying 'Impress me.'"

A blast of winter air greeted him as he walked through his own door. It was a cold but beautiful night out, and the quietness of the side streets seemed to focus his thoughts. Trent couldn't help thinking more and more about Katie Fiddler. Just yesterday he'd talked to her, held her, kissed her. Now she was dead. It had been so long since anybody important to him had died. Like many typical southern Ontario nights, there was a grey overcast sky hiding the heavens. And as the sun had set, the sky was opaque, as was his spirit. No stars followed him on his journey to meet with his wife.

Who and what had done this to her? She was so young. Had so much potential. What monster out there would do something like this? Feeling oddly impotent, Trent wished he could do something to help. But as a university professor of literature, his crime-fighting techniques were somewhat wanting. Somehow though, if possible, he wished he could find satisfaction for the memory of the young Cree girl. She deserved that.

Maybe, the man thought, he would dedicate his next book to Katie. In the grand scheme of things, it meant nothing, but still, her name would live forever . . . Well, as long as the book was kept in print. And it was his little way of making sure she would not be forgotten. For the moment, it was the least he could do.

Trent knew his wife was one of the leading realtors in the downtown core. With him being busy at university, first studying and then teaching, Sarah Trent had put all her available time into getting a licence to sell houses and land. At first, amongst their upscale friends, there was some humour about the non-Native woman, who was the wife of a Native man, making a more-thanhealthy living off selling land. Trent found it only marginally funny, but he'd forced a smile.

Mid-sized and trim, Sarah looked the part of an alpha realtor. Sharply dressed, and not a hair out of place, the woman had her role down to a science. She was as good at reading people as any con artist or psychologist. Her innate ability to look into people's souls, and his inability to hide his, had contributed greatly to their current situation. When first accused, Trent had differed, deflected, even feigned anger, but he had not lied. In the end, he hadn't denied it. That was five months ago.

The phone on Sarah's desk dinged. It was probably Trent, buzzing up. Taking a deep breath, she answered it. She hoped this whole interaction would not be unpleasant. Her husband didn't seem to envision the obvious outcome of their current personal relationship. Always the dreamer. Perhaps that came with the career mired in academic study. Without dreams, there could be little literature. Of course, the same could be said about reality. Meanwhile, her career in real estate made her more aware of the veracity of human nature.

"Hello." There was a pause as she drank her coffee. "You know where my office is." And with that, she hung up.

Trent entered the large, empty office, smiling broadly like this was a normal situation of a husband visiting his loving wife. Sarah's return smile was approximately a third of the wattage.

He'd been here a thousand times before, but he still took the time to look around the room to see if there had been any changes to the layout he needed to comment on. But unlike his life, it all seemed the same. "Hello. It's so good to—"

"These are what I need you to sign." Just as quickly, she opened the file with his name on it and turned it towards him. Sitting down, he glanced at the small pile of paper.

"I don't even get a 'good evening' or 'it's good to see you'?" He smiled a small, hopeful smile as he said that.

"You want pleasantries, talk to one of your lovers."

Right out of the gate, thought Trent. "Sarah, you know it's not—"

"Enough, Elmore. Just sign those papers. The one on top is the most important. I am separating our bank accounts. The others deal with some of our other investments, and the bottom one is that property we have down by Port Dover. The renovations we had applied for will, obviously, have to be postponed."

"Is all this really necessary? I mean, I think you're jumping the gun on—"

Sarah let out a very unfeminine snort. "You've got a Ph.D. in literature and all you can say is 'you're jumping the gun'? Trent, we will be having many important conversations—since you want to use clichéd terminology—'further down the road.' Right now, let us deal with this. Everything else will happen in due course."

At various times in their marriage, Sarah had shown this brittle and critical side, and as a result Trent had come to fear it. These days, she seemed stuck in that mode. The more he talked to his wife, the more he feared any romantic reunion he might have envisioned was disappearing down that so-called road his wife had just mentioned.

"Sarah . . ."

"Elmore."

They stared at each other for a moment—a contest of differing sentiments. Reluctantly, he grabbed a blue pen from Sarah's desk, and proceeded to sign the papers. "I should probably read these, but I trust you."

"Yes, you should read those, and I don't trust you. Bit of a problem, wouldn't you say?" There was silence for a second before she continued. "But don't worry about it. Those documents are exactly what I told you they were."

"Well, at least you've been busy."

"Indeed. I have a lot of 'me time.' And other than the obvious, I assume you've been keeping busy."

"I'm starting a new book." Trent didn't know why he'd just lied. It had just popped out of nowhere.

"Reading or writing one?"

"Both actually."

"It's about time. When was the last one you wrote, about seven years ago?"

Finishing his last signature, he placed all the signed documents back in the folder and shoved them across the desk. "It's an idea I've had for a while. I think I bounced some of them off you last year. About deconstructing Indigenous legends. Where they fit into today's society."

Trent watched Sarah double-check all the signatures, thorough as ever. "I got the idea from that book you gave me two years ago, about Christian parables and how they translate in contemporary culture. Same principle with our stories." He didn't know where all this was coming from. He'd had a few random ideas about the topic—sometimes a flash in the midst of class or while driving—but this was the furthest he'd ever developed the notion. "Look at the Haudenosaunee story of Sky Woman falling through the hole in the sky. The whole supporting story of the geese and the muskrat. I've got this theory—"

"Good for you, Elmore. Native stuff is still in. I don't suppose you'll have any trouble selling it. Your department head will be delighted, I'm sure." Sitting back, Sarah looked at him expectantly.

"You want to hear more?" Trent knew what she'd say, but there was always hope.

"I'll wait for the movie." Trent winced, and it looked like even Sarah found that a little cruel. "Sorry, that was uncalled for." In the background, the hum from some anonymous machine suddenly clicked on. "You know, Barbara told us Joshua is leaving at the end of next year. His position will be open."

This again, thought Trent. Even though he'd been raised in a residential school and spent the vast majority of his adult life in various temples of post-secondary education, it was his wife that seemed to think the academic ladder was something he was interested in. The years getting his Ph.D. had drained all the ambition out of him. "Yeah, I remember."

"You know you'd have a good shot."

Chair of the English department. That would mean a lot of extra work. A lot.

"You'd be a natural, Elmore. First Nations, published author, your students love you—some more than others." Ouch. "You excel in what my father called 'folksy academia.' It's practically sitting there, waiting for you."

They'd had this conversation before. Several times. Sarah, even at this stage of their marriage, thought he was too complacent. Life was a journey, and mountains were meant to be climbed. Why build your retirement home halfway up when you could do it at the top? He knew she expected to be running this office in five years.

"Put in a few years there, and then, possibly, Dean of Arts. A great way to end your career."

"Sarah . . ."

"I know. I'm wasting my time. It seems I always am." A familiar look of frustration crossed her face. "Go ahead, say it.

I know you want to." Trent refused to take the bait. "It's because I'm white. Right?"

"I've never said that. That's what you've always believed." Part of this was true. It was Sarah who'd pushed him to all his achievements. She'd proofed and edited his two books, pressed him to get his Ph.D. That sense of ambition that happened so frequently in her world. He had often wondered where he'd be if left to his own devices. Possibly a teacher of grammar somewhere, instead of a professor at a major Toronto university. Essentially, he was happy with what life threw at him. He was a gatherer, but Sarah wanted a hunter. She had spent twenty years trying to make him into a hunter, but with limited success. His ancestors might have been hunters, but Trent lacked that gene.

"Well, whatever. It looks like you're on your own now, Elmore. I won't be holding your hand anymore."

"You make things sound so . . . final. Sarah, if you want, I will definitely apply for that—"

"What I want is irrelevant. This is what you should want. Anyway, no use wasting time talking about these fantasies."

"I refuse to believe that we—"

"Look, Elmore. No histrionics. I am not ready to have these normal conversations like we used to. Too much has happened. I don't know if we'll ever get back on that path again. Maybe yes, quite probably no." Elmore's insides went numb, but Sarah continued talking. "Think of our marriage as a ship. There's a huge hole in the side, heavy damage, water is pouring in, and right now I don't know if that ship will sink or float."

He swallowed. "What can I do to help?" It was not like Sarah to use a metaphor to describe anything. Faintly, he thought that might be something positive. Metaphors sometimes conveyed good news.

"Well, leave me alone." Taking the folder, she put it in a large case sitting beside her desk. "I'll contact you when it's time."

"When it's time?"

"When it's time. To see where we end up. Goodbye, Elmore. You'll find the coffee shop at the end of the block has excellent tea. Feel free to avail yourself of some." It was obvious the meeting was over and she was waiting for him to leave. Trent racked his brain, looking for any bit of relevant information, gossip, or pertinent material to further engage his distant wife. Instead, he rose to his feet, adjusted his hat, and moved his chair back.

"I can do that, Sarah. Talk to you later. I look forward to it." He realized that in this meeting, like the last one, he had appeared weak. A small part of his intelligence told him he might just be better off without the woman known as Sarah Trent. Yes, there'd be a lot of paperwork, mess, and discomfort with a divorce, but once it was over, he'd be free to operate as he saw fit, totally unencumbered by a wife. But the problem with that philosophy was the fact Trent deeply and sincerely cared about this woman. She had been his guiding influence, inspiration, and motivation, something he hadn't had since Sister Beatrice at the residential school. Taken from his mother at a ridiculously early age and then situated in an environment run almost exclusively by bossy, aggressive, and opinionated women, perhaps there was a reason he had gravitated towards the young Sarah Ireland. What was that old saying? The devil we know is better than the devil we don't.

"Be safe, Elmore." And with that, she turned her back on him, forcing him into an unwanted retreat. Making his way to the exit, Trent passed a line of desks displaying numerous faces and places from family vacations and holidays. Some images taken on boats. Others in backyards. A few celebrating Christmas. Dozens of frozen people with frozen smiles watching him go out into the frozen night, leaving an uncaring wife and returning to a world where his mistress had just been killed. Were he to keep a diary, tonight's entry would not be a positive one.

Booch Go Nimaajaa

(Goodbye)

Sarah could hear her husband walk out of her office. A small part of her felt sorry for Trent. In all other instances, he was indeed a good man, whatever that might mean. Once, she had loved him. After all, he had given her the space to grow as a businesswoman, but even that sounded very patriarchal. She had given herself the space to grow, she finally acknowledged. At his core, Trent was weak. He found refuge and strength primarily in the writings of others. He had never written anything creative himself. His two books were merely the rehashing of stories by different writers and his attempts to understand them. He was content with the way things were. For the most part. His extramarital forays were merely his opportunities to do something exciting. Forbidden. Not safe. Perhaps a divorce would force him to do something different. Something uncomfortable. Something not so reeking of contentment.

Betrayal—that tended to eclipse a lot of a man's goodness. So instead, now, Trent was yet another philandering husband dealing with the consequences. Hardly an original story. In fact, there were probably two or three movies playing at nearby cinemas dealing with the fallout of such an act. Above all else, she hated being a cliché. But for the moment, it was time to deal with her current life. Some files had to be logged in the computer, and two phone calls had to be returned. It was indeed after normal business hours, but the real estate industry didn't really sleep.

Finally, it was time to go home—or the two-bedroom apartment that now acted as her home. But first, tidy up her desk, rinse out her coffee cup, turn out the lights, and put on her winter boots for the trudge through some of Canada's finest precipitation.

Sarah put her new jacket on. It had been a present to herself immediately after moving out of the house she shared with Trent. Tan, with a faux-fur collar, it fell to her calves—protecting much of her body from the bitter winds.

It was just after locking the second-floor door to the office when she felt the ambient temperature suddenly drop. Somebody must have opened the door downstairs, exactly when a gust of cold northern wind attacked the building. But nobody had buzzed up, and at this time of night Sarah was quite sure she was alone in the building. Had a window possibly blown in? It was then she noticed a second unusual effect in the hallway. There was no wind. It was suddenly, disturbingly cold, but there was no accompanying squall lowering the temperature. Like a light switch being turned on in a dark room, it was just cold. *Very unusual*, she thought. Had the air conditioning unexpectedly powered up? Looking above the staircase, where the vent was, the little strips of plastic attached to the metal grid were unmoving. There was no stream of air coming out of the aperture.

There would definitely be a strong series of words exchanged with the building manager first thing in the morning. Putting her hand on the staircase railing, her foot had touched the first step going down when the lights on the first floor went out. Not quietly, but with a very noticeable and discomforting crash. Someone was down there who had little appreciation for private property. Sarah Trent was not a woman who was faint of heart, but she was also not a woman who leapt into battles she quite likely had little chance of winning. There were people being paid to engage in those battles, many of whom were called police.

Swiftly, she pivoted on her left heel, fumbling for her keys again. There was another sound of something expensive breaking. Up until this moment, Sarah had not been aware of how many keys she had on her keychain. Finding the right one was proving time-consuming and unusually terrifying. In her panic, she could not help noticing a lack of human voices. If somebody, or more than just one somebody, had indeed broken in doing the amount of damage it seemed, there would be dialogue, even mutterings or screams of anger or rage. All she could hear was destruction, and perhaps a deep-throated raspy noise. But she was not sure if it was coming from outside, or if it was one of the random noises the aged building occasionally gave off. Regardless, she redoubled her efforts to open the door. There was another sound and the lights in the stairwell flickered, then died. Whoever they were seemed to be making their way up towards Sarah.

Finally, she found the right key for the lock, turned it, and quickly re-entered the office, just as quickly locking the door behind her. Once again this was a night of recognition for Sarah Trent, as it had never really occurred to her that the door, and the walls on either side of it, were glass. This was highly inconvenient, she thought. Then, she heard something along the stairway breaking. It might have been the drywall along the sides being crushed, or possibly the railings being bent or yanked.

There were going to be some serious renovations involved in this break and enter. Either the insurance or the intruder would damn well have to pay for this, and improve the security system at the same time. Well, might as well put an end to this insanity, she concluded. She pulled out her cell phone and was just tapping in the final 1 in 911 when something came flying through the glass door, sending shards in a hundred different directions. It all happened so fast Sarah couldn't tell what specifically was hurtling across the room at her, but for a brief instant it looked like that tree in the planter that normally stood at the top of the stairs. But it couldn't be. There was a good hundred pounds of soil in it, not to mention the tree and its terracotta container.

In that split second, behind the flying tree, the doomed woman saw what had made a mess of the building she had worked in. Oddly enough, despite her current situation, her mind refused to believe what she was seeing. She died not believing what was killing her.

A voice came on the cell phone, which landed three metres away from the mess that had been Sarah Trent.

"Hello, 911. What is your emergency?"

The only response was a growl, as a huge, furry foot came down on the phone, shattering it.

N'wanj Naanaagdawendaagwad Dbaajmowin

(The Story Deepens)

Trent had been to that coffee shop before, and he had to agree with Sarah. The barista there did serve excellent tea. Most of his relatives, the ones he knew back on the reserve—however casually—usually drank orange pekoe, affectionately known as black or Indian tea. But all these years in the city and with Sarah had made him into somewhat of a tea snob. So tonight, he was enjoying a cup of excellent lapsang souchong. Most of those he was related to would have difficulty pronouncing the term, and definitely wouldn't drink it. Last he had heard, green tea was growing in popularity back home.

In his hands he held Fabiola's book, almost halfway read. Earlier that afternoon in the other coffee shop, he had read just the introduction and the first three chapters. He'd found it nominally intriguing. But since then, his mind had been bouncing off walls as he processed thoughts of his life, of Sarah, and of Katie, and now he desperately wanted to focus it on something less painful. So, enjoying his third cup of tea after the meeting with his wife, he turned the page. Around him, the evening energy of this little café was coming to life, but Trent ignored it, intent on consuming the words before him. Her prose painted a picture of abandonment, fear, anger—a whole cornucopia of emotions she'd experienced while left alone in an alien environment. It was fascinating how she'd fashioned an ad hoc brace for her leg, followed by a crutch. What really impressed him was her foresight in creating a small snowshoe to keep the crutch from sinking too deep in the blowing snow.

Surviving for two weeks without any substantial food had been the next obstacle. When the pilot, Merle Thompson—Trent could fairly hear Fabiola spitting out the woman's name with anger—had gone over their supplies before abandoning her, she had neglected to go through the unfortunate young man's coat pockets. There Fabiola found three chocolate bars, some gum, and a single piece of beef jerky. Knowing it was going to be a long and boring trip, the boy had stored provisions familiar to teenage boys. Luckily for her. Under normal circumstances, it was hardly the cache necessary to survive fourteen days of blinding snow and formidable cold. But with the matches the pilot had left her, she lit fires and made tea from the cedar and tamarack bushes along her way.

It was coming across a winter road spreading across a frozen lake that had ultimately saved her life. At one point, as she lay under the shielding branches of an evergreen, she had reached the limits of her endurance. Right then and there she was ready to surrender to the strength and tenacity of the land. Closing her eyes, Fabiola had tried to remember her mother's face, expecting to join her in whatever post-life existence waited for her. But her eyes would not remain shut. Her body would not stay half buried in that snowdrift. Something deep inside her kept saying, "One more frozen bog. Another stand of trees. Somewhere over there, just a little farther, might be what you need." And then, in the process of pulling together what little resources she had left, she heard a decidedly non-wilderness sound. Engines of some sort. Distant, but growing closer. For a second it almost sounded like a motorboat, like the kind an old boyfriend of hers had at his cottage. Struggling, practically crawling through the deep snow, she followed the sounds. And just as that voice inside her had told her, just past that stand of trees, beside the frozen muskeg, she saw them. Three snowmobiles gliding across the glare of the snow. She could see numerous snowmobile ruts across the frozen water. It was a well travelled path it seemed. But in a matter of minutes the snowmobilers would travel past her, and she would be behind them, difficult if not impossible to see. If she were to be rescued, if she were to make them see her, Fabiola had to act now.

For the dozenth time, Trent reached for his tea, only to find it empty. He'd been meaning to get another, but the draw of the book kept pushing that thought from his mind. The prose was a bit lurid in places, overly dramatic in other spots, but all in all, many would find it captivating. She was indeed a survivor, especially considering her origins in a tropical country and her adulthood in a primarily urban environment. How much of it had she embellished, he wondered. A crutch with a mini snowshoe? A woman with obvious enjoyment of the finer things in life, quickly understanding the complexities of building a fire outside in near-blizzard conditions?

Putting the book in his backpack, Trent left the coffee shop. He debated catching a cab or Uber, but it was only a half-hour walk, and maybe along the way he could sort out some of the thoughts running through his head. Again walking down the street his wife worked on, he would turn left and then zigzag his way back to the house. It seemed oddly colder now than when he had first entered the café. The weak sun had set hours ago, taking with it what little heat it contributed to the city.

As he walked, Trent tried not to look up to where his wife's window was. She had probably left the office by now, doing the things separated wives of academics did. He turned the corner, about to make his first zig, but unconsciously he looked over his shoulder, unwilling to journey home without one last glance at his past. But what he saw was not his past. He wasn't sure what it was.

Being a cold winter's evening, on a small side street, there was not a lot of street traffic. So Trent saw what he saw, alone. Something big in the window. White. Possibly furry. Unreal. Then the window cracked, not enough to shatter, but it created a sheen of opaque spiderweb fractures, hiding everything behind it. Frozen not from the temperature but from the brief glimpse of whatever he'd just seen, Trent leaned against a red mailbox, hyperventilating. The thing he had momentarily observed was not possible. It could not have been a giant in a fur coat. Though he had only seen it for a second, he was sure whatever it was had glanced at him—directly at him. And it had black glowing eyes. The analytical person that had been submerged by the primal sense of fear somehow managed to tell him the colour black didn't usually glow. He wasn't sure of what he'd seen, but whatever it was, it was in his wife's office.

Dropping his knapsack, Trent started running for the building's front door, again glancing up to the second floor. All the windows were dark—including the damaged one, proving it hadn't been his imagination. Something had indeed damaged that window. Those things were tempered glass, designed to prevent people from jumping out of them, birds going through them, branches and gusts of wind showing who was tougher. Whoever—or whatever—had broken it, there had been some strength or weight behind it.

Immediately he noticed the door lock had been forced open. How something that was designed specifically for that not to happen had happened, he didn't have time to figure out. Leaping over the pieces of metal strewn on the floor, he bounded up the first set of stairs, barely noticing the overturned desks and torn fixtures. Arriving on the second floor, he saw the office was equally a mess. Desks, chairs, computers, bookcases, and oddly enough, a large planter and tree shattered into pieces. And across the carpet, a dark glistening stain.

Near the upside-down desk where Sarah worked, Trent spotted something on the ground. At first, he didn't recognize it; but deep inside, something seized. Kneeling down, he saw a hand with a ring that looked unfortunately close to a ring he'd given his wife some twenty-two years ago, and on that hand, fingernails painted a subtle shade of burnt amber . . . Sarah's colour. Farther up the hand, on the wrist, should have been an expensive watch he had given her on their tenth anniversary. Sadly, both the wrist and the watch seemed to be missing. As, it seemed, was most of what Trent assumed was his wife. It was very unusual for her to consider going anywhere without her left hand.

Near the Keurig he spotted what seemed to be a pile of . . . something. Flesh, it appeared to be. Intestines. A nest of bodily organs. Trent was no doctor, so his understanding of what he was seeing lacked context. Numb, bordering on panicked, he surveyed the mayhem surrounding him. What had happened here? Where was Sarah? That hand . . . and whatever it was, by the Keurig, could not be her, regardless of what he had recognized.

"Sarah?"

Some mechanical contraption located somewhere in the building answered with a hum, but other than that, silence. Desperately, he tried again, his voice getting weaker.

"Sarah?"

Silence. Not even the normal mechanisms of a contemporary office bothered to respond this time. Alone, in a destroyed room, surrounded by what just might be parts of his wife, Trent almost lost his mind. The only thing that allowed him to keep his faculties came in the form of an unexpected distraction, however unwanted. It was a low, throaty snarl, coming from the general direction of the office bathroom. Looking over, he saw what he had seen in the window, only closer. A lot closer.

Standing a good seven feet tall, perhaps an inch shorter or taller, stood a nightmare. Snow white, lean to the point of emaciation, but somehow radiating a dangerous sense of unnatural power, it stood, the head stopping just short of the ceiling.

Not eight feet away from him—maybe nine—it watched him. Dark black eyes, soulless and cold; sharp pointed teeth glimmering in the light coming from the streetlamps just outside the office, snapping together like castanets. Strips of desiccated flesh seemed to be hanging where lips would normally be found. In its hands, Trent saw a human thigh and calf, connected by a knee. There appeared to be a bite taken out of it.

Trent, normally a man of reason and education, found himself in an intellectual conundrum. What he was seeing he could not possibly be seeing. There in front of him was nothing that nature or any reasonable god could have possibly created. Therefore, it could not exist. But there it was, snacking on the leg of his wife. Looking directly at him. This was not good. So, he responded in the only possible manner left open to him as a man of knowledge.

He passed out.

Ezhi-Znagnak Ji-N'naandwi'igod

(The Difficulty of Healing)

Fabiola Halan had not slept well last night either. She was bored, yet at the same time on edge. That sense of being chased was constant, and wearing on her. Looking out the window onto the early morning city, she wondered if this winter would ever end. It seemed like all she saw was snow, clouds, and billowing steam emanating from buildings, cars, and people. This book tour across the country was happening when so much of the land was being held prisoner by the earth's rotation. Every town on her tour had snow. Even when she'd landed in Vancouver, a rare dusting of snow had greeted her there, forcing motorists into a state of panic. From the height of her room here in Toronto, the snow seemed to spread as far as she could see. And no doubt even farther. The woman could barely remember last summer. So many people from her homeland would give anything to build a life in this country. It was a land of opportunity alright, but also one consisting of a numbing chill.

Ever since that experience with the plane crash, her life had changed. Dr. Monk had told her there would be some after-effects of her experience. Dreams, flashbacks, possibly a fear of planes, perhaps even a distrust of Indigenous people. Luckily, little of that had come true. Sleep, when it came, was a blanket of unconsciousness. Flashbacks, though vivid and terrifying, were few and far between. Sometimes it did feel as if something deep inside her was struggling to come out, ever since the incident. It had probably triggered something that had started with her ill-fated boat journey so many decades ago, and added to it. A hidden trauma of some sort. Something not so obvious. Doctors like Patricia Monk loved things like that. She'd told her that if she wanted to get better, Fabiola had to let it out. The journalist countered with the simple fact that some things were hidden for a reason. Sometimes they were good reasons. The therapist disagreed.

This tour consisted of plane trip after plane trip, but luckily that aspect of her trauma was hardly an issue. As for any mistrust of Indigenous people, Fabiola had always considered herself far too intelligent to succumb to the hobbies of the less informed. Add to that the fact she was no stranger to ill-conceived perceptions due to her skin colour. And as her conversations with that professor had proved, Indigenous people were not an issue with her either. All things considered, she thought she was doing well. If she ever saw her therapist again, she would have to mention that.

But then again, the murder of that young girl at the university . . . It made her uncomfortable for some reason. Her breath went shallow, and very lightly, her hand pounded against the tempered glass. She'd been in a dozen situations where her life had been threatened, and only this time had it evolved into PTSD. This was the last stop on the book tour for a week. No more plane trips, no more public readings, only normal life again—until the next leg. She had told her publisher she wanted to spend a few more days in Toronto before heading on to the next venue. Why? She wasn't sure. It was a big city. Maybe she could get lost in it. That was as good a reason as any other. A peculiar sound pulled her out of her daydreaming. Looking up, she saw it was her nails clawing at the glass window.

Fuck, she thought, *this winter is getting to me*. Unconsciously, Fabiola looked over at the phone. She was half tempted to call Patricia. She could use some counselling, but for the moment, she was on her own. Dr. Monk really didn't like sudden calls unless they were emergencies. And acting just the way Patricia had told her to expect was not exactly an emergency.

Dr. Monk hadn't been her first therapist. There had been another, long ago, when she first got to this country. Adopted by a very white, very French Canadian couple named Suzette and Pierre George, in this new country covered in snow and cold, the young girl was very confused. And to add to that, she was bullied at school for her unique appearance and peculiar way of speaking French. Her adopted parents had thought she needed professional help, what with her constantly asking for her mother and father.

"Well, Fabiola . . . my, what a lovely name." Charles Blanchette was an expert in child psychology, according to the diplomas on his wall. "Tell me about yourself."

Fabiola said nothing.

"Surely you must have something to say."

She just shook her head. Back where she came from, there had not been a lot of these people with the not-dark skin, but here, they were everywhere. She'd been here two months and had maybe seen a dozen others who looked like her. The suburbs of Montreal in the 1980s could be like that. She didn't want to be there. She didn't want to be anywhere. Everything was different and new and unfamiliar. From the moment she got up in the morning till she went to bed at night, it was constantly something new. And it scared her. This man was new, and he smiled too much. Her original mother had told her people who smiled too much were not to be trusted.

Games and conversation failed to open the vault that was the little girl. She rarely looked him in the eye, and after a month of twice-weekly sessions, the psychologist admitted defeat. And the little girl went home with her new parents. Fabiola had been in this country less than six months, and it was beginning to dawn on her that this was her new life. No more mother or father. Just these two people and the land surrounding her.

One night at dinner, as she rolled around a Brussel sprout on her plate, the little girl made a decision. Her new parents, deep in discussion about politics, heard their normally silent new daughter speak.

"My name is Fabiola." Both parents looked at each other. It had been practically impossible to get the young girl to speak, other than to answer the most basic of questions, but there was now an unexpected and unrequested statement.

"Yes, it is," said the mother eagerly.

"Fabiola, yes, is there something we can help you with?" said the father.

In her thickly accented French, "Who am I now?" was Fabiola's question. Both parents weren't sure how to answer.

Gii-Mji-Nakmigad Maa

(Evil Was Here)

When it came to Paul North, first impressions told the detective the man did not have the classic indications of a homicidal nature. Birch could tell when someone was a liar—it helped with the promotion—unless of course they were really good and seriously believed the lie they were telling. But this Paul North; she doubted he was lying. He was nervous but not scared. But still, it was too early in the investigation. Yes, the man's fingerprints were on the vehicle, but so were a bunch of others.

But the brutal fact was that Paul North had been in town the night the woman died. Coincidence? Possibly. In a city the size of Toronto, a lot of people were in town the night Katie Fiddler was killed. Several million in fact. But Birch knew he may have been one of the last to see her alive. That was more than a coincidence.

She would keep him on her short list of subjects and wait for forensics to get back with whatever else they might find.

Now, Detective Sergeant Ruby Birch stood at the top of the wrecked stairs of the Dominion Real Estate Agency. She and her men had had a tough time getting up to the second floor, as practically everything on the first floor leading up to one second floor office had effectively been torn apart. As had the woman who she presumed worked there. It was easy to conclude this murder was connected to the Katie Fiddler case—as most of the body was missing, and what was left was scattered around what remained of the office.

It would easily take a half-dozen men to do this amount of damage. Or a handful of very big, very strong, and very agitated men. Things were bent, crushed, scratched, and thrown. Katie Fiddler had been caught outside. But this woman—the ID in a purse under an overturned desk gave the name Sarah Trent—had been caught here. A dozen people surrounded her, some taking pictures, others dusting for clues, the rest looking for potential forensic evidence. Coming up the stairs, Constable Wilson emerged into the second-floor hell. Birch heard him gasp when he saw the carnage.

"The bathroom's over there, Constable."

"Thanks, Ma'am, but I don't need it." She could tell he was trying to be tough. The second loss of a meal in such a short time would have branded him for sure. "It looks a lot like—the Fiddler case, from a couple nights ago."

"You noticed that too." Sizing up the room, Birch looked down and saw a lovely red pump on the floor, near Wilson's foot. It took her a moment to realize there was a foot inside the shoe, and only a foot. It seemed to have been overlooked by the crime scene investigators. For a brief second, she debated telling the young constable what literally lay at his feet, but instead she walked across the room to a more senior officer. No need to deliberately embarrass the man.

"Uh, Carl, there's a human foot over there by Wilson. I would advise you to tag and cover it before he notices, or we may have more DNA evidence contaminating the site than we want."

Knowing the detective sergeant, and familiar with Constable Wilson's projectile hobbies, Constable Second Class Carl Lee smiled. "I'm on it."

"Constable, we need some more rubber gloves. Could you please—" yelled Lee. Looking for any excuse to exit and personally regroup, Wilson nodded and practically flew down the stairs. Birch and Lee shared a smile as Lee kneeled over the red pump to process it.

Birch walked around the crime scene. The problem with locations like this was the number of errant fingerprints and other bits of evidence. After all, it appeared to be a working office. A quick survey of the room revealed at least a dozen desks. That meant a dozen people, not to mention various people who for one reason or another might find themselves in a real estate office. Clients, other agents, family members—and hell, noticing the garbage in the trash receptacle, food couriers.

Looking down, Birch noticed a series of numbers on the floor. The evidence team that had just left, doing their job, had noticed hand and footprints on the carpet, which was stained with soil from a demolished planter. Her mind traced the movements they'd told her about. Somebody had fallen, or passed out, then tried to get up. First crawling, then managing to rise to his or her feet. The erratic pattern of the prints seemed to indicate staggering. Was it an emotional staggering, born of the realization of what this person had done? Or was it physical, arising from exhaustion or psychic burden?

This crime had all the earmarks of the Fiddler case, but what worried Birch more was its similarities to a case she'd heard of in Edmonton. Birch had just skimmed the report that had come across her desk; unfortunately her workload made skimming a necessity. Something about a mutilated body. She'd have to find it again and do more than skim. This was the kind of situation that, if not handled properly, the press would have a field day with. And it was always better to be a jump ahead of the press.

Well, might as well start with the basics. For the present, disregarding the obvious similarities to the Katie Fiddler case, Birch decided to go back to basics. When somebody was murdered, and they were married or in a serious relationship with somebody, there was a statistical probability the partner was somehow involved. The hand under one of the towels wore a wedding ring.

Who and where was Mr. Trent?

Ezhi-Gchi-Zegendaagwak Mkwendmowinan

(The Horror of Memories)

A long time ago, Carl Benojee was dying, slowly. Tuberculosis. Unfortunately, this was quite common in most residential schools. Hundreds, thousands of malnourished kids packaged together in badly ventilated buildings for ten months of the year—the body count could become quite high. Lying in the infirmary, the large boy coughed and spit up blood. Every time one of the nuns went by, they crossed themselves, partially because they knew the boy was not much longer for this world, and also because of a deeper worry that whatever was eating the boy's lungs might find their white lungs just as tasty.

As luck would have it, Elmore Trent was in the bed next to him, nursing an infected buttock. It was the by-product of a whipping by one nun that had gotten infected. For two days Elmore lay prostrate on the mattress, listening to his nemesis cough and cry. Mostly he just closed his eyes and tried to close his ears, but dying children were difficult to ignore.

Early one morning, while they were both alone in the room, Elmore heard his name called. "Elmore, I need to talk . . ." It was coming from Carl. And most amazing of all, it was in Anishnawbemowin, Elmore's language.

"Did . . . did you call me?!" he answered in English.

Carl tried hard to stop coughing, but with little luck. Every cough was agony, his lungs both bleeding and tender from the effort. But slowly, he managed to get words out.

"Memengweshii . . ." More coughing followed. He was talking about the little people.

"What about them? You told me not to mention them ever again. And I haven't."

Shaking his head, Carl looked over at Elmore, his eyes bloodshot and his hair wet with sweat. "No."

"No what?"

There was a second while the boy struggled to find breath without coughing. Finally, he spoke again. "I saw them too. Once. A long time ago. The Memengweshii . . ."

Another coughing fit followed. Elmore tried to make sense of this. Carl Benojee had seen the Memengweshii too?

"Why did you tell me they didn't exist then?"

There was a faint smile as he held the coughing at bay. "They can't protect you here. It's better if you forget everything when you come here. Forgetting keeps you going. The more you remember, the badder they think you are." With that, he coughed some more, and didn't stop for several minutes. Then he was silent.

Later that day, Carl died. Not long afterwards, he was forgotten.

Later that year, the next and last time Trent went home, he stayed clear of the lake. At night he was sure he could hear them chattering away, like they were waiting for him outside. Nothing ominous; just to say hello. Normally the Memengweshii were friendly, if they liked you. Just as he'd been told, some would play tricks on you, others would help, and there was the odd story of them even acting somewhat maliciously. They could be varied in their actions and purpose, just like people.

But post-Carl, all thoughts of the furry little people who lived along the water's edge soon disappeared from Trent's imagination. Life in that school didn't allow for such frivolous and sacrilegious beliefs. There were more important things to be embraced.

Elmore Trent sat in his bathroom; legs extended the length of the antique tub his wife had insisted they buy. In one hand, he held the edge of the tub, gripping as tightly as his forty-nine-year-old physique would allow him to. In his other hand, he held a glass of Scotch. The two did not usually go together, but when he'd arrived home, his mind had demanded he take the bottle of Scotch, brewed on some faraway island he couldn't pronounce but concocted for just such emergencies, and find the safest place in the building. The tub in which he hid was cast iron and could quite probably survive a horrendous explosion of some type. His natural instinct had been to grab the bottle and lock the door and not come out until God himself (or herself—Trent was ambiguous on the gender of any and all deities unless specifically noted) gave him the thumbs up. But once inside his modified panic room, he noticed that he'd neglected to grab a glass or cup with which to consume the malted barley extract. So there he sat, drinking an awfully expensive imported beverage in a plastic cup usually used for rinsing his mouth after the brushing of his teeth.

Waking up on the floor of his wife's office, surrounded by bits and pieces of his wife, had been quite distressing. Whatever he had seen standing there—obviously the catalyst for the death and destruction all around him—had rendered him unconscious and had departed during his blackout, which according to his watch had only been a few minutes. Why it had left, leaving him alive and relatively intact, was just another of the mysteries surrounding this whole situation.

Crawling to his knees, and then his feet, Trent had seen more completely what was around him. The office in which his wife worked had been wrecked. Once again he saw the scattered remains of his wife, the index finger of the severed hand, pointing at him.

"Sarah . . ." A lump in his throat prevented him from saying anything more.

Standing with a definite wobble, Trent looked beside and behind himself, on the off chance that the creature was perhaps hiding on the other side of an office partition or supply cabinet. But for the moment, Elmore Trent was alone . . . possibly. Knowing this, nature supplied him with a suggestion on what to do in an environment like this—essentially, run like hell. Millions of years of evolution had taught any creature with a relatively well-developed sense of self-preservation that, when faced with a more powerful creature or situation that defied any rational method of defence, it was always better to seek safety and run away.

Man, with all his highly technical devices and the untold millions of psychiatrists and psychologists spread across the world, were still essentially primal creatures. So, when in doubt, running and hiding was always a good strategy to fall back on. Unwilling to fight against man's overall nature, Trent had stumbled out the door, desperately trying to remember how to get home. Seeing his abandoned backpack on a snowbank, it acted as the North Star and reminded him of the direction to safety. Somehow, he managed to make it home, every foot of the way flinching at bushes quivering in the wind or cats dodging out in front of him. Along the way, a growing sense of guilt concerning the abandoned and piecemeal state of his wife gnawed at him, forcing him to stop at a subway station. There, in one of the few remaining public phone booths in the city, he placed an anonymous phone call to the authorities about a mysterious disturbance.

Katie was gone. Sarah was gone. The two sides to his coin. Trent was alone again. Regret and remorse powered his legs as he found his way home, almost in a fugue state.

Now, one of Canada's leading experts on Indigenous storytelling and stories was marinating in a bathtub with a bottle of Scotch. What else does one do in a situation like this?

Z'nagziwin D'goshnoomgad

(Trouble Arrives)

It was an insistent ringing that woke Trent up. Fighting to reach a level of consciousness that might be able to deal with the annoying and persistent noise, his head lurched to the side, making forceful contact with a large chrome faucet. That made the journey to awareness a lot easier, but the reality of that awareness was quite puzzling at first. Trent was in a bathtub, with a queasy, empty stomach. Nestled between his knees was an empty plastic cup, and beside it, an equally empty bottle of fairly good-quality Scotch.

Hangovers never really gave Trent a headache. Sarah used to joke that it was because, like a muscle, he used his cognitive abilities too much to let anything limit his head's capabilities. Instead, the metabolizing of the alcohol in his bloodstream via his liver usually resulted in nausea of some sort. As it did this morning.

First things first—why was he in a bathtub? Fully clothed. Why had he been drinking enough to cause a hangover? Again, in a bathtub. And what was that ringing noise that was dangerously close to actually giving him a headache?

Slowly the neurons began to fire, gradually picking up speed, allowing him to immediately recognize it was the doorbell. The doorbell was ringing. Somebody was at the front door. Wanting to talk. So far so good. Secondly, back to why was he in a bathtub with an empty bottle of Scotch? He reached down to pick it up . . . and that's when he saw the stains on his knees. On the light brown pants he was wearing, it looked like he'd been kneeling in something dark. Almost like earth, or blood . . .

The light didn't just go on, it flooded his consciousness with a blinding supernova sense of recognition. It was indeed blood. Sarah's blood. She was dead. The woman he'd married and sworn to love forever . . . And he'd seen who . . . what . . . had killed her. Instinctively he crouched lower, head barely above the bathtub rim. Maybe it had been an alcohol-induced nightmare . . . but there was the blood on his knees. Again, the doorbell rang. At first, Trent was tempted to let whoever it was pressing the doorbell button continue until spring finally decided to show up.

Instead, he crawled out of the tub, landing on his side with a thud. Every journey began with a full-scale body thump on the floor, it seemed. Sitting there, the full-length mirror on the wall told the man he did not look how a qualified, well-respected university professor should. He was in socks that also looked tainted with what he assumed was blood, or earth, or both. The pants with the soiled knees were in dire need of washing and ironing. And his hair and hands—well, there was much that needed to be done for Trent to look like he belonged in this neighbourhood and hadn't just wandered in after some Indigenous rights parade.

After some serious negotiation with gravity, he managed to stand and don an incredibly quick change of clothes. Next challenge was the flight of stairs. Declaring success, Trent opened the front door to what appeared to be a blinding whiteness. The reflective nature of snow and hangovers didn't generally go together.

"Yes, hello?"

"Mr. Trent? Sorry to bother you this morning. I'm Detective Sergeant Birch. May we speak?"

Gradually his eyes adapted to the influx of white light, and he found the source of the voice. A smallish woman, showing a little grey, with piercing eyes that Trent could tell were intelligent and had seen a lot. And she was with the police. He didn't need the Ph.D. hanging above the fireplace to tell him this quite probably had something to do with what had happened to his wife. Aware that he no doubt smelled of Scotch, was definitely bleary-eyed, and had bathtub hair, he managed a weak smile and went into host mode.

"Good morning. Ah . . . come in."

A comb followed by two cups of coffee later—strong coffee that could quite easily be called dangerously toxic—Trent and Birch were sitting around the restored oak table in the dining room.

"My wife and I have been separated for several months now," said Trent, looking down at his coffee. The drink was helping settle his stomach. He was aware how closely the woman across from him was studying his every word and gesture.

"You have my condolences, Mr. Trent."

Maybe it was paranoia, but to Trent, Birch's condolences sounded a bit contrived and rehearsed. For a brief second, the professor wondered if they taught this kind of thing—how to deal with mourning individuals who just might be guilty, but not appear overly insensitive—in detective school.

"When did you last see her?"

The professor had seen enough movies and television to know what this meant. He was quite probably the immediate and logical suspect at the moment. He could lie and say the dinner they'd had two nights ago. Nobody had seen him in his wife's office . . . other than that *thing*. But he had spent a substantial amount of time in the coffee shop just down the street from there. And he'd used his debit card to get the tea. And there were those contracts he'd signed, dated yesterday. It seemed he was his own worst alibi.

"Yesterday. Evening." This earned a raised eyebrow from the woman. "There were some documents that needed signing. What with tax season rapidly approaching."

"How long were you there?"

Trent knew this did not look good. "Less than twenty minutes. That's about all."

"A short . . . very short visit. Was anybody else there? Did anybody see you leave?"

"I went to a coffee shop. They saw me there. I was there a while. Reading."

"Was there any animosity between you two?"

And the view was getting worse. "Not really. I was trying to suggest a reconciliation but . . ."

"What was the reason for the separation?"

A third coffee. He definitely needed a third coffee. Maybe with a syringe. Normally Trent would be drowning his sorrows in tea, but there were undeniably things in this world that tea could not fix. It was definitely a coffee morning. "We were having some personal problems."

"Who had the affair? You or her?" The way Birch asked the question, so matter-of-fact, disturbed Trent more than the question itself. He knew everything he was saying made him even more of a suspect. The fact he could easily identify the killer— there could not be more than one of those running around the city, he hoped—made this conversation much more difficult. For a period of time, one so short-lived and swift only someone well versed in the arcane understanding of physics could categorize its briefness, Trent considered volunteering what he knew.

"I don't really see how that is—"

"You really don't?" Birch raised an eyebrow. "You're the husband, separated, of a murder victim. I believe you were the last person to see her alive. You appear to have a fair understanding of the world. If you were in my shoes, wouldn't that make you ask the obvious question?"

Trent took a deep breath. "I had the affair."

"Are you still having the affair?" There was Birch's eyebrow rising again.

Briefly, Trent thought of Katie. "No." A roughly accurate answer.

"How would you categorize your relationship with Mrs. Trent?"

"I don't understand."

This time Birch sighed, giving her eyebrow a rest. "Were you on good terms? Did she hate your guts? Restraining orders? That kind of thing."

"No." Leaning forward, Trent faced his accuser. "It was difficult. Strained, you might say. But it was amicable. Definitely not what you're thinking."

"And just what am I thinking, Mr. Trent?"

"That I . . . did something . . . horrible to my wife." The memory of what he had seen flashed across his eyes. He tried to supress a brief shudder that rippled across his body.

"Interesting choice of words: 'something horrible to my wife.' How do you know it was horrible?"

"Isn't death, murder, always horrible, Detective?"

For the first time that morning, the detective sergeant smiled. "Yes, but I don't think that's how you meant it. That momentary look, the shudder . . . when you said horrible, you meant *horrible*, in every sense of the word. Not terrible. Not unfortunate. Not even tragic. Horrible."

Trent, a man of words, a writer, an academic, an analyzer of sentences and communication, looked at the woman. "I don't know how to respond to that. *Horrible* to me means . . . horrible.

I think you'll find the definition of *horror* as something causing an intense feeling of shock, fear, or disgust. Finding out your wife has been murdered—I think I'm allowed to feel that way. Do White people feel differently about the death of their spouse?"

That proved how stressed Trent felt. He had played the race card. He almost never did that, feeling it was a cop-out. Everything he had achieved had been based in innate ability, not his heritage. Frequently Sarah had urged him to use his ancestry more, even mentioning it herself in conversations as if it were a party trick, or an award he'd won. The fact he'd just uttered that last sentence was very un-Trent-like.

This caused Birch to raise both eyebrows. "Mr. Trent, whether you are Indigenous or non-Indigenous, the loss of a loved one is horrible. Sorry if I made you feel otherwise." The next question was obvious. "Sir, where do you work?"

"I am a professor, at a university in Toronto. I teach courses on Indigenous literature and storytelling."

"Wait, which university?!"

Immediately, Trent saw the detective blink, but he didn't know why. Instinctively he realized this was probably not a good thing. His insides seized up. Perhaps it was time to switch to tea.

From his upstairs office, Trent saw the police detective finally pull away from her parking spot. She'd been parked there a long time, no doubt digesting everything he'd told her. When she'd asked if he knew a Katie Fiddler, he'd answered honestly. When asked if it was her that Trent had been having an affair with, he was a bit less honest. Each minute Birch hovered outside his home made the professor increasingly uncomfortable, the business card she had left him burning in his hand. All the while, Trent kept telling himself that technically he hadn't lied to her about what had happened last night. He'd told her the truth, up until a certain point. That "certain point" being the admission of what he had witnessed.

And then there was what Birch had told him about Katie's body. That the flesh was not cut with any tools. For the most part, the body looked like it had been ripped, bitten, and chewed apart. Birch noted that there were sizeable . . . what appeared to be teeth marks, puncturing what was left of the young woman.

The description was too much for Trent to handle, and he had the odd thought that Birch was purposefully trying to catch him off guard. It worked. The creature. He did not know what else to call it. Several times it had been on the tip of his tongue, but he couldn't bring himself to share those final images of his wife and whatever killed her. Trent didn't know how such an admission would go over. Actually, he did, and that's what scared him. Regardless, it definitely would not have improved his situation. There was still too much uncertainty around what was happening and how he fit into it all.

He was still hungover and needed time to assess his situation. Under normal circumstances, Elmore Trent was a very law-abiding person. No outstanding parking tickets. Unlike many Indigenous people, his suspicion regarding law enforcement was negligible. But not today. The last few days had thrown his entire life into a chaotic storm. And in the midst of that storm was a large, extremely thin, snow white creature currently digesting his wife.

Something about that in itself, as odd as it sounded, was eating away at him. Trent was in the midst of a nightmare, one that was slowly dispatching the people he loved. He should do something about it. But what? What he saw wasn't possible. Looking up, he saw the Morrisseau painting on the wall. The man turning into a thunderbird. What an imagination that man had. Sarah had loved that painting, and Trent had loved Sarah. There had to be something he could do. These two women in his life . . . somebody had to do something. The only problem was he didn't know what he should do. Or could. For the moment, he closed his eyes.

Geyaabi Bmi-Nakmigad Damnowin

(The Game Continues)

Somewhere in the distance, Paul North could hear a siren. Several of them. But that wasn't unusual. Here in the city, that's practically all you ever heard, whether it be police, fire, or an ambulance. This metropolis always seemed to have an accident or tragedy in waiting. And then happening. There'd been a couple of cousins and one aunt living here at various times in his life. They usually returned home, accompanied by tales of woe. At home, it was only the wind in the trees, or some opinionated birds that usually called you forth early in the morning.

Wherever those sirens were heading, Paul was positive there were tales of regret involved. But for the moment, he snuggled down deeper into his bed, sheets pulled up around his neck.

Across the room, Jamie also slept peacefully. Practice was in a few minutes. Experience had taught the man from Otter Lake to milk as much sleep out of a situation as possible. His reaction to the cruel and noisy world around him, a pillow firmly placed over his head. Whatever was out there causing so much fuss—let it stay out there.

The vast majority of the problems of this world were not his.

Everybody on the team was talking about the death of Katie Fiddler. One person on a Manitoba team was even distantly related to her. That afternoon, all the players in this semifinal game were wearing red armbands in her honour. Black would normally have been expected, but at a First Nations hockey tournament, everybody agreed red would be more appropriate. A collection blanket had gone around the arena just before the game, with the contributions being sent home to her family out west. The customary rivalry between teams at the tournament was lacking at this game. All the First Nations and Métis who were in the arena understood that poor Katie Fiddler was another example of missing and murdered women, a phenomenon all too familiar in the Indigenous community.

Somewhat rested, Paul North stood at centre ice, head bowed, looking down at the blue spot in front of him. Seventy-two minutes. That was how long he had known the woman. One meal at a Toronto Korean restaurant. He'd told no one other than that policewoman that he had met Katie. Why he didn't mention it to Jamie or any of his friends, he didn't know. It was just a random fact in a tragic story. And now they were there to play hockey.

He could barely hear the Elder saying a prayer in Cree. Or the drum group that quickly followed. All he could think of was her laugh. That sounded ridiculously romantic, but it was true. She had laughed like a real Cree woman. And now, he and everybody else were being expected to play a hockey game. A particularly important one, but still.

Herbie Tort, standing erect at the end of the line, looked anxious. Shifting his weight back and forth on his skates, he was fidgeting, waiting for the game to begin. Each game was sixty minutes, broken up into three periods, setting up the rest of his life. Waiting back home on his reserve was a father—overweight, diabetic, and highly critical of his son no matter how well Herbie did at anything. In fact, the better he became at anything, the more judgemental his father was. Though not well-versed in social studies, Herbie was aware there were essentially two types of fathers. Those that dreamed and encouraged their sons (and now daughters) to do better than they ever had. And the other type, who thought a successful child was disrespectful and should be punished for daring to supersede the father. That was Gerald Tort, Herbie's father. Regardless of what happened with the scout and the NHL, Herbie was never going to return home again. He had a cousin that had played for three years in Sweden. He'd move there and herd reindeer before he'd lock eyes with his father again.

Glancing down his team line, he saw Paul North at the end, looking distracted as usual. People like Paul bothered him, even annoyed him. The man didn't know how important these games were—not just for Herbie but for everybody who put on a pair of skates and battled their way up the leagues. Yes, this was a game. It was also a preparation for life. It was an opportunity for success. A way off the reserve. It was many things to just as many people. But Paul, he didn't care. That was obvious. It was something to do. Kill time as the years went by. He just naturally gave off the impression that it was either this or work at the grocery store back home. But in hockey, you got more women.

Herbie had known too many people like Paul. Life was not a mountain to climb. It was a plateau to saunter over. The centre wanted to be the next Bryan Trottier, Fred Sasakamoose, or George Armstrong. All great players of the game. All great Native men. His father knew all their names. Herbie Tort would sound just as good. Teams had come knocking, and Herbie had already sat down in discussions with three very well-respected teams. Come next season, there would be no more Indigenous Hockey League for him. If all went well, he would be on a professional team shovelling down poutine in Montreal or salmon in Vancouver or even clam chowder in the States. It didn't really matter where he ended up. As long as it wasn't home. Or playing in these "let's try and be proud of who we are and adapt as best we can" hockey leagues, or showering next to people like Paul North.

The drum song ended. All twenty hockey players from each team evacuated the ice surface, and the game began. Seven minutes into the game, Paul was hit by a defenceman from the opposing team, the Dead Rat River Rez Dogs, sending him flying into the boards and stopping the play. As he crawled to his feet, Herbie skated by, a broad grin splitting his face. Once again, Paul found himself hating the man. There but for the grace of too much beer, hamburgers, and— more beer, go him.

"You okay, man?" Jamie helped him to his feet.

No, he was not. "Sure." There was something about his shoulder.

"You don't look good."

"That's not what your mother said." Yep, definite pain coming from his left shoulder. Where he had hit the wall. He skated to the bench and tried rotating his arm, resulting in an unexpected grunt of pain.

From his right, the coach suddenly appeared. "North?"

Smiling brightly, Paul smiled his best smile. "Hey, Coach, how's it going?"

Experienced with hockey injuries and knowledgeable about a player's vanity, the coach laid his hand on Paul's shoulder and gave a little twist.

"GAAAA . . . FUCK!" and a single, lone tear flowing gently down Paul's cheek was the immediate response.

"You're done. Go see the doctor."

Two, maybe three years earlier, Paul might have argued with the coach. He might have not flinched when his shoulder was perturbed. He might have jumped up immediately after the hit, without Jamie's assistance. But at this very moment, a shower and a lie-down were looking very good. And maybe the doctor might give him some interesting pain pills. There just might be a silver lining to this after all, he tried to tell himself.

In the shower, Paul sighed as he washed his hair with one hand. Not his best day, or week. Luckily, he'd just bruised his shoulder, nothing permanent. Just a simple matter of inertial force hitting an inanimate object. Simple physics, the physician had told him. He was to stay off the ice and limit any strenuous physicality for at least three days. Normally Paul would like the time off, but if his team won the game today, the final was in three days. That definitely sucked. Still, the shower felt good.

Showers frequently provided Paul with his best thinking time. There was a slight chance the coach might let him play, should the Otter Lake Muskrats survive this elimination game. After all, he was still the best right winger on the team, seeing as Tom Thomas was a borderline alcoholic and Bradly Samson had a trick knee. With enough painkillers, the ache in that shoulder could be muffled. He wouldn't be the first athlete to attempt this, and God knows the coach had twenty years of sniffing out scenarios like this. But with a game this important, even the coach might be willing to bend some of the rules. And Paul was a rule-bender from way back. Nodding his head in the empty shower, that seemed to be his best option.

He heard a loud cheer echo through the building. Somebody had scored a goal. Paul hoped it was his team. But not Herbie.

Madsaad Skweyaang

(The Past Visits Someone)

Fabiola Halan was hungry. In retrospect, maybe she should be reading that book on PTSD that her therapist had recommended. But it seemed to agitate her more than help. The nightmares were returning. More tossing and turning. She had heard voices in the hallway and feared they were coming for her. Surviving a hell of a plane crash and its aftermath seemed to have dubious benefits.

She'd tried to start writing another book, this time dealing with the after-effects of survival. Hell, by now she was an expert. The PTSD angle could be an interesting take. Enduring what both the ocean and the north had put her through had provided her with a unique perspective few living people had. But the words would not come and the file in her computer hard drive remained empty.

Instead, she closed her eyes. It was a technique Dr. Monk had suggested, to quiet her mental chaos. She was to concentrate on something distinct but harmless. If she was lucky, it would focus her mind and help her sleep. Fabiola thought about her watch, her hand circling the dial. It had been a gift from her adopted parents when she graduated university.

She still remembered seeing both of them sitting in the audience, smiling proudly as she sashayed across the stage. They were good people. She knew that. They had tried very hard to get through to this strange little girl from a faraway place, and for the most part, they'd been successful. Was she not graduating from a very reputable university with a degree in communications? She recalled blinking twice at them—a family way of saying "hi" or "I see you." They'd blinked back. It was a good day. That night, at the celebratory dinner, Pierre and Suzette George had congratulated the new graduate. Fabiola was enjoying the beef Wellington, basking in their appreciation, when her mother said something that caused her to put down her fork.

"Fabiola, this may be of interest to you." Suzette had a small piece of paper in her hand.

"What is it?" she asked. A small part of her hoped it might have something to do with a new car, but there was no such luck.

Pierre answered her question. "Now that you're out of school and have the time to explore your life, we thought this might be important to you."

Unsure what they were getting at, Fabiola took the note and opened it. At first, she didn't understand what was being given her. "It's a name . . . and . . . is this a phone number? A foreign one?" Written in her mother's distinctive handwriting, the note said *Emmanuel Desir.* "Who is this, Mother?"

Suzette took a deep breath before she answered. "We believe that is your uncle. We can't be sure. It took some investigating, but that man is the only blood family of yours we could find."

"We thought you might like to . . . contact him," added her father.

For a few seconds, Fabiola looked down at the name and number in her hand. Her delicate hand shook a bit. She almost never thought about her origins, and other then a fleeting image in her dreams, never her mother. This was scary. She didn't know what to do. Folding the paper delicately, Fabiola gave the Georges her best smile. "Thank you."

For a long time afterwards, she thought of the paper and what it meant. For two months, the young woman wondered about the name and the man. An uncle. She couldn't remember anything prior to that experience on the ocean. Once she dialled the first three numbers but lost the nerve to complete the call. In the end, she never called the number.

Deep inside, Fabiola knew that was then. This was now. Fabiola wanted to look forward, not backwards. The slip of paper with the handwriting of her mother had been deposited in a wastebasket.

What would she say to a man she didn't remember? He probably thought she was dead. She might just be a painful reminder of what the man had lost. Just like he was to her.

Naag'ajge

(She Follows a Trail)

Detective Sergeant Birch had spent the last half-hour hovering over her desk. Spread across it was an array of photos, reports, and her own notes about the two murder cases. Sometimes seeing them chaotically arranged over a flat surface allowed her to see patterns, coincidences. But so far, nothing was really drawing her attention.

Both women. Both essentially rendered into body parts. That was where the similarities stopped. One Native. One not . . . but married to a Native man. One young. The other not. One a student. The other an established realtor. One killed outdoors. One indoors. What was the connection? What was Birch missing?

And then there was that case in Edmonton. She'd been meaning to pull the file on that. She doubted there was any connection, but better to have too much information than not enough. But first she'd have to . . .

The ding on her computer drew her attention. An old friend on the Winnipeg police force, Sheila Martin, had sent her an email. "See you guys have been having some fun out there. Sounds kind of familiar. We've had some weird shit happening here too. Thought you might be interested in some of the stuff I've dug up. No thanks necessary, just a nice bottle of rum next time you go to Cuba. Oh, and Jeremy says hello."

They had done their early training together, before Sheila moved west in search of less dampness. In the attached file were a series of crime statistics put together by Sheila. This was the kind of research Birch would have done once she had the time. But luckily, here it was now, all tied up in a nice bow.

Many of the things she read were vaguely familiar. Reports she had glanced at quickly over the last few weeks, including the Edmonton case. But she had not seen the forest for the trees. She had not connected them with her cases. She had no reason to . . . until now. Inside, she felt a cold chill.

In Vancouver, blood had been found smeared along the shores of the False Creek. Again, no leads. Two people had been reported missing several weeks ago. One was a runaway girl, and that was never easy to confirm.

In Edmonton, two legs had been found floating in the Saskatchewan River. Judging by the shoes it had been a male jogger. So far, no leads. And as always, with Edmonton's down-and-out population, there were reports of several missing people. It was nearly impossible to follow up on. Also, the down-and-outers did not frequently jog.

Thunder Bay had several missing person reports, but so many disappeared into the accursed river that ran through that city. There were many questions, specifically about two teenagers that were not accounted for, but for their own reasons, the police seemed reluctant to investigate.

In Winnipeg, a human head had been found, along with a left arm, on the outskirts of the city. Most thought some rogue coyotes had found a drunk and made short work of him, but even Ruby Birch, city born and raised, knew coyotes didn't do things like that. At least not Toronto coyotes.

And in Regina, the remains of a hacked-up woman had been found in a rundown hotel, but the police had a suspect. Her husband had a history of violence, and he had disappeared. A national warrant had been issued for him.

Again, these notes sounded oddly familiar to Birch. A coincidence perhaps, but she didn't believe in coincidences. All similar, but different enough to not really draw any attention to a pattern.

A serial killer, she thought immediately. Possibly. Maybe. If so, judging by the distance involved, one that collected air miles. And if that was the case, the timings of the murders indicated the killer was heading east. All this had happened in the past six weeks. Maybe there was more to this, proving it wasn't all a coincidence. Where this was going to take her, she wasn't sure. But at least she had a direction in which to go. The division head was breathing down her neck, and she was beginning to get calls from the media. That was never good.

Somewhere, in all of this, was a killer. An incredibly unique murderer.

Nisidawendaan

(He Understands)

Trent was scared. *Terrified* might be the more correct term. Not just because he was a prime suspect in the murder of his wife—and if he'd been reading the detective lady correctly, possibly Katie too—but because his subconscious was finally beginning to process his experiences. The thing he'd seen last night, in his wife's office, consuming part of Sarah . . . it had left a memo light flashing in his subconscious. Finally, that message was playing. Though he struggled not to remember the *thing*, it kept forcing its way into his consciousness. A purple faux-fur throw draped over the sofa now looked ominous to the professor.

The really scary thing was—the creature he'd seen looked . . . familiar. Trent was sure he couldn't have seen anything like it before in his life, but still, there was something about it that tugged on his memory. It was screaming "remember me" to a man who did not want to remember anything from the previous night. But it was something Trent couldn't ignore.

Sitting there, silent and alone, his mind began playing whack-a-mole with information, memories, and possibly his mind itself. He would think of something, then immediately discard it as unimportant and misleading. And then re-examine it. The murderer—monster . . . whatever it was—something about it was hiding deep in Trent's hippocampus. Something that would stop his journey into insanity while at the same time drive him insane, but for totally different reasons. And like his ancestors, he was hunting it down.

The figure he had seen was huge. Sasquatch huge. Seemed white, with some fur. Sharp teeth. Bizarrely thin but radiated strength. No lips. Black glowing eyes. Trent suddenly remembered seeing a lump exaggeratingly sink down the creature's throat. In retrospect . . . a chunk of his wife's flesh? It had seemed voracious—incredibly hungry—and that's when it hit the professor of Indigenous literature and storytelling. What he had seen. What he could not possibly have seen in any sane world.

His first reaction: did he have another bottle of Scotch hiding somewhere in the house? As if proving the intensity of the shock, the privileged connoisseur in him would even have consumed one of those horrendous American blends.

Shaking his head, Trent refused to believe what his memory and knowledge was forcing him to consider. It was unreal. Unimaginable. Not possible. No more than seeing Dracula or the Loch Ness monster at a bodega. There were no such things as . . . could he think the word, let alone say it to himself? The W-word? They were creatures of legend. Metaphors to keep his ancestors in line. Fanciful stories created for cold winter nights. They most certainly were not walking the streets of Toronto, hanging out behind a Tim Hortons or an Indigo.

He was thinking about Wendigos.

Two hours later Trent had torn his personal library apart. The room was scattered with books of all sizes, pages open and passages highlighted in yellow marker. One of the benefits of being an academic was that you didn't need the internet to research your area of study. The accumulation of topic-related books was part of the job description. He was reading selections from Thomas King, Basil Johnston, Gerald Vizenor, and a host of other Indigenous writers who had documented Indigenous beliefs and written about such creatures.

Sometimes called the Weetigo, Wiindigoo, Wiijigoo, or Windikouk, it was a terrible creature born of frigid winters and fears of starvation. Details varied from legend to legend and nation to nation, but essentially it was a cannibal spirit that would invade the body of somebody—or take shape itself—and plague villages with an insatiable hunger. The more it ate, the bigger it grew. And the bigger it grew, the bigger its appetite grew. It was an eating machine that could never be satisfied, and it preferred the flesh of humans. As horrifying as it seems, all the evidence Trent had pointed to that. But it couldn't be . . .

Most contemporary authors tended to approach the legendary creature as more of a metaphorical creation. Though not specifically stated, it was implied that one of the characters in Joseph Boyden's well-written but contextually questionable *Three Day Road* had been overcome by the spirit.

Three of the books he'd looked through had images of the so-called creature. Unusually long arms, long snow white hair, teeth that would make a tiger jealous. The pictures didn't look exactly like what Trent had seen, but close enough. Few who had seen an actual Wendigo were likely to live long enough to sketch a reasonable facsimile. Trent, being a believer in truth, tried desperately to find an alternate theory. An escaped ape of some sort?

Completely foolish, but apparently less foolish than a Wendigo. It had worked for Arthur Conan Doyle's Sherlock Homes. But apes did not do well in cold, didn't eat flesh, and weren't seven feet tall. A homeless man or woman? Very unlikely. A person in a costume of some sort? An emaciated bear? All theories were severely flawed in their reasoning.

A momentary hallucination might be possible, thought Trent. He had been under a lot of stress recently. Maybe seeing his wife eviscerated had snapped something deep inside his mind, and as an academic he had forced something from his studies to take shape and take the blame. But even though the police detective had never actually said it—in fact, she had implied everything except that—the implication was that Sarah had been partially consumed. A figment of his imagination could not have done that to her. Nor to Katie.

Then there was the most terrifying possibility of all. Maybe it had been him. Maybe Elmore Trent, respected professor and author, had indeed killed his wife and eaten her. As Sir Arthur Conan Doyle had also said through his creation Sherlock Holmes: "Once you eliminate the impossible, whatever remains, however improbable, must be the truth." After all, he had awakened this morning covered in her blood. That was a big issue.

Several small problems with that hypothesis: first of all, Trent had no recollection of the event. In fact, he could account for all his time after the meeting with Sarah, if those were indeed accurate memories. It was difficult to understand why he would fabricate two hours in a coffee shop, but again all things were possible. Second, for the last four years, both he and Sarah—except for the occasional fish, and of course lamb rogan josh—had been essentially vegetarians.

But perhaps the strongest reasoning against this possibility was Trent's devotion to Sarah. Yes, he had cheated on her, but not because he had lost interest in her. She had frequently pointed out that he was weak in that way, but he had always believed she made him strong. He was a romantic at heart, and romantics didn't kill and eat their wives.

At the thought of her and her fate, Trent fought back tears. But first he needed to deal with this, and then he could properly mourn the woman he'd spent a good chunk of his life with.

And of course, there was Katie and her untimely demise. Was it happenstance that he knew both victims? It was all sounding uncomfortably plausible. Even he was doubting himself. Eating people though, human flesh . . . that possibility was a tough one to swallow. Somewhere amidst all this information and conjecture was an answer.

When faced with a conundrum, Trent—like so few of his academic kind—went to battle. The man could wield his chosen weapon mightily and do great damage or great healing depending on the situation. There were thirty years of expertise accomplishing mighty scholastic feats with it. But he had never needed it as much as he had today. Sitting in his office chair, he turned his computer on, immediately hearing the comforting hum, and opened up a search engine. The entire world existed on the other side of his keyboard. And he only had himself to figure things out. Trent started typing those seven terrifying letters that spelled an equally terrifying concept.

Somewhere to the north, a complex system of air currents, high pressure, and low temperatures started its peculiar dance, bringing a cold front drifting towards Canada's largest city. Something merciless, frigid, and cruel was descending upon Toronto. Many would say it was too late in the season for such an anomalous and severe weather manifestation to develop. Spring was technically just a few weeks away. Then there were those who were frequently ignored, but whose understanding of the world was far older, and they would say the icy climate was being called, beckoned even.

In the age of science, who had ever heard of such silliness. Regardless, the cold came. And something, deep in the city, was delighted.

THE SUN BREAKS THROUGH

N'dawenmigon Na? Maage'sh N'dawenjige Na?

(The Hunter or the Hunted?)

Alone, the Native woman seldom noticed the pile of discarded sunflower seeds she left behind. She wasn't allowed to smoke in here, so the sunflower seeds helped with the craving. Also, her mind was elsewhere. On the dirty screen of a twenty-year-old television, attached to the wall high above the communal living room, the news of the day dashed quickly by for those with limited reading or attention capabilities. There had been a second murder. Rumours around the building said the first one had been gruesome, practically demonic. The victim . . . a Native woman. But this woman knew that tales in the hostel were seldom anything but stories. For the last few days, she'd tried to ignore the gossip, let it flow past her like she was an island in a river. But if white people had started talking about it in the media, there had to be some truth to these stories. And now there was a second death. Details were scarce, but she knew it was a piece of the mosaic that had become part of her life. No matter how far she travelled, sometimes blindly it seemed, it was there. Waiting somewhere. It was like that thing was a part of her.

Some people cracked their knuckles. Others blinked repeatedly. She had even known one man who wet his lips with unconscious abandonment, his tongue constantly flicking out. Her, she ate sunflower seeds. It was a new habit. Cracking them and spitting them out like every shell was a breath of oxygen. She was never aware of doing it, nor the amount she consumed, nor the trail or piles of emptied shells she frequently left behind. It was just something her subconscious demanded in lieu of nicotine. And you could seldom say no to your subconscious.

It was like Vancouver again. Winnipeg. Edmonton. Now Toronto. No matter where she was, there were always murders. Deaths. Even the disappearances, accidents, or "misadventures" as the authorities frequently called them, were all the same thing. It was hungry. It was always hungry. And it would always be hungry. Luckily—or unluckily—it lived in a country of thirty-six million people.

"Hey!" The woman looked around to where the sudden voice had sprung from. Unsurprisingly, it was coming from that Salish woman. The two of them made up half of the Native people that were staying at this hostel. "Those things you keep spitting out. You know Bella doesn't like that. You better stop or you'll get in trouble." The Salish woman turned her attention back to the television screen. "Not that I care."

"Thanks."

Looking down, the woman noticed that, indeed, there was a substantial circle of split shells extending away from her chair. She never knew where she got the sunflower seeds, but there always seemed to be a bag or two tucked away in her pockets, her purse, her bag. One of these days she'd have to figure that little mystery out. But for the moment, there was the matter of all the dead people. And what she should do about it.

She placed another seed in her mouth as she watched more of the news. That action was quickly followed by the sound of a small crack, as her teeth split the shell for the flesh underneath.

It was sometime later when the Native woman realized she was cold, which was odd. The woman had grown up in places so cold no Torontonian would dare build a cottage there. And it seemed it was getting colder. Currently the coat she wore was not designed for temperatures like this. Underneath she had on two sweaters and a pair of men's long johns, but still, the cold ate its way into her flesh, on course directly for her bones. This wasn't normal cold. This was abnormal cold. It carried a message, or maybe a promise. Either way, it was here and when it left, it would leave a scar of some kind.

The place where she was staying sent its residents out looking for jobs, or to get experience, or to just give some semblance of being proper members of society. The problem was this woman was no stranger to working, having worked hard for most of her life, since her mid-teens. Through most of her youth and adulthood, she had experienced many kinds of abuse and difficulty. Pain and disappointment were commonplace in her life, but she would not let those obstacles interfere with her journey. Her grandfather, who had told her many tales and stories in the few years she knew him, had also taught her that our journey in life was to impress the Creator. So far, the woman felt like she wasn't exactly succeeding.

Unfortunately, the world frequently neglects to be as supportive as is wanted. This woman, who was perfectly capable of finding and keeping a job in any of numerous different fields, purposely made herself undeserving of regular employment. A job would tie her down. It would limit her mobility. She'd be tethered in a story that needed freedom. As a result, she knew she was wearing her welcome out here and would have to move on soon, which was fine with her. It was time—she could tell.

In this city was a hunger. And there was a big, golden-brown bannock wrapped around her neck.

But where to go next? And when? Mobility required money and energy. Both of which were diminishing. She'd find a way though. That had been her primary drive for the last year. But for the moment, she was very cold. Standing on the street, grabbing a delicious smoke, did little to generate heat. As she headed into the hostel, the woman looked up. High above, leaving twin snow white trails, a plane flew over the city. With a sense of longing, she watched it for a few seconds, until the burning sensation in her cheeks forced her in through the door.

Dreaming and nostalgia were for those who weren't cursed.

Pakaan Dibaajmowin

(A New Kind of Storytelling)

Doing media always made Paul uncomfortable. The pretence, the artificiality of it—even though it was supposedly the news—made him regret agreeing to the coach's request. And he always looked fat. Paul's coach didn't want his other players distracted by the fancy cameras and lights, nor did he want them jockeying for position in front of the pretty female reporter. So that left Paul, with his injured shoulder still healing.

Behind him he could hear players whooshing past on the ice, the coach's whistle blowing, and muttered grumbling from the players, who were doing their best to hone their skills. Jamie waved from between his goalposts, giving Paul a thumbs up. Normally an Indigenous hockey tournament wouldn't generate much interest from local sports media unless it was in a small town with little other news happening. Here in Toronto, it was the reporter from the Aboriginal network, showcasing the growing popularity of the Indigenous Hockey League. So, Paul tried to look taller, glad he'd washed his hair that morning.

Standing at a 45-degree angle to the rink, Paul was leaning against the penalty box. Behind him were a dozen of his teammates practising passing and doing power skating drills. In front of him were two members of the media: one a female reporter holding a mic, the other a cameraman. Looking at ease was more difficult than Paul thought.

"So, tell us who you are and who you play for." Her name was Laura Bear, she was thirty-ish, wearing an abnormal amount of makeup. *Probably for the camera*, he thought. She looked kind of Native.

"My name is Paul North, and I'm a winger for the Otter Lake Muskrats." His eyes kept darting back and forth from her to the camera. He'd already forgotten the name of the cameraman—Tim, Kim, something like that. (As for the cameraman's blood quantum, one of those DNA tests had told him he had 11 per cent Indigenous ancestry. That was good enough for a decent job with the network.)

"So, the big game is the day after tomorrow. Are you excited?" Most of the questions asked by reporters, he thought, were stupid. Of course he was excited. His team had made it to the final. This was the big game. If they won the next game, they'd be champions. How else did she think he'd feel? Sometimes he just wanted to . . .

"Yeah, pretty excited. The team is out there practising. You can almost smell their sweat from here." The reporter managed a small smile at his small joke. "We all know the White Lake Wolverines have taken the trophy home the last three years in a row, and they're favoured to win their semifinal game today, but we think we've got a good shot at beating them and taking the tournament ourselves." He added a forceful nod of his head to accentuate his assertion.

"Why is that?"

Paul faked a casual look behind him at his teammates. "Well, we're hungry. We want it. We've worked hard for it. Jamie Dawson, our goalie—it's impossible to get anything by him. So, if the hockey gods are with us . . ." He managed a modest shrug.

"And Herbie Tort is on your team. Word has it he's pretty good. This may be his last year in the Indigenous Hockey League. Rumour says he's been scouted by some pretty impressive NHL teams." The reporter left it at that, without a specific question, hoping Paul would vomit forth some pithy and usable comment. Instead, Paul managed his own wan smile.

"Yes, we're pretty proud of him. What happens to him after Saturday's game . . . well, you'd have to ask him. I'm not his manager or publicist. Just a fellow hockey player."

Paul saw her tap the cameraman's elbow, and the camera panned left and filmed the Muskrats taking turns shooting on Jamie. "I notice you aren't suited up for practice." Again, no explicit question.

"Uh, no. Bit of a shoulder problem. I'm sitting out practice today. But both the doctor and the coach say I'll be good for the big game though. Looking forward to it." Once again, he gave the woman his best smile. Unfortunately, it felt as fake as it was. God, he hated doing this. He noticed the camera swinging back to him. It had missed his smile.

"In the Indigenous community, how important would you say hockey is?" An actual question, forcing him to think. Not usually his best talent. But somewhere, probably on a long bus ride to a game somewhere far away and not that long ago, he'd found a magazine on the bus. In it was an article about the popularity of the game amongst Native people. Obviously, it was something he was familiar with; he'd been playing the game practically since he came out of diapers.

It was estimated people spent a third of their life sleeping. Paul was sure he'd spent another third of his life balancing his body and mind on a narrow expanse of steel. The remaining hours—a combination of eating, partying, bathroom stuff, and women. Twice he'd spent some time on a beach in Mexico, but he wasn't sure how that fit into the overall mathematical equation that was his life.

"There is a reason, I think, why we like hockey so much." The reporter leaned in closer and Paul could see the iris deep inside the camera tightening. "We were a warrior people. Playing hockey is an extension of that. When I put on my gear, it's like I'm putting on my warpaint. At the other end of the ice are our enemies. Out there, we compete. We battle each other for possession of the puck. Frequently, there are fights from that. Hockey sticks are our tomahawks. It's how we do battle today. I'm thirty-five years old. A lot of my family back home who are about my age and don't play hockey, they're overweight, battling diabetes or some other health issues. This game called hockey . . . they call lacrosse Canada's national sport, and yeah it was invented by Native people, but for every Indigenous lacrosse player you can name, I can name a dozen Indigenous hockey players. Every player out there, behind me and especially me, is a warrior. This is our game." To give his words emphasis, he nodded his head firmly.

Wow, he thought to himself as he finished his speech. He'd have to read more articles. He'd actually remembered most of it. And it sounded good. More importantly, it made *him* sound good.

"Alright Marshall, let's wrap up. I've got four hours to package this." The cameraman—Marshall was his name it seemed—started packing up the equipment.

Ms. Bear stuck her hand out, and automatically Paul shook it, trying not to show his disappointment. "Nice clip. Thanks, Mr. North. This will be on tonight." Absent-mindedly, he wondered if she had a tattoo of a West Coast–style killer whale spread across her torso. "Just about ready, Marshall?" The cameraman nodded and lifted his big canvas bag and case. Over her shoulder, the reporter gave Paul a grateful smile. "Good luck."

"Thanks."

And then she was gone, climbing the stairs, out of the sweaty, masculine atmosphere. Turning, Paul saw Jamie look at him, raising a quizzical eyebrow. Shaking his head, Paul gave his friend his best hangdog expression, making the goalie laugh. For a few seconds, Paul watched his teammates practice. As usual, Herbie was by far the most talented man on the ice. In other physically related fields, the man could have been a successful ballet dancer, he was so quick and balanced.

Was that a sufficient reason to hate the man, Paul wondered? Oh well, it would have to do for now. Moving his shoulder gingerly, he felt a twinge quickly grow into a spasm. His shoulder had less than twenty-four hours to heal.

Otaminwin

(Playing Games)

Since this part of the book tour was over, Fabiola Halan had spent the morning moving into a smaller, less expensive hotel. From this moment on, accommodation costs were coming out of her pocket. Still, her need for more than mere comfort demanded a privileged hotel environment. So, here she stood, once again gazing out at Canada's largest city. The view via her new window was not nearly so amazing. Her room faced west and was only on the sixth floor. These were difficult times though.

Roughly thirty metres below her, and just off to the right, was a large building. She noticed several dozen people milling about its entrance. Even from this distance she could almost smell the cigarette smoke. The pilot who had abandoned her had smoked. Others she noticed were walking in and out of the large domed building. Obviously, something was happening in there. Fabiola was now curious. It was a curiosity conceived by boredom. She needed something to do. Fabiola put her jacket on. This was a big city with lots of people in it. Somewhere amongst those people, and in that building, might be a distraction.

As expected, the closer she got, the more pungent the cigarette smoke became. The irony that it was in front of an athletic arena made her smile briefly. Once she had done a story on one of Montreal's most successful anti-drinking organizations, which was sandwiched between two bars. Irony like that amused her.

A sign near the arena's entrance said it was a semi-final for the Indigenous Hockey League trophy. Fabiola had never heard of the league, but during her years in Canada she'd developed a basic understanding of both Indigenous people and hockey. Also, her career in journalism had taught her a lot about a few things, and a few things about a lot. Hockey had never interested her. Again, it was that Canadian fascination with all things cold. Hockey, curling, dog sled racing, ice carving, and numerous other sports that perplexed her.

The weather report she'd listened to that morning had said a massive cold front was slowly moving in. Wasn't there always one approaching? The woman could already feel it beginning to seep through her cashmere coat. Quickly, she slalomed her way through the smoking people outside, most of whom seemed to be Indigenous in appearance, on her way into the building. Subconsciously, she kept her eyes open for the pilot, not really expecting to see her—though random chance seemed to both favour and curse her. Fabiola had no idea why she was on her way to see a hockey game—and not even a real one, an Indigenous one. Still, it beat sitting in her hotel room watching real estate shows.

The game was already in play, but most of the seats in the arena were empty. Those that were occupied revealed a cross-section of the Indigenous community—some urban, while others had travelled hundreds of kilometres to watch the games. Scattered about, purposely attempting to look uninterested in the game, were a small group of teenagers. Clearly there because they had to be there, and dedicated to letting the world know that. Around them, men and women of varying ages sat in seats consuming hotdogs, popcorn, and a variety of soft drinks, all the while cheering on the players on the ice. And everywhere else was a pandemonium of numerous children running up the steps, through the aisles, and along the boards in glorious anarchy.

Making her way down a flight of cement steps, Fabiola managed to dodge two kids playing tag between the seats. Their agility in their own private game almost matched the dexterity of what the players were accomplishing on the ice. Finding a seat that gave her a good view of the game, about eight rows up and overlooking one of the blue lines, Fabiola sat back to watch the game. Glancing at the scoreboard, she saw it was the middle of the second period. The White Lake Wolverines in brown versus the Fox Island Arrows in yellow. The Wolverines were up by three. Nine minutes and forty-two seconds left in the period. Most of the people in the arena seemed to be Wolverines fans.

The game puzzled her. Both its origins and the devotion people had for it. Especially the Indigenous people surrounding her. It was a game unfamiliar to their ancestors, but it was clear that everybody, sans the teenagers, revelled in the game—an unusual symbol of their colonizers. Scattered vendors were busy selling t-shirts, sweaters, and posters.

At a multicultural seminar Fabiola had once been forced to attend, the lecturer had theorized the Potlatch Ban had deprived all the Indigenous nations of the land of their traditional pursuits. And since nature abhors a vacuum, the First Nations people in Canada quickly gravitated towards hockey, embracing it with a seldom-seen fervour. The end result being this particular game she was now watching.

Down near the ice, leaning against the battered and scuffed boards separating the rink from the seats, she noticed a man. Fairly tall. Good-looking. Mature but still carrying the vestiges of his youth. Wearing a worn jacket and even more worn jeans, and he looked good in them. First Nations probably. And a hockey player, judging by his physique and apparent familiarity with his immediate surroundings. The journalist in her noticed he was favouring his right shoulder by leaning over the . . . what did they call it . . . the penalty box, with his left. More than likely an injury of some sort. A different man, in full hockey regalia, burst out laughing at something the man she had spotted said. This got a stern look from another man, who seemed to oversee the same team as the penalty guy—the Fox Island Arrows.

The man in . . . she wanted to call his lack of hockey equipment "civilian wear" . . . smiled, and stepped away from the guy doing time, knowing he was interfering. Leaning against the Plexiglas that circled the rink, the man lifted a can of pop, but didn't drink. Stifling a yawn, the man casually looked up into the sparsely filled seats. His eyes darted from one group of people to the next, nonchalantly seeing if there was anybody scattered in the arena he might know.

Paul immediately noticed somebody who looked out of place, sitting one section away. She wasn't dressed for a hockey game. She was alone—and hockey was a communal sport, both on and off the ice. And for a game consisting entirely of Indigenous players, this woman was definitely not Indigenous. She was indeed dark, but not Indian dark. She was . . . duskier. A person of substantial aesthetic appearance. More interestingly, she was looking back at him. They held each other's gaze for a few seconds, both wondering why the other was looking.

Ten minutes later they were in deep conversation. The game, now in its third period with the Wolverines up by two more goals, was forgotten.

"I've never heard of . . . Otter River?"

"Otter Lake. It's a long way up north. And you?"

"Oh." She smiled. "I come from an even farther place, down south, and a town so small many would say it doesn't exist."

"That sounds kind of cryptic." Around them the ambient noise was getting louder as the end of the game approached and the Wolverine fans could taste victory. Even the teenagers had pulled back on their disinterest and were glancing at the time and score.

"Do you want to hear something even more cryptic?"

"Sure." Paul slid just a bit closer, his left elbow leaning on the armrest.

"Do you know how or why I'm sitting here?"

"An insatiable interest in Indigenous hockey?" He had hoped for a laugh but only scored a bemused smile. Still, entire weekends had been built around bemused smiles. Paul decided to count that as a point.

"Up until fifteen minutes ago, I didn't even know it existed."

"Okay then, why are you sitting here?" Behind them, a huge roar erupted as the Wolverines scored once again. The Arrows were being utterly demolished, registering just one lone goal. Oddly enough, Paul—for his own personal reasons—had lost interest in the game. The louder the crowd got, the closer he could lean into his companion, to hear her soft-spoken voice.

"I almost died twice." As she spoke, he noticed her eyes wandering down to the game. For a brief second, she seemed lost in time and place.

The conversation had suddenly gone in a different direction. "Okay, I don't know how to respond to that."

"It doesn't need a response. Just thinking out loud. I do that a lot."

"Confessing you almost died twice isn't thinking out loud. At least not where I come from."

"I remember. Otter Lake." She seemed cold, and pulled her coat tighter. "Hey, do you know a guy named Elmore Trent? He's a professor at a local university."

"Nope. Why?"

"No reason. Thought you might. I talked with him a few days ago. He's Indigenous too. Thought you two might have crossed paths."

"Because we're both Native? There are supposedly seventy thousand in this city alone. And we all know each other? I think there's a few thousand left that I haven't borrowed money from yet."

"Does my assumption make me racist?"

They both shared a smile.

"Nah. I've heard people think there are—what do they call it—six degrees of separation. In the Indigenous community, it's gotta be down to possibly three. This Trent guy, was he Anishnawbe?"

"That's your tribe . . . nation, right?" Her brow furrowed as she struggled to remember. "You know, I don't know. I didn't ask." Rising half out of her seat, she tucked her left leg under her bottom, shuffling around as if to get comfortable. "A sad bit of trivia for you. Where I come from, in the Caribbean, there are no more Native people. All gone. Killed by white men or disease, or a combination of both."

"Yeah, that happened a lot I hear."

Again, Fabiola looked out at the game. The Wolverines' lead was essentially insurmountable. By this point, they were just playing out the clock. "I take it the team in brown is winning."

"Those are the Wolverines. Best team in the league. We play them day after tomorrow."

"Think you'll beat them?"

Paul paused for a moment, seriously considering her question. "Sure. Why not? You should come to the game." There, he'd put the offer out, now to see what she did with it. Much like hockey, this was a game too—one he'd played innumerable times over the years. He was almost better at this than he was at hockey. For a brief second, a flash of him making the same offer to Katie a few nights ago occurred to him. Now a little morose, he waited for this woman's response.

Suddenly standing, Fabiola started buttoning up her coat. "I'm hungry. Want to grab something to eat?"

That was not the answer he had been expecting, but as always, it beat "go fuck yourself."

"Uh sure. Where do you want to go?"

"I feel like something . . . ethnic." It was an ironic statement considering the multicultural heritage of both people.

Paul put on his own coat. "As long as it's not Korean."

As if on cue, the buzzer went off, indicating it was the end of the game. And the beginning of another.

Niizh Ndawenjigewninwag Noopnadamwaad Bmikwaanan

(Two Hunters on the Trail)

It was obvious. There was a trail of dead and missing people spread across the country, ending here in Toronto. Detective Sergeant Birch was sure of it. As clichéd as it sounded, she could feel it. A painstaking examination of the material Sheila had sent her, and a little follow-up checking of her own, had made her positive. She had mentioned it to her superiors, but what she had wasn't exactly hard proof. A good part of policing was intuitive—that was a given. But evidence frequently helped in presenting an argument. Theories required proof. As they'd told her, there were plenty of deaths and missing people in Toronto to worry about. Should the detective sergeant find anything more substantial, their office doors were open.

The problem was the murders and disappearances all seemed so random. Still, this job was like being an archeologist. The answer was there, buried somewhere. It was just a matter of knowing where to look, how deep to dig, and for how long. There was an old saying her ex-husband had used to describe her: she was the job. Wherever her mind and body were, that's where her office was located. That was possibly one of the reasons Karl was an ex-husband.

There were two things that needed to be done now. First, she wanted to review and then re-interview all the witnesses so far attached to the two murders in Toronto, in light of this new theory. Maybe there was something she had missed or forgotten to ask. While the concept of promotion didn't really matter to her, recognition did—for her and her gender. For the most part, the force was still an old boys'— and new boys'—club, and every time a woman police officer succeeded, Birch felt the world became a better place.

Secondly . . . Birch checked her watch. It was getting late, but she didn't care. Her shift had long since ended. She never knew why she kept such a constant surveillance of the time. Essentially it was a nervous habit, and like all nervous habits, had no practical use. Still, it was three hours earlier in Vancouver. On her desk was the name and phone number of the detective involved in the False Creek murder. It wouldn't hurt to touch base, she surmised. Maybe there was something left out of the official report.

Picking up her phone, she dialled the number of Detective Chatterjee. As it rang, she arranged files in order. Birch shifted her behind on her seat, trying to find a zone of comfort in the police-issued computer chair.

That night, still hunched over his computer, Trent was now sure of the impossible. All afternoon and evening he had been focusing his memory on the creature he'd seen in that office . . .

was it only two days ago? He'd even done a fairly accurate sketch of what he'd seen. What truly terrified him was how close it came to the other images he had come across in his research. Maybe he was crazy. Maybe he was psychotic. Maybe there were several other, more explainable, reasons why Trent was so sure of what had killed his beloved wife. But now, none of them made any sense.

It was a Wendigo, and even thinking the word made him uncomfortable.

As weird and impossible as it seemed, that was the only answer. The thirty years of academia in him had desperately tried to provide another explanation, but with little luck. He was a man of academia. Of the real world. The Wendigo was a creature of legend. A legend no different than a Yeti or Chupacabra. Unconsciously, he glanced into the living room, half expecting to see a portly white man, dressed in a red suit, emerging from the faux chimney.

The legend had different manifestations, depending on the source material. In some it was an actual creature, cold and vicious, that came down from the north, causing mayhem and disaster as it consumed everything in its path. In other versions it was a spirit that could enter and overcome an individual, transforming them to do its evil deeds. All the stories said it was insatiable. Transforming it into a context the dominant culture might understand: it would never leave the buffet table. It would just get bigger and hungrier. It also could be a combination of both legends. Or there could be different kinds of the creature—it was all mindboggling.

But what was it doing here? The Wendigo wasn't exactly a creature of an urban environment. City streets and an excellent transit system were not really of interest to it. The last recorded case—if it could be called that—had been in northern Manitoba, almost a hundred years ago. The creature, in the form of a man, had been shot by an Indigenous man who recognized it for what it was.

Regardless, the hand-drawn images he was looking at were unmistakable. And even more odd, something deep inside Trent told him he was right. Though schooled and successful in the dominant culture's ways of understanding, at his core Elmore Trent was an Anishnawbe man, his ancestry and heritage guided by untold generations of his ancestors. That innate sense told him there was a Wendigo prowling the streets of Toronto.

Trent accepted that. He didn't know how or why, but that was the truth. The next question was what to do about it. How did a university professor destroy such a creature? Now that was a question, and not a moot one. The Manitoba case said it could be done with a gun. There was a slight problem with that possibility. University professors didn't own guns. Yes, he knew many of his relatives back home had rifles. Such weapons were a part of everyday life on the reserve. But Trent was sure some sort of law would be broken if somehow he convinced one of them to courier a rifle to him. And that seemed unlikely anyway, considering how little he knew them.

Perhaps he could buy such a weapon. But at a faculty function a few years back, an adjunct professor who exercised a more libertarian approach to life had complained long and bitterly about the paperwork necessary to purchase a rifle. Handguns were notoriously more difficult. So much for that.

But Trent was getting ahead of himself. There was another relatively major problem. He was forty-nine years old. A good stiff walk was the extent of any cardio he was doing on a regular basis. Tangling with this seven- or eight-foot-high monstrosity would definitely tax his abilities as a combatant, with or without a gun.

Earlier in the evening, as he'd gone through the motions of making himself a sandwich—mortadella with tomato and mozzarella—Trent had turned on the television as white noise. Essentially, he had forgotten about it as he returned to the living room to sort out his research results. But sitting there in his chair, overwhelmed by fantastical problems, his eyes began to droop. Hours spent hunched over a computer, added to the previous night's wrestling match with a Scotch bottle, on top of the sheer physical and emotional exhaustion of the previous few days, was taking its toll.

Sandwich on one lap, sheets of paper on the other, head leaned back. As a large pale pink canvas by Maxine Noel, extolling the virtues of Aboriginal women watched from where it hung barely two feet above his head, Trent began to nod off.

The voice was soft at first. "Elmore." It came again. "El?"

"You're being too soft. You want Elmore's attention, you have to take it. ELMORE!"

Like a door flung open by a gust of wind, his eyelids snapped open. The problem was that nothing he was seeing made any sense. He was in his parents' house, and it wasn't dilapidated. It looked like it had when he was a child. It still smelled of bannock. And sitting across from him, on the other side of the worn table, were Sarah and Katie. They were staring at him. Each looked as beautiful and special as he remembered them.

"Oh for God's sake, Elmore, don't cry."

He was having trouble breathing. "I'm so sorry. You're dead . . ."

Sarah raised an eyebrow. "You don't think we know that? That Ph.D. might just be an overestimation of your cognitive abilities."

Katie interjected. "You're so mean to him."

"Oh, he can take it. You don't spend twenty years with a man so you can be mean to him. You spend it with him because, when it's necessary, he can take it. Am I right, Elmore?"

Trent did not respond. "Sarah . . . you deserved so much better . . ."

"Well yes, I did, but let's not get into that now. Now, I'm not exactly sure what's going on. I'm getting the impression this is some sort of Indigenous thing . . ."

Katie nodded, adding, "She's talking about the Wendigo. Or as my people call it—"

"Yes yes, big hairy monster that eats people. Trust me, I have some personal familiarity with the topic."

Trent opened his mouth, not sure of what exactly was going to come out. "Why are you here? This . . . this is my parents' house . . ."

"That is a good question. Work with me here, Elmore. I remember when I used to help you with research for your thesis, and I would come across references indicating Indigenous people having connections to the dream world, and on occasion communicating through it. Do you remember those? I think it was—"

Shaking her head, Katie almost snorted derisively. "Don't be silly. That's just romanticism. The objectification of Indigenous spiritualism. You know, making us into 'the other' . . . so-called mysterious powers the dominant culture think we can utilize . . ."

"Okay, Ms. Perky Boobs and only two dozen years of life experience. Then why are we here?"

Katie paused for a moment. "It could be his subconscious. Maybe we can find a Freudian or Jungian approach to this . . ."

"No. I know Elmore's subconscious and I don't think this is it. He's not that innovative."

"Let's ask him."

As if on queue, they both turned to Trent, who was sitting there silently. All he could think of was wanting to reach out and touch each of them. To hold them. To hug them. It had only been a few days but he missed both of them so much.

"Elmore, focus."

He couldn't. Katie put her elbows on the table. It rocked slightly, just as he remembered it doing so long ago. "Let me try. The Wendigo. You think you saw a Wendigo. That it killed us. Am I correct?"

Somehow, the professor managed to nod.

"Good. We're getting somewhere. Work with me, El. What is the natural evolution of this narrative? What usually happens to the Wendigo?"

Trent didn't respond. He could smell Katie's lip balm.

"Elmore! If you found the time and interest to sleep with the lady, you should be able to answer her question! Well?"

"It . . . uh . . . should be killed. Destroyed."

Katie nodded. "Yes, or it will keep killing, and eating, and growing."

"Charming. My father's side was Irish and my great-grandfather was really Irish. Used to tell me all sorts of scary stories about Banshees and Dearg Due and other things. I never for a moment thought they could be true. How about that? You live and learn . . . or die and learn."

"Do you mind?" Katie said to Sarah before turning back to Trent. "So you have to kill it. Do you understand, El?"

"She's right. If you want our deaths to have any purpose, Elmore. You have to. Not just for us, but for yourself."

In the window overlooking both women's shoulders, Elmore thought he could see something coming from the lake. But he couldn't quite make it out . . .

"Elmore!" snapped Sarah.

"I can't!" he yelled. "I'm scared. I just teach at a university. Write books. I can't. I don't know how."

"El, yes you do. You know everything you have to. It's not a matter of you can do it, it's a matter of you have to do it. Remember what you told us those old legends meant, on a deeper level."

Katie waited for an answer and Trent struggled to give her one. "Sometimes they were stories about the weaknesses of people. Their flaws. That kind of thing."

"And . . . ?"

"Their strengths. What they were capable of. Sometimes they were stories of challenges being overcome."

Katie slapped the table, startling Sarah. "See, he's pretty smart."

"Yes, but smart people often do the stupidest things."

"Yeah, that kind of attitude will definitely help."

This couldn't be happening to him. If he were dreaming he didn't want to wake up. "In three months I'll be fifty. This thing is almost two feet taller than me. There's no way . . ."

At the same moment, both women said the same thing: "Find a way."

"If you can't do it, find somebody who can," Katie added.

"From what you and this sweet young thing here say," Sarah began. Katie flashed her an angry look. "It's been done before. Therefore, it can be done again." He felt her soft, delicate hand land on the top of his hand. It felt so good. "For us, El. For me."

Sitting back on their chairs, their message delivered, each woman became silent and stared at the professor. In the window behind them, he saw what had been coming up from the lake. A handful of tiny faces were peering at him through the glass, their hairy little faces watching him closely.

Sarah looked over her shoulder, puzzled at the odd noises the little people were making. "Leprechauns?"

"Memengweshii. Cousins," corrected Katie with a smile. "They remember you, El. They're no fans of the Wendigo either, but they think you can do it too. They've been watching you. They think it's your time. They want to help." All dozen of them nodded at the same time.

The sound of a plate with a half-eaten sandwich crashing to the floor woke him with a start. His heart in his throat, he looked around, not sure what he was looking for. Alone, in his house, he tried to calm his pulse. It had been a dream. Only a dream. In dozens of books by Indigenous authors, he'd read about the power and importance of dreams. Cherie Dimaline had even written a successful young audience novel about it, *The Marrow Thieves*, where the dominant culture had lost the ability to dream and were kidnapping Indigenous people for their marrow, which allowed them to still dream. An obvious metaphor for residential schools, but . . .

He was getting off-topic. Was the appearance of the two women and the little people something supernatural? Or psychological? He wasn't sure. In the last three days, his life had been turned inside out. Nothing made any sense.

Looking up, he saw the large plasma screen mounted on the wall. It took him a moment or two to fully fathom what was playing on the Indigenous network news.

"We were a warrior people. Playing hockey is an extension of that. When I put on my gear, it's like I'm putting on my warpaint. At the other end of the ice are our enemies. Out there, we compete. We battle each other for possession of the puck. Frequently, there are fights from that. Hockey sticks are our tomahawks. It's how we do battle today."

A handsome young Indigenous man was being interviewed. Sturdy, fit, this man—underneath his face it listed his name as being Paul North—looked interesting. Possibly . . . no . . . could it be . . . ?

"Every player out there, behind me and especially me, is a warrior."

He was a warrior. Paul North. Katie had been right. He'd have to find somebody to help him in his quest, however bizarre it might be. Maybe this Paul North guy. Evidently there was some Indigenous hockey tournament happening at the university arena. Just maybe . . .

All of this was sounding crazier and crazier. But sometimes in life, the world became crazier and crazier through no action of your own. And coincidently, leaning in to the absurd was the only way you could fight back. In the frozen blizzard of the conundrum that had suddenly enveloped him, Elmore Trent could see a trail sketched hesitantly ahead of him. The question was: would he be walking it alone?

Giigdowin Pishmowining

(Pillow Talk)

His eyes still closed, a dozy Paul was sure something was missing. But he was warm, comfy, and didn't want to re-enter the world just yet. Trying to figure out what was missing was dangerously close to waking up. So, he rolled over onto his side, content to let the waves of sleep roll over him again. Then, out of the blue, he realized what was missing. Jamie, his roommate, wasn't snoring. A thousand hotel and motel rooms over the years they'd played on the Muskrats made their bodily functions very familiar to each other.

Instead, he heard a slight wheeze. It was the kind of noise that might come out of somebody almost half Jamie's size, with a smaller set of lungs, nasal passages, and everything else. Now curious, Paul opened his eyes. Directly in front of him was a cream-coloured wall. The bedspread and pillow both looked and felt a little more upscale than the rental rooms he was used to, let alone a university residence. Slowly, he looked over his shoulder and saw Fabiola Halan, lying face down in the sheets, eyes still closed.

"Oh yeah." He'd almost forgotten about that.

Though by now familiar, the sharpness of her cheekbones still struck a note of awe in him. The way the morning light glistened on her darker skin. Her stylish short hair that framed her face. "I find long hair very inefficient," she'd said at one point last night. All packaged up, Fabiola Halan certainly cut an impressive image.

After they'd left the game, they had gone to dinner, had some wine, and talked and talked. He'd found her life far more fascinating than he'd thought he'd find any individual's life story who couldn't skate backwards. *Fascinating* was a mild word for her. Fabiola had been to countries he'd only ever heard of. She'd done things that definitely would've made him nervous. This woman had done so much more with her life than he ever could have imagined for his own. Once, playing in northern Quebec, he'd been in a bus accident. In Australia, she'd been in a boating accident, managing to swim away with little more than a twisted ankle. During an attempted mugging in Winnipeg, Paul had fought two guys off, leaving him with two broken fingers to show for it. Dodging bullets in a Middle Eastern dust-up had left stone chips lodged in Fabiola's scalp. She was indeed some kind of woman.

Paul doubted she even knew what a puck bunny was.

"Hey . . ."

There was a brief flicker, then the woman's eyes opened, looking directly at him. "You."

"Yep. Me."

She stretched a stretch born of a deep sleep and a need not to go anywhere. He watched as, rolling onto her back, she stretched again. Of course this made Paul want to stretch, but halfway through it he felt the now-familiar twinge in his shoulder. Fabiola noticed the wince.

"Pain? Did I do that?"

"No, all my fault. The by-product of an angry defenceman and Father Time." Delighted that had elicited a smile, he looked around the room, his hand caressing her thigh. "I like your hotel room. Better than we get."

"Just moved in yesterday. My publisher had put me in a better room, but I'm on my own dime now so I have to make do. I'm still earning out my advance, so got to cut costs when and where I can."

"Wow, if this is your version of cutting costs, I'm impressed."

Under the sheets he could see her flexing her toes. "I guess. Over the years I've stayed in some real shitboxes. Places where you shake the sheets—if your room has sheets—before crawling in. So, you learn to grab luxury where you can. Right now, to me, this is just another hotel room in a long string of hotel rooms."

Across the room Paul spotted a coffee maker on a small stand near the bathroom. "Been on the road long? Must be some big story you're chasing. Mind if I make some coffee?"

"Brilliant idea. By all means, go ahead." The woman extended her left foot off the side of the bed, and then raised it so it was perpendicular to the rest of her body with little effort, showing an amazing flexibility. *Impressive*, thought the hockey player.

He'd never been with a woman of her race before. Admittedly, there weren't a lot of people like Fabiola Halan on the Indigenous hockey circuit.

Paul filled the coffee machine with tap water, added the coffee to the filter, and stepped back, unsure if his shaky command of modern-day appliances would embarrass him in front of his new friend.

"Not a big story, an old one. I wrote a book about my experiences surviving a plane crash in northern Ontario last year. I started it in the hospital. It was published two months ago, and I've been promoting it for the last month or so."

Now to deal with other bodily functions. Paul opened the door to the bathroom as Fabiola's words sunk in. He gave her a worried glance. "You, ah . . . you didn't end up eating anybody, did you?"

"What?"

Paul gave an embarrassed shrug. "I hear that sometimes happens in these plane crashes. No food. Gotta survive somehow. You know, like that soccer team in South America. That sort of thing."

They locked eyes for a moment. Finally, she answered with a disarming smile. "Well, you'll have to buy the book to find out. I can't give you all my secrets."

"Well, with that kind of attitude, I'll have to keep a few secrets myself. Excuse me." With that, Paul disappeared into the bathroom, leaving behind the sound of coffee gurgling its way into existence. "Keep talking, I can hear you."

"From the bathroom. How romantic." Throwing the covers off, she rose from the bed like Aphrodite from the foam of the sea.

"You want romance? Maybe that was something we should have discussed earlier."

Clearly wanting to change the topic, Fabiola answered his earlier question. "Let's see, I've been to Vancouver, Saskatoon, Edmonton, Thunder Bay, Regina, Calgary, Winnipeg, and here. I'm just about ready for a good period of nothing but sleep, with a few hours of laundry thrown in."

"Thunder Bay!? Who the hell goes to Thunder Bay??! I mean, I've been there many times, but I had to. That's a lot of travelling in just one month. Nothing out east?" Paul exited the bathroom, drying his hands on a powder blue towel.

"Next week. My publisher is graciously giving me some time off to recover. Maybe the snow will have melted by then."

Paul stopped in front of the window and looked out at the city outside the building. All the universe looked cold. Very cold. Like walking into a freezer, the frigid temperature had landed last night with a thump. They'd felt it as they'd got into the cab, and twenty minutes later exited onto the street in front of the hotel. In that short period of time, the mercury had dropped noticeably. This morning, it was a good ten, more likely fourteen degrees colder than the evening before. Even true Canadians were truly cursing this morning. The familiar cry of the country was being heard all over the city: "Will this winter never end?"

"I'll have to pick up a copy of your book. Get you to sign it." Paul, lost in thought, was still standing in front of the large plate-glass window, naked.

"Perhaps you should stand back from the window. While I might enjoy the view, others might not." With barely a shrug, Paul stepped away from the window and turned. Thanks to twenty years of mastering a sport built on speed and reflexes, his left hand caught a book that came flying at him through the air. Glancing at it, he saw immediately it was the one she had written.

"I'll sign it later."

Jamie aside, not many Indigenous hockey players were heavy readers, but Paul made a personal pledge that he would start the book, and if it was a giving and noble world, he just might finish it.

"Does it have a happy ending?"

She smiled. "Again, I can't tell you everything."

There was something so mysterious and enticing about this woman. He wanted to know more about her. "Well, tell me this, do they play hockey where you come from?"

"Montreal? I believe so."

"I meant, before then." Paul prepared two cups for early morning coffee.

"I don't think so. Too poor. Too hot. It's been a very long time since I was last there. Soccer is the national sport. I seem to remember some baseball too."

"When was the last time you were home?"

Fabiola was quiet for a moment. "I don't have a home." The coffee maker finished its last gurgling. "Experience has taught me to live more 'in the moment.'"

"Hockey is a very 'in the moment' sport." Paul began pouring the coffee. "Ever slept with a Native person before?"

"That's certainly a change of topic. Can't say that I have. Consider yourself an ambassador. Dare I ask you the same question, about women with my particular skin hue?"

He handed her the steaming coffee. She wrapped her hands around it. "Looks like it was an evening of firsts for everybody." They both sipped their drinks. "Used to be, back home, people thought the lighter-skinned you were, the better off things would be for you."

"Same where I came from. Also Mexico I believe. India too. Many places."

"I had a white girlfriend once."

"Once?"

"Yeah, lost her in a snowstorm."

This elicited a good-sized chuckle. "You're funny."

Paul glanced at the book in his hand once more. "You're, ah . . . you're not going to write about this, are you?"

"Unlikely. I write about extraordinary events or things."

It took a moment before the implication of her comment registered. "Hey!"

Amused, Fabiola handed him her empty cup. Momentarily, Paul was amazed she had downed the scalding coffee so quickly. She began to pick up her discarded clothing, giving the hockey player the impression their time together was soon ending. "So, you gonna come to the big game tomorrow?"

"Will you be playing?"

"Hey, I'm their best player." He wasn't, and his shoulder didn't seem to be interested in healing. Active participation in the game was looking less than likely. But this woman didn't need to know the truth just yet. One thing Paul had learned over the years was that miracles did happen. Sometimes they were fake miracles, or momentary miracles that quickly fell apart. Regardless, that was an issue to be faced tomorrow. Right now, he wanted to see more of Ms. Fabiola Halan. There was something about her, above and beyond her passion. "Well?"

Standing there, in all her naked glory, the woman looked past Paul, out the window, and to the world waiting for them outside.

"Sure."

This produced a genuine smile from the man.

Nwanj Go Mshkawpide Sabaab

(The Rope Tightens)

It would be the first shower Trent had had in three days.
Between his original bout with the Scotch, and then his almost-
constant research into the nature of the Wen . . . he didn't even
want to say the word. Anyway, he'd had little chance for personal hygiene. Barely eating, going out only to replenish his
dwindling stock of coffee. Tea was a drink for civilized times
and normal problems. For Trent, coffee was his drink for battle.
Too many people frittered away its power on casual life. For the
professor, it focused his mind and energy. But for the moment,
he had grown aware of his bodily aroma asserting itself in the
house, and that had to be dealt with.

Few things eased both the mind and the body like a hot steaming shower, especially from an unusually powerful showerhead

that pushed the hot water directly into the pores. While the house had a generous hot water tank, frequently he came dangerously close to taxing its abilities. Once he was clean, he was ready for his next step in this ongoing nightmare. He had a clear mandate from Sarah and Katie. He had things to do. Fresh underwear and a white t-shirt, followed by brown cotton pants and a respectable pullover, and Trent was ready to do battle with the day and whatever else he could find to fight.

Looking in the mirror, Trent realized practically all the clothes he was wearing had been purchased by his wife. Top-quality with a quiet elegance to them. It was Sarah through and through. Though they had been separated for some months, it was only now he was realizing how alone he truly was. She was gone, never to complain about the raccoons she constantly saw on their deck, the boring university functions he dragged her to, or even his unused family house up north.

His dream, or whatever it was, had whetted his emotions for his wife. Seeing her there . . . or imagining her there, next to Katie—however real it had been—had reminded him of what he had lost. Real or not, he had a mission to complete for them.

There was also a funeral to prepare but the police were reluctant to release her body—what was left of it—until after the coroner had done his job. Part of the professor was a little relieved. There was work to be done regarding the creature: tracking it down, and figuring out what to do with it. Afterwards—if there was an afterwards for him—he could properly bury and grieve for his wife. And as ironic as it may seem, for Katie too. But he had a more immediate purpose now.

That's when the doorbell rang. During the last two days, there had been a flood of flowers, packages, letters, and a floral wreath delivered to the house, all from well-wishers and friends of Sarah's. The interruptions to his work had been most annoying, but to honour the memory of his wife, he had smiled through gritted teeth as he signed this and accepted that. One end of the living room was awash in flowers. This time, though, it was not a delivery man.

A woman stood at his door, shoulders hunched against the cold breeze that was desperately trying to make its way past her to set up lodgings in his house. Recognizing her, he managed to utter "Detective . . . ?"

"Detective Sergeant Birch, Mr. Trent."

"Professor Trent, if we're doing official titles. What are you doing here . . . Detective Sergeant? Again."

"Freezing. May I come in?"

Not knowing what else to do, Trent stepped back, gesturing Birch in through his door. "Feels cold out there. I thought it was supposed to get warmer."

"That's what I'd heard. Mr. Trent, I have a few more questions."

Being a gentleman and master of the house, Trent took her coat after she'd divested herself of it and removed her shoes. "Well, I hope I have the answers." He could feel the cold emanating off her jacket. If he was going to go outside, he'd have to make sure he wore a pair of long johns. He was sure he had some packed away somewhere.

"I have to say, Professor Trent, you certainly seem to be in a better state than at our first meeting."

"What do you mean?"

Birch prepared her notepad and pen, getting comfortable on the couch. "Well, to put it bluntly, you seemed to be somewhat hungover when I was last here, perhaps even still somewhat drunk."

"I wasn't drunk, Detective. I may have been a little intoxicated."

"What's the difference?"

"Income and education. Coffee? Tea?"

Birch smiled at Trent. "Clever, sir. No thank you."

"My wife had just died. Everybody grieves in their own way."

"I suppose they do. Now, Professor Trent, do you travel much?"

"Some. Not a lot."

"When and where was your last trip?"

On the glass table in front of them sat a number of framed photographs. Trent turned one around to face the detective sergeant. It showed Trent and Sarah, smiling, on a sandy beach, a palm tree just behind them. That had been barely a month before Sarah found out about the affair, so her smile was genuine. "Ever been to Mazatlán, Detective Sergeant? Lovely place. Gives you the real feel of Mexico. A lot better than a place like Cancún. This was early last fall . . . seems a lot longer though."

Seeing the photo again brought another wave of anguish, one that he likely couldn't hide from the detective. For reasons he couldn't explain, nothing short of a court order would let the frame out of his possession.

"You . . . both of you . . . look happy."

Delicately, Trent put the picture down in the exact same place he'd picked it up from. "Yes, we were."

"Any other recent trips?"

Forcing his attention away from the picture, Trent thought for a moment. "Last spring, an Indigenous literature conference in Minneapolis. I think . . . May. And a few months before that, Veradero, with my wife again."

"That's all? No trips to Thunder Bay, Vancouver, Edmonton, Calgary, Saskatoon, Regina, or Winnipeg maybe?"

Trent shook his head. "Nope. Not for a few years. I'm sure a woman with your resources can confirm all that. So, why are we having this conversation? You could have phoned and asked me all this."

"I'm a people person, Professor Trent. Phone, Skype, and Zoom leave something to be desired. I'm sorry to have bothered you." Closing her notebook, the woman rose, and Trent followed, grabbing her coat.

"Glad to have been of help."

He held out her coat, expecting her to put her arms through the sleeves, but Birch paused, caught in a thought. "Something wrong, Detective Sergeant?"

Her brow furrowed, then she turned to face him. "You didn't ask how the investigation was going."

"What?"

"Your wife has just been murdered. One of your students too, in much the same grisly manner. Yet I sit in your home, and am about to leave, and you didn't inquire about what was happening in the case? Most people in your situation would. That's very puzzling."

Not sure where exactly this was going, Trent tossed her coat on the couch. "I just assumed you would tell me you weren't allowed to comment on ongoing investigations. But fine, how is the investigation developing?" Trent could see Birch's mind filing and decoding information. Academia and police investigations, it appeared to Trent, worked completely differently. His deduction of thoughts, concepts, and themes took place over a long period of time, with few "eureka" moments such as this.

Birch shook her head. "Too late."

"Am I under suspicion again, Detective Sergeant?"

"You were never not . . . but . . ."

The professor began to feel nervous. "But what?"

They stared at each other. Birch stood in the living room and he could feel her studying him, as if wondering what he was capable of. "I'm sorry, but that's privileged information. I'm not allowed to divulge information pertinent to the investigation. Goodbye, Dr. Trent. Till we chat again."

Trent stopped in front of the Noel painting, forming his next question as the detective put her boots on. "Detective Sergeant Birch, I have a question for you. What do you believe in? Or maybe more accurately, what are you willing to believe in?"

"I'm a homicide detective. You have no idea the things I've seen."

The naïveté of Birch's comment made Trent laugh out loud.

Once again, Birch sat in her car, marinating on what Elmore Trent had told her. A thousand years ago, when she'd been a little girl, she had been sure there was a monster in her closet. The door had a habit of frequently swinging open for no reason and she was almost positive she could hear something rustling within. But no monster was ever found. She remembered putting traps inside once—tripwires and a crude attempt at a snare. But nothing ever worked . . . except the time her mother tripped on a wire, bruising her head.

A Wendigo . . . that was a new one. And the look on the man's face told her he believed every word he was saying. That in itself was scary. Turning to her right, she could still see the Trent house through the rapidly frosting car window. Maybe this was a Native thing or something. In recent years, Canadian law and order had taken it upon themselves to occasionally grant special dispensation to traditional Indigenous methods of justice and sentencing. Birch had learned that in a multicultural seminar. Regardless, she doubted the Minister of Justice would shrug off a double murder in the interest of better Indigenous relations.

For a brief second, it looked like Trent had actually expected her to help him in his quest. He was Don Quixote, tilting against cannibalistic windmills, it seemed. Still, it was worth investigating. All legends usually had their origins in reality, and maybe somewhere in his story were a few pebbles of useful evidence. She'd have to check out that Manitoba case he'd mentioned. Also, this could be some weird and bizarre way of confessing and setting up a justifiable insanity plea. Too bad, her gut instinct told her it was unlikely Trent was on the hook for the death of the two women. Well, you can't always be right, she told herself. Getting chilled, she started up the car and drove away.

From the upstairs of his house, Trent watched her leave. It was a long shot, he knew that, but it needed to be taken. The good news was he felt better having actually uttered the words to another individual. As weird as it may have sounded, speaking the words and the explanation had validated him. The bad news was . . . a police detective investigating the murders of two women he knew might now think him guilty of those same murders, or at least of having developed some sort of psychological alternate explanation for what had happened.

Birch didn't believe him. Instinctively he knew she never would. But she knew he was hiding something. What she would do with all the info he had shared with her, Trent didn't know. But it was out of his hands now. However, there were other things to do.

The Wendigo wasn't going to hunt itself.

Mji-Dbaajmowin Minwaa'sh Mnaajmowin

(Good and Bad News)

Despite the creeping cold, Paul entered the arena in a pretty good mood, hands deep in his pockets. Even his shoulder seemed less angry. The Muskrats were looking good for tomorrow's game. There was a rumour that two of their players had come down with something drastic, but that was all that was known. And to top it off, Paul had enjoyed the company of a rather unusual and stunning lady for the night.

On his way to the arena, he passed the parking lot where he had escorted Katie Fiddler to her car. The Lord giveth and the Lord taketh away, it seemed. Though the whole tragedy had happened just a few days ago, Paul was flooded with the memory of that night, and the next morning when he'd heard the news.

Pausing for a moment, he looked at the parking lot where he had last seen her, momentarily wondering what could or might have been. Not normally a man who thought particularly far into the future, recently he'd found himself pondering thoughts along those lines. His day-to-day existence was now transforming into a longer perspective. Not two months ago he'd actually considered opening an RRSP. What was up with that?

Perhaps he should put some tobacco down in her honour. Checking his pockets, Paul was disappointed to discover he wasn't carrying any. There was a cousin of Paul's who was a lot more spiritual than him, frequently giving Paul tobacco, sweetgrass, and sage for use when he needed it. Generally more interested in a pitcher of beer, he understood there were times when a pinch of tobacco or a smudge of some sort was better. In a small, tiny pocket on the inside right of his jacket, he usually had something for emergencies.

But not today. Maybe . . . if he got the chance, he might try to pick some up on his way back to his room. It was the least he could do.

But at the moment, all was good in the world. The arena was warm. He felt well. The lovely Fabiola had said she just might come to the game tomorrow. Hopefully, the coach and doctor would clear him to play. Otherwise, it might get a little embarrassing sitting beside the woman rather than playing to impress her.

He took the stairs up to where his team would be suiting up for practice. As he opened the door, Paul could hear the team with their voices rising high, and the adrenaline began to pump. Ah, he'd missed this. As much as he'd loved the deep and warm bed of the sexy and exciting Fabiola, he was a hockey player—and decades of training had made this environment his natural habitat. As he walked down the hall, he could smell the sweat from the generations of players that had come before him.

"Paul! There you are!" It was Jamie, struggling with his huge pads. Most of the team looked up as he entered the change room. "Man, I was almost getting worried."

Spreading his hands, Paul gave the occupants of the room an exaggerated bow. A few clapped and some whistled. Herbie Tort seemed to prefer to tighten the laces on his left skate, barely glancing at his teammate.

Raven Magneen, second-line centre and second-oldest member of the team, groaned as he stood up. He'd had back surgery the year before, and though it was unspoken, his departure from the team after the season-ending game was pretty much acknowledged by everyone. "How's the shoulder?"

"What shoulder? This one?" Paul flailed his arm about, ignoring the smaller but still-present twinge that went with it.

Jamie stood, reaching for his goalie stick. "Not that you really want to know, but the coach is looking for you. You broke—"

"Curfew. I know. How mad is he?"

"What do you think?"

Paul didn't have to think. He knew perfectly well how angry the coach would be. Breaking curfew was a very serious offence. The team was expected to think and act like a team. Going off by yourself, getting your jollies off, daring to act like an individual, infringed on the harmony of the team. But on occasion, when women like Fabiola Halan appeared in your life, rules tended to become transparent—practically invisible. Still, there was no point in avoiding the inevitable. "On the ice?"

Jamie nodded. Sighing, Paul left the change room. The fabulous feeling he'd been having that morning was being replaced with something dark and foreboding.

Walking through the corridor the hockey player took out his phone and saw three messages waiting. The only calls he ever got were either from Jamie, informing him of a get-together or change in plans, or from the coach, chewing him out. All three were from the coach's number. Paul's phone was so old, the volume button for the ringer had long since worn out. At some point, he'd definitely have to get a new one.

He found the coach flipping through pages on a clipboard, sitting on one of the team benches. Taking a deep breath, Paul emerged from the access tunnel, making his way towards the stern-looking master of the team. "Hey Coach, I know what you're gonna say. And I'm sorry—"

There was no reaction. The coach flipped another page, oblivious to his player's approach. "Coach? I said I was sorry. It won't—"

Putting the clipboard down, the old man looked out onto the ice. It shone with an early morning brightness, freshly Zambonied, ready for a new game in which men would give their best and people would cheer for their favourites. Before long, it would be scraped, pitted, and abused. "Just like life," the coach would frequently tell them.

"Ah, North, I wondered when you would bless us with your presence." Stopping beside the man, Paul opened his mouth to continue with his apology/explanation, but the oddest thing happened. The coach, a man famous for seeing only the bad side of practically everything, smiled. That was more unnerving than anything Paul could have envisioned. "Sit down. Keep an old man company." Seeing the man who had spent the last six years berating the him acting so calm and . . . benevolent, for lack of a better term . . . was disquieting. Afraid to say anything, Paul sat down. For a few seconds, the coach watched a family of six descend some cement stairs and take up some seats, waiting to watch the practice. Most wore the hockey jerseys of their favourite professional hockey team; two had sweaters bearing logos from the Indigenous Hockey League.

"See those youngsters over there?" Paul glanced over at them. "I can almost guarantee some of those kids might someday want to grow up and play hockey. Professional or semi-professional. Even from over here I can tell they love hockey. Why else would they get up early on a Saturday and come all the way down to watch an early practice? Because it's important to them. They want to watch. They want to learn. They want to understand as much of the game as possible. They"—the coach paused as he chose his words carefully—"are more of a hockey player than you are, North."

Sitting there, listening to his coach, Paul was realizing there was no possible way this speech could do a one eighty and come out in any way positive for him.

"That might have been you once. A long time ago. I like to think so. Everybody on this team wants to win. They will do what they can to win. Yeah, you've got some natural talent, and when necessary, I've seen you try. But I gotta say, North, I get the feeling you're on this team because you got no other place to be. And that's not fair to the rest of the boys. Or those kids over there. They want to see real hockey players."

"Are you letting me go, Coach?" Paul could barely get the words out.

Now the coach stood up, finally looking down at the sitting Paul. "No. If you had been with the team last night, or taken my calls, you would have heard that Roger King's wife went into early labour and he had to leave." The benevolence was gone and the fearsome coach was back. "I had to talk him into leaving. Do you hear me, North? That's a real hockey player. And it looks like Marshall Lake ate some bad shrimp last night. Been on his knees over the toilet for four hours. I'm short, North. I need you. And you have no idea how demoralizing that is for me."

Paul could feel his thirty-five years of life being put through a meat grinder. At some point a moment like this was going to happen—he'd known that, and in his own way had been expecting it. But he'd thought he had two or three years more to go. Whether another team might pick him up was difficult to say. Maybe all the other teams in the IHL had this same opinion of him. If that were true, the right winger might have to practise saying "Would you like fries with that?" for some future career.

"How's your shoulder?"

"It's good. I'm ready."

"Have the doctor look at it and contact me. If it's okay, you can play tomorrow. Think of it as your last hurrah." With a grim smile, the coach moved down the seating aisle and disappeared into a tunnel taking him to the rest of the team.

What had started out as a fabulous morning had quickly morphed into one that was not so fabulous. Potentially the end of his career would happen in—Paul checked his watch—thirty hours. Sitting down on the bench, he glanced across the wide expanse of ice to the family the coach had indicated. Two parents, three boys, and one girl. From over here, they looked Native. And they were dressed for hockey. The coach was right. That had indeed been Paul twenty years ago, eager for all things hockey. Then he'd lost his mother in a car accident when he was starting out on his Junior A team, and his one sister never really forgave him for not being there. Everything he'd once been taunted him from behind a Plexiglas barrier.

Paul North was alone in spirit and career.

Twenty-three minutes later, Paul was now sitting in the stands, leaning back, weighing his options. He knew at some point he would have to go see the doctor, but for the moment that wasn't a priority. Actually, he had no priorities at the moment. So instead, he sat there and watched his team go through the motions. Jamie, as always, was solid between the pipes. Above all, Paul was sure he'd miss his buddy. Of course, there was Herbie Tort skating rings around most of the other players, handling his stick like Bruce Lee handled nunchuks. Providing the man had no serious injuries, there was a definite future for him beyond the IHL. Paul lamented the possibility of, somewhere in the distant future, seeing his little cousins wearing hockey jerseys with Herbie's number on them. The rest of the team he would miss. But he would worry about that tomorrow.

From behind him Paul heard somebody approach. The vast majority of the seats were empty, but whoever it was came closer until they stopped one level up, just to Paul's left. An awkward silence followed. A little annoyed at being disturbed, Paul looked up at the mystery person, visibly annoyed. Standing there was a well-dressed man, maybe somewhere in his mid-forties. "There's lots of space here, dude."

"I'm sorry. Are you Paul North?"

"Yeah. Why?"

There was an urgency about the man. "My name is Elmore Trent. I need to talk to you about something."

People seldom needed to talk to Paul about anything, let alone with a look of such importance. And if they did, it was usually something bad. After this morning, Paul hoped that whoever this guy was, he had only good news to share.

Paul's day had started off so well. Ensnared in the arms of a beautiful woman, playing on a team guaranteed silver in the IHL final. But then the cold came, followed by the coach with his annoyingly accurate opinion of Paul, and now this guy. Was it possible this was the kind of day that would be perfect for crawling back into bed . . . with or without Fabiola?

"A Wendigo, huh?" Checking his watch, Paul saw it was almost eleven in the morning. Far too early to start drinking. Whoever this guy was sitting beside him—Trent was his name— might have had a few already. In an odd way, Paul was comforted by the knowledge that even well-to-do Indigenous people could have overactive imaginations, possibly powered by something that had been fermented.

The man nervously glanced over his shoulder, perhaps knowing exactly how he sounded. "Do you know what one is?"

"Of course I do. Every Cree and Ojibway does."

"Well, it's not just them. The stories are told by—"

"I don't need a history lesson," Paul snapped at Trent. He was very uncomfortable, and equally annoyed.

"Technically it's not a history lesson. More of an anthropological—"

"I DON'T CARE!" This was enough for Paul. The doctor—he had to find the doctor. That meant leaving this spot, and this man. "Gotta go. I think I saw the Loch Ness monster over by the women's bathroom."

"Look, Mr. North, I'm serious."

"Believe it or not, that's even more scary. Go away." Moving quickly, Paul jumped from seating level to seating level, in an obvious hurry to get away from this guy. But the man was persistent. He followed, not willing to let Paul get away.

"If you'll just listen—"

"There are no such things as Wendigos. Scary stuff from a scary time, but I think the Department of Indian Affairs banned them."

Trent stopped. "It's already killed two people here in Toronto. And I am sure more will follow. And then more. And more after that."

Paul stopped, puzzled by the rational and focused voice coming from the man. In his travels, Paul had come across a lot of hallucinating drunks, addicts, people who had been hit a little too frequently in the head, or just your general paranoid type of person. This guy actually sounded fairly coherent. Once more, he looked the man over. His suit jacket and winter coat looked pretty expensive. As did his haircut. "You do know they don't exist. Seriously. They're just some sort of Aboriginal boogeyman."

"I used to think that too." A loud smack came from their right as two players smashed into the Plexiglas before skating off. "Five minutes, Mr. North. That's all I ask." Looking closely, this

Trent guy kind of reminded Paul of his uncle Guy, just a bit shorter. Every fibre in his body was telling him to keep walking away. Nothing good could come from continuing this conversation.

"Please."

With a weary sigh, Paul looked up at the arena rafters. "I need a Coke."

Half an hour later, hunched over in a small concession stand located at the end of the arena concourse, Paul finished his fountain drink and a tray of fries. Elmore Trent—what kind of name was Elmore, he had wondered briefly—had gone all-in. A dead mistress and dead soon-to-be ex-wife. Already the red-alert warning was going off in the back of Paul's head. All this guy had was a brief glimpse of the supposed Wendigo, in the half-dark, as the shock of discovering his ex-wife's body was washing over him. "I swear, by everything I know, that was what I saw."

The doctor was probably waiting for him somewhere in the medical room. He should get going. Jamie would love this story. "Well, I'm sorry to hear all this, but I'm not sure what I can do. I just play hockey."

"Yes, I saw your interview last night. That's why I'm here." Paul had almost forgotten about that. "I need you to help me find it."

"The Wendigo . . . ? You want me to help you find it . . . ?"

"And maybe . . . kill it. If you would . . ."

What had been annoying, then briefly fascinating, was now becoming severely uncomfortable. Even insane. Paul gave the man his best smile. "Sorry, not in my job description. But I wish you the best of luck. Try throwing some celery at it. Vegetables might scare it off." Once again, he rose to leave. And once again, Trent managed to stop him.

"I know this sounds insane."

"No. *Insane* would be a kind word. Now back away or I'll forget you're my elder."

Looking defeated, Trent sat back down, his will visibly evaporating. For a moment, Paul felt a twinge of sadness for the man. Whatever had driven him around the bend—oh yeah, those two deaths—he could see the older man being overcome. "Look, I'm sorry. I really am. But there's nothing I can do. Maybe the police—"

"The police can't help Sarah and Katie. I'm sure they're even more skeptical than you are."

"That—that was their names?"

Trent nodded. "Sarah Trent and Katie Fiddler."

All sound in the arena stopped for the younger man. The mention of Katie Fiddler grabbed Paul's attention with the speed of a lunging animal. He knew that name. He knew the woman. But was it the same woman? Could it be? Quickly, he sat down again. "Katie Fiddler? Cree, from Manitoba. Taking some sort of Indigenous—"

"—literature course. Yes. Did you know her?" For the first time, their eyes met, and a world of feeling passed between them. This was all becoming too coincidental. Paul knew she was dead. And this guy knew her, and was saying a Wendigo ate her.

"I think so. We had dinner. Actually, we met at dinner, bumped into each other at a restaurant and started talking. I heard the next day . . . she was dead." Emotion washed over him. "She seemed really nice. And smart." Suddenly, all the varied parts started coming together in Paul's mind. He looked at Trent with a new perspective. "And you were having an affair with her?!" For a moment, he couldn't identify what he was feeling. It seemed to be a combination of anger, sadness, concern, and maybe a little smidge of jealousy. In a brief expanse of time, Paul had developed a bit of a crush on the woman, despite only knowing her for less than an hour and a half. And this guy had been nailing her. Behind his own wife's back.

Looking embarrassed, Trent nodded.

"If you knew Katie, then you have to help me. She would want it."

That elicited a small chuckle from Paul. "She'd want me to help you hunt down a fictional creature?! Somehow, I doubt it. Aren't people at university supposed to know better?"

"This may sound strange, Mr. North . . ." Whatever the man had to say, Paul felt, could not be stranger that what he'd already said. "Other than the obvious, do the cities of Vancouver, Saskatoon, Thunder Bay, Regina, Winnipeg, Edmonton, Calgary, and Toronto mean anything to you?"

Paul blinked twice. "Sounds like a rock band tour."

"Close. That's it?"

Paul nodded after almost adding: "or a book tour." Oddly enough, Fabiola had cited those same cities not more than a few hours ago. But mentioning it would make this professor guy even more annoying.

"I'm sorry for bothering you, Mr. North." Standing, Trent reached into his pocket and pulled out a business card, handing it over. "Here's my contact info. If for some reason you change your mind . . ." Reluctantly, Paul took the card, glancing at it quickly before depositing it in his coat pocket.

"Unlikely, but stranger things have happened. If I see Scooby-Doo and the gang, I'll give them your phone number." With that, Paul turned away, desperate to be lost in his own thoughts. There were a lot less monsters in them.

"It looks like you'll live to play again." In the arena's little medical room, Dr. Sprung took off his latex gloves, smiling. "But the question is, do you want to? It'll still hurt. A lot. Sure you don't want to sit this game out?" The short, rotund man, complete with glasses, never struck Paul as the poster boy for the medical profession. He felt sure that, twenty years ago, Dr. Sprung would also have been sporting a cigarette.

"Tomorrow's the last game, Doc. If I miss that, what's the point in showing up?"

After washing his hands, the doctor popped a butter tart in his mouth. "I've seen players go out onto the ice with fractures and concussions. It's just a game, Paul."

"I had a girlfriend who told me that a lot. But I always said that if this is just a game, then I don't know what anything is anymore." He tried not to wince as he put his shirt back on.

"And I guess that's why you're not with her anymore?"

"I told her it's the same with architects. All they do is draw interesting pictures on paper. Actors just pretend to be people they're not. Psychiatrists listen to people talk about their friends, family, and problems. But people still think what they do is important, don't they?"

Palming a second tart, the doctor smiled. "In my office we have this ongoing debate about butter tarts. There is the pro-raisin faction of which I am the president. There is the delegation for pecan, which my nurse is a strong proponent of. And then there are those that do not like either. My wife. They are happy with just the syrup and pastry. I guess different things are important to different people." He bit and swallowed half the tart. "I myself would not go out onto the ice with a shoulder like that."

"But you're clearing me."

"So I am." The second half of the tart disappeared into his smiling mouth. "I never said I was a particularly good doctor. Witness the luxury I work in. Give it a bit more time to heal, so no practice today. And Paul, tomorrow, try not to hurt yourself."

"Will do. And thanks."

Opening the door, Paul was struck with an unusual question he wanted to ask the doctor. Maybe it was a by-product of his encounter with the weird professor. Paul turned to face the doctor.

"Dr. Sprung, just a quick question. I'm sure you know this stuff so . . . Physical therapist, kinesiologists, those kind of professions, do you—"

"Do you want me to recommend one for you? I can. Let me—"

Paul shook his head. "No. Uh, does it take long to learn to be one of those things? I mean, does it take lots of schooling?"

"A few years. Why, Paul? Are you looking at what to do for the second part of your life?"

"Yeah, somebody suggested I might be good at those. You know, because of the hockey thing. Just following up on the idea I guess."

The doctor sat down wearily on his wheeled stool. "I think it might be possible, Paul. But you'd have to apply yourself. It can definitely take some effort."

"Yeah, I've heard that's popular these days. Thanks. I'll let you know, Doc."

Out the door and into the hallway, Paul managed a little skip in his walk. There had been a deep valley in his morning, but once again, he was climbing the mountains of good cheer. If tomorrow was going to be his last game, the man was going to give it his all. Herbie Tort would remember his name. Paul would make sure it would be the best, most amazing game of his life. Afterwards, he would have the rest of his life to worry about his shoulder.

No practice, which meant he had the afternoon free. But first, there was business to attend to. As far as rink washrooms went, the university's were above average. After doing up his zipper, Paul washed his hands and was about to leave and put all the evil medicine of the day behind him, only to discover the evil medicine of the day was not finished with him. In through the door walked Herbie Tort, fresh out of his hockey gear.

Instantly they glared at each other. Next door, in the women's washroom, a toilet could be heard flushing. Otherwise, all was quiet.

"North."

"Tort."

Choosing to ignore the younger man, Paul headed for the door, wanting to avoid a scene, but the centre refused to move. "You missed practice. You broke curfew."

"I already got this lecture from Coach. Do you mind stepping aside?"

"Everybody is saying this is your last game."

"Yeah, I've heard those rumours too. I've heard people think you're a good centre. Well, guess you can't believe everything you hear. I gotta go."

Still not moving, Tort smiled grimly. "There are some of us who love this game. Respect it. I talked with my mother last night. She mentioned you." For a second, the most obvious, sexually based comeback teetered on the edge of his lips, but that would have been Paul from his late twenties. "She remembers when you started out. Said she used to like watching you. Now, she agrees with me, you're just going through the motions. Just killing time." Another sexually based retort came to mind, but once again, Paul resisted the urge. "I know we're supposed to respect our elders . . ."

Christ, thought Paul, *he's only twelve years younger than me. That's fighting dirty.*

". . . but no matter how much I try, I can't find much to respect. Go join the Ice Capades."

Paul's left hand, hard and callused from a career of physicality, lashed out, jabbing Herbie Tort on the right cheekbone, knocking him back into the door frame. This was a test of experience versus age. Unfortunately, experience was nursing a sore shoulder, and a lacklustre right hook came up noticeably short. Two punches to Paul's midsection—one directly in his stomach, the other more liver-oriented—had him on his knees, breathing harshly, trying not to throw up. Tort hovered over him, rubbing his cheek and deciding if he should follow up his defence.

"Go home, North. We have serious work to do here." Deciding he didn't need the bathroom after all, Tort turned and left the room.

Using the sink, Paul gradually got to his feet, groaning all the way. Gazing in the mirror, he looked upon his sweaty face. This is what his life had come down to? He had felt something odd about one of the punches. Reaching into his pocket, he saw his cell phone was now in two parts. Though he'd said it a hundred times before, time to get a new one.

As of yet, Paul North's day had not gotten much better.

Geskna Go Aanjibde Miiknaans

(The Trail Takes an Unexpected Turn)

Staring at the blank television, Fabiola answered the phone in her room on the second ring. Her cell phone was silent, so this meant somebody in the hotel was trying to get a hold of her. "Fabiola Halan."

"Hey, it's Paul North. I'm downstairs in the lobby." At first, she was silent. She checked her watch; he had left only four hours earlier. What was he doing back? While she never considered herself a fan of casual sexual practices, they had left the next step in their . . . affiliation? . . . blank when he left, already late for practice. In truth, she would be happy to never see him again. The state of her life, her emotional makeup, her everything did not leave her open for any type of relationship. Things were too unfocused now for any attachments. But the man was on the phone, six floors down, and needed to be dealt with.

"Hello Paul. Back so soon?"

"Yeah, thought you might be hungry."

Fabiola was indeed hungry. Much like sex, it was a primary urge that was difficult to resist. Besides, she had nothing else planned for the afternoon. If nothing else, this man was an interesting distraction. "I'll be right down."

"Wear something warm. It's freezing outside. I'm by the hotel phones."

Fabiola hung up, but didn't move from the chair opposite the bed. Somewhere amidst the three million people that lived in this city, and the other three million in the surrounding area, was the woman that plagued her memories. Almost back where things had started, the journalist could feel the end coming closer. They had been playing tag across the country for so long, she'd forgotten who was chasing who.

Pushing it out of her mind, she rose from the chair and put her jacket on. It wasn't a particularly warm one, but it would have to do. Besides, she was sure she had been colder.

The pasta was good. It was a little heavy for the time of the day, but neither party seemed to mind. Fabiola slowly and sensuously consumed her fettuccine in clam, garlic, and white wine sauce in an almost obscene manner, while Paul wrestled with twirling his spaghetti Bolognese around a spoon.

"You should taste my gnocchi. Took me forever to master but I'm told its divine," she said, between bites. Paul nodded, his mouth full.

"Gnocchi, yeah, that's good stuff. Ever had hangover soup?" She shook her head. "Canned tomatoes, hamburger, and elbow macaroni. An Indigenous staple. And much like cheese over in France, it changes as you travel. One community will add, I don't know, onions. Another some tomato soup. Where I come from, a little garlic or garlic powder."

"Sounds so simple."

"Some of the best things in life are simple. Like me!" He gave her his best hundred-watt smile. Again, she laughed. She liked laughing. She hadn't laughed in a long while. Grabbing another piece of garlic bread, she wiped up some of the remaining sauce on her plate.

"You know, it feels so great to do nothing. To just enjoy a conversation. A simple lunch. This is good." Fabiola looked into her wine glass. "I miss this."

"Yeah, I know what you mean. I got the afternoon off before tomorrow's game. And an afternoon off in Toronto—think of all the mischief we can get into!" Putting his utensils down, Paul continued. "I'd almost forgotten—you've been on the road for a while too, haven't you? That's one of the things we have in common. Geez, in the last month I think we've been to Sudbury, North Bay, Orillia, Peterborough, London, Kingston, Timmins, and a bunch of other places. Just hotels and hockey. Sounds like a country song."

Taking a small sip of wine, she looked out onto the street. Just a fleeting glance, like she was afraid of someone finding them. "Life in a suitcase, huh? Yes, Edmonton, Vancouver, Calgary, Winnipeg, Saskatoon . . . and . . ." For a moment, her mind wandered, captured by a woman walking by the big restaurant window. But it was a different woman, and Fabiola's mind returned to the table in the charming Wellesley Street Italian restaurant.

". . . Thunder Bay," said Paul.

"Oh yes, I mentioned this already?"

Paul nodded. "Thunder Bay seems to be a popular place these days. Never thought I'd say that."

Fabiola could tell something related was bouncing around inside the man's head.

Chuckling to himself, he finished his wine. "What's so funny?" she asked.

"Oh, this bizarre guy I met today. You would not believe what he told me."

She leaned forward across the table, enjoying the turn the conversation had taken. "Tell me."

"Okay. There's a monster running loose in Toronto." The pleasant smile on her face froze, but Paul was too engrossed in telling the story to notice. Grabbing a breadstick, he used it to illustrate points in his tale. "More interestingly, an Indigenous monster. It's called a Wendigo; a cannibal spirit that sweeps down from the north and gobbles animals and people up. This spirit is a part of my people's legends, and also the Cree and a handful of other Native Nations. And this guy—and he's Native too—tried to convince me one is eating people here, in the city. I don't mean to laugh at horrible things, but he's basing this on the death of two people he knew. He says he saw it, but who knows what he saw. He says this thing has been leaving a trail across the country. Cities like—"

"All the cities I mentioned . . ." Her voice was barely a whisper.

"Yeah. Funny, huh?" She didn't respond. She couldn't. Her face felt flushed, and she could tell by the way he looked at her that she wasn't hiding her fear particularly well. "Hey, don't worry. He was crazy."

"That would be nice, wouldn't it?" Looking up, Fabiola signalled to their waiter across the room, wanting another glass of wine. Paul grabbed her hand between his in an attempt to comfort her, but her hands were numb with cold. She was scared. Very scared.

"What's wrong? Do you know this guy?"

"Oh no, not at all." She managed a quick, fleeting smile, totally unconvincing.

"Okay, you may not know him, but you know what he's talking about, don't you?" She took a deep breath, as if trying to hold something deep in her chest. "Fabiola . . ." said Paul.

Silent, she squeezed Paul's hand with a desperate ferocity. "What if . . ." The waiter arrived with the wine and she grabbed the glass before he could put it down. "What if . . . what if he wasn't crazy? What if he wasn't lying? What if . . . he was telling the truth."

Paul responded in the only way he could. "Huh?"

"I can't keep living like this. I think I need help." Looking deep into his eyes, a piercing stare that could cut glass, the woman looked like a little girl being scared by a thump in her closet. A real noise that no parent could dismiss. "Paul, what if there were such things as monsters? And what if they were chasing you?"

Nkweshktaadwin

(The Meeting)

The card said Professor Elmore Trent, and it had an address handwritten on the back. That was where Paul North and Fabiola Halan now stood, ringing the doorbell. The porch was attached to a standard, early twentieth-century brick house, two storeys, nice latticework up the side complete with ivy. It looked expensive without looking pretentious. This was the kind of house his mother would comment on when watching television back home, Paul remembered fondly. Fabiola, on the other hand, looked over her shoulder nervously.

Paul waited a few more seconds, stamping his feet in the uncomfortable cold, before ringing the doorbell again. Finally, both could hear the gradual thumping of feet coming down a flight of stairs, getting closer. Then the door opened and there stood Trent, buttoning up a white shirt. Recognition passed instantly between the professor and the journalist. "Ah . . . hello?"

"Your name . . . Trent! I didn't make the connection."

"Ms. Halan! What . . . what are you doing here?"

Quickly, the woman looked at Paul, instantly suspicious, and backed up. "Okay, Paul, what the fuck is going on?"

"You two know each other?"

"Mr. North, I'm not sure what's going on here."

"Me neither." Trying to process the situation, Paul turned to Fabiola, trying to explain. "This is the guy I told you about. Really. But where the hell do you guys know each other from?" For a moment, all three were silent, then the climate reality of the situation forced the uncoated professor to break the silence.

"God Almighty, it's freezing out here. Come on in, maybe we can figure this out." Finishing buttoning his shirt, he retreated into his house. Paul stepped back, waiting for the woman to enter first.

Suddenly defensive, Fabiola was not sure what she should do. This was way too coincidental. Essentially these two men, who evidently knew each other, had suddenly and apparently randomly shown up in her life. Both Native. Both knowing way too much about a large cannibalistic monster roaming the streets of Toronto. It would make any woman a little nervous.

Though indoor and outdoor rinks were in his blood, Paul wished the woman would hurry up and decide what she wanted to do. He wasn't too enthralled with the situation either, but at least inside were answers—and warmth. "Fabiola? I don't know what's going on, but I'd sure like to." For the first time since they'd met, he could sense timidity in her— a sense of wariness, fear even, of what might be on the other side of the professor's door. Knowing the truth could frequently be more terrifying than hiding from it.

Taking a deep breath, she walked through the door. Paul, having no real idea what was happening, followed. It was not in his nature to leave a terrified woman behind, regardless if it was on a house stoop or in an Italian restaurant.

Cups of steaming herbal tea sat on the table in front of them. Paul, raised on orange pekoe, hid his distaste for the tea that tasted like a boiled salad. Fabiola held hers in her hands, trying to warm them up. Trent sat back in his chair, waiting for one of them to explain why they were sitting in his living room. The ticking of a clock could be heard. On the wall near the front door was such a clock, operating on batteries, making the swinging lever at the bottom a sheer affectation.

Around them were walls of books. Lots of them. Some were even in other languages. Names and titles Paul had never heard of. "You have a lot of books." Times like this, he felt almost . . . inferior . . . to a man like Trent. It was evident the man read a lot, knew a lot, and could probably beat the hell out of him at Trivial Pursuit.

"Tricks of the trade. Can I get anybody anything else?" said Trent. Paul shook his head while Fabiola drank from her cup. Trying a different tack, the professor addressed the hockey player, no doubt hoping she would chime in when properly motivated. "Mr. North. I was not expecting to see you again. You made that very clear."

Shrugging, Paul responded, "Yeah, well, you know . . ."

"Actually, I don't."

This get-together was rapidly going nowhere, thought Paul. This race in which he really didn't have a horse was predicated on Fabiola and what she had told him. Right now, he didn't know what to believe. She, however, did. "Fabiola. Tell him what you told me."

The professor leaned forward expectantly, but the woman, lost in her own thoughts like they were a frozen tundra, seemed not to hear Paul. Deciding the best attack was straight down the middle, he decided to push the metaphorical envelope. "Okay,

I'll drop the puck. Trent, Fabiola here says she knows something about your Wendigo. Not only has she seen it herself, it's chasing her."

This warranted two raised eyebrows, and a look of interest from the educated man.

"All across the country. Those cities you mentioned . . ."

"I've been to all of them, within the last few months. On my book tour. And so has . . . it. I keep trying to stay ahead of it. But it's always there. Just out of sight. Breathing. Hiding. Wanting."

"Fuck" was the only response—colloquial as it was—from the man with a Ph.D. in English.

"Yeah," responded the hockey player.

"Very fucked," added the journalist.

"Why is it chasing you?"

Fabiola's eyes froze on a painting on the wall. An image of a lone woman against a white background, signed Ioyan Mani, an Indigenous woman otherwise known as Maxine Noel. "It wants me."

"Why does it want you?" Trent had expected to deal with the whole Wendigo issue alone, battling against the winds of disbelief. But now, not only did he have two possible believers sitting at his table, but one had a direct connection with it. Theory had become reality.

"Go ahead, tell him." To Trent, the hockey player was still a wild card. Originally, he had wanted Paul to help him track the creature down, but now he wasn't sure where the man stood in the big picture.

"The plane accident. Up north." The thought had just occurred to Trent, and then he spoke it aloud. Eyes still on the painting, the woman nodded.

"Yeah, I only heard of that yesterday. I think—" said Paul.

"Shut up."

Okay, thought Paul—*is this guy too old, does he qualify as an Elder, or can I beat the shit out of him?*

"Ms. Halan, please talk to me." As if with effort, Fabiola took her eyes off the painting, levelling them at the older man.

"You read my book?"

Trent nodded.

"Not everything that happened is in the book. Or as it actually occurred. I opted to leave some . . . *things* out. And add other things." His tea forgotten, the professor listened intently as the woman's voice lowered to a whisper. "That woman who left me there . . ." She closed her eyes intently, as if feeling the pain of her broken leg once again.

"Merle Thompson. The pilot." Trent said this to Paul, to make sure he was following the story.

"Yeah, I caught most of this at lunch. That's why we're here."

Deciding to ignore him, Trent returned his attention to the journalist. "Continue."

"She . . ." Fabiola still stumbled over the mention of her name, barely keeping her bitterness in check. "She did abandon me, like I wrote. I stayed in that plane for . . . I don't know how long. In the book I think I said three days, only because my editor wanted a concrete timeframe for the reader to understand. But I don't really know. All I remember is how cold it was, and how hungry I was becoming. That's when she returned . . ."

Trent immediately interjected. "She *did* return then. Why didn't you include that in the book?"

Taking a deep breath, Fabiola continued her story. "I misspoke. She didn't return." A quiver affected her voice. "It did."

"It? The Wendigo?"

Ignoring the professor, she looked down into the bottom of the cup that had held her tea. "Somewhere out there, she had somehow run into it. Or it had run into her. I'm not sure how these things really work. I tried to do as much research as I could, once I recovered and could piece things together, but legend is a difficult thing to explore scientifically. As I'm sure you know."

Trent did not respond. Behind the professor, on top of a cabinet, Paul spotted a half-bottle of something light brown. Possibly rum, or maybe a whisky of some sort. That, he thought, would help the situation quite a bit right now, but it was no doubt an inopportune time to suggest it. Besides, it probably wouldn't go so well with this weird tea.

"At first, I could feel it close by. A cold that seeped quickly down to your bones, that made your teeth chatter. Then I heard it. Moaning and groaning like the trees outside the plane. But it wasn't the trees. It was that creature. It was hungry—which I know is a stupid thing to say since that's all it is, hunger personified. It wanted to come in, but I had built a small fire from all the salvaged wood she had found before leaving. It doesn't like fire and it stayed away. But it was there constantly, circling the fuselage. I found myself burning everything within reach. But I was running out, and I could feel it getting closer. It wanted me. Its hunger wanted me. I didn't know what to do. I didn't want to die; I was willing to do anything to survive."

That final comment elicited a rueful smile. "I wonder how many people in dire straits have said that and then had to live with the consequences."

"What happened next?"

Suddenly, her hand went over to Paul's, grasping it like it was a branch over a cliff she was about to plunge into. "Like I said, I was willing to do anything to survive." There was a pause. Paul squeezed her hand back. "I had an idea. You must understand, I had no clue what was going on. I'm not Native. I knew nothing of Wendigos. But somehow, in some way, maybe it was some primordial instinct, I knew what it was and what it wanted. I also knew how to trick it. There was another person in the plane wreckage with me."

"The young boy who died."

"The young boy who died. Jeremy Acapetum." Her voice was almost lost in the creaking of the windows as a gust of wind suddenly came up. "He looked so scared in the plane. So out of place. In my life, I knew that feeling, so well. I thought maybe . . . I tried making friends with him but it was too little, too late. He died, scared and alone. And I lived, scared and alone."

For a moment, the two men could almost see the image of the terrified young boy. "I'm not sure but the creature must have gotten hungry or bored or something, and gone off to hunt. Whatever, I could tell it wasn't nearby. I'm not sure how but I managed to find the strength to move about in the shattered remains of the plane, and then outside too. Crawling across the snow, I uncovered as much of the boy as I could. He still looked so young and innocent. Dragging him into the interior of the plane, I waited for it to return. It wasn't gone long . . . and if I'd left when I'd wanted, it would have found me, I'm sure of it.

"As it scrambled around the outer fuselage, God help me, I pushed . . . half . . . the boy out the side door. I could see him sliding down the snowy hill, to a small gulley about ten metres away. He lay there, his parts frozen stiff like a log. Almost immediately I could hear the thing approaching. I could feel its eagerness. And then I pushed his other half, the legs, out in another direction, I guess hoping it would take twice as long to find him. I built up the fire with the last wood and paper I could find in the plane, and then crawled out the back, where the plane had been ripped apart."

The house remained silent as her words sunk in. Paul had heard a synopsized version earlier, but now, at this table, with the funny tea, he could visualize what the woman had gone through. The stories his grandparents had told him of the Wendigo coloured his imagination. Was the wind outside, the cold, suddenly clamping down on the city, announcing its presence?

"From there, as it did . . . whatever it did to the boy, I crawled away. I stumbled. I fell. I pulled myself along the ground, desperate to get away from that . . . what do you call it?"

"Wendigo," said both Trent and Paul.

"Wendigo. With the fire going as hot and bright as I could make it, hopefully it thought I was still in there, and once done with the little Native boy, it would be sated for a while, then wait for the fire to die out. By then, I would be as far away as my broken body would allow me. The pain, the cold, the fear—my therapist says it's normal for me to have PTSD, but I couldn't tell her it all. She wouldn't believe me. Nobody would."

Trent glanced at Paul, who seemed obsessed with something high up over the professor's right shoulder.

"Can I have some more tea, please?" Fabiola held out her empty cup. Immediately, Trent jumped to his feet, grabbing it.

"Of course." He disappeared into the kitchen, and Paul and Fabiola heard the tap come on, gushing into the electric kettle. Suddenly, his voice rang out. "And . . . and it's been chasing you since?"

"Yeah. I spent a month recovering—my leg. Then I sat around and stewed in my apartment for another month, trying to convince myself this didn't happen the way I recalled it. But all the while, like there was some sort of unholy connection, I could feel it. Just on the edge of my mind. It was there, like something you see out of the corner of your eye. And the thing is, it was gradually becoming clearer. More in focus. Possibly closer."

Would he mind, thought Paul, fidgeting in his chair, *if I got up and helped myself to a glass?* Or maybe I should ask first. But Trent seemed so involved with Fabiola's story. He might consider it rude. But this wasn't the kind of story you sat through without some sort of stiff drink for fortitude. This might be normal for professors and journalists, but for a hockey player—Native or not—it was kind of stressful.

"And you think it was this Merle Thompson? Did you actually see her?"

Though Trent couldn't see the journalist, she nodded, adding, "Yes. And no. Like I said, I could feel her, waiting. It must have gotten her somewhere out there and, I don't know how to explain it, made a deal with her as she lay ready to die . . . or just invaded her. From what I understand, it can take over your body, giving you strength to survive, but eventually it will absorb your body and you will never be human again. Out there, somewhere in that frozen hell, it found and possessed her."

Fabiola paused a moment, as if reliving the memory. "To answer your question—yes I saw her body, as she hunched down over that poor boy. I saw Merle Thompson, but she was so much more than that."

Trent returned with three more cups of tea, including another funny-tasting one for Paul. "According to some legends. So, when . . . and how did you know it was after you? I mean, I know you say you felt it was coming after you, but at what point—"

"At what point did I know this wasn't all part of my imagination? When I was in Banff."

"Banff?" The professor seemed puzzled.

Finally, it was a chance for Paul to add something to the conversation. "It's a town in Alberta. In the mountains I think."

This earned a stiff glare from Trent. "I know it's a town in Alberta. But why were you in Banff?"

Once again, she cupped the hot tea in her hands. "While I was in the hospital, I received several calls from publishers wanting my story. First, I imagined it as a detailed series of articles. But it was my editor who suggested it might make a good book. I knew of the writers' retreat in Banff, put in an application almost immediately after I got out of the hospital, and was accepted. Luckily, there'd been somebody who'd cancelled recently.

"Banff is far away. So up I went, into a cabin, and I polished and re-polished the manuscript in less than a month. That was ten months ago. But while I was there, towards the end, several elk were found dead and partially eaten. It was assumed a grizzly bear had wandered into the outskirts of the town. It was unusual for full-grown healthy elk to be killed in such a way, but stranger things had happened, they said. The thing is, not long after, they found a dead, partly decomposed grizzly. That's when I started putting two and two together."

Paul could smell the unique aroma of the tea wafting up to him. It was amazing how people drank this stuff. Then he saw both Trent and Fabiola taking sips, reacting as if it was enjoyable. Not wanting to be left out, he forced a little through his lips. The Scotch would have been better.

"So, I left Banff soon afterwards, book completed."

"What then?" asked the professor.

"Wanting to strike while the proverbial iron was hot, the company I chose to publish the book managed to shoehorn it into the spring season. Normally it takes a year for a newly written book to come out, but they were in a hurry. So, it came out in nine months."

"What did you do in those nine months? If that thing was after you?"

"I moved around constantly. Told people that after almost dying I wanted to see more of my adopted country. So, I would fly here, stay a couple weeks. Drive somewhere else for some additional time. Always on the move. Always remaining difficult to find. Then the book came out and I managed to convince the publisher to put me on this punishing book tour. Have you noticed how haphazardly my book tour is set up?"

Familiar with book tours, Trent nodded. "I've done two. From what I gather, yours followed no linear path. It was all over the place."

"That was the deal I made with my publisher. I would tell them where I wanted to go with only a week's notice. That was part of the deal. Needless to say, I am no longer their favourite author, because doing the tour that way is expensive, it limits the amount of advanced publicity they can do, and generally makes no sense, which is what I was after. They refused until I offered them a smaller royalty rate for myself. But that way, she couldn't follow me quickly."

"Sounds like it was harsh."

"Not as harsh as the critics. I poured my heart out into that book and I'm told its 'overwrought and melodramatic.' It's easy to criticize, but harder to create."

Paul raised his arm. "I got a question. If you were on the run, isn't it kinda impossible to fly under the radar when you're being publicized in newspapers and doing public readings!? Doesn't that sort of shine a bright light on you and where you are?"

"Yeah, I agree. It wasn't the most logical manner to . . . I believe the term is 'go on the lam.' But you'll have to excuse me. This is the first time I've ever been chased by a Wendigo. Regardless, it isn't very quick-moving and I've been able to stay ahead of it, but the unfortunate truth is, everywhere I go, it turns up sooner or later."

"If it's been following you all this time, why hasn't it attacked you?"

The journalist shrugged. "Maybe I have actually managed to stay ahead of it. Or it's trying to scare me. Make me nervous. I don't think it's a matter of just eating me. I think it wants to make me suffer."

"Do Wendigos do that?" asked Paul. "I mean, do they have personal vendettas? That doesn't seem right. I don't remember anything in the legends about that." Both of them looked at Trent.

"I don't know. I'm not exactly an expert on them. I'm not sure who is."

"I thought you were knowledgeable about these kinds of things. I mean, if this thing is what you say it is, it was you that ID'd it."

Trent took a deep breath. "I'm winging it like everybody else here."

Fabiola spoke again. "Well then, what do you think we should do?" It was an obvious question with an obvious answer.

"Find this woman. Merle Thompson. If she's here."

Paul was becoming a little uncomfortable with where the discussion was heading. "And then what?" Trent and Fabiola shared a look that did not comfort the hockey player. "Never mind. Don't answer that."

All three sat in silence as the wind howled outside.

At least, they hoped it was the wind.

Mizhisha Gaazowin

(Hiding in Plain Sight)

The Indigenous woman sat in a room of other less fortunate members of the country's social network. Some were here because they were homeless. Others jobless. Others just did not fit into the larger mosaic of Canadian society and ended up here as a result. However, she was sure no others were here for the same reason she was. So there she sat, listening to her umpteenth life skills lecture on how to develop a resumé.

At the moment, she was antsy. The wind howling, trying to get into the building, reminded her of her troubles. It also contributed to them. Outside it was too cold and too blustery to enjoy her one remaining vice. As her body craved nicotine, she sat there learning about the importance of format. Worse, she was out of sunflower seeds.

Her time here was running out. There were already two deaths in the city, possibly more, but it was hard to say—especially when the best way to get rid of evidence was to simply digest it. And that woman was close. So close. But where to go next? People would be noticing it, and maybe her. Should she continue heading east, or maybe double back and return west? She wasn't sure it mattered, as the result would probably be the same.

As the resumé instructor droned on to the drones in the room about the potential power of proper spacing and tabbing, her mind wandered. To her left, on a foldout table, she could see the coffee vat, half full of weak industrial coffee. Perhaps that's what she missed most of all since this had happened to her. Good strong coffee. Stuff that could fuel an airplane. This concoction they pumped into you in these social assistance environments could barely be called coffee. But there beside the faux coffee, glowing in the fluorescent light, sat Timbits and crullers, glistening in divine caloric abandon. In addition to existing on the edge of nicotine withdrawal, she was hungry. Her diet was a victim of her circumstances.

Mumbling "fuck it" to herself, she arose during the man's presentation about the importance of proper headings. The pastry knew its days were numbered.

Until the Wendigo was stopped, this was the woman's life.

Geyaabi Bmi-Nakmigad Ndawenjigewin

(The Hunt Continues)

The two men dropped Fabiola off at her hotel. After her afternoon of confessions, she appeared drained. No amount of herbal tea seemed to revive her. So, on the ground floor of the hotel, Trent and Paul found the bar and settled down. Soon, a nice Pinot Grigio and a nut brown ale took possession of the table. Many of his team members had teased Paul for his taste in beers. Most preferred more mainstream lagers, but Paul believed he might as well enjoy some of the more unconventional tastes of the world. He would have the rest of eternity in hell to drink non-craft Canadian beer.

"You're pretty possessive of that backpack. What's in it?" he asked the professor.

"Cellphone, notebook, tablet, things like that. Things I might need."

Paul took a drink, savouring the taste. "I have what I need right here. Shouldn't you be teaching or something?"

The professor shook his head. "I only teach on Tuesdays and Thursdays, but I've cancelled classes for the week. Especially since Katie . . ." Silence enveloped them. For a few seconds, the young Cree woman was alive again. Across the bar, somebody laughed. Trent took a sip of his South African ambrosia. "How well did you know her?"

Katie's smile played in Paul's memory. "Not very well. We were just two Nish bumping into each other at a restaurant. I guess we could smell the reserve coming off each other. We were a little home away from home for each other."

Forcing a wan smile, Trent nodded as Paul continued. "You . . . I don't get that same vibe from you."

"I wasn't raised on the reserve. Residential school, then university. I think I've only been home . . . maybe six times since my parents died when I was ten."

"Why?"

Trent looked deep into his white wine, as if the answer was somewhere in there. "Several reasons."

"Give me one."

"I've been away too long. It's not home." There was a quick cheer from the bar area as somebody scored something on television. "I have a house there. Been meaning to . . ." Trent never finished his sentence. If pressed, the professor could come up with a dozen different answers to Paul's question. Some logistical. A few possible. And some even accurate. What the truth was about why Elmore Trent felt removed from the community that had created him . . . even he couldn't say. All he knew was he wasn't comfortable there. He used to think that maybe someday he would be again . . . but as of this minute, that day had not yet come.

In the silence, their minds wandered.

There were six other people in the bar. The late-afternoon office crowd hadn't shown up yet. Paul couldn't help wondering what these people would do if they knew what was running around this city. Most of the patrons looked white—or 'colour challenged,' to use a politically incorrect term, though he wasn't sure what that meant in today's day and age. So many people with such light complexions had a claim of marginalization: Jews, Irish, any number of smaller religious denominations, vegans, etc.

Trent wondered if, in a different time and place, he and somebody like Paul might have been friends. Though more than twenty years apart, he envied the ease with which Paul entered a room. Both Anishnawbe from roughly the same part of the country, they were like polar opposites. But oddly with the same objective. A Wendigo in Toronto. What had this world come to?

"Do you believe her? Fabiola, I mean." It was Trent asking the question.

"I don't know what I believe. Something's troubling her. But a Wendigo . . . that's a huge leap of . . . not just faith . . . of reality."

Opening his backpack, Trent pulled out his tablet, opening a file. "As strange as it may sound, there have been cases of Wendigos in Canadian jurisprudence."

"Jurres . . . what?"

"Jurisprudence. Canadian law."

"What, they got ticketed for speeding or something?"

Putting the tablet on the table, Trent pushed it towards Paul. "Regina v. Machekequonabe. 1897. A man was charged for shooting another man he claimed was a Wendigo."

Curious, Paul picked up the tablet. "Was it? A Wendigo, I mean."

"The Canadian court system wasn't interested in validating what they believed to be a pagan belief. As the cliché goes, 'just the facts, ma'am.' The Indigenous man was found guilty of manslaughter. The victim was his own foster father, it turned out. There are other similar cases . . ."

"So, you can shoot a Wendigo? With a gun and bullets?" That would make things incredibly easy, Paul thought as he scrolled to the next page. If it was indeed an actual Wendigo. There were a lot of words in this file that didn't normally roll off the tongue of the average hockey player, but he got the gist. Regardless, he was still on the proverbial fence regarding the issue. Three years ago, he'd met two people who belonged to the Flat Earth Society. Who knew they also believed in Indigenous hockey? The couple had sworn up and down that globes were a massive conspiracy. Just because two people believed something didn't mean he had to.

"I don't know. Many of the ancient stories predate firearms. So, it's hard to say. Machekequonabe might have shot a Wendigo. He might have imagined having seen one. Maybe you can shoot them when they're in human form, or in the early stages. Maybe he just wanted to kill his foster father. It's a tough call."

"So basically, we don't know anything. That's what you're saying."

"I'm saying we do what we can. We take the information we are sure of and use it to deduce our next move."

Frustrated, Paul shouted out, "What information? Fuck man, I'm beginning to think this is all a big mistake." The half a dozen people in the bar glanced over at them. Looking around and still frustrated, Paul stared them all in the eye. "What!!!" he bellowed. Just as quickly, everybody looked away.

Keeping his voice low, Trent did his best to calm his new friend down. "Well, for one thing, what Fabiola told us, about Banff. It was early spring when she wrote the book, remember. The dead and missing elk and bears? Spring and summer could be its weak time. It needs the cold to survive. Maybe that's why it couldn't attack people. It's inhabiting this Merle Thompson, gradually getting stronger as it feeds, waiting for the cold to return, and it has. A policewoman told me that, not in those particular words mind you, but it has been feeding all across the country. Getting stronger and stronger. Pretty soon, it might not . . ." The professor paused.

"Might not what?"

"Right now, if we're understanding what's going on, it's taking the shape of Thompson, or living inside her, something like that. But once it gets stronger, it might not need to do that."

"And that's not good?"

Trent shook his head. Shoving the tablet back across the table, Paul surveyed his newfound companion. The man did not strike him as a potential Wendigo warrior. He was wearing expensive winter boots and corduroy pants. "So, what do you think we should do now, oh great man of learning?"

"As with any hypothesis, investigate and test it out."

"And just how do we do that?"

"Like I said, find the woman. We know her name was Merle Thompson. It seems this whole thing pivots on her."

"You know, this is all insane."

"Totally. The American intelligence services used to experiment with clairvoyants trying to psychically influence goats. There are entire religions and belief structures based on only the barest amount of proof. Money is essentially paper and ink, but there is a belief that somewhere in the country there is enough gold or other precious material to validate it. Belief runs this world. What is one little cannibal spirit amidst all that insanity?"

Paul weighed the words of the man across from him. "One time, in Espanola, I was in this game. Overtime, because we were tied. Everybody was exhausted. But my teammate, a Cree guy named Barry, took a shot at the net and hit the post. It bounced off, tumbling towards me. Nobody else saw it, but I swear to God, it seemed to practically hover in front of me, in the air, like a present . . . for, I don't know . . . a little less than half a second. I went for it, using my stick like a baseball bat, whack, and sent it sailing past the goalie's right shoulder. We won. That was the closest I ever came to believing in God."

The confessional was not as complex as Trent's argument, but it was enough. "What are you saying?"

"I'm saying . . . what the hell! I've got the evening off. I hear Wendigo-hunting is good cardio." Paul finished his beer with a certain amount of gusto. "But we got to be done by morning. Got a big game tomorrow." He looked around the room for a second, wondering if he should ask his next question. "Katie . . . did she read a lot? I mean, was she into books?" Though she was gone, he found himself wanting to know more about the mysterious Cree woman.

"Yes, she was. She thought the world could be found between the covers of a book."

"Yeah, I kind of got that impression. Don't think I've read a book since . . . since high school." There was an odd tone of regret or possibly embarrassment in his voice.

Both men were silent for a moment, aware of the chasm that separated them. "Uh, you strike me as a man who might have been fond of comic books. Back in the seventies and eighties, Marvel comics introduced a uniquely Canadian villain called, as you might guess, the Wendigo. Ironic, huh? Huge white monster, amazingly strong, very prescient. Its main opponents were constantly the X-Men or the Hulk. Good news is . . . it always lost. That bodes well for us I think."

Paul gave a deep sigh. "So how do we find this Thompson chick?"

"I was hoping you would know."

"Me? Why me?"

Clearing his throat, Trent looked a little embarrassed. "Uh, I would assume you would know more about this level of society than I would. I mean, how would you travel about the country while keeping a low profile? That's not exactly in my wheelhouse of experience."

Paul raised an irritated eyebrow. "Mine either. The team manager makes all our travel and hotel connections. I just play hockey. Do I look like a homeless Indian cannibal?!"

"Then we're screwed." Both sat in sullen silence until the door to the bar opened and a couple dressed for an evening out entered. Looking around, they spotted and secured seats near Trent and Paul. Dimly, Paul could hear them talking about some play on King Street they were going to see. Both seemed quite excited. The woman had been listening to the soundtrack for the past month and knew all the songs practically verbatim. Her favourite musical was still *Sweeney Todd*, but this was coming in at a close second. Conversely, the man seemed curious to see what the big-time actor, who had a few Hollywood movies under his belt, would do with the role. He had his reservations, he said. Film and theatre acting were very different, like watercolours and oil painting. As he took his coat off, he glanced over at the two Indigenous men sitting glumly at their table, looking quite miserable.

"Hey Tamara, remember back in university, when we saw that play . . . *Rez Sisters*?"

Abruptly, Trent reached for his tablet and began typing madly on it. "What's your brainstorm?" asked Paul. Trent waited a few seconds before showing him the fruits of his typing. On the screen was the image of a woman, cropped from a newspaper article. She was Native, mid-forties, overweight, and looking very uncomfortable about having her picture taken.

"This is Merle Thompson. I thought maybe we should know what she looked like."

Paul studied the picture closely. "Actually, she looks like an aunt of mine. Great, so we know what she looks like."

Trent nodded eagerly. "That's a beginning."

"Yo, Trent, quick question. How many people are in Toronto?"

"Three to six million, depending if you include the boroughs or not."

"And how many of those are Indigenous people?"

Trent paused for a moment as he seemed to pull that fact from his memory banks. "It's estimated . . . maybe eighty thousand." The professor's shoulders slumped in realization. "Okay. I see what you're saying." The silence at their table returned.

Meanwhile, at the next table over, the two theatregoers were still deep in conversation. The man was weighing in on the Tomson Highway question. "I thought *Rez Sisters* was the better play, but *Dry Lips* had the better scenes. The way it showcased misogyny."

Tamara was having none of that. "Now that's where things get interesting. Many would say, including me, it was more a misogynistic play than a play about misogyny."

"I totally disagree, Tamara. Or is this part of your 'men can't be feminists' rhetoric?"

Looking out the big picture window, Paul saw the world pass by. All completely oblivious to the issues the two men inside were dealing with. His grandmother used to say, "Ignorance is bliss." She might have believed in Wendigos, but regardless, Paul missed those blissful days.

Across the road, next to a row of newspapers, he saw a panhandler doing what he could to solicit money from the passing hordes. About every fifth or sixth person would contribute to the homeless man's wellbeing. Watching him, an idea popped into Paul's head.

"Hey, when I was young, I had an uncle living here in the city. I wanted to send him a Christmas card, but for some reason he didn't have an actual address. Finally, after some whining to my parents, they told me I could send it to this address. It was some organization that promised to deliver it to him."

Trent did not see where exactly this was going, but hopefully, at the end of the story, there would be a direction.

"I didn't actually know what the word meant, but I sent the card off. It was a hostel of some sort."

Immediately, the professor grasped the point of the story. "Yes, of course. She'd want to keep a low profile, in a place with food and lodging, and with easy accessibility and exits." He paused, still thinking. "Know any?"

"Check that pad thing of yours." Grabbing it, Trent's fingers became a blur as Paul stood. "I'll be right back." Quickly, he ran outside to the homeless man and dropped ten dollars in his worn Tim Hortons cup. The man, with a heavy unfamiliar accent, eyes wide in surprise, thanked the hockey player.

"Thank you, kind sir."

Leaning in, Paul smiled, adding, "Enjoy. And stay safe. Stay inside if you can. There are things prowling this city."

Nodding in agreement, the ragged man whispered back, "Yes. Americans."

Rushing back across the street, Paul found the professor putting his jacket on. "Success?" he asked Trent.

"Found three hostels, and four hostel-like environments. Do you have a car?"

"I don't live here. Do you?"

Shaking his head, Trent buttoned his coat. "I'm a true Torontonian. No car. I guess we're Ubering it."

This bit of news seemed to delight Paul. "Cool. I've never been in an Uber."

Outside it was, they noticed, colder. Waiting for the Uber, Paul saw a bookstore across the street. In the window were pages and pages of dreams, fantasies, realities, truth, and magic.

Thoughts of Katie again fancy-danced across his consciousness. Tomorrow, life as he knew it would effectively end. The day after tomorrow . . . it was time to start thinking about the future. "Hey Trent, I got a silly question for you. If I wanted to start, like, getting into reading more. Getting more worldly. What would you suggest? I mean nothing heavy or weird, just a good beginner book. And by 'beginner,' I don't mean a kid's book. Just something that might"—Paul seemed lost for the right word—"help me understand things."

"Ever read *Indian Horse*, by Richard Wagamese?"

"Like I said, I haven't done a lot of reading. Is that a good book?"

"A very good one. About a young Native man who grew up in a residential school and finds salvation through the game of hockey. It has a bit of an unfortunate shocking ending, but overall, nicely written. One of his best. I thought, with you being a hockey player . . ."

Both were silent again. "*Indian Horse*. I'll remember that."

The Uber arrived, to take them to a place neither had ever been before.

Mii I'nake Ezhi-Nendang Ndawenjigewnini

(How the Hunter's Mind Works)

Detective Sergeant Birch wondered if she was reading too much into the seeming disappearance of Paul North. There were more questions that needed to be asked and the man wasn't answering his phone. Nobody on his team had seen him since the morning. The doctor had said the man had passed a physical with flying colours. His teammates, including his roommate, had stated he'd walked out and had said he'd be back later. The coach had seemed especially angry. She'd noted there had to be some history of animosity between the two. Reading people was part of her job, and what she saw in the coach told her Mr. North was not long for this team. Not answering his phone seemed to be a favourite pastime of the man. Luckily, one thing was true: Paul North was set to play in tomorrow's final, which was seeming like his actual final game. She would definitely talk with him there.

Some of the forensics were back on the two murders. As expected, there was some weird stuff. Hair fibres had been found at both sites but, as of yet, had not been identified. The lab said they needed more time for that, and that was never a good sign. Also, parts of the remains had repeated puncture wounds, very reminiscent of animal teeth, but of a much larger size. Bones had been broken randomly, bizarrely shattered. Whoever had done this was strong and strange. Part of detective work was figuring out motive. Humanity primarily consisted of several emotions that patterned activity. But what was the motivation behind chopping up two unrelated women, possibly consuming them or just carrying them off, planting animal hair, puncturing the remaining flesh with implements? Was this a man—crazy actions like this were usually, if not always, the privy of white men—trying to make it look like some bizarre animal attack? The human mind never failed to surprise the detective. But that was why she was getting paid the big bucks, as she kept telling herself.

It was getting dark out. Birch decided she might as well head home. Maybe tomorrow she would catch a break and find the missing key to the case. *Wouldn't that be nice*, she thought, warming up the car. And maybe, just maybe, this cold spell would break.

Ninety minutes later, Birch sat in her tub—one of the few luxuries she allowed herself. Showers were necessary in the rapid-paced life of your average crime fighter, but when time and circumstance allowed, a slow soak in an oversized tub reminded the woman she could, on occasion, feel pleasure. Her male colleagues might grab a beer and turn on some competitive sports event, but not her. Surrounded by three candles, a glass of a

Chardonnay recommended by a friend, and some innocuous soft jazz in the background, Detective Sergeant Birch had traded in her profession and title and become just a woman enjoying her surroundings. Or so she'd hoped.

The forensic results were weighing heavily on her, however. It seemed no amount of hot, scented water would still her active mind. What was worse, it was worrying how the forensics—she was not sure how to put it—matched her earlier conversation with Elmore Trent. About his monster. Murder investigations were essentially a massive game of Snakes and Ladders, with people like her going up ladders based on evidence, only to slide down the snakes after finding out they were false leads. At present, she wasn't sure where this investigation was going. All evidence seemed to point to a large animal of some sort. But it couldn't be.

What had Trent called it . . . a Wendigo? Birch had counted three framed university degrees on the wall with his name on them. Being well educated did not necessarily mean you couldn't be a homicidal maniac, though. Birch knew this for a fact. In her career she had met people who thought they were omnipotent god-like creatures taking lives they deemed unnecessary. Others who thought they were doing God's work. Or the Devil's. Or the coffee maker's. It was a complex world for sure. But there was something about this case . . .

"Wendigo . . ." She muttered. The academic had been oddly reticent about certain details in his theory, if she could call it that. Reading between the lines, Birch got the impression he might be protecting somebody, or was reluctant to accuse anybody directly. Try as she might, Birch did not have a bead on him yet. He kept changing, as did the nature of this whole case.

One of her candles was going out. Maybe that was a sign. And her wine glass was empty. Another sign. Grudgingly, she rose from the water, struggling to get out of the tub, letting the liquid drain. Unfortunately, her body was not quite at peace with the world as she'd hoped, and it was it was becoming increasingly unlikely she would achieve aquatic nirvana tonight. Her cell phone was in the living room, and she wanted to check with the lab. See if there had been any progress on those unknown fibres.

One of the things her superiors had told her when she was promoted was that you could always go home, but you never left the office. Birch blew out the two remaining candles and turned off the soft jazz.

Waya Mkaajigaazo

(The Hunt Finds Somebody)

The Native woman couldn't take it anymore. Her body was crying out for nicotine, and no amount of obsessing over monsters, icy weather, and sunflower seeds could placate her cells. She simply had to have a cigarette. Others in the shelter applauded her. Most—those equally addicted—had given up doing battle with the elements to get their fix. But not this woman from the north. Smoking had been a part of her life since her mid-teens, and no personal crisis or polar vortex should interfere with that.

With a heavy coat and only her conviction to keep her warm, she stood in the darkness of the building doorway, huddled against the north wall as the wind did its dance, trying to reach her. Maybe this was just as good a way to die as any other, she couldn't help thinking. At least she was doing something she loved. So many of her friends had given up smoking. Wimped out. Yes, she had seen the propaganda, telling her ad nauseam how bad it was for you. It created all sorts of health problems, but it was the only thing she could still count on. A long time ago she'd had a boyfriend that was far more damaging and a lot less pleasurable than cigarettes. That longish tube of tobacco was her only true friend these days, and it got her through each and every single day. She had suffered a lot over the years, and by god, she was not going to give this up.

Nights like this, she'd try to have two before heading in. It was so incredibly cold out, she would try to oversaturate her system, hoping that would limit her trips outside. She made a mental note to put a letter in the suggestion box, for a recognized smoking room. It was an unlikely possibility, she knew, but at least doing her bit to fight in an unjust war helped her sleep at night. And she needed all the help she could get sleeping.

Not that her notes to management would help her directly. If the woman stuck to her plan, she would be gone in a day or two, having legally and less legally amassed some travel money. She had been here, in this city, this location, too long. Deciding where to go next had been at the forefront of her mind during the boring workshops—by now she could produce a competent resumé, backwards and forwards and possibly in her Indigenous language.

Maybe Montreal. Possibly Kingston. There was also the possibility of going farther east. St. John's. Halifax. Charlottetown. Goose Bay even. She found herself entertaining the thought that she was going about this the wrong way. Staying in small towns might make more sense. Staying off the beaten path. Problem was, smaller towns seldom had hostels and shelters like this. Finding a place to stay could prove a little difficult.

But at least she knew how to fill out a resumé. Everybody here seemed to believe that would help. Looking around, people deep into living their lives jumped on buses and texted on their phones. This was all normal for them. The Native woman longed for normalcy. She wanted the everyday. She wanted boring. She wanted what most people tried to avoid. She had adventure, and excitement, and danger. The novelty wore off pretty quick.

If she were a child and believed in Santa, she would have wished for everything she'd had—which hadn't been much—a year ago. Not to wake up in fear. To have her old job. To have more than two sets of clothing. To be who she had been born to be. And to smoke as many cigarettes as she wanted. Small but seemingly impossible dreams for this woman.

Finishing the last of her cigarette, she dropped it to the ground, but the wind grabbed it and took it away, a red spark disappearing into the growing darkness. Just like her, she thought glumly. As she idly followed the spent cigarette's airborne trajectory, she noticed two guys getting out of the back seat of a new car. Both seemed Native. One was tallish, with a nice physicality to him, and a seeming familiarity with cold like this. The other guy was better dressed, with a high-end backpack, vainly rewrapping a scarf around his neck as if to protect his urban-conditioned skin.

An odd couple. She wondered what they were doing in this part of town together. Maybe they were gay. She had seen odder matches—and as the cliché went, opposites did attract. They seemed to be searching for something, both sets of eyes scanning storefront names. One, the taller fellow, suddenly pointed at her hostel. The other nodded and their pace increased. For some reason, they had business in the place she was staying. They did not appear to be potential clientele.

As they got closer, the well-dressed man spotted her and stopped. The one with the athletic build noticed his friend's sudden halt. Turning to investigate, he saw the direction of the other's eyeline, straight to her. Then it was his turn to stop. Both were looking intently at her. This was not good. She had spent the last year hiding and avoiding attention. There was no logical reason why these two men would be interested in her. Therefore, she immediately engaged in the only reasonable course of action. She started running.

This was not how she'd expected her life to end, chased by two men, both relatively good-looking. Many a night she'd pondered how her particular story would end, but this possibility had not occurred to her. Turning the corner, she ran up the street a short distance. Reasoning logically, there was a poor chance of losing the two men on a broad street where they could easily follow her by sight. Her best chance was in the alleys, dodging between buildings, dumpsters, parked trucks, and so forth. So, the first small laneway she came to, she plunged into it, not sure where it led. She couldn't hear them; the wind was in effect creating a huge sound blanket over the city. But she could feel them somewhere behind her.

Down the laneway, through a parking lot, and then she stopped behind a parked Lays potato chips van. An ironic thought came to her as she looked for somewhere else to run— smoking and running for your life were not necessarily good companions. Breathing heavily, the woman surveyed her options. Across the street was an open lot, and behind it were two secluded avenues to escape through. Normally a woman rushing into such a dubious environment might not be a good idea, but this wasn't a normal situation. And at the end of one of those two potholed pathways, her salvation might lie. It was better than standing there, waiting for them.

So, she ran again, crossing over the street, her feet flying like they hadn't flown since her thirties. One minor problem robbed her of her anticipated victory. In the near-darkness, she had miscalculated the height and angle of the curb. Her speed and ungainly gait, added to the poor lighting, set the stage for a very unladylike misstep. The result being a rude re-acquaintance with the laws of gravity and angular momentum. Falling face forward, her remaining breath was knocked out of her with a seeming vengeance. Unable to move, she lay there on the sidewalk, somehow finding the energy to roll over. If she was going to meet her death, or whatever malfeasance those two men had brought with them, she would do it facing them, albeit from the ground amidst the litter of Toronto life.

Her vision slightly blurred, she saw the two men on the opposite side of the street. The athletic one saw her, tapped the other guy on the shoulder, and pointed. After safely checking the traffic in both directions, they slowed their pace as they crossed the street. What seemed odd to the woman was that neither man walked with any seemingly evil intent, or showed any type of violence towards her. But they did look intense, even a little worried.

"Are you Merle Thompson?"

It had been a while since Merle Thompson had heard her name spoken. For the last year she'd been travelling across the country under a number of assumed names and histories. She had been an abused wife on the run from her husband. Once, just to shake things up, she'd said her wife. She had told organizations she'd stayed at that she'd been mugged, her apartment had burned down, something about witness relocation—a plethora of reasons why she didn't have any proper ID. But she'd never used her birth name.

In between ragged breaths, she replied to the two men. "No. She died. In a plane crash."

Paul and Trent realized they had finally found her. Though her hair was longer and a different colour, she looked like the picture they had found online. The address they had just showed up at was the third place on the list they had assembled. Neither of them had realized how difficult it was to try to find somebody in hostels and shelters. Many did not take names. Others were confidential, on a strictly need-to-know basis. Some did not have access to that specific info, telling them to check with the program coordinator. The evening had been rapidly turning out to be a waste of time.

What little information they had managed to get—essentially that no place so far had heard of Merle Thompson—had come at the cost of several expensive donations to the hostels, courtesy of Elmore Trent.

Dejected and losing hope, they'd stopped at the Dawning of the Sun shelter. There they saw a familiar woman, smoking and looking uncomfortable. And now she lay prostrate before them, seemingly on the edge of a heart attack.

Paul kneeled, unsure of what he was looking at. This woman, heaving so painfully, hardly seemed to be a demon from the north. "Sorry, but no. We know for a fact Merle Thompson—you—did not die. Any more than Fabiola Halan did."

As if struck by an electric shock, Merle backed away from them, scurrying like a crab, only stopping when a mailbox blocked her path. "She's not here, is she?" The men could see panic in her eyes. "No! Don't let her near me." This terrified woman was not the monster they'd been expecting to see.

"Why not? Haven't you been following her? Across the country? Don't you want to kill her . . . and eat her?" Even as he said it, it still sounded weird to Paul, even though he was completely conscious of the fact that's why they were here. Luckily, there was nobody else on this side of the street to hear him.

Trying to get up, the woman stumbled, still struggling to draw a decent breath. "It's her. It's her. Not me. Leave me alone. I've got to get away from here." Once more, she tried to run, but this time she fell to her knees in front of a park bench. If this was indeed the Wendigo, Paul thought, he'd seen tougher bantam players.

Trent could tell something was amiss. "What do you know about her? About Fabiola?"

Looking over her shoulder at them, Merle Thompson took in enough breath to answer his question. "She's not Fabiola Halan," she said in a husky tone. "I mean she is, but she isn't." The fear in the woman's eyes was replaced by a sense of fatality. A chill ran down Paul's spine, but it had nothing to do with the frigid weather surrounding them.

At a Tim Hortons half a block down the street, Merle Thompson sat with Trent and Paul, telling them a different version of the tale to the one they'd heard from Fabiola. On the table were two large and steaming cups of coffee, and one—Trent was not going to argue the point though he personally considered it a case of false advertising—tea. Not thoroughly convinced, both men watched her closely. Since neither was a seasoned Wendigo hunter, there was no point in letting their guard down.

"Why should I trust you? I have no idea who you are. You could be working with her. You could be under her spell." She sipped her coffee. "Can we get some donuts here? I just ran two blocks."

Trent looked at Paul, who rolled his eyes as he got up. Merle watched the hockey player as he approached the counter, eyeing him with an "I like to window-shop but seldom waste time and money on buying anything" attitude. "He's cute."

"I think the question was, how can we trust you? Everything Fabiola told us says you're the Wen—" Suddenly conscious of where they were and what they were discussing, Trent looked around. Tucked in a corner, they were afforded a certain amount of privacy. "The Wendigo. And don't say you don't know what we're talking about. You wouldn't have run. That look of fear on your face when we caught you, that was real. You knew we were on to you. You are part of this whole thing, aren't you?"

Merle wasn't sure what to say. All this time she had been expecting Fabiola to find her, not these two guys who seemed really out of place. It had been a long time since she had trusted anybody. Her grandfather used to always tell her that when she had a nightmare to share it with him. A nightmare shared was a nightmare weakened, he would say.

"How do I know you're not . . . 'it'?"

"Do we look like Wendigos?"

Merle flinched at the mention of the word. "Do I? Does that thing you call Fabiola Halan look like one? Early on, they hide inside you and only come out in order to eat. It's not until later . . ." The woman shuddered.

Carrying a tray of multicoloured donuts, Paul took his seat. "Okay, you weren't too specific on what kind of donuts you wanted, so I got a selection. Help yourselves." Quickly, Merle grabbed a maple-drenched one and immediately took a bite. Then she saw Trent eyeing her peculiarly.

"Hey, this doesn't mean anything," she added defensively.

"What do you mean it hides inside you?"

Finishing the donut and reaching for a second one, this time one with sprinkles on top, Merle used it as a pointer as she talked. "It's a spirit. It doesn't have a body, but it has horrifying hunger, a hunger so strong it eclipses anything else. But, as I was told, spirits are spirits and therefore they can't really eat things or people. It needs a physical body so it can eat. Keep in mind those things have been wandering the wilderness since time immemorial. That makes it kinda hungry. So, it has to find a host body that will accept it. Didn't your Elders teach you anything?"

A little awkward about revealing his residential school past, Trent wasn't sure how to respond. Paul, however, had been told such stories. "The legends I heard said they were actual things, physical monsters that came out of the north and ate up all the deer, moose, beavers, everything, until there were only people left to eat. They were, like, actual monsters. Not just spirits."

"Yeah, I can see that. I hear those too. Maybe. I don't know. What I was told though, once it's been in the human for a long enough time and has eaten enough people to get really strong, the human host gradually turns into the Wendigo and stays that way. Travelling across the land eating and killing as it goes."

"Hey, looks like you were right!" Paul slapped Trent on the back, making him spill his so-called tea.

"These are good," Merle exclaimed. Trent wasn't eating and Paul was still working on his first, leaving the woman to reach for her third donut.

"Hey," said Paul, "these people aren't known for the chicken soup."

Merle eyed the younger man for a second, chewing slowly. "You, I get. I know you." Her attention turned to Trent. "You, I don't. What's your story?"

"What do you mean . . . you know him."

Sipping more coffee, Merle smiled. "He's a Nish. It's coming out of his pores. I got cousins, two brothers, uncles just like him. We could be in a bar in any city across the country, spot each other, and immediately start a conversation. But you . . ." She stopped, shaking her head. "You're different."

"I'm Anishnawbe too," Trent said, almost defensively.

"Well, just because you're dressed like a boxer doesn't mean you can fight. So, what's your story?"

It occurred to Trent that the woman they'd been chasing, who might be at the centre of this whole tragedy, was now asking the questions. He was having doubts about her participation in everything Fabiola had confessed. And Merle now wanted the Rez breakdown of Trent. From him. *Where to begin*, he thought.

An hour later, they were all sitting in a Vietnamese restaurant. Merle had never had pho before and was quite enjoying it. Beef in a good steaming hot broth with some noodles. Just a slight variation of hangover soup minus the tomatoes, she commented, making Paul laugh and Trent request an explanation. In between bites, Merle continued with her tale. And as she spoke, both men noticed there were fewer chills running down their spines. Reluctant to admit it, those chills had happened only when the journalist had been speaking.

"I got about three kilometres away when I came across flat tundra. It should have been littered with small trees, tamarack, that kind of thing. Instead, just a field of white."

Slurping loudly, Paul managed to say, "A frozen lake."

Nodding, she continued. "I didn't trust it. Could be fast-flowing water, meaning the ice could be thin. I'd step out on it and I'd go right through. That thought didn't appeal to me. And the lake, if it was a lake, seemed to go around the spit of land I was on. Evidently the plane had landed on either an island or a peninsula. So I headed back. I was confused, half frozen, despondent. I wasn't sure what to do. But eventually, the next morning, I made it back to the plane."

Both men took everything in when she stopped talking. Though perhaps not consciously, they were believing what she was saying. When Fabiola had been speaking, it was like a journalist telling somebody else's story. Here, they were getting gospel.

Merle twirled a noodle around in her steaming bowl. Her thoughts were far away in time and place. Then she started again. "I can't tell you how much I really mean this, but I swear to God, and every god that is worshipped on this stupid planet, that I wish I had walked out onto that lake and taken my chances."

"What did you see?" Trent spoke but Paul pulled his chair closer, the spring roll in his hand all but forgotten.

Closing her eyes, she spoke with a slight tremor. "At first, looking through the small plane window, I couldn't quite make out what was happening. I don't even know why I was looking through the window. I was practically frozen, desperate for some shelter, but as I approached the wreckage, something told me to look inside before entering. Most of the windows were covered over with frost, only a small hole in the centre of one was clear. She . . . it . . . was hunched over that young boy. Kneeling over the body. I had my hand up to knock on the fuselage when that thing lifted its head." She put down her chopsticks. "It still looked like the woman, as far as I could tell, but it had something in its mouth. I couldn't tell what, but looking down to the floor, I saw what remained of that poor boy. And then I saw what remained of her. Her eyes were . . . almost glowing, framed in black. There were parts of her that looked bigger than they should, like her arms and legs . . . and her teeth. Christ Almighty, her teeth. They had eaten away at her own lips. Suddenly, all the stories my grandparents told me so long ago came rushing back. I knew what had happened. And I knew what could happen to me." Merle stopped talking. All three quietly sat as her confession weighed on all of them.

Trent broke the silence. "And you left the crash site again?"

"I went in the opposite direction, as fast as I could. Turns out we were on a peninsula. I ran. I walked. I crawled. The next day, just about ready to lie down and give it all up, I came across a mining road cutting through land. I couldn't continue, my tank was empty. I just sat there, on the edge of consciousness, for I don't know how long, struggling to stay awake. If I fell asleep . . ."

"Hypothermia," said Paul, no stranger to cold environments.

"Yeah. As long as I wasn't eaten. That's all that was important to me. Every wind that came, every branch that creaked, I thought it was her. Then, as if sent from heaven, one of those big ore trucks came rushing from the horizon, almost hitting me. The man driving it saved my life. I don't even know who he was. He dropped me off at the clinic on this small reserve. And then left."

The Vietnamese waitress dropped off the cheque. Several times in his younger years, Trent had been mistaken for having some sort of Asian background. Same with Paul—but not Merle, who'd spent most of her life up north where Chinese, Japanese, Korean, etc. people were few and far between, and more importantly, where people could tell the difference. Both men were busy digesting her story, so Merle thanked the waitress.

"Thank you. Uh, is anybody going to pay this? I live in a hostel, remember?" It took a moment for that to register before both men quickly reached for their wallets. Once the cheque had been taken care of, Merle continued her story.

"I don't know why, but I pretended to have amnesia, or maybe I did actually have it, or something like it. The point being I told people I couldn't remember my name or how I ended up in the middle of nowhere. The plane crash was still big news, but I'd lost so much weight and the whole situation had made me look different. When they started asking me more questions, and were going to get the police involved, it made sense for me to disappear. I suddenly remembered who I was, gave them a fake name, and got the hell out of there. That's when Merle Thompson really died. I figured if that thing thought I was dead, she wouldn't come after me."

Trent and Paul shared a glance. "But she did."

The woman took a deep breath. "But she did. I ran and I ran. I started out in Thunder Bay. All was good for a couple months. I actually thought I might have a life again. Stupid me. Then, I don't know how, but I could feel her . . . somehow. She was there. And she knew I was there. I saw a poster advertising Fabiola Halan and her new book at a local bookstore. So I ran to Edmonton. Same thing. Vancouver, Winnipeg, hopscotching across the country, trying to stay alive. And there she was, always one step behind me. You caught me just before I was about to leave. I would have left a couple days ago, but you need money to run and I keep finding myself constantly, embarrassingly short of panic funds." She added more hot sauce to her pho. "So, what do you guys think? Montreal, or should I see what's happening in Moncton?"

An hour later they were at Trent's house in the Annex neighbourhood of Toronto. The fake fire was roaring and Paul was on the couch with Merle when Trent entered the room with a tray. "I've never been a big fan of Scotch," muttered the woman.

Paul took a glass and picked up the bottle for closer examination. "I can't even pronounce this name."

"That's how you know it's top-quality. The harder it is to pronounce, the better it is."

Putting the bottle down, Paul looked into his glass, then smelled the contents. "Good to know. Hell, my reserve should try and make their own. Slap an Ojibway name on it, and people would think it was the best in the world." Merle burst out laughing while Trent faked a smile.

Sipping her own drink, Merle sat back in the comfortable sofa. "Oh man, this is the good stuff. I haven't felt this at ease in a long time. I take it you don't think I'm the big, bad Wendigo anymore?"

Paul spoke first. "I don't know what I think. This is all pretty weird. I play hockey for a living. My usual life conundrums are deciding whether I should go left or right on the ice. I'm not sure how much of this I really believe. I'm giving Trent, my man here, the benefit of the doubt because somebody we both knew . . . well, it looks like that thing may have killed her. That's got me a bit riled up."

"It killed my wife . . . ate my wife . . ." Unconsciously, he looked over at the picture of him and Sarah on the beach in Mazatlán. Much happier times. She hadn't deserved what had happened to her. She'd been a good woman. She deserved justice. In the story he was currently hip deep in, Trent wasn't sure what justice was. Again, he felt those pangs of yearning for her and the life they had shared. The creature had taken the only two women that had welcomed him into their lives in a very long time. "And as for your question, about you . . ." He paused, "I'll . . . I'll be honest, I don't know."

"Okay, I got a question, and I'm not saying anything about anything, but, just pissing into the wind here, if she's not the Wendigo . . ." Paul pointed at Merle while he posed his question to Trent. "Who is? I mean, she says it's Fabiola. But it can't be."

Listening to the sound of the ice tumbling around in her glass, Merle disagreed. "Yes it can. And I swear that on everything

I believe. Spray me with holy water, wave some sweetgrass over my head, I don't care. But that woman is not a woman. I have never been so sure of anything in my life. I mean, in her book, she says she managed to hobble across kilometres of snow and brush to find safety. But she had a broken leg. Not just a broken leg, but a compound fracture. With breaks like that . . . it's very difficult, if not impossible, to stumble across ice, or limp through knee-deep snow. At best, she might have made it up that ravine wall, but no way she could have hobbled all that distance. That thing was inside her, giving her power."

Paul shook his head. "But she's not Anishnawbe, or Indigenous of any kind. She's from the Caribbean. How can—"

"I don't think the spirit asks to see a status card. You only hear of these monsters in Native traditional stories because there used to be only Native people that far north. And most people up there aren't on the verge of starving, or so desperate they'd let a thing like that enter them. But every once in a while, the door to hell swings open."

The situation was spinning out of control for Paul. Fabiola was a remarkably interesting and amazing woman. They'd laughed, they'd spent time together, they'd even fucked. Those were not normally the actions of a cannibal spirit. At least none he'd been told about. This was all so confusing. "I can't believe it. She can't be."

"Paul," Trent's voice took on a professorial tone, "like all cultural legends, there's a lot more to these stories than just what you think. Wendigos, yes, we're all familiar with the ravenous appetite, endless hunger, horrible monster imagery."

"Isn't that enough?"

"There's more. Like an onion, there are larger metaphors within even larger metaphors."

"Oh great," muttered the hockey player. "I like those even less."

"Think of it this way: hunger is just the most obvious characteristic of want. At its core, these stories are about appetites, in all their many forms, growing and consuming you first. The Wendigo approaches you when you are at your weakest. The most common stories tell us about starving people desperately wanting to eat something. That's its way in. But it can and frequently does also refer to ambition, greed, desire, essentially any type of self-indulgence or insatiability. As with any and all of those, the more you want, the less you'll be satisfied with."

"Yeah, yeah, yeah, I got the metaphor. But one more question." Paul leaned forward, a scant two feet from Merle's face. "Why did this spirit Wendigo go for Fabiola and not you?"

Nervously Merle put her fingers to her mouth, shushing the younger man. "Okay, first things first. Stop saying its name out loud."

"Why? Afraid it'll hear you?"

"Yes. I am. Whatever we may think of it personally, it's old. It's ancient. It was born of this land long before our people were here snowmobiling about. As strange as it may seem, it deserves some respect. It is of this land, and you know how we feel about our Elders—well, this thing was here before all of us. We're not supposed to mention the Trickster's name in summer remember? It's kinda the same principle here. Throwing its name about . . . might call it. Might make it angry. I don't know . . . Just stop throwing the W-word around. Better safe than sorry." The two men looked at each other. Even with Trent's extensive research, they clearly had a lot to learn about the creature.

"And secondly, to answer your question—maybe . . ." Merle thought for a moment, her mind trailing off to a long time ago, to a place far away. "Maybe we weren't the right match. Maybe I wasn't hungry enough. Or desperate enough. Or ambitious enough. It doesn't just look for physical hunger to survive, but maybe somebody with a hunger of some kind as strong as itself. That's its doorway into the soul and body. And do I look like I was made for climbing the corporate ladder?"

"And Fabiola was?"

Merle shrugged, finishing her Scotch. "That suit and winter jacket I saw her wearing didn't come from Goodwill." Both men pondered the implications of her words. The hockey player who only put enough effort into his career to get by was silent. The professor who had relied on his wife to guide him through the academic forest gazed into his fake fireplace. And then there was the mysterious woman from the Caribbean who wore expensive clothes, travelled, and wanted the world to know her name. Both men had felt her ambition.

"Speaking of goodwill, more Scotch please." Merle held out her empty glass to Trent. "I have to say, Elmore, you're spoiling me. Donuts. Vietnamese soup. Good Scotch. I should have run to Toronto a long time ago. Always thought I hated this city, but it's growing on me." She watched him pour her another glass. "Pity I have to leave again. I hear Val-d'Or is an interesting place."

"Look, I'm having some trouble here. Fabiola. You. This is not adding up," Paul said.

"What's wrong there, young man? You got a crush on her or something?"

Deciding to ignore the uncomfortable ramifications of her inquiry, Paul asked his questions. "If this is Fabiola, why did she eat . . . kill people like Katie and his wife? Why them specifically? I'm having trouble putting this puzzle together. Why make friends with the both of us? Why not just eat us? Why write a book about her experiences? Why is she chasing you across the country? Why is this happening now, in this city, with us? Why does she get her nails done? Why should I believe any of this? I mean . . ."

"Merle, you don't have to answer . . ."

Answering in an almost-maternal tone, the woman leaned over and took the bottle from Trent, pouring some into Paul's glass. "Simple answer, young man. I don't know. I don't have all the answers. This is my first time dealing with this insanity too, remember. Secondly, you're asking me to psychoanalyze a . . ." She looked over her shoulder uncomfortably and whispered, ". . . a Wendigo. To come up with logical reasons why it does what it does. Explain its methodology. I'm not sure anybody can." Then, topping up her own glass, she gave Paul a rueful smile. "For those kind of answers, you'd have to ask the Creator. Otherwise, this thing does what it does."

This thing does what it does. That phrase reverberated through Trent's head. It had been bothering him—why Katie and Sarah? Why did it attack two people he knew personally? Maybe the first one, dear sweet Katie, could have been a coincidence. But the next night, Sarah too? Identically? Far too coincidental. And if it was indeed Fabiola at the heart of all this . . . in that coffee shop, he had mentioned Sarah to her. His wife. Who was a successful realtor in the local area. How difficult would it have been to track down a realtor with the last name Trent, within blocks of that café?

And Fabiola's cryptic words to him as she was getting ready to leave: "Not everybody deserves to be abandoned." Was that a hidden message? Had she been telling him something? Was he directly responsible for the demise of his wife? All uncomfortable thoughts. Ones that for the moment, he would keep to himself. Still, his conundrum did present an interesting question.

"Well . . ." commented Trent, as he took a sip.

"You got some ideas?" replied Merle.

"Maybe, just maybe, it's still a mash of both Fabiola and the W—" Merle scowled. "And the thing. I don't know. Maybe she . . . it . . . liked us . . . as simple as that. Fabiola had enough control. There was still enough of her in charge to make decisions. Paul, do you think Fabiola liked you?"

For a brief second, the hockey player remembered her warm embrace, her kisses on his neck. Yeah, he was pretty sure she liked him. He nodded.

"But for how much longer would she be in control?"

"Not much, I would say. The more she eats, the stronger that thing gets." Merle inserted her index finger into her glass of Scotch, then sucked the flavour off it. "And don't forget, she hates me." Silence descended on the room. The unfathomableness of the Wendigo mindset had them all mulling their own questions.

Trent noticed Merle scanning the books on one of his shelves, then grabbing one. She looked surprised. "You write this one?" He nodded.

Leafing through it, she smiled. "Well, maybe there's even a simpler explanation for you. You wrote a book about Native legends . . ."

"Two, actually."

"He teaches a course on them too," added Paul.

"Nice picture. Maybe there's a reason for you writing and teaching this stuff. Maybe it's on purpose."

"*Maybe?*"

"You say you don't believe in this stuff, but you're surrounded by it. Maybe . . ."

Trent was beginning to hate the word *maybe*.

". . . you have a connection. One more than most. Maybe it knows that. Have you ever had any other experiences with . . . strange things or beings?"

For a fleeting moment, there was a fluttering in the back of Trent's brain. "No." Unconsciously, he looked out the back window to the obsolete koi pond, not sure of what he expected to see.

"Then maybe I'm wrong." Putting the book down, Merle took another sip of her Scotch. Once again, they were all lost in their own thoughts.

Finally, Paul broke the silence.

"So, what are we gonna do about the fucker?"

Eshkam Go Nwanj Nshkaadzid

(Anger Grows)

In her hotel room, Fabiola tried Paul's number for the ninth time. Once again, there was no answer. She was becoming annoyed, even angry. This was his number. He had given it to her. Why wasn't he answering? His automatic messaging service came on, but by then she had hung up. Maybe his silence was hockey-related. Maybe something had happened to him somewhere in the city. Or maybe he was just ignoring her.

Sitting in the dark, she dropped her phone on the carpeted floor. The weather report said tonight was supposed to be a record for the lowest temperature for this time of year. Even though windows like the ones in her room were specially designed not to ice up, there were small tendrils of frost along the edges. Not that she noticed.

Paul was supposed to be her friend. Same with Trent. Both had said they'd help her. Help her find the woman who'd abandoned her.

She let out a small, frustrated utterance, which if there were other people in the room, would have sounded suspiciously like a growl.

The next morning, walking slowly, Fabiola Halan entered the arena. She surveyed the crowd for Paul North, but with no luck. He said he'd be here, and currently the place was full of Indigenous people of all shapes, sizes, and ages. Two days ago, he had said this would be a big game, so there was no way he would miss it. A winger of some sort—that was how he'd described himself. So he'd be with his fellow team members. She remembered that, when the game that she'd watched with him was over, the teams went into those cave-like entrances. The showers and change rooms were somewhere deep in the bowels of this edifice. That was as good a place as any to start.

Aazha Dbishkooseg Ji-Maajtaayang

(It's Game Time)

All three woke almost simultaneously when Paul's knee, damaged repeatedly over the years by fierce hockey interaction, jerked suddenly in the midst of some dream, knocking one of two empty Scotch bottles over onto the table. The ensuing noise made them sit up with a start, still groggy with sleep and post-Scotch syndrome.

"I'm here, Coach!" Paul yelled, snapping erect from his slumped-over position. Trent, equally afflicted, stood up, weaving slightly in front of the chair he'd spent the night in. Merle, being the lady she was, merely yawned and stretched before opening her eyes.

Trent looked at his two companions, not fully understanding the current situation. "What . . . what . . . huh?" The fireplace was still going, but it was the light streaming in through the broad windows that made everybody blink.

"Oh Christ, it's morning," said the woman, suddenly feeling the after-effects of the night. Noticing the bottle, she added, "So this is what a high-priced hangover feels like." She leaned her head back. "Gotta say, not that different."

"Morning . . . it's morning! Oh shit!" Paul had missed curfew for the second night, and was in a piss-poor condition for the final that was due to start in—checking his watch—an hour?! "Crap crap crap!!! I'll miss the game."

Still trying to focus on his surroundings, Trent muttered, "Sarah . . . ?" before recognizing the two on the couch. "Oh, right."

"I got a game. I gotta go." Standing up quickly, Paul found himself just as quickly leaning over on the arm of the couch. Standing used to be so easy.

"What game?" Using her foot, Merle pushed her drinking glass to the other side of the coffee table. Hair of the dog was definitely not what she needed this morning.

"I'm a hockey player. I play hockey."

"I used to be a pilot. So?"

"Where's my coat? I need a taxi. And a blood transfusion. Oh, he's gonna be so mad." Quickly, Paul checked his pockets. "I gotta phone him . . . Son of a bitch!!!" The two no-longer-attached portions of his phone were still in his jacket pocket, awaiting a future. The hangover, plus the sudden stress, added to him standing up too quickly again, making him woozy. Leaning against the wall, Paul looked less like a seasoned athlete and more of a little boy out of his element. "Anybody got a phone I can use?"

"How many homeless people do you know carry phones, hockey boy? You really need to get in touch with your people on the streets."

Sitting back down, Trent struggled to regain his faculties. Slowly, the previous evening's conversations dribbled back into his consciousness. Wendigos. Running. Fabiola. And their final decision, before the Scotch took hold.

"Fabiola." The utterance of that name silenced the other two, making them remember the reason they were all here. Far better than a cold shower, or realizing you were in bed with a cousin. Paul and Merle sobered up. "Paul, where do you think she'd be? About now?"

Desperately trying to focus his cloudy attention, Paul looked at the older man. "I . . . we could try her hotel, but . . . she said she'd try and come to my game."

"Right. You said that last night. I guess we should go to the game."

"And when we get there . . . and if she's there . . . what then? There are so many ifs and maybes here, and this is so serious. For the sake of argument, what if she isn't the Wendigo?"

"Hey," Merle interjected.

"Ya ya, I know. Do you know how embarrassing this will be?" Paul's brain was slowly gaining momentum.

"That's a chance we'll—"

"And for the sake of argument, let's say she is. What then? Do we try and kill her . . . it? Try and talk rationally to the cannibal spirit? Explain the vegan lifestyle to it? And just to set the record straight, Trent, I've never killed a Wen—a cannibal spirit before. I've never killed a man. Hell, other than a handful of deer and moose and mosquitos, I don't have much experience in that line of work. I am asking you right here and now . . . what will we do when and if we see Fabiola Halan and she is what we seem to think she is?"

Most days in the class, Trent saw all those eyes looking up at him, wanting answers and wisdom. Or, if nothing else, to be told what to do and how to think. He saw it again in his living room now. And for the first time in a long time, he didn't have the answers these particular students were looking for. "I don't know."

"Great plan, Professor."

"Everybody including her agrees she's a part of this story. Let's go and find out how the rest of the story ends. Am I wrong, or does that make sense?" Trent looked for a response from either person in his living room.

Paul's only reply was to put on his winter coat. Accepting that as agreement, Trent did the same, before noticing Merle had not moved from her place on the couch and looked like she had no intention of vacating.

"Merle? We need you."

"No, you don't. It's not you she's hunting. You boys go have fun."

The men turned to face her. Afraid to meet their eyes, she grabbed a cushion and hugged it. "I don't want to."

"What's wrong? Last night you said, and I quote, 'Let's go get the bitch.'"

"Trent's right, Merle. You did."

She was silent for a moment before answering. "I was drunk. You've never said anything stupid and volunteered to do something suicidal when you'd been drinking?"

For Paul, that was most of his twenty-second and twenty-third years. Trent's walk on the alcoholic wild side had been substantially tamer, practically boring. Both could see genuine fear in her eyes, and they began to realize the potential danger they could be putting this woman in. And themselves.

"I have spent the last year running from this woman, and now you want me to turn and run *to* her. That . . . that does not sound like a good idea. In fact, it sounds downright stupid. There are lots of ways to die in this world. Being eaten by a skinny bitch with amazing cheekbones is not the one I want."

Kneeling beside her, Trent took her hand. "It has to be done. Otherwise you'll keep running and running. From what I know, they never tire. She will find you. I think if we face her, together, maybe we can appeal to whatever humanity might still be in there. I met her. Talked to her. So did Paul. She's still very much human."

"You didn't see what I saw."

Trent squeezed her hand. "Yes, I did. I saw two women I was very fond of, one irreplaceable in my life, destroyed by that creature. Since then, it's been a constant battle to stay sane and composed. I am going to miss them so much . . ." For a moment, the professor became quiet and his eyes watered.

Paul hadn't realized how much of an impact these events must have had on the man. "I've been hanging on by a thread," Trent added. "My parents . . . Sarah . . . Katie. I'm alone." Tentatively, Paul reached out and put his hand on Trent's shoulder.

Shrugging it off, Trent stood and did up his coat, finding strength at the prospect of revenge. "My skin is crawling right now at the thought of what happened to them. It may be after you now, but it's only a matter of time before Paul, me, and God knows who else will be next." The two men shared a stare. "When Fabiola's human, she appears very human. We've both felt her charm." Paul nodded. "And I think she's a little afraid herself. Maybe she's not totally aware of what's going on. Maybe something like a split personality disorder. And if she's the Wendigo, we can hope her human part might still be approachable. We can tap into that. I know it's a long shot but . . ."

Trent stopped talking. Merle's sense of self-preservation was doing battle with an equally strong understanding that Trent was right. Running was draining. And expensive. Literally in the last year she'd done nothing with her life except hide in somebody else's room and shiver in fear. And eventually, there would come a point when she couldn't run any farther. That meant she would die alone, and far away from home. These two men were willing to go into battle with her. Fight with her. Negotiate for her. Stand beside her. Not bad considering she'd only met them about twelve hours ago.

Making up her mind, she stood, firm and tall (for a short person), and a little woozy.

"It's better than no shot. Ah, fuck it. So, what's the game plan for this X-File? But I need a smoke first."

"Excellent. I'll call an Uber. Paul, can you grab my backpack, over by the bar?"

Paul did as he was told.

In the Uber they discussed their plans. "Did anybody bring some tobacco?" asked Merle.

"I thought you had a cigarette already?"

"Not for me. As protection. And maybe some sage and sweetgrass. You know, like Christians and their garlic for vampires and werewolves."

Closing his eyes, Trent tried to keep his voice less irritated. "I don't think it works quite that way."

"Are you sure? How do you know? You keep talking like you know stuff." Merle responded with a little anger of her own.

"What's this?" From out of his backpack, Trent pulled a mickey of Scotch. "This wasn't in here? Is this mine?" Putting two and two together, he glanced at Paul.

"What? I thought it might be a good idea. You know, to do some sort of toast when we win. That's one of the things we practise in sports—the power of positive thinking." Trent continued to stare at him. "And regardless of what happens, I know we may need a drink when this is all over—again, regardless of what happens. Care to disagree with me?"

"When the boy's right, the boy's right," said Merle.

Dropping the bottle back in the bag, Trent rested his head against the window. The city rushed past them as they raced towards their destiny.

"My life is fucked anyways." Looking out his own window, Paul was trying to figure out how to include these new influences in his life into today's game. "I'm supposed to be playing in this morning's game. I'm supposed to be there already. It's the final, against the best team in the league. It's our chance. I missed curfew. I'm missing the warm-up. This is also supposed to be my final game. I'm gone. And now we're going off to look for a cannibal spirit hiding in the body of a beautiful sexy woman. If this is how my day starts, I'm terrified to see how it ends."

"Grow a pair, will you? It's me she's after. I'm sure she's spent the last year dreaming of sucking the eyeballs out of my skull."

Concerned, the Uber driver glanced in his rear-view mirror at his fare.

Nwanj Go Daa-Gii-Biiskaan Ji-Wiisginesik

(He Needed Better Safety Equipment)

Herbie Tort was feeling good. His future was essentially in the bag. Provided he didn't end up injuring himself somehow, after this game and tournament he would spend the off-season negotiating the rest of his life. Even if they didn't win the tournament, there was a good chance he'd be named MVP. All was fabulous in the world. And better yet, Paul North hadn't been around lately to annoy him, and judging by the coach's language, North was in shit so deep, he'd need a coal miner to get out. So, all was good in the world.

As he made his way to the bench, there was an unmistakable jaunt in his step, which was difficult considering he was in skates.

"Excuse me. Do you know where I can find Paul North?"

The asker of the question impressed Tort. She was tall, dark, and remarkably striking. His first impression had been that she was more than likely one of North's puck bunnies, but looking at her closely, that seemed unlikely. There was something about her that, for a brief moment, made the man jealous of his rival.

"Uh, he's supposed to be here. But I guess he's late." Why would a woman like this be asking for a guy like Paul North? "Why? If you don't mind me asking."

Another player came around the corner, and the woman's eyes momentarily fixated on him. Looking disappointed, she turned her attention back to Herbie Tort. Smiling, she said, "I have a hockey question."

Smiling back, Tort took off his big, clumsy hockey glove and extended his hand. "Well, my name is Herbie Tort, and I have a pretty good understanding of the game. Maybe I can help."

Something, it seemed to the young man, flashed across her eyes. For a brief second, it was almost as if somebody else was looking through them, at him.

"Maybe you can," she said, still smiling.

In the background, the crowd roared as the Zamboni came onto the ice.

Aazha Gii-Bgamad

(The Storm Has Arrived)

Arriving at the arena, Paul, Trent, and Merle exited the vehicle, leaving the driver to drive off rather quickly. "The driver, he was weird," commented Paul.

Trying not to show her fear, Merle found herself standing close to Trent, eyeing the public warily. Trent was also scanning the crowd.

"Awful lot of people here. Great place if you're a hungry Wendigo."

Without looking at his newfound friends, Paul hastened to the front doors of the building. "Sorry for being part of a very popular sport."

"He's touchy," commented Merle. "Maybe he needs to get laid." Trent didn't hear her, as he was next through the doors. Not wanting to be left behind, the shorter woman struggled to keep up. "Hey, wait for me."

Once inside, Paul moved as if a man on a mission. He knew he should be upstairs getting into uniform, but for the moment the question about Fabiola filled his mind. Despite what Trent and Merle were saying, he was praying to a God he hadn't interacted with since Sunday school decades earlier, hoping that it was all a misunderstanding. Locating the escalator to the changing area, his fast walking turned into a jog as he ascended the steps. Barely hearing the "Paul, wait up," he landed on the third floor.

Almost immediately, Paul heard a familiar bellowing voice, dripping with anger and judgement. "North! Where the fuck have you been?! You are so off the team. Tamarind is replacing you."

"Tamarind!? But he's got asthma! And he's fat! And he's the equipment manager!"

"Yeah, but he was here, and he's still a better option than you." Suddenly, Trent and Merle came through the doors. For a second, a look of anticipation flashed across the coach's face, but then he realized he didn't recognize them. "Shit. On another matter, North, you seen Tort? He was around here an hour ago. Said he was going to warm up . . ."

"I just got here."

Sneering, the coach walked away. "You just got here . . . of course you did. And you just left."

"But Coach . . ."

Ahead, to the coach's left, was the change room for the Otter Lake Muskrats. The coach stuck his head in the door and the banter died immediately. "Any sign of Tort?" A slight pause, followed by a myriad of *no*'s. Looking back over his shoulder, Coach locked eyes with Paul. "You still here, North?"

As the man walked away, Paul muttered to himself, "Well, I'm fucked."

"Focus, Paul. There are bigger issues here," Trent snapped.

"Says the man with a job, an Uber account, and a fireplace in his living room."

Merle's attention was elsewhere. "She's here. Close. I can tell." Her eyes wandered upwards, towards the ceiling. "Paul, is there somewhere in this building where we can get a bird's eye view? Someplace we can look at the crowd without them seeing us."

After thinking for a moment, he nodded. "I think from the lighting booth possibly. I haven't been there, but I've heard . . ."

"Do you know how to get there?"

"I guess. I think it's somewhere up on the fourth level. There's an elevator over there I think." Paul pointed, and grabbing Merle's arm, started down the narrow hallway. At the end, Trent spotted the elevator and increased their speed, forcing Merle and her smaller legs to pump faster.

Paul was the first there, pressing the up button repeatedly. Looking at the elevator door and the lights above it, people might think the elevator was so old, the arena had been built around it as a way of maintaining it as a late nineteenth-century landmark. From behind the door, they could hear heavy creaking and moaning as the car made its way to them.

"I hope you guys know what you're doing," said Merle.

Paul, his life and career in ruins, leaned against the cinder-block wall, wondering what had happened over the past few days. Tomorrow, what would be left of him would greet the dawn. Gazing down at the floor, he sighed. Such was his life.

Across the hallway from him, he saw something seeping through the a few millimetres between an unmarked door and the floor. It looked like red liquid. Instantly, his testicles shrunk, trying desperately to disappear up into his abdomen. Fearing the worst, Paul stepped forward, reaching out to grasp the doorknob. Every part of his body screamed for him not to open the door. But regardless, his hand turned the knob, and slowly the door creaked open. Leaning forward, careful not to step on the red liquid, Paul North peered into the room.

"Come on, come on, come on. Hurry up." Trent's fist anxiously knocked against the painted cinderblock walls beside the elevator.

"You know, I actually took a year of university. History." Why Merle said it, then and there, she didn't know. It just popped out of her. "I'm just sayin'."

Puzzled, Trent looked at her, trying to comprehend her thought process, but stopped when he saw Paul. The man was peeking into a room a few feet away. And now he was stepping back, his face pale and stunned. Closing his eyes, the man fell back, held up by the opposing wall.

"Stay here," Trent said to Merle, as he scurried over to Paul. "You okay?" Reflex made the professor glance over his shoulder at the semi-open door. It seemed to be beckoning, as if wanting to show him something.

"Don't. Don't." Trent could barely hear Paul's voice. In retrospect, that quite probably would have been the best advice, but their situation, the crisis at hand, dictated that Trent investigate everything to do with their mission. Hesitantly, he looked through the door into the fluorescent-lit room.

The normally dull cream-coloured cement walls were awash with red. Blood was spattered and smeared everywhere. Bits of yellow fabric and plastic thrown in every direction. Paul would later tell him yellow was the team colour. On the floor, what at first appeared to be a hunk of meat attached to some long, thin bones. Underneath a bench he saw something that would haunt him for the rest of his life. It was a round object, encased in plastic. A human head wearing a hockey helmet. Blankly, the eyes stared at him. As advertised, the helmet had indeed protected the head.

It seemed the Wendigo had been here.

Behind Trent came Paul's voice. "That was Herbie . . . Herbie Tort." Witnessing the consumption of his wife had happened so quickly, and in such bad lighting. But here, all the trauma, all the horror—it was well lit and thick on the ground, inches from him.

Merle could tell both men were deeply affected by something inside that room. "I don't want to look in there, do I?" Both men violently shook their heads. "Told you she was here."

Behind Merle, the elevator door opened.

Bi-Dgoshin

(It Arrives)

The elevator let them off on the fourth, which was in the middle of hundreds of assembled hockey patrons there to see the final.

"Oh great," said Merle. The men had not yet regained full use of their faculties. Ahead of them in the stands were rows upon rows of people—innocent men, women, children, mostly Native, all completely unaware of what was potentially in the arena with them. "This was your idea. So, what do we do now, oh brilliant one?"

About nine thousand urban and Rez Natives had travelled here to see these two great teams battle it out for the IHL trophy. Even though the game had not yet started, the noise was already deafening. Somehow it forced Trent to his senses, making him

332

lean over to Paul, whispering loudly into his ear. "Merle has been with us since last night. Your friend Herbie . . . it looks like he was killed recently. Really recently. The blood hadn't had time to congeal. It couldn't have been Merle. It had to be—"

Suddenly pointing and cutting him off, Paul whispered, "Fabiola." There, about a dozen rows back from the centre ice line, three sections over, was the journalist. She was easy to spot in the crowd—wearing her familiar coat—and for reasons they could only surmise, she practically radiated energy.

Instantly, Merle Thompson's mouth went dry, and a couple drops of urine escaped her bladder as panic flashed across her face. Every fibre in her body told her to run. Instead, she gripped Trent's arm, yelling, "Oh Christ, it's her. It's her. What do we do!?"

Gently, Trent sat her down in an empty seat. "Stay here. We're gonna go . . . investigate."

"We are?" said Paul.

"We are," replied the professor, trying to sound confident. Trusting the younger man would follow, Trent started down the stairs. At the same time, the two opposing teams began to emerge from their dressing rooms on to the ice, to thunderous applause. Around the arena, the multitudes stood and cheered, waving foam fingers and handmade signs. There was a definite sense of excitement in the building.

Desperately trying to keep up with Trent, Paul found himself pinballing his way through people filling the aisles and thoroughfares. Some were trying to find their seats; others were taking the last opportunity to pee or grab some food. Regardless, several times Paul almost lost sight of his companion.

Gradually, both Trent and Fabiola grew closer as Paul tried to make up the space separating them. Then, out of the chaos, an arm grabbed him, almost bowling him over. Adrenaline already flowing, he turned to do battle with his assailant.

Detective Sergeant Birch stood holding his arm. "Mr. North, you're a hard man to get a hold of. Can I have a few moments of your time?"

"Here? Now?"

"We're both standing here. Why not? You've got someplace else you'd rather be?"

"Oh yeah, a million places actually." Looking over her shoulder, he saw Trent arrive directly in front of Fabiola Halan. Paul made a mental note to ask the professor if there were any schools of philosophy that said life was merely a series of ill-timed coincidences and uncomfortable occurrences. Nothing more. Then Birch, following Paul's eyeline, spotted Trent.

"Professor Trent . . . why am I not surprised?" Her attention returned to Paul. "Are you part of this whole Wendigo theory of his?" Instinctively, Paul flinched at the utterance of the name, something he must have picked up from Merle.

"What do you know about that?"

"Enough to have a fair number of questions. Perhaps the three of us should chat," the detective said. After decades of not understanding the phrase "between a rock and a hard place," it finally made sense to Paul. "It seems those fur samples at both murder sites have a mixture of human DNA . . . and something Toronto's best forensic analysts can't place. They are very, very puzzled. Curious, isn't it?"

Overwhelmed, Paul could only comment, "Not really."

A few sections over, in this arena built specifically for a different kind of confrontation, Fabiola greeted Trent.

"Professor Elmore Trent. How delightful. I wasn't expecting to see you here." Fabiola's smile seemed honest and forthright. Hardly the look of a woman who had just overpowered and eaten an athlete in the prime of his life, with a dozen kilograms of protective equipment covering his body.

"Fabiola. What are you doing here?" It was then Trent realized he was alone. Instinctively, he stepped back.

"I came to see Paul play with his team. Look at all these people. I guess it's going to be a good game. Have you seen Paul?" Again, she smiled sweetly, and for some reason it elicited a cold sweat from the man. Legitimately scared, Trent looked around and spotted Paul talking to some woman, visible from the back, one section over. *What the fuck could be so important right now*, he thought.

"So, Mr. North, regarding these new developments, your friend has some interesting theories concerning the murder of those two women. Where do you stand on that?"

"You should really talk to him about this. He's the smart one." Paul's eyes darted back and forth between the woman in front of him and the woman one section over. He wasn't sure which one made him more nervous.

"You seem a little on edge. Well, I've been trained to believe in a theory called Occam's razor. Are you familiar with that term, Mr. North?"

"I . . . I don't believe so."

"Basically, it states that the simplest answer is most often the correct one. Luckily for me, most murders also agree with that school of thought, and for the most part that makes my job a lot simpler. But for reasons I don't understand, this theory does not seem to apply in this particular case."

"Uh, yeah, that could be a problem." On the ice, Paul could see his friend Jamie taking position in the crease. And there, filling his spot, in his ill-fitting uniform, was Tamarind. He looked like he was already out of breath and the game hadn't even started yet. A third-pairing defenceman was taking Tort's position. The coach was indeed desperate.

When Fabiola asked the professor about Paul's location, his natural impulse was to glance again over his shoulder at Paul. The woman followed his gaze and, in a few seconds, found him amidst the hordes of fans. "There he is. But he's not in uniform. I thought he was supposed to be on the ice?"

"We've been busy."

"Busy? With what?"

Trent, a man with three degrees including a doctorate, author of two books, and one of the most knowledgeable academics in the country concerning Indigenous storytelling, did not know what to say. His mouth opened . . . then closed again. Thinking this out better might have been a good idea, he found himself thinking.

"That woman. Merle Thompson. Her. Is that part of it? Did you find her?" Fabiola's voice suddenly got faster, noticeably more eager, as she leaned forward in her seat, finally standing up. Located a step above the professor, she towered over him. Her personality seemed to have changed right in front of him. "Is she here? She's here, isn't she?" Forgetting the man, she started looking around the arena.

"Fabiola . . ."

"Where is she? Tell me."

Something dark and deep had changed in the woman, Paul could tell. Standing erect, her head twitching slightly on her slender neck, she was looking around—and from where Paul stood, Trent looked intimidated if not outright terrified.

"Mr. North, do I have your attention? Perhaps we should carry on this discussion at the station."

Paul looked back towards Merle and saw her sitting there, staring at him, then at Trent, then back at him. Something was happening, and it wasn't good.

From her seat, Fabiola saw Paul's head turn upwards to the rear seats. There! She saw her, finally. The woman who had left her to die in the frozen north. Sitting there so warm and comfortable. The journalist's heart started pounding and her vision got hazy with the realization. She stepped down onto the stairs, moving quickly in the direction of Merle Thompson.

Trent stepped in front of her, saying "I don't think . . ."

Fabiola backhanded him with ridiculous ease, sending the man flying into the seats below, causing two hot dogs to soar and spilling several boxes of popcorn. Her eyes fixed like the cross-hairs of a periscope, Fabiola walked forcefully towards the other woman. Several people unfortunate enough to be in front of her found themselves flying through the air, landing haphazardly against walls, seats, and other people. Reacting to the commotion, everybody in the arena looked in her direction. A fight had broken out at the hockey game, except this time it was in the stands.

"Shit." Paul, seeing this, dove past the policewoman, intent on intercepting Fabiola.

"Mr. North," shouted Birch, but he was racing up the steps towards an altercation that seemed to be occurring. Following him, she wondered to herself why her ex-husband was so fond of this game. Tennis was her game.

Not sure what else to do, Paul jumped in front of Fabiola, putting on his best fake smile. "Hey Fabiola, how's it going?" Recognizing him, she briefly stopped, blinking rapidly.

"Paul . . ."

"Yep. So, what are you doing?"

"You . . . you invited me . . . ?"

If Paul could be classified as a charmer, he pushed it into overdrive. "Yeah, I did. Glad you could come, but like . . . so what're you doing up here? If you want, I could give you a tour . . ."

"You didn't answer my calls yesterday."

"Yeah, sorry about that. My phone was broken. Haven't had a chance to get a new one. But hey, hungry? I've heard . . ."

Distracted for only a moment, Fabiola saw the Thompson woman dart from her seat and scurry down a flight of steps, in the direction of the ice. She was trying to escape. Fabiola would not allow that.

"Sorry Paul, I have to go. Business, you know."

Instinctively Paul stood in front of her, blocking her from chasing Merle. It only took two seconds for the journalist to figure things out.

"You're with her. You don't want me to —"

"We're all a little excited here. I think the best thing we can do—"

Fabiola's hand instantaneously found Paul's throat. She was strong. Way too strong. Insanely strong. Paul outweighed her by about eighty pounds, most of it muscle, and try as he might, he could not dislodge her fingers from his neck. As the darkness settled over his consciousness, Paul found himself acknowledging the fact this was not normal. If he had been doubting Trent's theory before, that doubt was disappearing as quickly as his mental awareness.

Suddenly he was released and fell back onto a row of seats. His vision clearing, Paul saw Trent rise from the cement, having used his heavy backpack to hit the backside of Fabiola's knees, knocking her onto her rear. "Come on!" Trent yelled, helping Paul up. They descended the steps in the direction they'd seen Merle go. Neither had any idea what to do next but they were confident there was strength in numbers.

Climbing to her feet unharmed, Fabiola looked around. All were now fair game. Down near the boards, she saw Merle approached by the two men. Meanwhile, all around her, people were milling about, both puzzled and mildly amused by the physical interaction they had just witnessed.

"You go, girl!" yelled one tattooed teenager.

"What now?" asked Merle.

"I'm open to suggestions," responded Trent.

"Does anybody remember the Lord's prayer?"

"Paul, I don't know if that covers Wendigos."

Fabiola was getting closer, and the trio found themselves backing up. Looking to her right, Merle spotted a door leading onto the ice. *Any door in a crisis*, she thought, as she lifted the latch and jumped through it. With no better idea, the two men followed her. Suddenly, they were standing between two competing hockey teams, who were somewhat perplexed at this civilian invasion. Immediately, the referee skated over, blowing his whistle angrily.

"Hey, you're not allowed on the ice. Get off!"

"North! Is that you? What the fuck are you doing? I told you you were fired." Practically screaming, the coach angrily threw a hockey stick at the trio. It slid across the ice, stopping at Paul's feet. The crowd started booing, upset at the potential delay in the game. It seemed all the world was angry at them.

One of Fabiola's expensive Italian leather boots stepped out onto the ice, followed by the second one. Of everybody in the arena, she seemed to be the only one not overly agitated. "Geez, who are you, lady?" yelled the referee. "Get off the ice." He gestured for one of the linesmen to escort her off. His name was Darrin Leach, and he left behind a wife and two children as the woman in front of him taught him the fundamentals of inertia and gravity. The crowd screamed as he landed. The referee screamed. The two teams screamed. Paul, Trent, and Merle were the only ones who didn't.

Fearing the unusual power of the woman, the ice was immediately evacuated, leaving only the trio and Fabiola.

"You left me out there . . ."

Hiding behind Trent and Paul, Merle's quivering voice was heard. "I came back for you. I did. But it was too late."

"Do you know what happened to me out there?"

Trent was the one to answer her question. "I think we all do."

"Do you?" A new voice was heard. "Okay, don't move. I've called this in and backup are on their way." Detective Sergeant Birch was on the ice, her standard-issue Glock pointed directly at the woman she'd just seen somehow make a volleyball out of a 190-pound man. At one end of the rink, she could see the ice was smeared with blood.

"Lady, you're under arrest. Mr. Trent, Mr. North, care to introduce me to your friend? I assume she's tied up in all this?"

Paul could see the pistol, fixed and steady, aimed directly at Fabiola. Oddly, it didn't fill him with comfort. "Uh, ma'am, that may not work."

"What?" That was the stupidest thing Birch had heard today. In her hand was a Glock 22, complete with fifteen rounds in the clip and one in the pipe. There were very few things it could not stop, especially at such close range. She'd been fortunate, having never had to use it in her career, but should the need arise, Birch knew how to use it expertly.

Fabiola looked at the strange woman, not really knowing who she was but then not really caring. She was just a speed bump, like the linesman had been, to achieving her final objective. "Fuck it," she said to herself. And with that, the safe and comfortable world most of the people in the arena normally accepted changed for them forever as they stared down at the events on the ice.

Trent saw it first. "Oh crap."

Then Merle and Paul. In unison they said, "Oh shit."

Birch didn't comment. She just held her breath as Occam's razor evaporated.

Fabiola's head jerked left so quickly it blurred. Her hands clenched repeatedly. Falling down on one knee, her head bowed for a second. Then she raised it. Her eyes were black, brilliantly black. Her dark black hair was suddenly developing strands of white, continuing until all her hair was white. This wasn't Fabiola Halan anymore. Whatever it was started growing taller, leaner. White hair, closer to fur, expanded across every part of its skin. Fabiola's jacket, pants, shoes, everything she'd been wearing was shredded. Seven feet, eight feet, until finally the creature stopped at what must have been a good nine feet, possibly ten, in height. With the speed of a switchblade, long savage-looking nails grew.

Every nightmare Paul had had as a boy disappeared in that moment. In front of him and the entire arena stood an incredibly tall and horrid-looking creature. Later, in the media, those not overly familiar with the Wendigo legend would describe it as a lean albino Sasquatch or a werewolf-like creature.

The last part of the metamorphosis was the appearance of long, pointed teeth. The thing bit its own lips off, swallowing them as an appetizer. Only its teeth showed below the dark, bleak eyes. A howl born of endless hunger and freezing spirit emanated from the former woman's mouth, sounding oddly like a gale coming out of the north.

The building erupted in a cacophony of shrieks, with many people running in panic to any available exit while others were frozen in fear. A few were mesmerized by what they were seeing and wanted to see more, daring to come closer, thinking the Plexiglas sheets might protect them. A few held up their cell phones, hoping to capture what was happening.

Suddenly, a series of loud sharp sounds echoed in the arena. Birch was emptying her gun into whatever was standing there twenty feet away. From this distance there was no way she could miss, and she didn't. Even drawing a gun in public led to a mountain of paperwork. Firing it in a crowded environment would lead to an investigation, but at this moment in time, Birch didn't care. Sixteen bullets hit the creature's centre mass, with the result being scarcely more than an annoyed growl. It was like shooting a frozen side of beef.

Trent turned to Paul, trying to analyze everything that was happening. "Yeah, I thought that was a long shot. Would have been nice though."

Birch, as a police detective, was a woman of logic. This was not logical. Not really comprehending its ineffectiveness, she looked at her weapon like it had betrayed her.

"I don't . . ." Almost instantly, the white door that opened onto the ice came flying through the air, hitting Birch and sending her flying across the ice. Sounding almost satisfied, the creature turned to the remaining three and let out a thunderous roar. Dust fell from the rafters forty metres above them.

Stepping back in fear, Paul almost slipped on the hockey stick his coach had tossed at them. Instinctively, he picked it up, ready to use anything he could as a weapon.

As it took a step forward, the creature's right foot almost slid out from underneath it. But, being a spirit from the north, its ability to adapt to frozen water was quick. The long claws on its toes dug into the ice, solidifying its stance as the surface cracked several inches in all directions.

A desperate and crazy thought came to Trent. "Paul, I have an idea." Both Merle and the hockey player looked at Trent in astonishment. A dozen feet to their left lay the dead linesman. Taking the hockey stick from Paul, Trent started moving right. "His skates. Put them on."

"Why?"

"It'll give you an advantage. We need an advantage. Any advantage! Do it!" For a brief second, Trent sounded like Coach, making Paul do as he was told. But unlacing skates from a dead man and then putting them on and re-lacing them was not a speedy task.

Looking up at Merle, Paul mouthed the word *help*. Eager for something to do, she ran to him, falling on her knees to help her new friend don the sharp skates of battle. Eager to distract the creature, Trent continued circling to the right, desperately trying to keep his footing. Slipping and falling right now would not be a good thing. "Fabiola!! Over here." He waved the stick then banged it on the ice, trying to make as much noise as he could. "Come and get me!"

The creature's eyes were still fixed on Merle, and it took another tentative step towards her. And then another. Under their breath, both Paul and Merle cursed the hockey gods for making ice skates so laborious to tie up.

Remembering his earlier conversation with Merle and Paul, and the notion that Fabiola might still have some consciousness not so deeply buried beneath the primal desires of the creature, the professor tried an unusual tactic. "Fabiola! Your book was embarrassingly overwritten and lacked any serious dramatic through-line. You should have stuck with writing articles people could read on the toilet." Now, standing on the opposite side of the rink, Trent finally got her attention. The creature's huge head, eyes blazing fiercer if that was possible, turned towards the professor. "Also, it was melodramatic and devoid of any serious narrative. I counted three dangling participles. Shame."

With a roar the creature lurched forward, clearly intent on doing serious damage to the professor. A few feet to the left of Trent was a small door that allowed the players onto the ice, but it was latched. Attempting to leap over it, Trent's feet slipped out from under him, landing him on his back. Scrambling to his knees, he narrowly dodged a huge hand with razor-sharp claws, which splintered the wood just above his head. Pushing off the wood, he used Newton's third law to propel him past the creature. Nearly falling due to misjudged momentum, the creature grabbed the Plexiglas, cracking it as it righted itself. Trent managed to make it to his feet, but fell again almost immediately. The Wendigo turned and stood over the prostrate man.

Thinking fast, Trent used the hockey stick to jab the creature in the stomach, again thrusting himself a small margin of safety away. Quicker this time, the Wendigo used all four limbs to cut the man off. Lying there a few feet away, he could feel the cold emanating from it.

It had been a hell of a week, Trent thought, as death literally hovered over him. Then, to his left, a blur came sailing across his peripheral vision and grabbed the stick from his hands. Like a gyrfalcon, the blur circled the both of them faster and faster. Suddenly, the blur shoved the stick between the Wendigo's legs and shoved, toppling the creature over onto its side. Then, extending the stick, the blur known as Paul North yelled "Trent, grab it!" Doing as he was told, Trent was towed to relative safety.

Paul and Merle helped him to his feet. "Thank you, Paul, thank you. You saved my life."

A roar of frustration rattled the building as the creature rose to its full height. Before it had been obsessed with Merle. Now it was pissed. Angry. At all three of them.

Feeling at home in his skates and with the stick in his hands, Paul said, "What now, Kemosabe? There must be some way to kick that bitch's ass . . ." Suddenly he looked at Merle. "Oh, sorry. I hope it's not a problem that I called her a bitch? I've gotten into trouble before, but I figure in this case . . ."

Looking at the Wendigo flexing its gigantic clawed fingers, Merle shook her head. "No no no no. I come from a long line of proud bitches, I think my father was one-quarter bitch, and let me tell you that thing over there is one colossal bitch and a half, if ever I saw one."

Despite the terror approaching them, they shared a smile.

"Well, Professor Trent—you started all this, you got a way to get us out?"

"Maybe. Can you keep her occupied?"

Paul nodded. Confident and fast in what could be called his natural element, he skated directly towards the towering monster. Repeatedly, the Wendigo tried to grab Paul. To claw him. To grasp his legs and tear him apart like a wishbone. But the man on skates was too fast. Dodging and weaving, he stayed just out of range. As he got closer, he went left then suddenly deked right, circling the huge mass and coming out in front as the creature, clumsy in its bulk, nearly tripped over its own legs. On the offensive, Paul hit its back leg with his stick, then its shoulder. Finally, reaching up, he managed to whack the monster across the side of the head with all his might, shattering the stick's blade. After all his efforts, the only damage seemed to be to the colossal creature's pride. But that was something.

"Merle, I need my bag. Where is it?" shouted the professor.

"I don't know! What am I, your valet?" Merle yelled back, her eyes still on the approaching creature.

Suddenly, Trent's bag slid across the ice, stopping just in front of him. Looking over to the side, he saw nobody in that direction. Then how had the bag . . . ?

"There it is. Got an academic grenade in there?" Merle asked, seeing it too. Instead, Trent took out the bottle of Scotch Paul had stashed away. "Hey man, I'm all for a good drink to ease the tension but do you think now is the right time? Oh, what the hell . . ." Merle's opinion on the issue was to grab the bottle and swallow several ounces. "Okay, I'm ready to die."

Frustrated, Trent took the bottle back. "Nobody's going to die . . . hopefully. The one constant thing I've read about the destruction of Wendigos is they are cold and frozen spirits from the north. If you burn them . . . their hearts, that might do it. We have to set it on fire." With that, he tossed the half-full bottle onto the ice, sliding it in the hockey player's direction.

"Paul!" Trent yelled, pointing at the amber-coloured bottle, conveniently located on a big blue circle in the ice. "There's your puck. You have to douse her in the Scotch so we can set her on fire. Can you do it?"

Gripping his stick, Paul looked down at the bottle, then up at the Wendigo. "'Can I do it?' he asks . . . This is what I do, Professor." In his mind he was doing the hockey math, assessing angles, calculating speed and anticipated trajectory. The problem was that the blade of his stick was broken. Smiling grimly, he grabbed the bottle in his left hand, and stood there, calmly, eyeing the approaching monster. Both Trent and Merle's hearts were in their throats. "Do something, you idiot!" she screamed.

With the creature a scant dozen feet away, Paul tossed the bottle in the air and up it went. Then gravity grabbed it and, as it fell, he swung his broken stick at it, this time like a baseball bat. The result was a resounding crash as the glass broke, and a shower of expensive amber liquid splashed across the front of the Wendigo's torso, drenching it. Merle cheered. Instinctively, Paul pumped his hands in the air as he did when he scored a goal. Even angrier, the creature lunged for Paul, but the ancient spirit was no match for the settler culture's crowning achievement in technology: steel on ice.

"So, what now?" yelled Paul.

"Uh . . ."

"Uh?"

"I think we're fucked."

Amidst the screaming of the increasingly frustrated Wendigo, Merle grabbed Trent's lapels angrily. "Just like a man. You promise a happy ending, but in the end we get fuck all."

"I, ah . . ." Trent hesitated. "I was going to douse your scarf in the alcohol first, then wrap it around the blade . . ."

"But you forgot. You got any more Scotch in that bag?"

"No. I'm sorry. This is all happening so fast."

"For fuck's sake!" Angrily, Paul backed away, urging the others to follow him. "Any chance you think she'll lose interest?"

Trent tried to follow, but Merle grabbed the hem of his coat.

"Don't you dare leave me here. You brought me here, you better damn make sure you take me out of this place." Another roar from the creature told them it was barely ten metres away, and getting closer.

"I'm sorry, Merle. We never should have tracked you down."

"Agreed. What a way to go. Wish I could have one final—"

Like a hockey puck bouncing off her head, she was hit by an idea. "My scarf . . . give me your stick!" Waiting for Paul to do as she'd yelled, Merle rummaged in her pockets. Barely conscious of what he was doing, Paul handed her the stick, his eyes never leaving the glowering creature two dozen feet away.

Taking the stick from Paul, Merle wrapped the flimsy, sheer scarf around the remaining three inches of blade, then pulled something small out of her pocket.

"Where did you get that?"

In her right hand, Merle held a silver lighter. "A fringe benefit of being a smoker. You should consider taking it up." When she flicked the wheel, a small flame ignited. Holding it up to the makeshift torch, it immediately started to burn slowly, the fabric having been designed to be non-flammable. But Merle had a solution. She flipped the lid on the lighter and poured its contents onto the scarf and stick. The fabric exploded into flame, turning the broken hockey stick and scarf into a torch.

Merle handed the weapon to the hockey player. "Go get her, Paul."

Once again smiling grimly, Paul left his friends. His legs pumping like mighty Indigenous pistons, Paul North, right winger for the Otter Lake Muskrats, skated faster than he'd ever skated before, bearing a flaming hockey stick of salvation. For a sliver of a moment, Paul thought he could see fear in the glowing black eyes of what had once been Fabiola Halan. Then, like a knight on horseback wielding a lance, Paul hit the Wendigo dead centre where basic anatomy said a heart should be, knocking the creature down. A pillar of flame erupted as Paul rolled clear. There was a scream, and then several more as the flames grew. All those remaining in the arena watched as the creature crawled to its feet, hidden behind a curtain of fire, the hockey stick still protruding from its chest. Huge hands tried to beat the fire out, but the flames seemed to feed on its evil spirit. Falling to its knees, one hand seemed to almost reach out to Paul, as if seeking forgiveness and help.

Though happy the creature was no longer a threat to anybody, there was a moment—or more—of sorrow in Paul's own heart.

Then it fell backwards, onto the melting ice. The Wendigo was no more. The flames flickered for a few seconds longer before extinguishing. The arena, now with only a handful of people still in the stands, was silent. Getting to his feet, Paul skated over to what remained of the Wendigo. Trent and Merle joined him. A few seconds later, Detective Sergeant Birch arrived beside them, nursing what would turn out to be a broken shoulder.

The body of the creature was burned—scorched in some places, charred deeper in others. It appeared the conflagration had triggered a transformation, but not completely. The torso and most of the body remained Wendigo-like, but the extremities . . . The feet of the massive creature were small and delicate, with pink painted toenails. Hands that had once caressed Paul could be found at the end of long, furry, muscled arms. And atop the massive burnt chest, the beautiful, unfortunate face and head of an orphan who had cheated death twice, but not for a third time.

Birch was the first to break the awed silence. Leaning in, she appraised the face of Fabiola Halan, sounding oddly matter-of-fact. "I don't suppose somebody would like to fill me in on what just happened."

Without looking at her, Trent answered. "We just killed an ancient Anishnawbe spirit using a mickey of Scotch and a hockey stick. How's that for a day's work?"

"Shhhh" was Merle's response. Not used to being shushed, Birch glanced quickly at the unknown woman. She looked Native, and was now kneeling down, putting what appeared to be a broken cigarette on the ice, near what was left of the . . . creature.

"What are you doing?"

"I'm putting tobacco down."

"Why?"

"Because I'm still alive to be putting tobacco down."

Birch watched the woman as she seemed to close her eyes. "I take it this is a Native thing?"

Merle nodded. In the distance, sirens could be heard, getting louder. Turning to the hockey player and the professor, the Birch said, "You guys do this a lot?"

Letting out a weary breath, Merle opened her eyes and offered her hand to Trent, opting not to answer the question. She had the rest of her life to answer questions. She had a future again. But first things first. "Oh, Christ I need a smoke."

Trent was silent, hoping the dead figure before him might let Sarah and Katie rest, if not in the afterlife then at least in his conscience. His missed them just as much as before, but now there was closure of a sort.

Then, out of the corner of his eye, he saw something move. Adrenaline still pumping, his head swivelled. There, where the ice met the scarred wooden boards, he briefly saw a little furry face peeking out of a crack. A tiny hand gave him a thumbs up. It seemed the little people had evolved and migrated, as had their Indigenous cousins. It had been the Memengweshii that had slid his bag to him across the ice, saving their lives. Katie had been right . . . they were still keeping an eye on him.

Paul's only comment on the situation was a long and protracted bout of projectile vomiting.

And from deep in the rafters, high above the arena, currently awash in smoke from the still-smouldering figure lying on the ice, the sprinkler system came on.

Ezhi-Giizhichigaadegin Niw Dgaajmowinan

(Loose Ends)

The shoreline where he stood looked the same, albeit with the trees having grown bigger and what appeared to be an evolving subdivision on the other side of the lake. Trent took a deep breath and smelled the essence of the land floating on the breeze. It smelled intoxicating. It had been years since he'd stood in this spot, taking in the scenery, filling his lungs. But he was back now.

The house he'd grown up in and that his parents had died in . . . well, there wasn't much left to salvage. Bears could be surprisingly thorough when they were in a destructive mood. But all things could be repaired and salvaged. The past few months had taught him that.

The world was still trying to process what had happened. Cell footage from the few who had stayed behind in the stands had gone viral, inspiring a multitude of theories. The body, once the literal dust had settled, had been taken away by the authorities for examination. There had been a few press releases issued by the government revealing surprisingly little. Most, including Trent, were smelling the beginning of a conspiracy. One of those rare Canadian ones.

There were calls that this Wendigo, or whatever it was being called, needed to be examined, classified, and demystified for the public's own sake. Few suspected it would ever be seen again, despite the public protests. Quite probably, it would simply cease to exist and disappear into legend . . . maybe.

Trent, attempting to avoid all the publicity, had come home. Not including the brief glimpse at the ice rink, it had been decades since he'd seen or even wanted to see the little people. But times—and he—had changed. If they would have him, he wished to re-establish communications. Kneeling down, he put some tobacco in the water, just an inch from the shoreline, and closed his eyes in silent prayer.

It might take a while, but that was okay. Elmore Trent had brought lunch.

There were four kids skating loops on the indoor rink. Paul North was watching them from halfway up the bleachers. All were around eleven, maybe twelve. Paul was never good at guessing kids' ages but that felt about right. Here in this anonymous community rink in some anonymous town, he had stopped in to watch the next generation of skaters—perhaps future hockey players. Somehow, it gave him a quiet sense of purpose.

The taller boy had potential. He knew how to lean when he took the corners and could skate decently when looking over his shoulder to talk to what appeared to be his younger brother. Once he'd even skated backwards. The youngest of the four, a girl, was still trying to find her equilibrium. She tended to try to walk with the skates in an awkward shuffling motion, not pushing off in a smooth glide. She seemed the least comfortable. The other two, both boys, fit somewhere in the middle.

Paul offered up silent suggestions for form and practice. Things he might say if he was closer and actually communicating with them. All their mistakes seemed so obvious to him. But nothing that couldn't be handled with a little guidance.

Since the . . . incident . . . he'd kept a low profile. He'd always enjoyed being the centre of attention, but not because of something like this. Now he just basically hung out, travelling to some of his familiar haunts, keeping his mind occupied, and trying not to remember.

It had taken a while, but just a few weeks ago he had talked to his sister. She had been madly trying to track him down, concerned after seeing him on TV doing battle with the creature. But because he'd been trying to fly—or skate—under the radar, it had taken a while. Once they connected, however, the result was that he might just be heading home. Sisters and brothers, regardless of family disputes, were still sisters and brothers. With everything that had happened, that made him happy. It had been a long time since anybody had really been concerned about him.

Watching the youngsters do their best on top of the frozen water, the conversation he'd once had with Katie began to creep into his mind. Something about training or coaching. Paul had lost interest in playing the game and he was pretty sure the IHL teams were treating him like a bad smell. He had to do something with his life eventually.

The little girl fell and the older boy helped her get back up. The other two laughed, not cruelly but joyously.

Paul realized he couldn't just keep hanging out in rinks watching little kids skate. People might talk.

Merle Thompson was as happy as a pig in shit, as her father would have said. The humming of the engine as the plane climbed altitude was akin to a kitten purring in her ear. She'd missed this. This was where she belonged.

Of course, getting her licence back and proving she wasn't dead had been an incredible headache. The bureaucracy involved made her re-evaluate her time of non-existence in a more appreciative light. Being dead involved less paperwork.

Luckily the small airline she had worked for before the tragic events—the thought of everything that had happened still made her shiver—had immediately vouched for her identity and helped her get her life back in order. For that she was grateful. More importantly, they had allowed her to climb back in the cockpit.

So here Merle sat, looking down at the land far below her approaching and receding, depending on which direction you looked. Throttling up the engine and enjoying the effect it had on the plane, she'd spend her life high in the clouds if she could. After all, there were no monsters in the sky. She was fairly sure of that . . . except for maybe—what had her grandmother called them—thunderbirds. But they didn't exist, of course. Just a story.

Suddenly her grip on the throttle slackened. That's what they'd said about the . . .

Birch enjoyed the feeling of the sand between her toes. She much preferred the beaches of Pacific Mexico to the Caribbean side. Down here, nobody knew who she was. Just another Canadian tourist, except with haunted eyes for some reason. The detective had needed to get away. There had been months of questions and investigations where she gave the same answers over and over again.

It was time for a vacation. Leaving in the middle of an investigation, under normal circumstances, that was something Birch would never even have contemplated. But these were not normal circumstances, and she had told all different levels of government and law enforcement all she knew—repeatedly. It wasn't her fault none of it made sense, from a bureaucratic or any other perspective. And more of the inquisition was probably waiting for her upon her return.

So here she was, feet buried in the sand, watching the waves come crashing in, waiting for that guy who sold coconuts to walk by again. She'd bought one every day for the last four, enjoying its fresh water and the flesh.

The detective had also heard there were some interesting alcoholic drinks that could be made with coconut water. She wasn't a heavy drinker, but maybe it was also time to explore that possibility. Numbness could have its benefits. After all, there were definitely worse things in the world than a hangover.

Though the sun was burning high in the cloudless sky and winds were blowing hot, Birch shivered.

A Note from the Author

Amongst the Anishnawbe/Cree people, the Wendigo is a creature that can inhabit both the real and spirit world. As such, it should be respected and honoured, as perhaps a particularly aggressive manifestation of our culture. In weaving this story, I meant no disrespect, I merely wanted to tell a tale our ancestors would have been proud of.

I also meant no disrespect to hockey players or university professors. You know who you are.

Drew Hayden Taylor
Curve Lake First Nation
April 2023

Acknowledgements

No book is born alone, at least none that I know of. They are usually the product of a life filled with conversation, gathering knowledge and experience, then transmuting it into a magical tale that will hopefully take the reader to someplace they've never been. Hopefully.

So, keeping with that spirit, I would like to thank everybody that I have ever come into contact with, conversed with, argued with, agreed with, and more importantly, shared a story with. But of course, there are a few special people who provided specific help in the development of this story, and aided in its long gestation. This book is dedicated to you.

Twenty years ago, I first told my brand new agent, Janine Cheeseman, about this cool idea I had for a contemporary Indigenous horror movie, called *Wendigo*. I told her the tale in about 15 minutes, having worked out all the characters and plot devices. She loved the concept. So, I wrote it as a movie.

If there's one thing I have realized in my varied career, it's that sometimes stories are either birthed too soon, or in the wrong medium. That could be said of *Wendigo*. Much like the creature in the title, I don't think it was ready to be seen or experienced just then. So on to the shelf it went, for a very long time, where it matured.

Jump forward fifteen years or so. I'm in Dawson City, Writer-In-Residence in the Pierre Berton House, when famed author Lawrence Hill showed up in town, doing research for a new project. We met and ended up having dinner at the only Greek restaurant in town. I came away from our time together feeling invigorated by our discussion of writing, to the point of sitting down that night and banging out the first 1,700 words of a new novel. Thus began the epic rebirth of *Wendigo*, or as it is now called, *Cold*.

The story and characters were all there, waiting. Maybe, I conjectured, it wasn't meant to be a movie. It was meant to be a novel. That had been the case with *Motorcycles & Sweetgrass*. *The Night Wanderer* too had been an unsuccessful play. So converting *Cold* into a novel became the project for the next year and a half. While writing it, I had to rely on the wisdom and guidance of several people in both its iteration as a movie script and as a work of prose. Herbie Barnes and my cousin Ryan Taylor had provided me with more intimate hockey lore than I retained. I know . . . bad Canadian.

Cousin D. J. Fife provided help with the Anishnaawbemowin language, along with Jonathan Taylor (another cousin). Alok Mukherjee and Constable Steven Lee, 14 Division in Toronto, assisted with information regarding various police procedures and practices. I'd also like to thank all the authors whose work I mention within the context of *Cold*. Such a delight to read your work and help share it.

Of course there's my editor, Joe Lee, and the powers-that-be at McClelland & Stewart, who came willingly into the dark and humorous world of Anishnawbe cosmology and there found something of interest.

Finally of course, there's Janine Willie, who would patiently bring me up water or something to fuel my imaginations as I sat for hours slaloming through a strange world of my own creation.

She also provided a wealth of understanding—if that's possible—regarding the academic world.

While some may consider this book a bit of a scare, be it known that it is full of love and my thanks to those who supported this effort of mine.

Ch'meegwetch.